the MEPHISTO KISS

the Mephisto Kiss

BOOK TWO:
THE REDEMPTION OF KYROS

TRINITY FAEGEN

EGMONT
USA
NEW YORK

EGMONT

We bring stories to life

First published by Egmont USA, 2012
443 Park Avenue South, Suite 806
New York, NY 10016

1 3 5 7 9 8 6 4 2

www.egmontusa.com
www.trinityfaegen.com

Library of Congress Cataloging-in-Publication Data

Faegen, Trinity
The Mephisto kiss : the redemption of Kyros / Trinity Faegen.
p. cm. -- (The Mephisto covenant ; bk. 2)
Summary: Sasha, a descendant of Eve, and Jax, a son of Hell, must try to stop
Eryx from using the President's daughter, also a daughter of Eve, to take over
the country.
ISBN 978-1-60684-171-6 (hardback) -- ISBN 978-1-60684-379-6 (e-book)
[1. Good and evil--Fiction. 2. Christian life--Fiction. 3. Supernatural--
Fiction. 4. Love--Fiction. 5. Presidents--Family--Fiction.] I. Title.
PZ7.F132Mep 2012
[Fic]--dc23
2012004025

Printed in the United States of America

Book design by Torborg Davern

For Mike.

I love you more than John Lennon loved guitars.

"I AM PART OF THE PART THAT ONCE WAS EVERYTHING,
PART OF THE DARKNESS WHICH GAVE BIRTH TO LIGHT . . ."
—MEPHISTOPHELES, FROM GOETHE'S *FAUST*

ONE

KISSING MATTHEW WAS ONE OF JORDAN'S FAVORITE THINGS to do, but tonight was different. Instead of enjoying the feel of his arms around her and the slow, gentle slide of his mouth over hers, all she could think about was the argument she'd had with her father before she came to Matthew's house.

In the middle of the kiss, she sighed, and he pulled back a little, gazing at her from soft brown eyes. "It's not something you could have prevented. You didn't even see the e-mail until . . . after. Don't beat yourself up about it."

"It's not that. Not entirely, anyway. It's Dad. After the news hit about that girl's suicide, he told me I have to quit doing the TV spots for STOP, that I can't be their spokesperson anymore, and we got in an epic fight about it. Why does everything I do have to be about him?"

With long, warm fingers, Matthew smoothed the hair at her temples. "Well, he *is* the president, and you've said yourself that your family lives in a fishbowl. STOP is a great thing, but every time it doesn't work, the newspeople make a big deal about your involvement. As long as you're part of it, they're going to focus on you instead of the kids it's supposed to help."

Pulling away from him, she sat up on the sofa. Across the room, the closing credits of the movie they'd just watched rolled across the screen. "When I turned seventeen, Dad asked me to do some of the things a First Lady does, since Mom's gone. I had lessons about how to greet state visitors and which fork to use and how to talk to reporters. Dad's press secretary wanted me to get involved with breast cancer awareness, since that's how Mom died, but I wanted to work with STOP, because of Holly." Volunteering to do public-service announcements for the Suicidal Teens Outreach Program had been her way of dealing with her friend's death, and now Dad was telling her she had to quit. It felt like a betrayal of Holly's memory.

"Maybe it's not a bad idea to step back. Those e-mails eat you up, and since you aren't allowed to respond to any of them, it just frustrates you and makes you depressed."

He had a point. She'd had notes from kids that sliced her soul to ribbons. Some managed to work through their problems, but some didn't. Like the girl who e-mailed Jordan in the middle of last night and said she was all done, that she was giving up. By the time Jordan saw it, the girl was dead from an overdose of sleeping pills.

As the First Daughter, she received hundreds, sometimes thousands of e-mails every week. It was White House policy that each e-mail receive a reply, and most were a generic response sent by Carla, the press secretary's assistant, or one of several staffers who worked under her, but they always flagged the e-mails they felt needed a personal reply from Jordan. Since Jordan had become the public face of STOP, she also received e-mails from desperate teens, and those received a reply expressing concern and compassion, along with the phone number and e-mail address for STOP. It wasn't that she didn't want to respond personally; she wasn't allowed. The press secretary was adamant about it, because of who she was. If she counseled someone who still killed himself, it would be a PR disaster for Dad. Everything was always about the presidency. Most of the time, she didn't mind, but sometimes it really got to her. "I told Dad that the news will call me a quitter, and it'll look worse."

"And what did he say?"

She turned her head and looked at him over her shoulder. "He said it wouldn't be the worst thing said about him." Sucking in a deep breath, she let it out slowly. "It's so bad, Matthew, like everything Dad does is wrong. He said every bill he signs to fix a problem seems to create another one. Unemployment is higher than it's ever been. His approval rating is almost as low as Nixon's the day he resigned from office."

"My dad says he listened to the wrong people and took bad advice."

Just that morning, she'd noticed Dad looked really old. "After Mom died, he shouldn't have run for a second term, but he did, and now it's all wrong."

Matthew rubbed her back. "Come on, Jordan, don't be so down. Let's do something that'll take your mind off of all the negative."

"Like what?"

"We could go upstairs to my room."

"Are you serious?" She turned her head again and saw the look in his ordinarily calm eyes. "Oh, wow, you *are* serious! Geez, Matthew, way to be inappropriate. I'm supersad and bummed out, and you're saying we should have sex?"

"It's not like we haven't been going out forever, so why not tonight? It'd be something to remember from this day that isn't a bummer."

She turned away and tucked her hair behind her ears. "I just got through telling you what a bad place my dad is in. Can you imagine if I got pregnant? It'd kill him." She sighed again. "Not to mention the field day the newspeople would have with that."

"You won't get pregnant."

"Says you. Nothing's for sure, and it's not a risk I want to take." She focused on the movie credits and waited for Matthew to tell her she needed to stop running everything she did through the filter of living in the White House. Other than going off about Auburn football, it was his favorite lecture.

Instead, he asked, almost in a whisper, "Do you love me?"

Ohmigod, he dropped the L word. Out of nowhere, when she least expected it. Her friend, Tessa, said he'd do it eventually, that it was every guy's last-ditch effort to get a girl to say yes. Jordan told her Matthew wasn't like that. Sure he asked—he was a seventeen-year-old guy, after all—but she always said no, rolled out some variation of the Speech, he gave her the Lecture, and they moved on. Rinse and repeat.

Now he changed everything by asking if she loved him. Inwardly cringing, she held the do-you-love-me grenade gingerly while she debated what to say. What if she said yes, and he didn't say he loved her, too? It would be out there, with no way to take it back. She'd die of humiliation.

But what if she said she wasn't sure, and he broke up with her? She wasn't ready for life without Matthew. Other than Tessa, he was her best friend, and yes, she *did* love him, but not necessarily like that. Not enough to sleep with him.

The credits came to an end, and the menu screen popped up. Turning to look at Matthew, she lobbed the grenade back at him. "Do *you* love *me*?"

He reached for her arm and tugged until she was back against his side. "I've never known a girl like you, Jordan. You think the only reason everybody likes you is because your dad's the president, but it would be the same if he was a garbageman. It's not him. It's you, and whatever's inside you that makes everybody want to hang with you." He pulled her closer and kissed her forehead. "It's part of the reason I keep asking about sex, because it'd make me feel more sure about us, that you'd be less likely to bail on me."

Lifting her face, she met his eyes. "You worry that *I'll* break up? Seriously?"

His arms tightened. "All the time." Sincerity was all over his face, and his smile was crooked, like he was embarrassed. "I love you, Jordan."

She almost couldn't breathe. *This* was romantic. This was *awesome.* Pressing a kiss to his soft mouth, she was about to whisper, "I love you, back," but didn't get it out before there were two loud pops from the street, just outside the window, making her jump. "Somebody has firecrackers."

Looking completely freaked out, Matthew grabbed her hand while he shoved away from the back of the sofa. "Those wern't firecrackers."

A loud crash came from the front hall, and she whipped her head around just as the door flew open. Two men in ski masks rushed inside, each with an arm extended, holding a handgun.

Matthew was already lunging from the sofa, pulling her along as he booked it toward the kitchen. In those few seconds, all she could think was, *Where is the Secret Service?* There were two agents, one in front of Matthew's house, one in back, and they were constantly in contact with police patrolling the area, so help had to be on the way already. But why weren't the agents inside? Had these guys shot Maggie out there on the front steps? Where was Paul? He had to have heard the shots. He should be coming inside, right now, but as they cleared the swinging door into the kitchen from the den, there was no one.

Matthew was headed for the back door. An alley ran behind the row of town houses, and once they were outside, in the dark, they could run and find somewhere to hide until—

Her heart skipped a beat when she heard another gunshot.

It broke into pieces when Matthew stumbled and let go of her hand.

⁓⁓⁓

Snipping the last of the wayward tendrils from an ornamental orange tree, Key stepped back and surveyed his work. "Why won't you bloom? It's time. You need to give it up. The bees are hungry."

The tree stood there in the dark, small and silent.

His gaze moved across the lush interior of the greenhouse while he inhaled deeply of the warm, moist air, heavy with the scent of vegetation and rich earth. The greenhouse smelled like life. Situated in the rambling garden to the east of the house on the Mephisto Mountain, all but buried in late December snow, everything within the walls of glass and steel depended on him for survival, right down to the earthworms. His care was rewarded with a slight easing of never-ending restlessness.

Sometimes, when the sun shone through the glass at just the right angle, when the blue of the sky above reflected against the tiny waterfall in the middle of the south wall, he could almost forget what he was, what he did, and imagine happiness.

But those times were rare.

Tilting his head, he looked up at the bowl of stars suspended above the greenhouse and wished God could hear him.

Jax's voice on the intercom above the greenhouse door cut through the perfect silence. "We have a situation. War room in one minute."

Damn.

With a heavy sigh, Key walked toward the door, setting his green shears on the potting bench before he disappeared. A few seconds later, he stood in the room at the center of a maze of computer banks and offices housed in the basement of the Mephisto mansion. One wall of the war room held an enormous plasma screen; on another was a gigantic map of the world and a whiteboard, and the center of the stone floor was dominated by an ancient oval table, three identical chairs on either side, and a new, smaller one at the end.

His brothers were all there, in varying states of dress. Key noticed that Sasha, the latest addition to the Mephisto, wore one of Jax's dress shirts, her long, slender legs ending in a pair of white socks. She had her blonde hair up in a ponytail that somehow made her more beautiful than if she'd had it all fixed and perfect. He wished he had a girl who'd wear his dress shirts as pajamas.

He focused on Jax. "What's going on?"

Jax picked up the remote control from the table. "This was recorded about an hour ago." The plasma screen was filled with an image of the president and his daughter, standing side by side on the steps of the White House, greeting the King and Queen of Sweden. The scene changed, and Jordan Ellis was handing out Easter baskets to a gaggle of little kids. Key watched impassively, but he definitely noticed she was beautiful. Small, barely over five feet, with long dark hair and wide blue eyes, when she smiled, her lovely face lit up, and her eyes . . . he'd swear they twinkled. He enjoyed watching her, but began to wonder how the hell photo ops of the First Daughter warranted a Mephisto situation.

The voiceover reporter said, "No one has claimed responsibility, no ransom demand has been issued, but an inside source tells CNN the FBI and Homeland Security believe the two gunmen are Americans. Several militias are being questioned, particularly a group based in Texas known as Red Out."

Key felt sick. "Did the bastards kidnap her?"

From where he leaned against the map wall, Phoenix said, "They took out her Secret Service detail, broke into her boyfriend's house, shot the boyfriend, and stole the girl."

"No way. Maybe somebody could take out a couple of Secret Service agents, but they couldn't take the president's daughter farther than a few blocks before they'd have every cop and uniformed Secret Service agent in the city all over them."

"Just keep watching," Phoenix said.

The screen changed to a scene outside a Capitol Hill row house, yellow crime-scene tape blocking part of the sidewalk. Scores of people stood watching as medics rolled a gurney through the front door and into a waiting ambulance. The voiceover reporter said, "Matthew Whittaker, seventeen-year-old son of Senator Jim Whittaker of Alabama, is in critical condition at George Washington University Hospital. He remains unconscious, but FBI agents hope to question him when he wakes."

Jax fast-forwarded, then stopped when the White House press secretary was speaking. Various White House staffers stood just behind him.

"Two men affiliated with the Red Out militia in central Texas were arrested after law enforcement pursued the car seen speeding away from the Whittaker residence. Miss Ellis was not in the car. The Secret Service believes the car was a decoy and the president's daughter was taken by alternate means."

Narrowing his eyes, Key stared at the guy second to the left. "The guy second to the left is way too still. He looks like a statue."

"He's Ron Trent, the chief of staff," Jax said. "It wouldn't be so obvious if every other staffer wasn't fidgeting, or crying."

They knew the Skia by the dark shadow across their eyes, but it never showed up on TV. They had to see a face in person to know if he'd given his soul to Eryx. But there were other signs, especially with the newest Skia. It took a lot of practice to act like a human with a soul, to fashion a facial expression to fit the situation, whether happy, sad, or frightened. In a row of hyperemotional people, Ron Trent was completely impassive, not an ounce of feeling on his face or in his eyes. "Did someone check him out? Is he Skia?"

Phoenix said, "I did, and he is. Then I called M, who found out Eryx turned the guy about six months ago."

Key instantly began to consider the difficulty of taking out the White House chief of staff. Ron Trent was a high-profile guy, closest adviser to the president. "What are you thinking, Phoenix? How can we do this?"

Jax and Sasha exchanged a look before they both turned to Key. "Taking out Trent is definitely something we need to do, but that isn't the situation."

Looking around the room at the faces of his brothers, he realized they all knew something he didn't. "Okay, then, what *is* the situation?"

"Eryx is behind the kidnapping," Jax said. "That's how Jordan disappeared. We think he staged the break-in for show, because, just like us, he can't screw too much with reality. He had those guys, who're bound to be lost souls, give the cops a good chase, and in the meantime, he transported her somewhere he can keep her until Ron Trent coerces an oath from the president. To keep that from happening, we need to find her."

Key looked around at each face, hoping to see somebody break. This had to be a joke, a prank they cooked up just to screw with him. But no, he could see from their expressions that they were dead serious. "Have you all lost your minds? We *can't* interfere with free will. If the president caves, there's nothing we can do about it. It'll be dicey to take him down, but it won't be the first time we took out a head of state. Eryx has tried to take over governments before."

"Not exactly free will," Ty said from the opposite corner, one of his wolfhounds sitting next to him. "The man's daughter, the only family he has since his wife died, is in danger of being killed unless the president agrees to pledge his soul to Eryx."

"Do you know for sure that Eryx is behind Jordan's abduction?"

Phoenix said solemnly, "When I went to see if Ron Trent was Skia, I popped all over the White House, looking for him. I finally found him, with Ellis, in the Yellow Oval Room on the second floor of the residence. He was telling the president—"

"*Did Trent see you?*" Key stopped and took a deep breath. Under a cloak, no one could see them, even the lost souls. But Skia were different. Their immortality allowed them to see past a cloak.

"Do you *seriously* think I'm that stupid?"

Feeling heated glares, aware that all of them were as angry as Phoenix, Key took one more deep breath and shook his head. "No."

"Trent was telling the president about Eryx. Why would he do that if he wasn't planning to convince him to pledge?"

"It doesn't matter. If a man will give away any chance of Heaven to become a drone for Eryx, if he'll say out loud that he forsakes God, he's without faith. He's already lost."

Ty's big hand gently smoothed Greta's fur. "He's the leader of the free world. He has power, influence. If he belongs to Eryx, it's as if our oldest brother is president. Imagine the fallout. He'll appoint Skia and lost souls to judgeships, cabinet seats, committee chairs. He'll have every agency within the federal government stacked with his followers."

"He won't be in office long enough to do any real damage. We'll take him out immediately."

Denys was staring at the screen, at Jordan in a PSA for the teen suicide hotline. "An assassination will send the United States into a tailspin."

"Then let's hope the president's faith is stronger than his love for his child."

Twirling the diamond stud in his ear, Zee spoke up from where he stood, just next to the whiteboard along the east wall. "You're pissing me off, bro. Maybe you're in charge, but last I checked, we're a democracy. Majority rules. Six to one, Key.

"Unless majority wants to break Lucifer's law, in which case it's my call." He looked at each of them, searching for any sign of dissent. One flinch and he'd send that brother to Kyanos for six months to live in solitary. Until the spring thaw, he'd starve unless he could find something to kill on the frozen North Atlantic island.

"If he doesn't pledge the oath," Denys said, "Eryx will kill Jordan."

Key looked again at the screen. Jordan was accepting a posy of bluebells from a child in a London crowd. Her eyes matched the flowers. Her smile was captivating. Thinking of her death, he felt a twinge of regret before he said, "Everybody dies sometime."

"Except us," Denys said. "And the Luminas."

"We're not human. The Luminas are live angels. Doesn't count." He watched Jordan dance with her father at some formal White House dinner. "We're not going after the president's daughter. We're not going to interfere. It's Lucifer's law, and if we break it, there'll be hell to pay."

Phoenix huffed out an impatient breath. "I told them you'd never go for this on its own merit, but they insisted we try." He pushed away from the map wall and took a chair at the table. "There's a caveat to the law. Remember?"

What did he mean, on its own merit? "Of course I remember, but the exception is only if the human is Anabo, if interfering is necessary to protect her. This isn't—" He stopped talking, suddenly feeling as if a Toyota had been dropped on his chest.

Holy shit.

Jerking his gaze back to the screen, he saw Jordan coming out of a restaurant with a lanky brown-haired guy. They were holding hands, smiling and waving at the camera before getting into a late-model BMW, followed by Secret Service, and driving away.

"She's Anabo," Sasha said quietly.

The screen went to a video of Andrew Ellis taking his second oath of office, almost a year ago. His daughter stood with him, looking earnest and serious. "How do you know?"

"Jax and I saw her at the National Cathedral on Christmas Day."

"Are you sure? Maybe it was just a trick of the light."

Sasha and Jax exchanged another look before his brother said, "We're sure. She had the Anabo glow."

"Christmas was three days ago. If you found an Anabo, why am I just now hearing about it?"

Dead silence was his answer, which meant they were afraid to tell him. Good call. An Anabo, right there in plain sight—available for the taking by the Mephisto—gone, and most likely fated to die. "I'd like an answer sometime before *next* Christmas."

"We wanted to see who's her intended before we told anyone," Jax said. "It seemed . . . kinder."

Key shoved his hands into the pockets of his trench coat and told himself that strangling Ajax, while tempting, was counterproductive. They'd found another Anabo, a huge miracle, and her immediate recovery was imperative. "And?"

Sasha picked up a small plastic bag from the seat of her chair at the end of the table and pulled out a pale blue sweater. "Jax popped into her room and swiped this from her laundry hamper."

As she walked toward him, Key caught the scent of bluebells, reminding him of Yorkshire, where they'd lived for several centuries, until they lost Jane a hundred years ago and moved to Colorado. As much as anything in England, he missed the bluebells.

Darting a look around, he knew from their expressions that Sasha had shown Jordan's sweater to each of his brothers, and none of them caught the scent of bluebells.

All this time, he thought he'd be the last to find an Anabo, but the subtle fragrance of bluebells coming at him from that sweater proved him wrong.

He was so short of breath, he was seriously afraid he'd pass out, but he kept his face expressionless. Standing straighter, he forced a calm that came from centuries of practice. His brothers depended on him to keep it together, to be in charge. Any falter would give them reason to doubt him, lose focus, and let go of the tightly held control they kept on their dark natures. Humanity didn't deserve unrestrained Mephisto wandering the Earth. His leadership had never been questioned because he never wavered from who he was, and he wasn't going to do so now.

His brothers assumed he was in charge because he was oldest after Eryx, the first of them to become immortal when he turned eighteen. They didn't know Lucifer had appeared to him while he hovered between death and resurrection and commanded him to lead his brothers, or that he threatened annihilation of their father, Mephistopheles, if Key failed. Having the dark angel of death as a parent was heavy, but there was affection there, of a kind. Not to mention, they counted on M to help in their never-ending war with Eryx. If Lucifer decided to take out their father, Key wasn't going to be the reason. In a thousand years, he'd never lost his footing, and he wouldn't now, even though he was scared out of his mind. "Do you think Eryx knows she's Anabo?" he asked no one in particular.

"We don't think so," Jax said. "He can't see the glow, and unless he sees her birthmark, how could he know? It's doubtful she knows."

"I had no clue I was Anabo until Jax found me," Sasha said. "I'd never even heard of Anabo. Eryx had Jordan taken to use as leverage to get the president to pledge. It's just a weird coincidence that she's Anabo."

She held the sweater out to him. His hand closed around the soft wool and brought it to his nose while his gaze moved once again to the screen, to the face of the girl he'd dreamed of finding his entire miserable life. If they were too late . . .

Turning, he gave Phoenix a look. "How fast can you make a plan?"

His brother replied evenly, "Already done."

∽≋∾

She was going to die. Soon. Blindfolded and gagged, wrists and ankles bound, riding in what she was certain was the trunk of a car, Jordan tried to stay focused on life after death, on Heaven. Maybe it was morbid, but thinking of her own death was better than thinking about Matthew. So much blood. Rivers of it, pooling beneath him on the floor.

Underneath the blindfold, she squeezed her eyes more tightly shut and made herself think about God, tried to imagine what Heaven must be like.

Wiggling into her mind were images of Matthew on the first day he came to Oates Priory School, two years ago, after his dad was elected senator from Alabama and moved his family to Washington. Matthew was a new kid in a whole group of new kids, not a big deal at Oates. People moved in and out of Washington every year, all depending on how Americans chose to vote. It was a running joke that no one who started there ever graduated from Oates.

She was used to new faces, but Matthew's stood out. He made her think of romantic dead poets, with wavy brown hair that always seemed to be across his forehead; big, brown expressive eyes; and a soft drawl that made every word sound beautiful.

She'd nearly fainted when he sat next to her in English and asked if she'd liked visiting China. "I saw you and your dad on TV, standing in front of the Imperial Palace."

"I loved China, but it's really smoggy. I couldn't see much of the Great Wall because so much of it's hidden by pollution." Oh, wow, way to be Debbie Downer. She should have said it had been awesome to see the terra-cotta soldiers, or the Beijing opera. She should have said something positive.

While she desperately tried to think of something else to say, something witty and interesting, he said, "I thought the exact same thing. Maybe China should take a cue from your dad and try harder to control pollution."

He diffused her anxiety and endeared her to him in the space of two seconds. With her dad always in the hot seat, she tended instantly to like anybody who said something nice about him or his job.

Within three weeks, they were going out. He was a paradox: he was crazy about football and R&B, was a total computer geek, and wrote lyrical short stories. But maybe best of all, he never, ever asked her stupid questions about what it was like to live in the White House, or have a dad who was leader of the free world. To Matthew, she was just a girl. Other than Tessa, he was her best friend.

The image of him on the floor, facedown, and all that blood, came rushing back, and she cried so hard, she choked on the gag in her mouth. Was he dead? He must be dead. No one could lose that much blood and live.

Those beautiful eyes, closed forever. Oh, God, and for what? Jordan didn't know who these guys were, but there was no doubt they were doing this to protest something they didn't like. She would most likely be killed, and she hoped and prayed it'd be quick, that they wouldn't cut off her head and send the video to Dad.

A distant voice came from deep inside her memory bank. "If, God forbid, you're ever taken hostage, there's a chance you'll be tortured for information. As someone who lives in close proximity with the president, you will know things, even what you're not supposed to know. An expert interrogator can find things in your memory you may not consciously remember." Maggie Young had been part of her Secret Service detail from the start, when Dad first ran for president.

In her heart, she knew Maggie was dead. The gunshots she heard outside the window had ended her life. And Paul never came inside after those shots were fired, so chances were good that he was also dead.

Jordan swallowed back tears and more spit, the taste of the

cloth in her mouth causing bile to rise in her throat.

"Don't try to be a hero," Maggie had said. "If they ask you a question, answer it. If they want you to say something on a video, even if it's a lie, do it. Your number one goal is to stay alive as long as possible. No matter what they do to you, remember, we can fix you if you're alive. Nothing lasts forever except death. An abductor has wants and needs, same as anybody, and he's convinced he's doing something noble, something that makes him a hero in his own mind. Play to that, if you can. Do whatever it takes to stay alive."

Jordan started violently when she suddenly felt someone right behind her, with incredibly high body heat. How could someone get into the trunk with her when the car was moving? The more bizarre question: *Why*? She felt arms slide around her and caught the scent of a burned matchstick, then had the creepiest sensation that she was weightless. Seconds later, the very hot arms set her on her feet and released the bindings around her wrists. With her ankles still tied together, she was shoved until she fell backward, landing hard in the seat that caught her.

She heard the whine of a plane engine, and her heart raced from rising hysteria. How could she be in the trunk of a car one second, then sitting on a plane the next? Was she dead? Had those guys shot her and this was like *The Sixth Sense*, where she was dead and didn't know it?

A deep, resonate voice with a vaguely British accent said, "Remove the gag and blindfold."

She could feel the plane taxiing, knew they were about to take off, just as the gag was removed and her blindfold was jerked from her eyes.

Blinking in the bright light of the cabin, she hurriedly took stock of her surroundings. It was a small plane, without ordinary seats. Instead, she sat on a wide black leather chair that faced the other side of the plane, which was lined by a long leather bench seat. Two thirtyish guys in brown shirts and jeans sat side by side, staring at her with unreadable eyes. They weren't the ones who had taken her, she was certain. Those guys had been small and wiry, and these were tall and built. They also smelled bad, like sour BO and stale cigarette smoke.

Suddenly, her chair began to swivel, and she held tight to the armrests. A chair like hers came into view, and the instant she saw the guy sitting in it, her heart raced faster. Young, maybe nineteen or twenty, he was beautiful, with jet-black hair and the face of a god, dressed in a pinstripe suit. But his eyes. Oh, sweet Jesus, his *eyes*. They were the color of ink, solid black, lifeless, without a hint of humanity.

Instantly, she thought of vampires and ghouls and zombies. Dead people whose souls had left their bodies yet who still walked the Earth.

There was no such thing as vampires, ghouls, or zombies, but she knew for sure that this guy was not human. It had been him in the trunk of the car. He was the one who took her from there to this plane in less than five seconds. She couldn't look away from those eyes, and in the middle of fear so intense, she was frozen, she knew she was going to throw up.

He came out of his chair to reach across the space between them and cup her chin in his very hot palm. "You will not be sick."

The nausea left as quickly as it came. He leaned back and settled his arms against the chair rests, staring at her from those horrific eyes. She tried as hard as she could to look away, but couldn't.

"I'm Eryx DeKyanos. I won't harm you, Jordan. So please relax."

Her fear of dying had taken a backseat to horror of something that went far beyond pain and death; a fatal threat to her spirit, what made her human, her very existence.

"You're wondering who I am and why I've taken you from your father."

She stared and made no move, no reply.

He jerked his head toward one of the men, and within a minute, she was handed a heavy crystal glass filled with amber liquid that smelled like liquor. She never drank alcohol, mostly because her father was never far from her mind. Most kids who were caught with booze got grounded. If she was caught, she'd be on CNN.

"Drink it," Eryx said. "I realize you're afraid, but you can't fly all the way to Bucharest sitting stiffly like that. The whiskey will help you calm down."

Bucharest. Romania. She had been born in Romania, abandoned at four and left on the steps of a Bucharest orphanage, where she'd lived until Andrew and Connie Ellis adopted her. Was it only coincidence this lunatic living dead guy was taking her there?

Did it matter? Whatever hope she held out for rescue went down the drain. She took a sip of the whiskey. It was awful. "Why Romania?"

"My home is in the Carpathian Mountains. You'll be my guest until your father can give me what I want."

"What if . . . if he can't?"

"Then I'll kill you. But I don't believe it'll come to that. He's an intelligent man, creative in crisis."

"Who . . . what . . . who . . . " She'd never had so much trouble speaking.

"I'm the firstborn son of Mephistopheles and the Anabo Elektra."

"Meph . . . Mephist . . . the *devil*?" Her voice went so high, she squeaked.

"No, not the devil. Like Lucifer, Mephistopheles fell from grace and was banished from Heaven. He became the dark angel of death, charged with collecting souls bound for Hell."

Stiff with fright, Jordan took another sip. It was still awful, but the warmth of the alcohol began to thaw her insides.

"Do you know of the Anabo?"

Mutely, she shook her head.

"Before Eve gave in to Lucifer's temptation, she had a daughter, Aurora, who was lost when she wandered away from Eden. Her descendants came to be known as the Anabo, which is Greek for light, because they're born without the darkness of original sin. Over time, their numbers dwindled, but once in a great while, the spiritual line of Aurora is resurrected and another Anabo is born."

His words came to her as if from a great distance, echoing through her head, their meaning slow to catch up.

He wasn't finished.

"Elektra was Anabo, and when Mephistopheles found her, he tried to tempt the light from her soul, but she resisted. Instead of giving up, he fell in love with her. It was the worst of sins, a dark soul of Hell in love with a pure spirit of Heaven. If Lucifer had discovered his secret, Mephistopheles would have been extinguished—gone as if he had never existed. It's a strict law that angels, divine or dark, aren't to consort with humans, even if they're Anabo. He took Elektra to a tiny island in the North Atlantic and hid her behind a cloak of secrecy that came to be known as the mists of Kyanos. My mother and I were hidden from both God and Lucifer."

Clutching her glass in shaking hands, she took another swallow, the crystal clattering against her teeth. Her bones began to feel as if they were melting, and she slumped back against the chair.

"As the son of a dark angel and an Anabo, I'm not human,

but I live and breathe and am bound to the Earth until the end of time. I've spent the past thousand years convincing people to follow me, and when they die, their soul becomes mine. When I have enough, when I'm more powerful than Lucifer, I'll guard the gates of Hell." He never moved, his expression never changed, but his excitement was obvious. "Because of original sin, mankind is doomed to Hell unless people can rise above it and live their lives according to God's law. Lucifer allows free will, gives humanity the liberty to choose between good and evil. I won't. Every soul will belong to me."

Jordan whispered, "Then God will destroy the world."

He settled back in his chair. "It will be the beginning of the ultimate war."

Maybe her thinking was twisted, but she found herself wishing her kidnapper was an ordinary terrorist, a man with a mission that might be half baked and misguided but was based in reality. All that guy could threaten was death.

Eryx wanted to take on God.

She set the glass of awful whiskey in the cup holder in the armrest of her chair. "What does my father have to do for me to go home?"

His smile didn't reach his eyes. Nothing reached his eyes. "Pledge his soul to me."

Never. Dad was all about faith and doing the right thing. "He won't do it."

Eryx shrugged. "Time will tell. I think he'll be more open to the idea when he sees the result of your abduction. The American people will sympathize, and their dislike of his administration will be forgotten."

Maybe Americans would feel sorry for Dad, but they weren't likely to forget their unhappiness with his presidency. Most people were a lot more worried about their own problems, especially when times were hard. That was now. She'd heard Dad say he was afraid the country was headed for another depression, and his daughter being kidnapped wasn't going to divert attention away from that. Not long term, anyway. "Will they know I was kidnapped by a guy from Hell?"

"Of course not. To all the world except your father, you've been abducted by Red Out, a militant group angry with the president's agenda. In reality, they belong to me. They'll demand concessions for your release, which he'll appear to give them, right up until the FBI takes them out. If he does what I ask of him, you'll go home with no memory of your ordeal, no way to deny or confirm where you were during your abduction."

"I'm supposed to lie?"

"No, you really won't remember. I'll erase your memory of me, of everything, before I send you home."

He could make her forget. Could he control her mind? Her fear, if possible, ratcheted up another notch. "If I'm going to forget, why have you told me all of this?"

"To pass the time." His lifeless eyes stared harder at her. "Also, perhaps, because I want to convince you to follow me."

Her instant reaction was another wave of nausea, Maggie's voice repeating over and over in her head. *"Do whatever it takes to stay alive."* Telling Eryx she'd rather have her head cut off than give her soul to him would do nothing to help her. Swallowing hard, she managed to ask in a fairly normal voice, "How do you get followers? What would convince someone to give up God and hand her soul to you?"

"My followers recruit people by telling them they can have their heart's desire. Amazing what some people will ask for in exchange for their soul."

"How do you give them what they want?"

"That's the beauty of it, and the tragedy, I suppose. Most of the time, they don't get what they want, but they believe all of it, right up until they swear the oath. In that moment, they understand, but it's too late. They can never go back. They'll spend the rest of their lives serving me, finding new recruits; then, when they die, their souls are mine."

"So you'll lie to my dad to get his pledge?"

"On the contrary. If he does what I ask, he'll have you back."

He was lying, she was certain. No matter what Dad did, she was going to die. "He won't give up his soul, even if it means saving me. He's better than that."

Eryx chuckled. It had an odd sound to it, like rusty hinges on an old door. "No one is immune to temptation, except the Anabo, and there've been only two born in the past hundred years. If I knew what you wanted above anything, I would promise it, and you'd pledge, even knowing what you now know. Temptation is irresistible to every human because each one carries the sin of Eve. You'd gamble that maybe, just this once, I wasn't lying, that I'd give you what you want."

"Do whatever it takes to stay alive."

Maggie didn't know, could never have guessed, that something other than Jordan's life might be at stake.

TWO

IN HIS CLOSET, KEY SLID HIS SWITCHBLADE INTO HIS TRENCH coat pocket before he opened a drawer, selected two other blades from their felt-lined beds, and slipped them into the straps of his engineer boots. Turning to his dresser, he was scraping his hair back to fasten it into a ponytail when he was hit by an uneasy feeling.

What the hell would he say to Jordan when they found her? He was probably the least talkative of any of his brothers, and not always because he had nothing to say. It was just easier to keep his thoughts to himself and to speak only when he had to. He wouldn't be able to do that with Jordan. She wouldn't know anything about them, or Eryx, or that she was Anabo. At least, he didn't think so. How would he tell her? How would she react?

Jax told him Sasha had been afraid, but after a while, she accepted the reality of what existed on the other side, what ordinary humans didn't know. He said that because Jordan was Anabo, she'd feel like she owed it to humanity to join them, but what if she didn't? Key didn't know if he had it in him to be persuasive.

Annoyed with himself, he turned away from the dresser. His worry about what to say was pointless if they didn't rescue her before Eryx had her killed.

To conserve energy, he didn't pop downstairs but walked through the winding corridors of the second floor until he came to the grand staircase. His brothers and Sasha were waiting for him in the front hall of the mansion, forming a circle around the onyx *M* inlaid in white marble. Sober and silent, they watched him descend the stairs. He wondered why they were staring but decided not to ask. No way could he get through an interrogation about his feelings, and any dissection of his thoughts on finding an Anabo after more than a thousand years was not going to happen. To make sure no one said anything, he glared at them.

It worked.

As soon as he'd joined the circle, standing between Zee and Denys, Jax said, "We've done the White House before, so you're all familiar with exits and possible escape routes. You know which are yours, so cover and watch anyone who comes in or out. If you see Trent, take him immediately to the gates, but don't get carried away and send him down. We have to know where they've taken Jordan, and he's our best hope of finding out. Any questions?"

They all shook their heads.

Jax looked down at Sasha. "You stick with Phoenix. I'm going in with Key."

She frowned at him. "I can get there, Jax. It's the White House, and I know where it is."

He glanced at Phoenix, who shrugged, then looked down into her face and touched the mic curled around her ear. "If you have a problem, let us know, and Phoenix will come for you . . . wherever you wind up."

"I won't have a problem. You'll see."

Key noticed the looks exchanged among his brothers, luckily not seen by Sasha because she was focused on Jax.

Sasha had been in training the past year, but she still had a long way to go. She was awful at transporting, sometimes landing miles from the intended destination. Takedowns were a challenge because she couldn't resist engaging, even though she knew it was pointless. A lost soul would do or say anything to save himself from Hell on Earth. Reasoning with him, saying anything at all, was wasted effort. Also a recipe for rage. She lost it during one of her first takedowns and killed the lost soul before he could be sent to Hell on Earth. A win for Eryx, the dead guy's soul adding to his tote board, increasing his dark power. Sasha had been horrified. It spooked her, and in every takedown since, she hesitated just long enough to allow the enemy to wound her.

She'd learn, and get better at what they did. It would just take some time. Key wondered if Jordan would be a quicker study than Sasha. Once she was here, they could train together. Maybe Sasha would like that.

Jax looked around the circle, said, "Let's do it," and, as one, they disappeared from Colorado.

Moments later, Key stood with Jax on the roof of the White House, cloaked so no one could see or hear them. He glanced at the Secret Service countersnipers, who kept watch for any long-range threats, then looked across the lawn toward the street. Hundreds of people clustered along the fence, waving American flags, holding candles and flowers. "They may hate her father, but they love her."

Jax gave him a weird look. "Are you sure you're up for this, Kyros?"

"What are you talking about? Of course I'm up for it."

Jax stared for a while before he looked away. "If you say so. On three, pop down to the Truman Balcony. One . . . two . . . "

Before Key could say anything else, Jax had thrown out three fingers. Key had no choice but to follow.

They materialized on the balcony, to the left of the windows of the Yellow Oval Room. "Why did you ask me if I'm up for this?"

Jax moved toward the window and whispered as he peeked inside, "Your hair's down."

Son of a bitch. He never, ever went into the field with his hair down. He'd been so busy thinking about Jordan, worrying about what he'd say to her, that he'd forgotten to bind it. The slip rattled him, but he'd never admit it to Jax. "I ran out of hair bands," he lied.

Jax threw a look over his shoulder that called bullshit, but wisely didn't say anything.

"What's in there?"

His brother looked again, then stepped back and huffed out a breath. "Ellis and Trent, just like Phoenix said, but now they have company."

Key moved around Jax and did his own peek, sucking in a breath when he saw who was with the president. Looking around at the well-known, important, high-ranking people in the U.S. government, a sea of shaded eyes, he was stunned.

Eryx had been busy in Washington. Converting the president must be the final step in his plan to control the United States. It was brilliant, really. With enough of his followers in Congress and serving on the president's cabinet, he could alter the course of history. He would lead American citizens to desperate hopelessness, then offer them a way out—an empty promise of a better life in return for their souls.

The president was the only one in the room whose eyes weren't shaded by the darkness of Eryx. He stood next to the fireplace, looking like a man whose daughter had been abducted by terrorists—angry, confused, and scared shitless.

Key stepped back and looked at his brother. "Is that blowing your mind?"

"Totally blown, and Phoenix's head will explode, trying to dream up a takedown plan. But we'll worry about it later. For now, I'm throwing a freeze. Are you ready?"

Jerking a nod, Key waited for the count, and as soon as Jax said three, he popped inside, landing just on the other side of the windows. Jax appeared close to the door into the Central Hall, in case Trent tried to make a run for it. Thinking they were lucky that Ron Trent was the only Skia in the room, the only one who couldn't be frozen, Key headed for the chief of staff, stepping around the stone-still figures of the Senate majority leader and the secretary of the treasury as he went.

Their prey was an exceptionally smart man, and he clearly knew the sudden stillness of everyone in the room but him, coupled with the appearance of two giants dressed in black, meant he was very close to toast. A nanosecond after the realization lit his eyes, he stepped behind Ellis's still body and held a knife to his throat. "Leave now or I'll kill him."

Key made a snap decision to call the man's bluff. "It's nothing to me if you kill him, but I suspect Eryx won't be pleased. Ellis's assassination will land the vice president in the White House, and Eryx will have to convince all the new staff and cabinet members to pledge their souls." Key lifted one brow. "And you'll be executed for killing the president."

Looking triumphant, Trent said smugly, "I can't be executed. I'm immortal."

"To humanity, you're immortal. What Eryx gives, Eryx can

take away. Do you seriously think he'll let you live if you murder Ellis?"

Trent hesitated, determination shifting to anxiety.

"Tell us where to find Jordan."

Behind the dark shadow of Skia, a cagey look came into the man's eyes. "Leave and call me in an hour. Then I'll tell you."

Key sighed. Did the man really think he could get out of this? Maybe he wasn't as smart as Key thought. Moving at the speed of light, he knocked the knife from Trent's hand and grabbed him in a headlock. "Jax, you got this covered?"

"Got it. Go. Now."

Trent had just begun to put up a fight when Key transported him all the way to the other side of the planet, to the vast, barren desert of southwestern Saudi Arabia. The Empty Quarter. No-Man's-Land.

Throwing him to the patch of sand that hid the gates to Hell on Earth, he towered over him. "Where is Jordan?"

Turning his head from side to side, Trent looked more confused than afraid. "Where are we?"

"The gates of your own personal Hell. *Where is Jordan?*"

"What's it to you? I thought the Mephisto never interfered with humanity."

"Answer and I'll take you back to civilization, where you'll have a fighting chance of escaping us. You've got thirty seconds. After that, we're done and you're history."

Trent glared at him and said nothing.

The wind died abruptly, a gift from Lucifer, no doubt, and the dawn air was filled with the eerie sound of keening wails: the infinite misery only the immortals in Hell on Earth could know.

Losing his attitude, Trent's eyes widened, and he began to shake violently. "Is that . . . are those . . . ?"

"Your immortal brethren, calling for you. Are you ready to join them?" Key stepped back and raised his arms to the sky, prepared to begin the ancient chant that would open the gates.

His captive fought desperately, writhing against the sand, trying to get up, and when that was impossible, he tried to roll. The fear in his shaded eyes became terror as he finally realized he was no longer a man with power and influence, but just another sucker who had believed Eryx's lies, who handed over his soul in exchange for what he thought was an easy ticket. "Stop! Dear God, please stop!"

Key began the chant.

"She's with Eryx, on a plane to Romania!"

Key stopped the chant and dropped his arms. "Does he plan to kill her, even if the president pledges?"

"Yes. He says her abduction and death will garner sympathy and make America less critical of Andy's administration. It'll allow him to do some things he might not get away with otherwise. The people will blame it on his grief." He began to cry piteously. "Eryx said a lot of things."

"And you believed him." Key had never understood why, but it sometimes seemed the very best of men were Eryx's easiest converts. Maybe it was their decency that wouldn't allow them to recognize evil when it came calling.

"I've told you about Jordan. Can we leave now?"

Key answered by raising his arms to the sky. The wind returned, whipping his trench coat behind him, blowing sand across Trent.

"You said if I told you, I'd be given a chance!"

"I'm a son of Hell, Mr. Trent. I lie and cheat without any guilt at all. You of all people should know better than to trust the word of a guy like me."

"Have mercy! Kill me! Don't send me down there!"

"I can't kill you. Only Eryx has that privilege."

Trent looked up to the pearl-gray sky and begged God for mercy.

"He can't hear you." Key again began to chant, and beneath the sobbing, bitter regret of another Skia, the sand swirled, faster and faster, until it sucked him under. By the time Key lowered his arms, all traces of Ron Trent were gone, and the desert was barren once again, its silence broken only by the ghostly whistle of the wind.

When he popped back to Washington, the other Mephisto were in the Yellow Oval Room, surrounding the still-frozen president and lost souls.

Jax asked, "Did you send Trent down?"

He nodded. "Not sure how we're going to explain his disappearance."

"I've already asked M for a doppelganger," Phoenix said, "which will be in the cooler by lunchtime tomorrow. It'll look like all the stress caused him to have a massive heart attack."

Ty asked, "Where's Jordan?"

Hoping it'd calm him a little, Key took a deep breath. "Eryx has her on a plane, en route to Bucharest."

Sasha's voice was shaky. "Can we pop onto airplanes in mid-flight?"

"It's next to impossible," Jax said. "Best bet is to be there when they arrive and get her before Eryx transports them to his home in the mountains."

Phoenix grimly shook his head. "Transporting into a flying plane is dicey, but popping off of one to solid ground is easy. As soon as Eryx gets news that Ellis is a no go, he'll take her to Erinýes and kill her."

"He plans to kill her, either way," Key said, "but I think he'll wait until Ellis pledges. Otherwise, he loses his leverage."

"Then we need time. We need to make sure he goes all the way to Bucharest." Phoenix eyed the lost souls. "After the freeze fades, they're going to wonder what happened to Trent. If they realize we took him out, one of them will contact Eryx, and it's all over."

"We'll scrub their memories," Zee said, "so none of them, including the president, will remember Trent was already here. Ellis won't remember anything Trent told him about Eryx, and the lost souls won't dare say anything until Trent shows up."

"What happens when Trent is a no-show?" Ty asked.

Key looked at Zee. "Can you send a text and make it look like it came from Ron Trent?"

Zee nodded.

"Send Trent's assistant a text that says he's been held up, but he'll be here soon."

"Won't the president think it's bizarre that his best friend isn't with him right now? He'll want to know where he's held up, and it'll mean a back-and-forth we can't sustain."

"Good point. Okay, skip the text. This is just going to be one of those times when a guy disappears for a while and no one knows where he is. It'll work itself out when his body is found in the afternoon."

Phoenix looked a little less fatalistic. "Then, after Eryx gets Jordan to Bucharest—"

"I'll be at Erinýes, waiting," Key interrupted.

They all stared at him. The last time the Mephisto went inside Erinýes was to rescue Jane, over a hundred years ago. They had been too late. Eryx waited for them to arrive, then slit her throat while Phoenix ran for her, screaming like a madman.

A cold, empty pall fell across his brothers, everyone dropping their eyes to the floor.

Except Sasha. In her usual way of innocently blundering in where no one else would go, she said, "Eryx won't be expecting the Mephisto this time, so we have a good chance of rescuing Jordan."

Phoenix swayed a little but said nothing, didn't look up from the rug at their feet.

"I'll go alone," Key said. "I can get around the castle undetected, but all of us are bound to be noticed."

"We'll be cloaked," Sasha said.

"Eryx's staff and assistants are Skia, so a cloak won't help."

"Jax? Are you going to let him go alone?"

His brother had no expression on his face. "It's not a matter of letting him, Sasha. It's his call. And he's right. Alone, he has a chance of stealing her. With all of us there, it could mean . . ." He stopped and shot a quick glance at Phoenix.

"If I'm not back in Colorado by dawn, with Jordan," Key said into the pregnant silence, "it means she's dead and I've gone to Kyanos."

He disappeared, but didn't go to Romania right away. Instead, he popped himself to the Central Hall and looked in the West Bedroom, which was generic, then the East Bedroom, which he knew must be Jordan's. There was a giant bulletin board on one wall, and a collection of framed photos of her family and friends on the other. He needed something of hers to prove that he'd been here, that he wasn't aligned with Eryx, just in case she tried to run from him.

He moved around the room quickly, then noticed a pitiful-looking stuffed rabbit slouched against her pillow. As he picked it up, he wondered why she kept something so ragged and old? Surrounded by the scent of bluebells, he held the soft, pathetic thing and looked down at its missing eye, the stitching coming loose around its neck, and wondered: If Jordan Ellis, daughter of a president, child of a wealthy family, would keep something this old and tattered because she felt some strange sense of human affection for it, was it possible she'd overlook what he was and keep him around as well?

Tucking the ragged toy into the breast pocket inside his trench coat, he laughed at himself.

～∽〜

Jordan started when she heard what sounded like an annoying game-show buzzer. Eryx reached into the armrest of his chair, withdrew a cell phone, and bent his head to read the screen. Evidently a text message, and not good news. He scowled, and when he looked up at her, she expected to die immediately. He replaced the phone, then turned toward his minions, whom she'd begun to think of as Smelly and Stinky. "Carla says the Mephisto have altered our plans. She was in the residence living room when they showed up and threw a freeze."

Carla? Was he talking about übernice Carla, who worked for the press secretary?

"We were so careful," Stinky said. "How did your brothers find out?"

Eryx had *brothers*? There were more like him? God in Heaven, humanity was doomed.

"I don't know, but they interrupted Ellis's conversion and took down Ron Trent." He stared at her from those horrible black eyes and said with dull finality, "You're about to die, so make your peace with God." He glanced at Stinky. "Tell Bruce to take us down to ten thousand feet, then throw her off the plane." He stood and turned away. "Keep some of her clothing as proof we had her. I may be able to salvage the situation and convince Ellis myself, and he'll be more amenable if he's got nothing left to lose." He walked to the back of the plane and took a bottle of water from the galley. Smelly and Stinky remained seated.

Do whatever it takes to stay alive. If she could keep him talking, it'd buy time.

"Is Ron Trent dead?" she asked.

"I'm certain he wishes he was," Eryx replied, "but no, he's not dead. The Mephisto have taken him to Hell on Earth."

She didn't really care, because all she could think about was dying, but she wanted to keep him talking, so she asked, "The Mephisto? Hell on Earth?"

"I have six younger brothers," he said quietly, staring down at the label on the bottle in his hand, "collectively known as the Mephisto. Hell on Earth is within this physical realm, but not of the world. It lies miles beneath the surface."

"And that's where your brothers took Mr. Trent?"

"Yes."

Maybe he'd let her go to the bathroom. She looked toward the door beyond the galley. Was that the bathroom? Maybe it was a bedroom. Whatever it was, she could lock herself in there. If he or his minions couldn't get the door open, he'd have to wait her out.

The plane would eventually run low on fuel, and they couldn't fly around forever. Maybe when they landed, she could get away from them, somehow, and scream for help.

He was staring at her. "It's impossible to escape, Jordan. Even if you could get away from me, I have the ability to move through any obstruction."

Was she that obvious? She looked down at her hands, gripping her thighs, her mind constantly imagining what it would be like to fall ten thousand feet into the ocean. Would she pass out before she hit the water? She'd die on impact. Wouldn't she? Oh, God, she hoped so. Drowning would be so much worse because it would take longer. It would be horror like nothing else to be out there in the middle of the ocean, treading water until she was too exhausted to stay afloat.

She began to cry, more afraid than she'd believed possible, close to hyperventilating, her mind filled with a thousand memories, colliding against one another while a frantic voice screamed from deep within, *Help me, God! I don't want to die!*

"If you will pledge your soul to me, Jordan, I'll let you live."

"I can't do that."

"Your choice." He said to Stinky, "Tell Bruce to change course to London. By the time you land, they'll have investigated every plane that left Washington since she was taken and figured out this one is owned by one of the Red Out people. They'll arrest you. Remember, you're only the stooges in charge of the abduction and murder. You're to pin the plan on the Texas militia."

"What will happen to us?"

"You'll be executed, certainly."

Instead of arguing, or trying to save himself, Stinky merely nodded before he got up, went to the front of the plane, and opened the door to the cockpit.

Smelly stood and moved close, his rank odor nearly suffocating her. "Take off your sweater."

Like she was going to go meekly, a lamb to the slaughter? "You take it off."

He did, with relative ease, despite how hard she fought. Her legs were still hobbled, making the struggle worse. Breathing rapidly, she sat there in just her bra and jeans, crying, and silently asked God for a miracle.

Startling her, Eryx rushed toward her, and she cringed, expecting him to hit her. Instead, he went to one knee and reached for her, his eyes on her breasts. *Oh, God, why?* She squeezed her eyes shut while he ran his hot hand across her rib cage, beneath her right breast.

"Is this a tattoo?"

She opened her eyes and saw he was staring with total fascination at her birthmark. "No."

"You've had this your entire life?"

She nodded, sucking in deep breaths, for once glad she had a bizarre birthmark. She never wore two-piece bathing suits because it was so weird, a tiny, swirly *A*, surrounded by what looked like sunbeams.

"Anabo," he whispered. "You're Anabo."

She wasn't anything but scared to death.

Smelly was there, staring at the *A*, looking confused. "What does it mean?"

Eryx took the seat across from her again, still staring at her birthmark. "It means you should give her back the sweater."

Like a robot, Smelly did just that.

Not sure what was happening, or why, Jordan slipped the sweater over her head, pushed her arms into the sleeves, and hugged herself while she watched Eryx.

He appeared to be lost in thought. After several long moments, he met her eyes and said, "You can relax, Jordan. You're not going to die."

"I don't understand. If I'm Anabo, what difference does it make?"

"It's not just that you're Anabo. It's that I found you first, before my brothers."

"You're not making any sense." Frustration and fear made her cry harder. She'd been inches from death at the hands of a guy from Hell. Now he was looking at her like she was a winning lottery ticket.

Eryx went to the galley and returned with a Coke in a can. He held it out to her, but she was shaking too hard to hold it. With an impatient sigh, he set it in the cup holder of her armrest, empty since Smelly had taken the whiskey away.

He took his seat, then said solemnly, "Before I became

immortal, I was very close to my brothers, especially the next in line, Kyros, who we called Key. We all knew we were fated to die and come back, but I also knew that when we died, we'd lose whatever light existed in us. I wanted to save my younger brothers from what I was certain would happen to me, but I couldn't pray for help because neither God nor Lucifer knew we existed. The only one on Kyanos who could get their attention was my mother. I asked her to pray for me, for my brothers, but she said God couldn't hear her as long as she was behind the mists of Kyanos. I knew then that the only way to make God and Lucifer aware of our existence was to kill her. On my eighteenth birthday, I smothered her in her sleep, went to the cliffs, and jumped."

An image of her mother floated across her conscience: so still, thin, and pale, every breath painful, every last moment of life a prison of suffering. Every hour, she asked God to take her, to let her die. Dad broke down and had to leave the room. It was Jordan who'd held Mom's hand while she left this world for the next. She had been fourteen years old, but the enormity of her mother's death aged her. After that, nothing was the same. That anyone would kill his mother . . . it didn't compute. "How could you do that?"

"You could say it was my last act of compassion, sacrificing my mother for my brothers' immortal souls. It worked. The release of her spirit made God and Lucifer aware of them, of what they faced if something wasn't done. For me, it was too late. I was lost."

Tears continued to drip onto her jeans. Through no fault of

his own, he was a monster, a freak of Hell without a soul.

"With immortality came the ability to move around the world with just a thought. In the beginning, I didn't know where I was, but I found people, lots of them, and it didn't take long to cultivate followers. I had a certain power, a charisma some found irresistible."

Irresistible? How could anyone see past those horrible, dead eyes?

"Lucifer was aware when I gained another soul, knew what it meant to him in the long run. To prevent me from collecting more, he and God came to an understanding about my brothers. When they turned eighteen and jumped to immortality, God blessed them, allowing them to keep the light of our mother in their souls. In return, Lucifer promised they would spend their days hunting my followers. The mortals die when they're sent to Hell on Earth, but their souls are trapped there, a loss for me. The immortals live, but their existence is horrific." He leveled a sober gaze at her. "I granted immortality to Ron Trent six months ago."

No wonder Mr. Trent seemed so different. He'd been her dad's friend for as long as Jordan could remember, but lately it seemed like all they did was argue.

"How did you feel about Ron Trent?"

"I was afraid of him."

"You feel the threat of the lost souls and immortals because you're not like ordinary humans. I'm guessing you have a gift for making friends. You attract people."

What had Matthew said? *"It's whatever's inside you that makes everybody want to hang with you."* She didn't get it, had no idea why being Anabo set her apart from anyone else.

"You can't fathom what lies within other humans. They fight temptation, every day, every minute. Your father is a perfect example. He's a good man with noble intentions, but he's in way over his head, surrounded by people he doesn't realize have a different agenda. They've helped get him into trouble, and he's close to seeing no way out, no possible recourse for the United States."

"And you have all the answers?"

"I have solutions."

"That work to your advantage." She was overwhelmed with longing for her father.

"Unfortunately, my brothers somehow discovered my plan and interfered. I may have temporarily lost the president as a follower, but in a weird twist of fate, I now have an Anabo."

She felt as if her skin would slide from her bones and land in a heap of despair on the carpet beneath her chair.

"In the end, he'll give in. Every human, except the Anabo, will turn his back on God if the temptation is great enough. Your father prays for help, but in God's usual way of ignoring humanity, divine intervention won't be forthcoming."

"God doesn't ignore humanity. He just doesn't interfere."

"Then of what use is he? Your father will eventually understand this and agree to follow me."

"He'd never willingly turn his back on God. If he ever agrees, it will be because you coerced him, or tricked him."

"It's not within my power to do that, Jordan. If a human isn't sincere in his desire to follow, it can't happen."

"Then why did you kidnap me if it wasn't to coerce him?"

"To the world, Red Out kidnapped you. Ron Trent was to use them as an example of the resources available to your father. If he's with me, he can stage events to sway public opinion and eventually lead people to where I want them."

"Why would you think he'd hand his soul over to the guy who kidnapped his daughter?"

Eryx was smug. "I'm banking on President Ellis instead of your father. He's painted himself into a corner and sees no way out. I'll show him a way, and he'll choose saving his presidency over righteous anger."

Jordan felt cold all over. Dad was in major trouble, she knew, and everyone had a breaking point. She had hundreds of e-mails from suicidal teens to prove it. "Do you think you can convince me to follow you?"

"No, but you'll stay with me."

Everything he'd said was leading to this. She saw that now. Her fear of death was gone, and in its place was the realization that there really might be something worse than dying. Hugging herself more tightly, she asked, "What do you want from me?"

His lifeless eyes moved across her slowly, as if he were checking her out. "I want you to have my children."

God help her. "Why me?" Her voice came out in a whisper. "Why not one of your followers?"

"Neither I nor my brothers can have offspring with an ordinary human. An Anabo, if she becomes immortal, can bear our sons. We all want extensions of ourselves, the better to fight the enemy, but there are so very few Anabo . . . You see the problem."

She swallowed and leaned forward to stare at her boots, not sure if she was more grossed out or embarrassed. She had to figure out a way to get away from him. She had to escape. There wasn't anything she could do at the moment, but as soon as they landed, she'd take stock and make a plan.

He was so still, as if he was holding his breath. "A child of ours would have amazing capabilities. He could go my way, or he could go yours. I'll ensure, from birth, he goes mine."

"He?"

"Only a son can become what I need."

She didn't know why a girl wouldn't fit what he wanted, but she didn't care. She would never have his children, boys or girls. "How could you take the soul of a baby? How could he be sincere?"

"He'll grow up with me, see what I plan for the world, for Heaven and Hell. He'll become an immortal, but unlike any other. Powerful and influential, he'll have the light of the Anabo inside of him. People will follow him anywhere."

Every cell in her body revolted so violently, she was dizzy. Black spots floated across her vision, and the next thing she knew she was lying on the long bench seat, Smelly trying to pour water down her throat. Choking and coughing, she shoved it away. "Get out of my face!"

"So the Anabo has a temper," Eryx said, his face replacing Smelly's. "I realize you don't like the idea of giving me a son, but if your only other choice is death, why not accept it?"

Closing her eyes so she wouldn't have to look at him, she said, "You killed Matthew and tried to force my dad to turn his back on God. Twenty minutes ago, you planned to drop me into the ocean. You're evil worse than Satan, but you expect me to have your baby? You may be lost, your soul as dark as midnight, but you're not stupid. Why would you delude yourself into believing that I'd agree to it?"

"Why would you delude yourself into thinking that I care if you agree?"

Her eyes flew open, and she saw the look of triumph on his incredible face. "You're a monster."

"Am I, Jordan? How do you know human beings wouldn't be happier if they didn't have to try for Heaven, if they knew Hell was all that waited for them at the end of life? No one could pass judgment. Think of the wars fought in God's name. Take away the promise of Heaven and nobody's right, nobody's wrong. My son will go out in the world and preach a new gospel. People will listen and follow. The world will change, in some ways for the better."

What had Maggie said? *"An abductor has wants and needs, same as anybody, and he's convinced he's doing something noble, something that makes him a hero in his own mind."* So maybe Eryx wasn't going for noble, but he believed he was truth, God was useless, and

Lucifer was only a roadblock. He was like every other terrorist, determined to make others believe as he believed. The difference was, he was born of Hell, and his soul was without light. He didn't blow people up to prove his point; he collected souls.

She'd be damned before she'd help him.

THREE

SHE CRINGED WHEN HE BENT TO PICK HER UP. WAS HE GOING to take her somewhere on this plane and rape her? He'd said she had to be immortal to have his children, and she was still alive. Was he going to kill her?

Shaking with fear, she heard him say to Smelly, "Take a lock of her hair to prove that you had her, then cut the binding around her ankles."

Seconds later, she felt blood rush to her feet, her skin prickling at the sudden warmth.

"I'm taking her to Erinýes. You understand what you're to do when you land in London and are taken into custody?"

"I say we had instructions from Red Out to drop her over the Atlantic."

"That's right. They'll eventually execute the Texas group leaders, and you, of course, so this is good-bye."

Before Smelly could respond, before she could process that her fake death would be world news within a few hours and her father's heart would break all over again, everything went dark, and she felt weightless again. In other circumstances, like if he were an angel or some other benefactor of the paranormal, she'd think it was incredible to travel through the ether from one place to another. As it was, in the seconds the trip lasted, all she could think about was how she was going to escape. And that Eryx smelled like a burned matchstick.

When she could see again, he set her on her feet and stepped back. "I hadn't planned to keep you alive, so it'll be a while before a room can be prepared for you."

Just as she suspected, he'd been lying about letting her return home, regardless of whether or not her father pledged his soul.

Looking around at the stone walls and flagstone floor, at the massive bed with crimson velvet hangings, at the candles in sconces, the Renaissance paintings in gilt frames, and a fireplace so huge the whole graduating class at Oates could fit inside, she thought of Dracula's castle, which must be nearby, since Eryx had said he lived in the Carpathians.

She knew, without asking, that they were in his room.

"You should know, there's no possible way to escape. Outside, the grounds are under twenty-four-hour surveillance, and I have dogs. If you were to get past the edge of my land, your every move would be tracked by the GPS you'll have implanted. Once you become immortal and marked, we won't need the tracker because I'll have the ability to find you anywhere in the world. So I suggest you accept your fate and not exert yourself trying to escape."

She pretty much ignored him, already looking for ways to fight her way out. There was a collection of sabers and swords on one wall, but she shied away from those. She'd probably wind up falling on one. Glancing at the canopy railing around his bed, and the velvet ropes holding back the bed draperies, she wondered if she could tie him up while he slept.

"Here's Alissa, who'll show you to a bathroom where you can freshen up."

A petite young woman with long dark hair, dressed in a black sweater dress and killer shoes came to stand beside Eryx and glare at Jordan. "Isn't she the daughter of the American president?" she asked, with more animosity than curiosity.

"Yes. She's also Anabo, and I expect you to take good care of her. See that she has food and clean clothes, take her to Loren for a tracker, then bring her back to me."

Alissa looked up at him with a pout on her face. "If she's Anabo, she's never going to be what you want, Eryx. She'll never do for you what I do."

Eryx frowned at her. "And you'll never do for me what she can do. Retract your claws, Alissa, and do as you're told."

Wrapping her fingers around Jordan's arm, she pulled her

toward the door, and Jordan took one last look at the bed, at the velvet ropes, promising herself she'd find a way. Then they were in a wide stone corridor, lined with oil lanterns. Was there no electricity in this castle?

Jerking her arm free of Alissa's bruising fingers, she said, "It's not like I can run away. Back off."

Alissa practically hissed at her, but she continued walking, taking so many turns, Jordan soon became hopelessly lost. They climbed a winding set of narrow stone steps inside a tower, then walked down another long corridor, one wall lined with thin stained-glass windows, slits really, that cast red light along the opposite wall. They were in Romania, seven or eight hours ahead of D.C. It was midmorning here.

Toward the end of a long hall, where there were no more windows, where the gloom was oppressive, Alissa stopped at a rough wooden door that was straight out of a pirate movie, with heavy iron hinges and a serious iron handle and lock. She looked at Jordan with eyes full of hate. "I'll wait here for you to finish."

Deciding against telling Alissa that her jealousy was a total waste because Jordan planned to escape as soon as possible, she opened the door and saw exactly nothing. "Is there a light?"

Alissa reached around the doorframe and flipped a switch, bathing the room in the dim light from an incandescent bulb, hanging from a plaster ceiling. As soon as the light came on, ginormous roaches scurried under the claw-foot tub, behind the ancient-looking toilet, beneath the rotting wood of the cabinet below the sink.

Her heart nearly beat her to death. Irrational, maybe, but her fear of cockroaches bordered on phobia. "Eryx told you to take good care of me, Alissa. He's going to be way pissed that you brought me here."

"You need to learn how it's going to be. No one takes my place. Understand?" Alissa pushed her inside and closed the door. Jordan heard the key turn in the lock, followed by Alissa's laughter.

Horror kept her rooted to the spot. But not for long. The stillness faked them out, and while she stood there, the cockroaches began to emerge, despite the light. She unclenched her hands and leaped for the vanity, scrambling to get on top of it. Standing, she looked over into the tub and cringed. There were a zillion of them in there. Carefully leaning over, she turned the spigot on the bathtub pipes and watched rusty water run into the dirt lining the tub.

The roaches didn't drown.

Of course they didn't.

They swam.

Breathing hard, adrenaline pumping fast and furious, she watched in horror as more bugs poured out of the drain. She'd had nightmares about roaches that hadn't been this terrifying.

"*Alissa!* Open the door! Let me out of here, *now!* Hello? *Alissa!*"

A loud thump sounded against the door, then the key squeaked and the door opened quickly. Expecting to see Alissa, she caught her breath when she saw someone else standing there, looking across at her with an odd expression on his handsome face. He looked a little like Eryx. Actually, he looked a lot like Eryx. Young, with the same coal-black hair—except this guy's was long, past his very wide shoulders—and the same sharp cheekbones, but his face wasn't quite as beautiful. The most striking difference was his eyes—black as midnight, just like Eryx's, but these eyes weren't lifeless. This had to be one of his brothers. One of the Mephisto.

He was dressed completely opposite from Eryx and his Armani suit. This guy wore a black T beneath a black leather trench coat that ended just where his black biker boots poked from beneath black leathers. Mr. Monochrome.

He was staring at her, his gaze mesmerizing. "Why are you standing on the sink?" he asked, his voice deep, with more than a little bit of British.

"I'm scared to death of the roaches."

His gaze moved down to the floor, and she could swear he smiled. "You're a captive of unimaginable evil, but you're losing it over bugs?"

"It's not funny. I'm having a heart attack, I'm so freaked out. And more are coming out of the drain." She hated that her voice quavered a little at the end.

"They won't hurt you," he said, moving into the bathroom to stand just in front of her.

"I know, but it doesn't matter. If one gets on me . . . if it touches me . . . "

He reached out and lifted her from the sink, dropping her just to his waist. "Wrap your legs around me."

She did, and wound her arms around his neck, clinging to him while she silently thanked God for sending help. He was warm, and she instantly felt better. Closing her eyes as he turned and walked out of the bathroom, she inhaled the clean, fresh scent of him. He smelled like evergreens. Like the forest. "Thank you," she whispered.

He made no reply but kept walking, and she kept her arms around his neck, not knowing where he was taking her, not really caring. "What happened to Alissa?"

"She's unconscious and won't wake up for several hours. The rest of the castle is also unconscious, so getting out of here should be without drama."

"You're one of the Mephisto."

"Yes. I'm Kyros."

"The one they call Key."

"Eryx told you about me?"

"He told me a lot of things."

"Tell me later and I'll let you know what's true and what are lies."

"Why did you come for me?"

"Because you're Anabo. It's my duty to protect the Anabo."

"How do you know? Eryx thinks he got one over on you."

"My brother saw you at Christmas. As for Eryx, if he was

aware that we know you're Anabo, he'd have had everyone in the castle on full alert, to keep us from rescuing you. Since he has no clue, I was able to sneak in and take everyone out of commission."

"How did your brother know I'm Anabo?"

"You have a glow, an aura around you."

Just when she'd thought this situation couldn't get any weirder. "Why didn't Eryx see it? He didn't figure it out until one of his minions made me take off my sweater and he saw my birthmark."

"Only the Mephisto and others who help us can see the Anabo glow." He continued walking, but she sensed an urgency in him, as if he wanted to run. "Why . . . what was the reason he made you take off your sweater?"

She swallowed and clung a little harder to him. "They were going to drop me in the ocean. He wanted an article of clothing as proof that they'd had me on the plane."

His arms tightened so much, her breath left in a little whoosh. "But he saw the mark and called it off?"

"Right." She was so glad to be rescued, elated to be leaving this house of horrors. "Are you taking me back to Washington?"

"I'm taking you to Colorado, where my brothers and I live."

Had she just traded one nightmare for another? "But I want to go home. My dad . . . this has to be killing him."

Key said nothing.

"Why aren't you taking me back to my father?"

"It's complicated."

"Give me the short answer."

"Did Eryx mention why he let you live?"

"He wants me to give him a son."

He whispered a curse. "Now he knows what you are, there's nowhere on Earth you'll be safe from him except our mountain. He can't go there."

Panic rose up. "I'll have to stay with the Mephisto on a mountain the *rest of my life*?"

"Unless you want the rest of your life to last less than twenty-four hours, or unless you . . . " He didn't finish.

"What? Unless what?"

"You give up Anabo. If you do, you'll be like everyone else and of no interest to Eryx."

There was a way out! She could go home, to Dad, to her life. "How do I give up Anabo?"

"Through Lucifer." They were close to the end of the long hallway, but he slowed his pace. "It's not something to be done lightly, Jordan. You need to know everything there is to know before you make a decision like that."

"Okay." No contest. She would lose Anabo as soon as possible.

Moments later, he stopped. "This staircase is too narrow to carry you down. Are you okay to walk?"

"I'm fine." She slowly unfolded her legs from around his hips and slid down the front of him, looking up into his face when her feet touched the floor. He was way tall. The top of her head barely reached his shoulder. He was looking at her like he was in awe or something, and she wasn't sure if it was flattering or just kind of strange.

He nodded toward the stairs. "We need to go now."

"Can't you transport us away from here? Or is that unique to Eryx?"

"I can, but not from this castle or from his land. He keeps everything under lockdown. We have to make it to the fence line before I can take us to Colorado, and that's a mile-and-a-half hike across the side of a mountain."

Turning, she started down the winding stone staircase, feeling as if the cold, damp walls were closing in on her. At the bottom, he held a finger to his lips, then reached for her hand and took off in the opposite direction of what she thought was the front of the castle. But she was all turned around, and he appeared to know where he was going, so she hurried along with him and didn't say a word.

Eventually, they came to a large, oak door, which he pulled open with little effort, waving her through. When she was outside, she dragged the cold morning air into her lungs, feeling almost euphoric to be out of there. Looking up, she realized this was a side of the castle, not the front. "Eryx said he has dogs."

"I've already taken care of the dogs. The only one awake is Eryx. Unfortunately, he's also the only one who really matters. We have to run, Jordan. Are you up for it?"

She nodded, sucked in a deep breath, and whispered, "Let's go."

What followed was the most grueling physical experience of her life. She played volleyball at school and wasn't half bad. When she was younger, she'd taken gymnastics. She always thought she was in pretty good physical shape, but running with Key across the side of a mountain, on frozen ground, patchy with ice and snow, made it clear just how much of a lightweight she was. Her lungs screamed in agony, her feet were frozen, and she knew her boots were rubbing killer blisters on both heels. Still, he kept on, and she suspected this wasn't difficult for him at all. If anything, he seemed to be pacing himself so she could keep up.

He proved it when he slowed slightly, snaked out an arm, and hauled her up and onto his back. "Almost there," he said as he ran, not breathless at all. "We'll be gone in less than five, but just in case something goes wrong, will you promise me one thing?"

"Maybe. What is it?"

"Do whatever it takes to stay alive. Don't despair, and don't think you've been abandoned. I'll keep coming back until I can take you away from here. But you have to stay alive. Promise?"

"Do you promise to come back?"

"I promise."

"It's all beside the point anyway. There's the fence, just ahead." She could see wrought-iron spikes rising up from the forest floor. On the other side was freedom.

She felt Key's body tense at the same time she saw the figure appear in front of the fence. "You knew he'd be here," she whispered against his ear as he slowed to a walk.

"I can mentally search for him and know exactly where he is. I could feel him moving through the castle. Unfortunately, he also knows where I am, and he's as smart as his soul is dark."

Seeing those eyes again made her nauseous. "*Please* don't let him take me back." Panicking, she clung tighter to Key's neck, her legs in a viselike grip around his waist.

They were close now, so close she saw with perfect clarity when Eryx raised his arm, aimed a gun at them and fired one, two, three, four shots. Key's body jerked as each bullet met flesh, but incredibly, he remained standing. "Run, Jordan," he said roughly, lowering his arms from where they were hooked around her legs. "Run and hide."

She slid from his back, then turned and fled, flinching when she heard more shots. She glanced over her shoulder and saw Key fall to his knees, his body twitching as each bullet hit him.

Running faster, she dodged around branches, leaped over rocks, slipped and fell, scrambled back to her feet, and took off again.

It made no difference. She rounded a huge boulder, and there was Eryx, staring at her from those dead eyes. She skidded to a stop, gasping for breath, silently shouting for God to help her, to make this go away.

She expected Eryx to force her back to the castle.

Instead, he pulled a different gun from his pocket, raised his arm, and fired. The force of the shot knocked her backward, and as she fell, as her heart stopped, she looked up at the sky between boughs of evergreen and saw a raven swooping toward her.

FOUR

"I'm dead, aren't I?"

"For the moment. You can go back, but only if it's what you want."

"I don't feel dead." Looking down, she saw no blood, no bullet wound through her heart. She felt so strange. Instead of fear and horror, she actually felt . . . relieved.

"Death brings release of human anguish, Jordan. Everyone fears death, but for obvious reasons, it's lost after you die. There'll be no more physical pain, unless you decide to become immortal. Living forever in the realm of physical reality leaves you impervious to death, but as vulnerable to pain as humanity."

She was enchanted by the woman on the rock. In the half-light of predawn, they were perched on an enormous boulder, suspended above a snow-lined rushing stream. "Where are we?"

"In Colorado, on the Mephisto Mountain. It's lovely here, isn't it?"

"Who are you?"

Petite, with long, curling dark hair, olive skin, and the bluest eyes, wearing holey jeans and a faded Woodstock T-shirt, the woman was divinely beautiful. "I'm the angel, Mary Michael. I've been visiting you in your dreams all of your life, but you don't remember me after you wake up. I'm something of an adviser."

"Like a guardian angel?"

"There's no such thing as guardian angels. I was chosen to visit the Anabo, to help them navigate life. It's difficult to be pure of spirit in a world cast in darkness."

"But I didn't know I was Anabo until a few hours ago."

"You knew, in some secret part of your soul, just as others knew there was something irresistible about you. As attractive as you are to humanity, you're like oxygen to the Mephisto." Mary Michael smiled. "What you have to decide right now is if you'll accept immortality and walk the Earth until Eryx has been defeated, or until there is no humanity, whichever comes first."

"I guess the alternative is Hell?"

Mary Michael looked puzzled. "Why would you think so?"

"I saw a raven coming for me, and I'm certain it was from Hell."

Mary Michael's reaction was bizarre. She began to cry, turning her face away to stare out at the snow-covered mountains.

Jordan wasn't sure what to say—how did one offer comfort to an angel?—so she said nothing.

After a while, the angel appeared to pull herself together and gave her a watery smile. "Ravens live in the forests of the world, so it's not unusual that you saw one before you died. As Anabo, you were destined for Heaven from the day you were born. If you choose not to become immortal, I'll take you back with me."

Jordan narrowed her eyes. "What are you not telling me?"

Looking away from her again, Mary Michael said quietly, "The raven was Mephistopheles. He was there to protect you, but Eryx must have seen him and shot you before the raven could interfere."

"Why would Mephistopheles want to protect me?"

"Because death means you can never go back to humanity. It makes things difficult."

"And this makes you cry because . . . ?"

"I . . . I don't know. I apologize. This is about you, not me, so you need to make a decision. Will you accept immortality?"

"I'm not really clear why I would. What would happen to me? Where would I go? Wouldn't it be discovered, considering I'd never grow old?"

"Your time in the real world would be limited and for specific reasons. Most of the time you'd live on this mountain and help the Mephisto in their quest to find Eryx's followers. Others are here, good people who exchange mortality to become Luminas and help the Mephisto. If you stay, you'll be educated further and encouraged to find a job that suits your talents. Everyone on the Mephisto Mountain works."

"So what you said about my being oxygen to the Mephisto, is this what you meant? If I become a Lumina, I can help them?"

Again, Mary Michael looked away. "No, that's not what I meant."

"What, then? Why am I so important to them?"

Obviously trying hard not to cry again, Mary Michael said in a soft voice, "They've been alive over a thousand years, but forever eighteen. They're immortal, with certain abilities, but human in most every other way. They crave friendship, love, and affection. A companion. A soul mate. Because of what they are, humans are frightened of them, so they have only one another."

"What about the Luminas?"

"They're not afraid, but what they are precludes them from the ability to accept a Mephisto as a mate. Even though they're living angels, they still harbor a dark side. Minimal, for sure, but it's there. It's in the souls of all mankind, within the spirits of the angels. How do you think Lucifer fell from grace? He gave in to his dark side. Only the Anabo are free of temptation. Only an Anabo can find it within herself to love a child of Hell, to be close with him and not feel the pull of the dark. Unfortunately, there've been only a handful born in the past thousand years."

Understanding dawned, and she thought of Key, how he had looked at her as if she was amazing. Like he was in awe of her. In life, others wanted to be with her because she was the president's daughter. In death, the Mephisto wanted to be with her because she was Anabo. The only people who liked her just because they liked her were Matthew and Tessa. "So if I become immortal, I'll have six guys wanting to be with me?"

"Only one. It was part of the bargain Lucifer struck with God when the Mephisto were created. If an Anabo could be claimed by any of them, the fight that would follow among them would cause a rift no one could ever heal. What makes them strong enough to fight Eryx is their unity. So God insisted they would know which of them is intended for an Anabo."

The idea fascinated and repelled her at the same time. "How do they know?"

"By scent."

Remembering the scent of evergreen clinging to Key, Jordan said, "It's Key, isn't it?"

"Yes, but you have a choice. If you don't like him, if it doesn't work out, you don't have to accept him. You can find someone among the Luminas, and he'll wait for another Anabo." Her smile was soft. "But he won't give up on you easily. Just so you know."

"What if . . . I mean, wow, this is *so* weird." After a long pause, she asked, "What if he doesn't like me?"

"Everyone likes you, Jordan."

"Evidently, just because of the Anabo thing."

"I suspect Key will like a lot more about you than the circumstances of your birth. He's very serious, a loner, more so than his brothers, and he experiences things the others don't. You have what he values above all else, even if he's not fully aware of it." Mary Michael reached out and touched her hair. "Kyros leads the Mephisto. Every decision, every immortal life on this mountain, every move made is ultimately his responsibility. He can't be with a girl who's not equal to his strengths. You're what he needs."

"But maybe not what he wants?"

"He thinks he wants a pretty girl who'll admire, respect, and listen to him, appreciate his greenhouse, and stay out of his way when he's doing his leader-of-the-Mephisto thing. Kyros takes alpha male to extremes."

"This sounds about as romantic as cold oatmeal."

"Don't trip over romance, Jordan. I'm talking about deep, selfless *love*. Even though he can't fathom what it means to love a girl more than anything or anyone else, including himself, he longs for something he can't even name. It drives everything he does. Because of the events of the past several hours, everything for him has changed. He has something he never had before."

Jordan cocked a questioning brow.

Mary Michael whispered, "Hope."

"Do whatever it takes to stay alive." No wonder he was so adamant that she promise. But did she ever say it? Did she promise? "He was shot. Eryx shot him."

"He's recovered, and right now, he's struggling to bring you back to life."

"What about Eryx? If I go back, he's still a threat, right?"

"Yes, but he can't get to you on this mountain, and even if he could, he can't force you to have his child. An immortal Anabo can conceive only when she wants to."

The angel rose to her feet, bare in the snow on the boulder, and held out her hands. "Time's up, Jordan. Will you live forever and join the Mephisto in their fight against Eryx? Or do you choose to end your time on Earth and go with me to Heaven?"

"If I choose Heaven, will I see my mother?"

Mary Michael nodded.

"And Matthew?"

The angel's smile faded, and she dropped her hands.

Turning her face to the snowy sky, Jordan couldn't believe it. "He's all that's good, everything people are supposed to be. How could Matthew not be in Heaven?"

"Because he's not dead."

"What?"

"He lingers, Jordan." Mary Michael came close and bent to look into her eyes. "But it makes no difference. Don't make this decision based on anything but your own feelings. Even if Matthew lives, if he recovers, you can never be with him again. He's human, and, if you return, you'll be an immortal. It's forbidden for immortals to go out among the humans unless it's necessary." She straightened and looked toward the mountains. "You have to leave Matthew, your father, and your human life behind. Tell me you understand."

"I understand." But it didn't change that she was elated. Matthew was alive!

Standing, Jordan looked at the mountains all around, at the snow falling softly. It was breathtakingly beautiful, but could she spend the rest of eternity here? She watched a raven as it flew to the branch of a fir tree. The wind picked up, and within the whispers of the evergreens, she heard Key's voice, calling her name.

She went completely still, listening.

He was more than mournful.

He was desolate.

Turning her head, she looked to the angel.

With fresh tears in her incredible blue eyes, Mary Michael began to fade. "Now, Jordan. Make your decision now . . . "

FIVE

CLUTCHING JORDAN TO HIS CHEST, KEY TRIED TO BLANK HIS mind of anything except sharing his life force with her, but it was next to impossible to stop himself from replaying her death. He'd caught up to her just in time to see Eryx fire a shot through her heart, sending her to the ground. She had died instantly, and Key hadn't let a nanosecond pass before he was on Eryx with his switchblade. His brother thought Key was down, giving him the element of surprise. He cut Eryx's throat, then restrained him until he bled out, staring down into his flat, dead eyes until they closed, never letting go of the image of Jordan hitting the ground.

Half an hour later, she was still unmoving. Why wouldn't she come back? How could he convince her to wake from death to immortality? His energy continued to deplete, but he couldn't give up, wouldn't stop trying. "Don't go," he whispered into her soft, dark hair. "Not like this. Give me a chance and I swear you won't regret it."

He stilled when he heard her say, "What if I do regret it? Will you let me go?"

Her arms slipped around his neck, and she was there, with him, life coursing through her small body, surrounding him with the scent of bluebells. He wrapped his arms more tightly around her. "You came back," he whispered into her silky hair.

"I promised to stay alive. Remember?"

He held her tighter against him, and for the first time in his life, he knew what it felt like to be happy.

"Eryx?" she asked.

"I took him down."

"But I thought—"

"We're immortal, but we can be taken out temporarily. He thought I was down." He loosened his hold on her enough to reach inside his coat and withdraw the rabbit. "I don't know how, because its stuffing is so thin, but this took most of the bullets. I was barely hit." He looked into her wide eyes and could see she was shocked. Then he looked at the rabbit and mumbled, "I'll get you another one." Mister Bunny was in pieces.

"It's okay, Key. I don't want another one. It wouldn't be the same. He's all I had from before I was adopted. I was carrying him when I was left at the orphanage in Bucharest." She looked up at him. "He changed everything, didn't he?"

If Eryx had been the one to bring her back, he wouldn't have wasted a minute before marking her, and her immortality would have made the mark permanent. Even if Key and the Mephisto had managed to rescue her again, she'd have lived the rest of eternity with Eryx's mark. She could never become Mephisto, and no Lumina would touch her. As a pure spirit, she'd be tormented by the existence of his evil within her body.

Feeling light-headed, Key nodded slowly. "Everything." Instead of tossing the old thing away, he shoved the ragged pieces back in his pocket, then stood, still holding her in his arms. He swayed with the effort.

"Are you okay?"

He slowly set her on her feet and reached into his pocket for an energy bar. "I'm drained," he told her as he unwrapped it and ate it in two bites. Swallowing, he waited for a spike in energy, but it was way too little to get them over the fence and back to Colorado.

She was staring at him with a weird look on her face. "You're very pale."

"I gave you the bigger part of my humanity to bring you back. As soon as I get more food, I'll be good." And maybe twelve hours of sleep. He couldn't remember ever being this exhausted. "How about you? Feeling okay?"

"Mentally, you don't wanna know, but physically, never better." She reached for his hand and started walking toward the fence. "Can you take us to Colorado if I can get us to the other side?"

He hoped so, but it was taking all his effort just to follow her through Eryx's forest. With his free hand, he pulled out his cell and cursed when he saw there was no service, even though this was the middle of the Carpathian Mountains and it made perfect sense that there would be no service.

She saw him replace the phone in his pocket. "Can you get to your home, to one of your brothers, if you don't have to carry me?"

"I think so, but no way I'm leaving you here alone."

"Sure you are. Go home and tell one of the other Mephisto to come get me. Easy."

"Eryx will wake up, probably in another half hour. It wasn't easy to rescue you, but if he gets you again, it'll be . . . " He didn't finish, didn't tell her exactly how much jeopardy she'd be in if Eryx recaptured her. No matter what cost to himself, he had to get her out of here. "I can't leave you, Jordan. I'll figure something out."

"Key, you've got no choice. If you don't have the energy to carry me to Colorado, that means we're both stuck here."

He wanted to argue, but he didn't have the strength. The thought of leaving her here was screwing with his mind, making him lose focus. He tightened his hand around hers.

They reached the fence, eight feet of wrought-iron spikes with only three crossbars, which meant throwing a leg over and climbing down the other side was impossible without impaling themselves. They'd have to scale the top three feet, get a foothold between the spikes, and jump. Key eyed it, wearily thinking it'd be just as easy to scale Everest.

"You can do this," she said, already lifting herself up to the second crossbar.

"You can't jump to the ground without breaking something. Wait for me to get over so I can catch you."

Ignoring him, she grasped the topmost bar, walked herself up, and, with zero hesitation, launched herself into the air. She bent her knees at just the right moment, and the thick carpet of forest needles cushioned her landing. On her feet. No tuck and roll.

Key was incredulous. And way impressed.

She grinned at him. "When I was twelve, I was convinced I could be an Olympic gymnast. No way I was *that* good, but I did practice a lot." She came toward the fence. "Your turn, Kyros."

He grabbed onto the top crossbar and tried to heave himself up, but didn't make it. Sliding back to the ground, he stared at her through the fence. "This is humiliating."

"Like I'm judging you? You just brought me back to life. Come on, Key. Concentrate."

It took three more tries before he made the top of the fence, and his landing on the other side was way less nimble than hers. He crumpled into a bundle of exhaustion at her feet. While he forced himself to a sit, she knelt before him and said in a low voice, "I hear something. Go to Colorado now, and I'm going to climb a tree and hide."

Blinking away unconsciousness, Key admitted defeat and replied, "Climb the tree. Then I'll go for help."

Without another word, she stood, turned, and ran away from him. She took a huge leap and just made the lowest branch of a maple tree, then swung herself up to another and climbed until she was very high off the ground. Without leaves, the tree didn't hide her, but she was high enough that no one would notice her unless he looked up. Eryx wouldn't. He'd look ahead.

Despising the weakness forcing him to leave her, Key closed his eyes and transported to the Mephisto house. He fell in a heap on the onyx *M* in the front hall, rolled to his back, and used the last burst of energy in his body to yell, "Phoenix! Can you hear me? *Phoenix!*"

His brother materialized next to him, took one look at his face, and dropped to his knees. "Where is she?"

"A mile and a half from Erinýes, outside the east fence, in a maple tree. Eryx is after her." He drew in a breath and saw Jax appear next to Phoenix. "He shot her, and I brought her back."

Phoenix nodded and disappeared.

Key fought to sit up, but couldn't. He heard Jax shouting but was incapable of a coherent response, and in spite of his iron will to remain conscious, he slipped into darkness.

❧

From her perch high in the tree, Jordan watched Eryx materialize on this side of the fence. He looked bad, white as a ghost, covered in blood, but his voice was strong and loud, echoing through the forest. "I know you're out here, Jordan. Key is in Colorado, but you're not. He was too weak to carry you, wasn't he?" He walked away from the fence, away from her tree, talking as he went. "If you don't come out, surrender yourself, and agree to stay with me, the price you pay will be very dear."

What could he do to her? He couldn't kill her. She was already dead and resurrected. Mary Michael said he couldn't make her have his baby. She told herself she wasn't afraid, but the quiver in her belly made her a liar. She was scared out of her mind.

"The Mephisto will come for you, and if you go with them, those you left behind in your human life will suffer. Think about your father, the boy Matthew, and your friend Tessa."

He knew about Tessa? Did he know every nook and cranny of her life?

"Stay with me and they'll live the life God intended for them. Leave and I'll ensure they each belong to me before they die. Never underestimate my ability to persuade humans to follow me."

His voice became quieter as he moved farther away from the tree, but Jordan heard every word. Freezing, she clung tight to the tree's trunk, determined not to be swayed by anything he said. He was evil worse than Lucifer, made to deceive and cheat people into giving him what he wanted. If she stayed, he'd still go after Dad. Maybe Matthew and Tessa, as well. Her best bet for protecting them was from the side of the Mephisto.

"You're something of an idol in the United States, aren't

you? You receive hundreds, even thousands, of e-mails every week from young people, some of them looking for help or advice, and you spend hours replying to them. Carla answers most, but she pulls the saddest for you, doesn't she? Carla is mine now, Jordan."

She squeezed her eyes closed. No wonder Carla had texted Eryx when his plan to convert Jordan's father went south.

"You also get e-mails from kids considering suicide, and nothing is as desperate as a suicidal teen. I have all those e-mails, Jordan. The ones who chose to live are still at risk, and I know what they want, what they need."

She rested her forehead against the rough bark and wished for the millionth time that she wasn't the daughter of the president. All it had ever gotten her was pain and grief. Now, in the strangest twist of all, being the First Daughter meant all those kids who wrote to her were one step closer than the rest of humanity to having their souls annihilated.

"I'll send my immortals to work the hotlines, and they'll offer an alternative to suicide that'll be just what the sad, hopeless callers want—the promise of freedom from torment if they'll follow me. Remember Holly?"

Tree bark dug into her palms with the effort it took not to whimper.

"She needed help, but Carla said, even with all you did for her, she still chose to die. It must have been hard for you, being the one to find her. "

Crying would be the worst thing at this moment. She bit her lip and pressed harder against the bark.

"What if Holly had called the STOP hotline that day instead of hanging herself? Imagine if the voice on the other end had offered her a way out of the mess that was her life. She'd have grabbed at the chance because she thought all her other options were gone."

He has no soul. No conscience. No heart. She told herself these things, but it didn't relieve the pain he inflicted, or the harsh truth to his words. Holly would have done anything if she thought it would put an end to her misery, even give away her soul.

"I'll place immortals where they can influence the kids who wrote to you and didn't kill themselves. They'll go as educators, Scout leaders, spiritual advisers, dance instructors, music teachers, doctors, and coaches. I'll gain thousands of young followers, all thanks to your e-mails."

His voice had grown louder, which meant he was headed back toward her tree. Stiff with cold and anxiety, she watched him through limbs of evergreen and hardwood until he was just below where she waited.

That's when she saw the footprint in a patch of snow. Her footprint.

While she stood on the highest branch and prayed one of Key's brothers would show up *right now*, Eryx's head slowly tilted back until his eyes met hers. "What's it to be? Will you stay, or go?"

"I'm not staying."

"You care so little for your family and friends? For all those young people who look up to you?"

"My staying won't help you, Eryx. While I was dead, an angel told me you can't force me to have your children. I'm Anabo and immortal, which gives me the power to decide when and if I want to have a baby."

"To protect others, you'll agree to what I want."

"You're lying. If I agreed to give you ten thousand babies, you'd still use those e-mails to con kids into pledging their souls to you."

Before Eryx could respond, a guy with midnight hair, dressed all in black, appeared just behind him. This brother had a scruff beard and rage on his striking face. He never spoke, didn't make a sound, but she could tell Eryx knew he was there. He turned just as the new guy charged at him, and Jordan saw the glint of steel that caught the sunbeams knifing through the forest canopy, watched with morbid fascination when the Mephisto plunged his blade straight into Eryx's heart.

He shoved Eryx's limp body to the ground, then bent to wipe his dagger clean on Eryx's trousers. After he slipped it into a strap on his boot, he stood straight and looked up at her. "Let's go."

She was so ready to be gone, in her haste to climb down she slipped on a frozen limb, crashed through branches and twigs, and fell the last ten feet. He easily caught her in strong, sure arms, then looked down into her eyes. "Bad day?"

In spite of it all, maybe because her relief was so enormous, she smiled.

He didn't smile, but nodded and said, "I'm Phoenix. It's nice to meet you, Jordan."

Everything went dark. She had that same sensation of weightlessness, then ten seconds later, he was setting her on her feet. He stepped back and said solemnly, "Welcome to the Mephisto house."

She looked around quickly, astonished by the beauty of the circular grand hall. She'd been inside palaces that weren't this amazing. Rosewood and gilt, life-size portraits, and acres of white marble interrupted only by an ornate inlaid onyx *M* and the bottom step of a grand staircase. The domed ceiling was at least three stories above them, painted with angels and clouds. She took it all in within a few seconds. "Where in Colorado are we?"

"The San Juan Mountains, about ten miles from Telluride." He turned and nodded toward the stairs. "Come with me to see Key."

She walked beside him up the steps, then through winding wide corridors lined with masterpieces, lit by candles in sconces. "Why candles? Eryx has oil lanterns. Is there something about lightbulbs you guys don't like?"

"Our eyes are more sensitive to light than ordinary people." He glanced down at her. "But we also prefer the old ways of doing certain things."

They passed several doors, then he stopped in front of one and reached for the knob. "Prepare yourself, Jordan."

"For what?"

"To meet my brothers. They can be . . . intense." With that, he swung the door open and waited for her to step inside the room.

Calling it a room, however, didn't do it justice. She took a nanosecond to register a soaring ceiling, butter-yellow walls with more old paintings, silk drapes pushed away from a giant window framing the Rockies, French antiques, a wall of bookshelves, a beautiful rose marble fireplace, a cream wool rug partially covering gleaming wood floors, and a very huge bed with a very large guy lying in it.

Key was asleep, or unconscious, the covers just to his waist. Jordan blinked. She didn't see a lot of guys without their shirts on, except in summers on sailboats, but she could say with absolute certainty that none had ever looked like Key.

He had a cluster of bruises on the right side of his chest, above his heart. She shivered, imagining if he hadn't had the rabbit inside his coat. Those would be much worse than bruises, and she wouldn't be here right now.

She noticed he had a beautiful, ornate tattoo of an *M* on his right bicep; just below, in the crook of his arm, was an IV catheter.

Superfast observation over, she focused on the people in the room while Phoenix made introductions. They were all dressed completely in black, just like Key and Phoenix, including the girl, although she broke the monochrome with her blonde hair, which was pulled into a ponytail. She was gorgeous: tall, slender, and überfeminine, even in biker boots. Who was she? Eryx hadn't said anything about a sister.

"That's Jax." Phoenix pointed to the one who stood closest to the bed, next to the girl. "And his Anabo, Sasha. She came to us about a year ago."

Jordan felt enormous relief. Here was someone who knew what this was like, somebody who could explain what it meant to be Anabo.

Her joy was short-lived. Jax nodded and gave her a warm smile, but Sasha met her gaze and immediately started to cry. She turned away, toward the bed, and Jax slid his arm around her.

"This is Xenos, who goes by Zee." Phoenix nodded toward a guy leaning against the wall by the windows. He had a buzz cut, a diamond stud in one ear, and a tattoo of a question mark on his neck. Zee didn't smile. Or speak.

"Titus, we call Ty," Phoenix said, pointing at the only one seated.

His large hand stroked the head of the ginormous Irish wolfhound that sat next to his chair. "Hello, Jordan," he said, only slightly more friendly than a mother grizzly.

"Last, and youngest, is Denys."

This brother was the best looking, which was saying a lot, because every one of them was unholy hot. His dark gaze swept her from head to toe before he settled and stared at her chest. Geez, could he be more obvious? She was just about to threaten to poke his eyes out when he said, "Eryx didn't take any chances, did he? Looks like a nine millimeter."

"Forty-five caliber," Zee said.

Looking down, she saw a hole in her blue sweater, exposing pale skin beneath, without a wound or even a mark. The hole was right over her heart. No wonder she had died.

Denys asked, "What did you think of Eryx?"

Seriously? What kind of question was that? "I thought he was the scariest thing on the planet, then he shot me and I knew for sure he was."

"So you saw the real Eryx."

"Is there a fake Eryx?"

"Are you always this feisty?"

"It comes with being the daughter of the president." The tension in the room—almost hostility—set her teeth on edge. Had she totally screwed up by saying yes to immortality? Eternity with these people loomed large and awful. She wanted to go home, to Dad and her own room and Tessa and Matthew. But she could never go home.

Never.

She swayed a little as the enormity of it all hit her broadside.

Crap. She was *not* going to cry. Not now, not here. She suspected any sign of weakness would set the stage for the rest of time. Sucking it up, she asked Denys, "Are the Mephisto always this stone-cold?"

"It comes with being sons of Hell. We don't do jolly very well." He nodded toward the bed. "Especially today, with one of our own close to death."

Death? Key was *dying?* How? He was immortal.

Zee said, "We think it's because you took too much of his humanity. If he dies . . . " He didn't finish, but his meaning was clear. If Key died, they'd blame her.

"Tell us what happened," Ty said from his chair.

"After Eryx started shooting, Key told me to run, and I did, but Eryx caught up and shot me before I could hide." The finality of that made her short of breath. She stopped to draw in air and heard Sasha crying harder. "Are you okay?"

Sasha turned her face into Jax's shoulder and mumbled, "I'm so . . . sorry. I just feel so bad for . . . you. For Key. It's . . . I'm sorry."

"Go on and finish your story," Phoenix said with a solemn look. "She'll be all right."

"While I was dead, an angel brought me here." She nodded toward the window. "Out there. She explained things to me and gave me the choice of Heaven or the Mephisto Mountain."

"And you chose immortality," Denys said. "Just curious, but why?"

She looked toward the bed. How could she describe the way she'd felt, listening to Key calling her name? How could she explain what she didn't understand herself? One second, she was truly conflicted, and the next, it was no contest. Turning back to Denys, she simply said, "I promised him I wouldn't die." To Zee, who seemed the most angry with her, she said, "It's not as if I knew Key was in any danger."

"It's not your fault," Phoenix said. "Kyros undoubtedly did his usual absolute-ruler thing and tried to force you to come back."

Jordan shook her head. "I don't think so. He wasn't . . . it wasn't like that." She moved toward the bed to stand next to Jax and Sasha. Gazing down at Key, she thought he looked worse than he had in the forest. His skin was even paler.

His shoulders were broad, his arms contoured by muscle, and his chest . . . man, he was a big guy. She didn't want to do it but couldn't help making the comparison. Matthew was lean, with long, thin fingers. He had an artist's hands. Key was huge, and his hands, lying against pristine white sheets, were twice the size of hers. Other than the pallor of his skin, he looked the picture of health and fitness. But he was dying. Because of her. "He said that after he had more food, he'd be better." She glanced at the IV drip in his arm. "Isn't that the same thing as food?"

"It is," Jax said, "but it's not working, and we don't know why."

Stepping closer to the bed, she reached out, smoothed Key's hair away from his brow, and leaned over until she was right in his face. "I came back because of you," she whispered, "and I'm gonna be way pissed if you leave me."

He didn't move at all, made no indication he'd heard her.

The lovely scent of evergreens was much fainter now. She moved closer. "I'm going to see Matthew. The angel told me he lives, and I have to see him, one last time."

Nothing. Even the threat of leaving to see another guy didn't wake him up.

Sasha came close. "Will you kiss him?"

Turning her head, Jordan looked up into her eyes. They were an unusual shade of blue, dark and kind of smoky. "Why?"

"Just try, and see if it helps."

Jordan turned back to Key and kissed his cheek, the stubble along his jaw tickling her.

"No, I mean a real kiss, Jordan. On the mouth. Give him some of you."

Jordan faced the only person who could possibly be her ally at this moment. Intuitively, she knew this was crucial. "What will my spit do to him?"

Sasha swiped at the tears on her cheeks. "Maybe nothing, but isn't it worth a try?"

Glancing around at the other faces, Jordan felt like something was off, like they knew something she didn't. Meeting Sasha's eyes again, she asked, "What will Key's do to me?"

"Begin turning you to Mephisto. It's why you're here, isn't it?"

Jordan stepped back from the bed and looked toward Phoenix. "The angel said I'd become a Lumina. She never said anything about my becoming Mephisto."

He was obviously uncomfortable. "Did she tell you about Key? Do you understand why he was so desperate for you to become immortal?"

"I get it, but she said I'd have a choice, that if it didn't work out with Key, I'd be free to find someone else. Another Lumina. What will it mean if I'm Mephisto?"

"You're either single for all time, or stuck with Kyros," Denys said, looking like he wanted to laugh. "Good luck with that."

"Shut up, Denys," Ty said from his chair. He leveled a look at her. "If you're Mephisto, you'll go with us on takedowns. We do it all day, every day, and Eryx still gains ground. We need help."

"I can help if I'm a Lumina, can't I?"

"Yes, but your becoming Lumina would be like hiring Mozart to tune pianos, a complete waste of your ability. Only the Mephisto can take people to Hell on Earth, and only the Anabo can be changed to Mephisto."

She backed farther away from the bed. "I've known about Anabo, Eryx, and the Mephisto for less than twenty-four hours. I've been abducted, murdered, and brought back to life. My dad . . . my friends . . . the whole world thinks I'm dead, and, maybe if I'd picked Heaven, I wouldn't be so worried about that. But I'm still part of humanity, capable of feeling everything I felt before I died."

"And what do you feel?" Ty asked, looking a little less unforgiving.

"Confused. Sad." She darted a look at Key. "And so . . . scared." What if he died? She wanted to believe she came back for humanity, to help in the fight against Eryx, and that was true, but the main reason she chose to come back was because of Key, because she'd never forget the sound of his voice calling her name. But she didn't expect to have to make the decision about being with him forever fewer than thirty minutes after arriving on the Mephisto Mountain. "You don't even know if I can help him."

"No," Ty agreed, "but I don't know that you can't, and it's looking like you may be his only hope."

Turning away from all of them, she stared at the painting above the console close to the door. It was a beautiful manor house, majestic and stately, with mullioned windows and neatly trimmed ivy. She thought of all the times her father had been required to make a rushed decision that had the potential to change many lives, sometimes even at the expense of people's lives. She could picture him in his office, staring out the window up at the sky, asking God for guidance and strength.

She thought about Eryx and his determination to take Dad's soul. If he succeeded, if her father gave in, he wouldn't look at the sky and pray for help. He'd answer only to Eryx. The thought made her sick to her stomach.

"If I become Mephisto, can I convince people not to take Eryx's oath?"

No one answered.

Turning, she looked at Phoenix. "Can I?"

He slowly shook his head. "We aren't allowed to interfere with free will. All we can do is take out his Skia and lost souls, to keep them from recruiting new followers."

"Skia?"

"Eryx's immortals. In Greek, *skia* means shade, or shadow. The eyes are a window to the soul, and because the Skia have none, theirs are shaded. So are those of the lost souls, but not as much."

"What will happen to me? Will I be different than I am now?"

"You'll develop new abilities—like transporting, superhuman strength, and the capacity to see who are Skia and lost souls." He glanced at Sasha. "And who are Anabo."

"Those are all physical changes. Is it going to mess with my head?"

Zee spoke up from his spot by the window. "Becoming Mephisto is all about f'ing with your head. Right, Sasha?"

Clearly agitated, Sasha fiddled with the ear mic she held in her hand and said to the rug, "It's difficult to explain, but yeah, you'll see things a little differently."

"I don't even know what it means to be Anabo. How can I agree to become something else when I don't understand any of it?"

"You'll still be Anabo, still be certain of Heaven when humanity is gone, but you'll also be Mephisto."

"Do you regret it?"

Sasha jerked her gaze from the floor and met Jordan's eyes. "No, never."

"Give me *something*, Sasha. I'm lost."

The girl came a little closer, her eyes filled with tears. "If your father took the oath right now, you'd beg us not to take him. You'd be so devastated, it'd break your heart." She took another step closer. "If you were Mephisto and your dad took the oath, you wouldn't think twice about sending him down. I don't just *want* to take out Skia and lost souls—it's become an instinct that's hard to control."

Horrified, maybe even terrified, Jordan asked in a whisper, "If your father pledged his soul, you'd take him to Hell on Earth?"

Sasha's tears spilled over. "My father is dead, but my mother pledged, and yes, I took her down."

Jordan stepped back and bumped against the console.

"You have a choice, but if you're a Lumina, you'll work on a computer, or pop around placing records for us to look like legit people during field operations, or go out on fishing expeditions to look for lost souls. We can find ordinary humans to become immortal Luminas to do all that. What we can't find are more Anabo. In the last thousand years, only three have been born that we know of: you, me, and Jane, who Eryx killed before she could become immortal."

Jordan was even more confused. "If you want me to become Mephisto so much, why are you crying?"

Sasha stared at her for several heartbeats before she whispered, "Because I know *exactly* how you feel, except it's even worse for you, because there's no time, and you don't know him at all, and this is forever." She swiped at her tears again. "My heart's break-ing for you, Jordan."

This just got heavier and more depressing. Silently cursing her birthmark, she asked the million-dollar question. "If I'm Mephisto, can Eryx get to me?"

Sasha shot a look at Jax, who said, "Unless you're here, behind the Kyanos mists, Eryx can always get to you, no matter what you are. Since you're now immortal, he can't kill you, but he can keep you prisoner if he can get you to Erinýes, because you can't transport away from there."

She was well aware. "He's obsessed with what he believes I can give him. Before Phoenix showed up, he was threatening everyone in my life if I didn't agree to stay and give him minion babies."

She could tell by their expressions that she'd shocked them all.

Finally, Phoenix cleared his throat and said, "The only thing that can prevent any possibility of your having Eryx's offspring is if you carry Key's mark."

Jordan looked at Sasha. "I'm not going to like this, am I?"

Her counterpart in Strangeville dropped her gaze and resumed fiddling with the ear mic. "You get the mark through sex, and now that you're immortal, once you're marked, it's permanent."

Sasha had to be yanking her chain. "No way. I know these guys like doing things the old way, or whatever, but this . . . this is barbaric."

Sasha looked up. "It's part of who we are, Jordan. Sometimes it's important to know where each of us is, and the mark makes it possible—makes you one of us so you can do what we do. If Jax or any of the Mephisto were anywhere in the world, even somewhere remote like Antarctica, I'd know exactly where to find them. I'd be able to transport to where they are."

Phoenix said, "Theoretically, anyway. Sasha's still working on transporting. She knows where to go, but getting there is kind of a challenge."

Sasha's smile was wry. "I do suck at transporting, but the point is, the mark is what makes you permanently with us. Eryx could take you prisoner, but he can never make you have his baby if you have Key's mark."

She remembered Key said he knew Eryx was searching the castle for her. The idea made sense, but the execution completely wigged her out. She didn't know Key at all, and maybe she was connected to him because of fate, or because he brought her back to life, but did she want to be tied to him forever? He was an autocrat. He was huge. He was a little bit scary. The idea of having sex with him was awkward and freaky.

Unbidden, she was slammed with the memory of Matthew asking, almost every time they made out. She always said no, and admitted it wasn't only because she was afraid of getting pregnant. She just didn't want to. Not then, not now. Later, maybe, but she imagined it with someone she loved crazy, a guy who was not a giant, who wasn't the leader of a pack of sons of Hell.

While she stood there weighing the decision, allowing her imagination to take her places she really didn't want to go, Zee said, "It'd be great if you had all the time in the world to decide, but you don't. Key's starting to fade, so it's now or never."

Drawing herself up, she moved away from the console, around Sasha, and toward the edge of Key's bed. His breathing was rapid and shallow, and his hands had begun to shake. Whatever color had been left in his cheeks was gone now. There was no doubt he was in the throes of death. She'd seen it before, when her mom slipped away and left her.

The rest of them moved closer, circling the bed. Phoenix looked near to losing it; Zee looked angry; Ty was solemn; Denys had no expression at all; Jax was fighting tears; Sasha was staring at her. "He's what holds us together, Jordan. Please, do this for him, for all of us."

Taking the last step to the bed, Jordan bent low, held Key's face within her hands, and settled her lips against his. She forced his mouth open and gave him the wettest kiss ever, trying not to think of Matthew and how badly it would hurt him if he knew. He'd kissed her a thousand times, a thousand different ways, but always with feeling. Affection. Love.

This was nothing like that. The kiss was clinical, an exchange of saliva that might or might not help Key, but would change her forever.

SIX

SUSPENDED BETWEEN LIFE AND DEATH, KEY CAME TO awareness in the gardens at Kensington Palace. It was a particular favorite of his, so he supposed it made sense M sent him here to wait it out. Once he crossed over, he'd be with Lucifer in Hell, and while he had absolutely no idea what it might be like, he was certain it wouldn't be like this. Even in midwinter dormancy, the palace garden was a beautiful place.

Serene.

Which paradoxically elevated his frustrated rage to maniacal fury.

Good thing he was only a spirit. If he had solid form, he'd trash the place. As it was, all he could do was move through the beauty and hate it, resent it, curse it and everyone in it to withering death.

He passed a prissy lady in a hat who held the leash of a wee, yippy, defecating-in-the-pansies dog. He rushed at her, hoping he could shove her into the lily pond, but no luck. She walked on with the dog and left its business behind for someone else to clean up.

He continued to move through the gardens, hands clenched into fists. He'd waited over a thousand years for an Anabo, and after she died right in front of him, along with hope, he'd been desperate to bring her back. Incredibly, Jordan had come back, but now he was gone and would never see her again. The bitter irony ate at his soul like acid.

Without warning, his father appeared next to him, dressed in a black suit and red tie, looking almost as upset as he had the day their mother died. In the centuries that followed, Key had yet to see anyone lose it like that. Not even Phoenix went as far off the page when Jane died.

A photographic memory was sometimes essential. Other times it was a curse.

Right now, M's misery was so great, dark clouds began to roll into a perfectly blue winter sky.

"It's over," he said to his father. "I always knew this is where I'd end up."

"Of all my sons, Kyros, you were the one I *never* expected to end up here. You've always stayed the course, been a responsible leader, taken care of your brothers."

Hearing the grief and pain in his father's voice, Key slowed his stride. "All that means is I'm the one with the most on the line, the one with the biggest chance of pissing off Lucifer."

M dragged his hands through his black hair. "I swore on your mother's soul I'd never lose any of you, that I'd make sure you each earned Heaven. After so long, when there were no more Anabo . . . I decided . . . I asked . . . " He didn't finish, but the anguish in his voice sent all kinds of clues.

"What did you decide? What did you ask?" Had M done something to bring more Anabo into the world? Key had thought it was miraculous when they'd found another so soon after Sasha. Now he wondered if maybe it wasn't so much a miracle.

Instead of answering, M said, "Your mother . . . she'll never see you again."

Key couldn't say for sure, but he thought M was close to tears, and that blew him away. "Why are you acting like this is news? From the moment I jumped, I was doomed to Hell."

"No!" M grabbed Key's arm, forcing him to stop moving. "God gave you the Mephisto Covenant! He gave you and your brothers a chance of Heaven."

If Key wasn't so angry and despondent, he'd laugh. "A chance so slim, it's negligible. Not only are Anabo in short supply, none of us is designed for noble love."

"Ajax managed."

"Barely. And it's not the same for me. Even if I pull through and live, the odds of Jordan feeling anything for me but fear and revulsion are close to zero. You can't see it, or won't acknowledge it, but I'm the worst of the bunch."

"You're the only one who's never crossed the line, never been exiled to Kyanos."

True, but not because he was any less disturbed than his brothers. M didn't know the only thing keeping Key from succumbing to the unrelenting lure of wild, destructive lunacy was Lucifer's threat to obliterate Mephistopheles if Key failed. There was something within M that whispered of what he had been before he fell from grace. For his sake, and for that of the memory of their mother, Key walked the line, but it took all his concentration and self-discipline. So maybe he channeled his rage into taking out the Skia and lost souls, seeing to the needs of the Luminas and his brothers, and tending his greenhouse, but it was a tenuous hold at best. He had it in him to do things his brothers could never conceive, things that would turn Jordan away in horror.

He wasn't so sure he'd ever had a prayer of redemption, even with an Anabo served up to him on a plate. "I blew it, M. Accept it and let me go." He turned away and continued to move.

M fell in beside him, and they walked on in silence, waiting. After a while, as his father became more morose and anxious, the clouds became darker and rain began to fall. Key was pleased when the prissy lady's hat was ruined by the sudden cloudburst, but he felt kind of bad for the dog when she took off running and nearly choked it to death.

He tried not to think too hard about the reason behind the rain.

"It's not in me to be noble, either, you know."

"Yeah, Pops. I know."

M sighed and ran his hands through his hair again. "I loved her. It was madness, and I know what it cost her, but—"

"You've got to let it go."

"I just don't want you ever to think . . . you need to know that you and your brothers . . . I wish I . . . "

"We know, M. It's what it is."

His father stopped trying to tell him he loved him, which made him glad. Hearing M say it would take awkward to new levels. And he didn't require an apology for the circumstances of his birth.

"You're a good son, Kyros."

"Thanks, M." Let him have his delusion. What difference did it make at this point? He was about to descend into Hell for the rest of eternity. If his father needed to believe he was anything good in order to accept it, Key didn't mind.

They were close to where they'd started when M suddenly stopped. "Something's happening."

Key steeled himself for what was coming. He looked all around him and said good-bye to daylight, to the Earth.

"Jordan is trying to give back a measure of your humanity and keep you from death."

Hope rose up, unbidden and unwanted, but it came nevertheless. He faced his father. "How?"

"She's kissing you."

Key was stunned. Why would she do that?

"She must like you a little," M said.

Yeah. Right. "She barely knows me."

M looked up at the clouds he'd created. "Most of her life she's been asked to set aside what she wants for the sake of others, and she generally complied, maybe because she's Anabo, or maybe that's just who she is." He looked at Key. "I think she sees what your death would mean to the Mephisto and, by default, the rest of humanity. She's doing it for the greater good."

"That sounds real sweet, but I'm calling bullshit. They probably told her she could save me if she shared her spit, but failed to tell her the flip side of what mine will do to her."

"Whatever the reason, she's doing it."

Even as M spoke, he was fading. Key looked around and saw that the gardens were losing color, until they faded to black.

Suddenly, jarringly, he returned to his body, instantly aware he was in his bed, someone was crying, and Jordan was kissing him. The scent of bluebells was all around him. Instinct told him to lift his arms and pull her on top of him, but his muscles said no. All he could do was open his eyes. Hers widened, and she pulled away from his mouth. "Don't stop," he managed to whisper. "Not yet."

His brothers all began to shout at once—why were they always so f'ing loud?—and he heard Sasha gushing thanks to Jordan, but he ignored them and closed his eyes again, waiting for Jordan to kiss him. When nothing happened, he opened them to stare up at her lovely face, still close to his. "Please."

This time, he was awake. This time, he kissed her back. Other than her soft hands against his face, they weren't touching at all, but it was deeply satisfying. His anger dissolved, and he was enveloped by indescribable peace. When she pulled away again, he could see confusion and fear in her expression.

He wondered why she had brought him back from the brink of death, and, evidently, so did she.

She did the right thing, Jordan was certain, but instead of feeling happiness that he'd come around, she had an overwhelming desire to bolt, to run far and fast and never look back. The first kiss saved his life, but she felt nothing. Then he woke and asked her to kiss him again, and she'd forever regret going through with it. She imagined this must be what it felt like to be struck by lightning. Her body tingled, as if every limb was asleep, and she was infused with heat. Staring into his black eyes, she heard him whisper, "One more."

Run.

She had to get away from him. Pulling back, she stood up straight and moved away from the bed, all the way to the door, into the hall, and back toward the stairs. Miraculously, in spite of her speed, she didn't trip on the way down. She ran across the great hall to the gigantic front door and was opening it when she heard a deep, solemn voice from just behind her. "It is snowing, Anabo. You will find misery there."

Pausing with the door barely open, she glanced over her shoulder and saw an extremely tall guy in a turban and Aladdin pants, staring past her from dark eyes in a dark face. "I just need some air."

He nodded. "I will bring a coat." He disappeared, then reappeared seconds later, holding a leather bomber jacket. "You are smaller than the other Anabo, but this will suffice for now." He opened it and held it out.

Turning, she slid her arms into the sleeves of Sasha's jacket and asked, "Who are you?"

He rattled off a name she couldn't repeat if she tried, then added, "The Mephisto and others here call me Deacon. I am the butler."

"Are you a Lumina?"

"I am a Purgatory, one who is spirit only. Until I am able to forgive God for allowing my family's slaughter, I will remain in servitude to the Mephisto."

Facing him again, she noted he wouldn't make eye contact. Really old-school Muslim, a Moor, she guessed. "How long have you been a Purgatory?"

"Very soon to be nine hundred years."

She decided Deacon must be really mad at God if he still hadn't forgiven him after nine hundred years.

He stepped around her and opened the door. "Do not stray far, Anabo. The snow masks dangers for the unwary. Immortality won't ease the pain of a broken limb if you stumble into a crevice hidden beneath the snow."

"My name is Jordan."

"This is a boy's name."

"Maybe so, but as you can see, I'm not a boy."

"Indeed, Jordan, you are not."

She stepped outside and was struck by a blast of subzero air, but she still felt hot from the inside out. There were steps down to a curving drive that circled a frozen fountain and looped to a long alley of aspens and old-fashioned gas lamps, but she turned instead and headed around the house. It was huge and gray, with lead-glass windows and gargoyles, but she didn't pay much attention to the architecture, her mind completely absorbed with all that had happened to her since eleven o'clock last night. It was probably close to four o'clock in Colorado, already getting dark.

Not even twenty-four hours and everything was changed in a way she couldn't have imagined yesterday. She thought of her father and what he must be going through, but it was too painful, and so she shoved the thoughts away. She couldn't think about Matthew, either. Especially Matthew.

Determined to get a grip on her spiraling emotions, she focused on walking. The snow was up to her knees in some spots, and she welcomed the cold. Turning at the corner of the house, she saw a cluster of stone buildings across an open meadow and wondered what they were, but hiking that far through knee-deep snow wasn't possible right now. Not only was it almost dark and snowing, she was so hungry her stomach hurt. As soon as she cooled off and was a relatively safe distance from freaking out, she'd head back inside and eat. Then she'd go to sleep. The thought of unconsciousness appealed to her—and not only because she was exhausted. Sleep meant escape from reality.

Why had she kissed him again? She'd done what she intended, what his brothers and Sasha had asked of her, and he'd woken up. There was absolutely no reason for her to have kissed him again, so why had she? She could never again be with Matthew, but how could she kiss another guy this soon? Even if she was now an immortal, she was still Jordan Ellis, who didn't kiss somebody else while her boyfriend of two years recovered from a gunshot. No matter how much she tried to justify the impulsive kiss, she couldn't.

The unsettled feeling grew, along with the tingling and the heat. Was Mephisto like a virus? Was she changing already? She had so much to grieve for, it seemed incredibly cruel that she must now also mourn the person she'd been all of her life.

She reached the back of the mansion and drew up short, surprised to find what looked like an English garden buried in snow, but it was evident in the alignment of the hedges and smooth walkways, a frozen pond at the center. Farther out was a greenhouse, built in the round, the glass connected by elaborate swirls of beautiful metal joints.

The angel had said Key had a greenhouse, and here it was. Extremely curious, Jordan crossed the garden and had to shovel snow with her hands to get the door open. Inside was a tiny vestibule, designed to keep the frigid air from the interior. She closed the outside door, then removed Sasha's coat and hung it on one of a row of pegs that held gardening tools before she opened the inside door.

She expected the usual greenhouse, with staggered benches and rows of potted plants, but this was like no greenhouse she'd ever seen. There was design and order, true, but every plant, every flower, every leaf lived in perfect harmony, meticulously placed, the flowers thick, a riot of color and beauty even in the gathering gloom. Miniature fruit trees were heavy with lemons, limes, and oranges, and one section was home to an herb garden. She heard the soft buzz of a bee and watched as a peacock blue butterfly rested on a daylily. On the east side was a tiny waterfall that tumbled gently into a tiny koi pond. Outside, the snow was several feet high, but the drifts stopped inches away from the warmth of the glass walls.

She wandered all the way around, following a narrow, winding gravel path. How was this possible from a guy like Key? He was huge, hard, edgy. The investment of time within the walls of steel and glass was infinite, and she couldn't imagine him here, carefully and patiently tending the plants, the bees, and the butterflies.

A potting bench was close to the door. Except for a set of gardening shears in the middle, it was neat, with stacks of small clay pots lining the back edge and bags of soil and plant food on the shelf below. A silver watering can sat to one side, and she picked it up to read the engraving: *For the woods are full of bluebells and the hedges full of bloom.* Had to be from a poem. Not only did Key tend this greenhouse like a doting mother, he owned a silver watering can with engraved poetry. Unbelievable.

She set the can down and turned toward the door, then noticed a retro-looking glider on the other side of the entrance. After she took a seat there to stare a little longer, she heard a low hum and realized a hive was just a few feet away, in an apiary box. If she wasn't so tired, she'd be nervous about being stung, but as it was, the constant drone was oddly comforting. Bees making honey was so wonderfully normal, she gazed into the encroaching darkness and could almost imagine this had all been a horrible nightmare, and she'd soon wake up in her own bed, in her room at the White House, and Dad would be in the residence kitchen eating Betsy's scrambled eggs while he read the paper.

Closing her eyes, she tried to blank her mind, but uninvited thoughts and memories came anyway. Her heart was an aching thud in her chest while her brain forced her to confront the finality of her decision not to die and, instead, to stay with the Mephisto. People of Hell. Not only would she stay with them forever, kissing Key meant she would *be* one of them. The weight of it crushed her, and she fell sideways on the glider, curling into herself while she said an anguished good-bye to her old life and faced the reality of this one.

Mary Michael's voice was in her head. *"Living forever in the realm of physical reality leaves you impervious to death, but as vulnerable to pain as humanity."* Had she ever felt this kind of pain? She didn't think so. Discovering there was a greater evil in the world than Lucifer; knowing millions of people were susceptible; understanding she was to give herself for the greater good, to protect and save humankind; giving up all her hopes and dreams—devastating. She wanted to run away and pretend she didn't know any of it.

The agony of knowledge was unbearable.

She'd give anything to be ordinary, even to be First Daughter again. At least that would be over once Dad's term was up. Then she could have lived her life how she'd always imagined, in relative anonymity. Instead, she would live thousands of years in the world, but not a part of it, every day a reminder of what she had given up for humanity.

Powerless to stop, she descended into righteous anger and asked God, over and over, *"Why me?"*

❧

She ran from him. One kiss and she booked it for the door. Key stared up at the ceiling of his bedroom and ignored his family's celebration. Not that he wasn't glad to be alive, with another chance to avoid eternity in Hell, but he saw what lay ahead and it frustrated him.

In their usual way, none of his brothers noticed his mood, not even when Mathilda came in with a tray laden with food and he ate without a word. They talked about the D.C. takedown, throwing out all kinds of suggestions, until Phoenix said, "As soon as Key's feeling better, we'll make a decision. Until then, let's let him get some sleep."

He didn't want to sleep. He wanted to go after Jordan, but as soon as they all filed out of his room, he was sucked under again.

When he woke, it was past nine o'clock. He wondered where Jordan was, if she'd eaten, if Mathilda had put her in one of the third-floor bedrooms. Sliding out of bed, he went to the intercom and buzzed Mathilda, who appeared immediately. "Master Kyros, ye're out of bed!"

"Where is Jordan?"

"I don't reckon I know who ye're talking about. Who is Jordan?"

Dammit! He grabbed a pair of jeans from the bathroom bench and, while he put them on, dialed the intercom code that would send his voice throughout the entire house. "I want everyone in my bedroom, *now!*"

Less than a minute later, the room was crowded with Mephisto and Purgatories. "Where is Jordan?"

He was met with blank looks from the Purgatories, who obviously had no clue about Jordan, and the downcast eyes of his brothers. Even Sasha looked away.

"How is it that an Anabo arrives in our house, and *no one* knows where she is?"

"Earlier, she was at the front door," Deacon said. "I gave her a coat, and she left."

"And when she didn't came back, it didn't occur to you to wonder why?"

"I assumed she had returned and was with you."

He turned his wrath toward the Mephisto. "What is *wrong* with all of you?"

Phoenix said, "I didn't realize she was gone. When we left, I thought she was still in this room."

The rest of them nodded in agreement. Denys said, "It's not like we blew her off, Key. It's just a screwup."

Taking a deep breath, Key said as calmly as he could manage, "We have to go out there and find her, immediately. If she's not found within the next fifteen minutes, sound an alarm for the Luminas to help search."

Turning back to his bathroom, he went through to his closet, pulled on his boots and a coat, then headed downstairs. Outside, Phoenix, always the organizer, had just sent everyone in different directions. He looked like he was going to say something to Key but must have thought better of it. Instead, he disappeared.

Despite feeling back to normal, Key didn't want to expend too much energy by transporting, so he took off around the house through the heavy snow, calling Jordan's name as he walked. All he heard in return were the distant sounds of others calling her name and the whistle of the wind through the pines and firs. She'd been gone long enough that her footprints had been erased in the snowfall, which was coming down fast and showed no signs of stopping. Maybe she couldn't die, but she could be miserable, and if she was lost in the dark, there were all kinds of painful dangers waiting for her besides the cold.

He felt awful, knowing she must be so scared, and confused, and now she was out there, alone on the frozen mountain, maybe lost, probably starving.

At the back of the house, he saw no sign of her and was about to head across the meadow to the gym and stables when he noticed the door to the greenhouse wasn't shut all the way. Hurrying across the garden, he reached the door and saw a leather jacket hanging on one of the pegs inside the vestibule.

Quickly shoving snow away with his foot, he opened the door, stepped inside the vestibule, then into the greenhouse, where he sucked in a deep breath of relief. Jordan was curled up on the glider, fast asleep.

Scooping her into his arms, he carried her through the snow back to the house, and went in the door to the mudroom, and hit the intercom button with his elbow to call off the search. Mathilda appeared and instantly began to fuss. "Puir lamb! Where did ye find her, Master Kyros?"

"In the greenhouse. Tell me which room to take her to."

"The blue bedroom at the top of the stairs. 'Tis clean and fresh."

She followed him all the way up two flights of stairs, then watched while he laid Jordan on the bed. He started to draw her sweater over her head, but Mathilda elbowed him aside and frowned at him. "She'll be embarrassed when she wakes up, if she knows 'twas you who undressed her. Step over there and light the fire while I get her comfortable."

He supposed she was right, so he did as she said and set about lighting a fire. The room was cold, so after he had the fire going, he went out into the hall and turned up the thermostat that regulated the heat on the third floor. Back in the bedroom, he saw Mathilda was just tucking Jordan in. "She's mighty tired, I reckon, because she didn't wake up at all." She bent to the floor and picked up Jordan's clothes. "Should I launder her things?"

"Burn them. I don't want her reminded of what happened today." He set the screen in front of the fire, then said, "Send Mercy out to buy her some new clothes. She'll need everything, obviously, and Mercy may as well go ahead and buy her some takedown clothes. Jax will want her dressed for the field when she starts training."

"Seems to me she needs to settle in and get used to things here before she starts to work."

"We'll let her decide, but make sure she has everything she needs."

Mathilda looked once more at Jordan, her kind eyes reflecting sympathy. "I'll check on her every half hour, Master Kyros. You go on back to bed, and don't worry none about her."

Even though he had no intention of not worrying, or going back to bed, he nodded, and the housekeeper disappeared.

He moved closer to the bed and stared down at Jordan's beautiful face, thankful all over again that she had come back, had saved him, that he still had a chance. But what of her? What price had she paid for his life?

Bending slightly, he gently stroked her silky hair and silently promised her she wouldn't regret it. He had absolutely no idea how he'd go about it, but he'd figure it out. He'd talk to Jax and ask him for advice. That wouldn't be easy, but he'd do it to learn what he needed to do to make her happy. It would take some time, but that was okay. Time was one commodity they had in spades.

❧

She came awake with a start and sat up quickly, blinking in confusion. She was in a bed in a small, beautiful room with pale blue walls, yellow silk draperies, and a petite wingback chair next to a fireplace with a cheery fire. Several sconces around the room held lit candles, and a simple candelabra sat on a small secretary before the draped windows. Where was this room, and how had she come to be here, in bed, *naked*?

The door opened, and a heavyset woman in clothes straight out of a Dickens novel stepped inside. She saw Jordan sitting up and immediately smiled. "Ye're awake!" She came toward the bed, long skirt rustling, and smoothed the covers. "I'd be Mathilda, the housekeeper. Would ye care for a bath, Miss Jordan? I can run one for you quick as a rabbit. Or mayhap you'd prefer a shower. I sent Mercy to buy you some clothes, and they're all washed and pressed, ready for you. Master Key instructed us to burn what you were wearing. Said he didn't want you to be reminded."

Mathilda must be another Purgatory. Why else would she be wearing an outfit like that? "How did I get here?"

Mathilda stopped fussing with the bed and stood straight, folding her hands together beneath her large breasts. "After Master Key woke, he asked after you and was mighty angry when no one knew where you'd got to." She sniffed, as if she disapproved. "I wish I'd known you were here, Miss Jordan. You had a bad time of it."

"Thank you, Mathilda, but you still haven't told me how I came to be in this bed, naked."

"The brothers went out to look, and Kyros found you in the greenhouse. He carried you here and put you to bed."

Jordan felt herself blush. "He took my clothes off?"

"Goodness no! I did that, and ye never once woke up."

"How long have I been asleep?"

"About ten hours, I reckon."

It must be somewhere close to three in the morning. "I'm sorry you've had to stay up this late to look after me."

"No need for sorry, Miss Jordan. I'm a Purgatory, a spirit with no need of sleep or food. Speaking of food, I'm sure you must be terribly hungry. Hans, the cook, has a nice stew simmering, if ye like, or he can make breakfast."

"Stew is fine." She was so hungry, she'd eat lima beans, and she hated lima beans.

Mathilda turned away and went to a door on the other side of the bed, evidently a closet, and when she turned back again, she held a white terrycloth robe in her hand. "The bath is through there." She nodded toward the door on the left side of the bed as she handed the robe to Jordan. "Your clothes are here in this closet. I'll fetch yer supper now."

"Thank you." Jordan watched her head for the door. "Where am I?"

The woman stopped with her hand on the knob and glanced over her shoulder. "Third floor. Ye've the whole of it to yerself. The brothers stay on the second."

"Is there somewhere I can watch TV?"

"The brothers all have TVs in their rooms, but no one ever stays up here, so there is no television. There's a great big one on the first floor, in the TV room. After you eat, I'll take ye there." She nodded toward the bathroom. "Take your bath, Miss Jordan, and ye'll feel better."

As soon as the door closed, Jordan climbed out of bed and headed for the bathroom. Flipping the light switch, she blinked against the brightness. When her eyes adjusted, she thought of the bathroom Alissa had taken her to in Eryx's castle. This was like a palace in comparison, with white marble, a separate shower and tub, and plush rugs. Best of all, no bugs.

She looked in the mirror, half expecting to look different, but she was herself, with messy hair and eyes swollen from sleep. Drawers in the bathroom vanity offered up everything she needed, including a toothbrush. At no time in her life had brushing her teeth felt this good.

Thirty minutes later, she was squeaky clean, wrapped in the terry robe, sitting in front of the fire while she ate maybe the best stew in history. There was also French bread, a mug of hot tea, and apple pie for dessert.

Mathilda, she discovered, was a kindhearted woman with an agenda. She busied herself smoothing the covers on the bed, tucking them in so tightly, Jordan was sure she could flip a quarter off of it, military style, and all the while, she talked about Key, pointing out his multitude of sterling qualities. The matchmaker song from *Fiddler on the Roof* kept playing in Jordan's head.

When she was done eating, she dressed in a pair of long boxers and a long-sleeved T-shirt, then dried her hair and pulled it into a ponytail. Mathilda led her into the hallway. "I put you in this room closest to the front stairs. It's easy to get lost in this house, but ye'll find your way quick enough." They descended the stairs, all the way to the grand hall. Deacon was there, straightening one of the gigantic old portraits. "Who are all these people?" she asked Mathilda.

"Mostly Luminas, but that one closest to the door is Jane."

Jordan stopped to look. Dressed in Victorian clothes, seated next to a small secretary with a spaniel at her feet, Jane was very pretty. Blonde and blue-eyed, she looked delicate, like a porcelain doll.

"She was Phoenix's intended, but the night she was to leave her life behind and become immortal, Eryx kidnapped her. The brothers went after her, but they were too late. Eryx waited, and as soon as they arrived, he cut her throat. Phoenix has never been the same."

"Why didn't he bring her back, like Key brought me back?"

"He tried, but Eryx had marked her, so he was the only one who could."

She felt queasy. "Eryx wanted to keep me so I could give him children. If he had Jane, and had already . . . why did he kill her?"

The light in Mathilda's eyes dimmed. "She carried Phoenix's mark, and, just to be cruel, Eryx replaced it with his own. He could have killed her as soon as he marked her, then brought her back to immortality to have his sons, but Jane was the first Anabo the brothers had ever found, and I think all Eryx could think about was making sure she didn't become Mephisto. And there's no doubt he got evil enjoyment out of waiting for Phoenix to show up, then murdering her right in front of him. Eryx is smart, and cunning, but he's as much a son of Hell as the brothers, and sometimes reason isn't what drives them."

The front hall wasn't especially cold, but Jordan shivered. "I thought the mark was permanent. How could Eryx replace it?"

"She wasn't immortal." Mathilda gave her a look. "You are, so it's all important you don't fall back into Eryx's hands."

Thinking of the possibility turned her blood cold. No wonder Key had been so determined not to leave her.

Deacon turned and said to a spot somewhere over her shoulder, "You could be held captive and coerced into bearing his sons, but this will never come to pass because you are strong." His eyes met hers, and the look he gave her was so intense, it was all she could do not to look away. "The truest test of strength is sacrifice. For mankind and God, you've tainted the purity of your soul with the darkness of Mephisto."

"He was dying, Deacon. I did it only to save him from death."

"You knew what it would cost you. No matter what befalls

118

you in the future, you won't be subjugated. I tell you this to relieve your fear." He looked away then and disappeared.

Mathilda petted her hair. "He's an odd one, child, but sincere, and he's taken to ye, which is novel. Deacon thinks he's above everyone, always judgmental and lecturing." Turning away, she said, "Come along, and I'll show you to the TV room."

Jordan followed her to a corridor that led off of the great hall, across from the dining room. Several doors down, she stopped. "Here we are. Everyone's asleep now, so ye're on your own with all the controls and such. I don't much care for TV, except to watch a movie now and then, so I'm no help to ye."

Moving into the room, Jordan said, "I'm sure I can figure it out. Thank you, Mathilda."

The housekeeper smiled as she left.

The TV room was black and white, with several black leather couches, a couple of deep, comfy-looking chairs, thick white carpet, and a bar that stretched across the back of the room. There was a popcorn maker, just like at the movies, fountain sodas, and baskets full of boxed candy.

She spied a tray of remotes on the low coffee table and fished around until she found one she thought would work. It didn't. She tried another and another, until she'd gone through all of them. Frustrated, she sat back, only to realize she was sitting on a remote. That one worked.

Steeling herself, she went straight to CNN. It was pretty much just what she had expected, with political pundits talking about Red Out, and the economic crisis that had brought on such a desperate move as kidnapping and murdering the president's daughter. They mentioned Ron Trent's death from a massive coronary, which confused her. Hadn't Eryx said Mr. Trent was taken to Hell on Earth? How could he be dead?

The pundits discussed a White House leak about how the president and his chief of staff had lately begun to disagree. They didn't suggest Mr. Trent had anything to do with her abduction, but his death added another element of drama they clearly savored. *Jerks.* She'd grown to despise reporters, pundits, and everyone else on the news.

While they blabbed on, the screen was filled with images of the White House, legions of people standing along the fence on Pennsylvania Avenue holding candles, flowers, and flags. The crawl at the bottom said President Ellis was set to give a speech at nine a.m. EST, but nothing was said about him personally. He was undoubtedly in the residence, pacing the living room like he always did when things got to be too much. Over the past six months, he'd nearly worn out the rug.

She tried to shove thoughts of her dad and his grief from her mind, but it wasn't possible, especially when the screen went to a still shot of the two of them in the Oval Office, not long after Mom died, him working at his desk and her doing homework on the floor. Their last words to each other had been angry ones, and she regretted them with all her heart.

"It's not a good idea to watch," Key said from the doorway.

Looking toward him, she saw he was wearing a pair of faded jeans and a T-shirt from the American Indian Museum. His hair was pulled back, and his color had returned. "How're you feeling?" she asked.

"Good as new." He came in and closed the door, then moved to the other end of the sofa and sat down, resting his bare feet on the coffee table. "How about you?"

The scent of evergreens wrapped around her, a reminder of who he was and what fate had in mind for her. "Better since I slept and ate." She returned focus to the TV. Now that they'd discussed their health, would he strike up a convo about the weather? Could this be any more awkward? At least he didn't mention the kiss. She'd slide into the sofa cushions if he did.

"Why did you run, Jordan?"

Oh, boy. He *was* going to mention it. "I just needed to be alone for a while." Kind of like now. As much as she didn't want to talk about kissing him, she wanted to watch every image, hear every bit of what was happening. The screen went to an aerial view of the Red Out compound in central Texas.

Suddenly, the picture went dark. She looked down at the remote in her hand and pressed the power button. As soon as it came back on, it went dark again. Jerking her attention to Key, she frowned. "You're doing that, aren't you?"

He nodded. "It's making you cry."

"Maybe I need to cry."

"Why would anyone *need* to cry?"

She looked away from him. "Don't you ever cry?"

"No, because it changes nothing. Better to move on and do what has to be done."

"Is this your not-so-subtle way of telling me to buck up?"

"I need to discuss something with you."

Still holding the remote, she stared at the dark television and accepted that he was going to talk about the kiss. "Okay, so discuss."

"After you were abducted, we went to the White House to find Ron Trent; we knew he was a lost soul and figured he'd know where you were. We expected to find him with your father, trying to convince him to pledge the oath to Eryx, but we didn't expect to find so many others there with him."

Anxiety over the kiss discussion forgotten, she turned her head to look at him, shocked. "Like who?"

He listed ten names, and with each one she felt more sick. "That's almost half of Dad's cabinet, the Senate majority leader, and people on the White House staff! How is that possible? How did Eryx convince all those people to hand their souls over to him?"

"The same way he gets anyone else to follow, with charm and empty promises. We're certain he'll try again with your father, and if his closest advisers are lost souls, it'll be that much more difficult for him to resist. They've lied and given him bad advice, which is a big factor in why the United States is on the edge of another depression."

Tossing the remote to the table, she turned to face Key fully. "What do you want me to do?"

He didn't answer for a while, staring at her from those black eyes, as if debating how best to tell her. Finally, he said in a low, sober voice, "Sasha and my brothers want you to go back."

"Like I wasn't killed?"

"Right. They think, with you in the White House again, you can help them with the takedown plan Phoenix has dreamed up. Do you know what happens when we take out a lost soul?"

"Eryx said you take them to Hell on Earth."

"The problem is, if everyone we took out just disappeared, people would panic, so our father provides us with doppelgangers. We figure out how they're supposed to die, and the stand-in body fits the plan, to look realistic."

"That's why they think Mr. Trent had a heart attack."

Key nodded. "But there are so many more to take down in Washington, we need a believable way for all of them to die at one time. Gatherings are always prime for takedowns of multiple people, and my brothers and Sasha want you to go back, because they think the president will have something to celebrate if you're still alive."

"I don't think Dad will throw a party, Key. He'd be more likely to take me to Camp David."

Surprising her, he looked relieved.

"You don't think I should go back, do you?"

He shook his head. "It's too dangerous. Eryx is still a huge threat, and now that you know what's on the other side, you'd be forced to lie and put on an act. I think there are other ways to go at this."

"Like what?"

"We'll take them out one by one. A heart attack here, a car wreck there."

"Won't that look weird, so many D.C. big names dying that close together? And you've already used a heart attack on Mr. Trent."

He leaned his head back on the couch and stared at the ceiling. "Maybe they could all catch a virus."

"A virus that kills? Talk about panic. People would totally freak out."

"True." He rubbed his chin, deep in thought.

"It's morbid, but what about planning something during the memorial? Dad's bound to have one for me."

"You're right; it is morbid, but it could work." Turning his head to look at her, his expression was dark. "Whatever death we fake for the lost souls is going to be bad, and your dad will already be upset. This will be hard on him."

"It'll be harder if those people hang around and somehow convince him to pledge to Eryx." Most of them were friends of Dad's, people he trusted and counted on, and he had no idea they were working against him. "I want to get them away from him as soon as possible, so even though it's totally creepy that it'll be at my funeral, I think it's the best idea."

"Would all of them attend your memorial?"

"I'm sure they will, as well as lots of others, which might make it more complicated. How do you take some out and leave others behind?"

"With the exception of Skia, we can freeze people for short periods of time, so we can take away the lost souls and Skia and stage their deaths. When the freeze fades, people are confused, and assume they saw things that didn't actually happen."

"I want to be there."

Instantly, he shook his head. "It's too soon, Jordan. The changes in you will take a while, and you've had no training."

"It'll be at least a week before a memorial, and I'm a fast learner."

"Your first takedown shouldn't be this personal. You need detachment and no emotion to be effective."

"Sasha explained what it's like for her, and she didn't seem detached. What's emotion got to do with it anyway? If I'm angry at these people for what they've done to my dad, wouldn't that make me more motivated to take them out?"

"You'll want to argue with them, which is one of Sasha's problems. There's no time for arguing, and it's pointless anyway. Once someone pledges, it's a done deal and there's no going back."

His refusal to let her take part in this only hardened her resolve. "Tell me what I have to do to be included, and I'll do it."

He gave her a level look. "Train with Jax, every day. Learn all there is to know about us and about Eryx from Phoenix. Don't watch the news, and don't spend time crying or feeling sorry for yourself. Grieving is a waste of time."

"Have you always been a robot, or is this a result of your near-death experience?"

"I don't have the luxury of basing decisions on emotion. My brothers have a little more latitude, but for me . . . I have to be the one who remains calm and gives them stability."

He hadn't been calm when he begged her not to die, not to leave him. So maybe he put this hard-ass face on to keep his brothers in line, but that's all it was—a face. "So you think the only way to be an effective leader is to be made of stone?"

"For the Mephisto, yes. This isn't a team sport, Jordan. We're all sons of Hell, and maybe we still have a little of our mother in us, but it's not enough to change what we are." He nodded toward the TV. "You can sit here and watch the news and make yourself depressed, but it changes nothing. All it can do is suck away your energy, and if you want to go with us on this takedown, you're going to need all of your energy for training."

They sat in silence for several long moments. She thought about the people who'd pledged themselves to Eryx, people her dad trusted, who he considered friends. What would someone say to a man like Mr. McCall, the Senate majority leader, to convince him to turn his back on God? How did someone even start that conversation? Most people were fairly private about their faith and spirituality. Maybe they had a public side that went to services, bowed their heads during prayer, gave money to charity and things like that, but how they felt, deep inside, what they believed—it kind of came down to something between them and God. "Key?"

"Yeah?"

"Why now? Why is Eryx working so hard to take over the U.S. government now? Why didn't he try it years ago?"

"He did."

She was stunned. "When? What happened?"

"Since the beginning, when he first became . . . what he is, he's tried to stack governments with his followers. His first try was in Greece, but he failed because he didn't understand their religion. He figured out it's easier to convince someone to follow him if he understands what they've been raised to believe in the first place. Later, he worked to convert the aristocracy of Russia under Catherine the Great, but we made sure he didn't get too far there. During the American Revolution, he collected a decent percentage of the House of Commons in the British Parliament. In the American Civil War, he made a lot of conquests on the Confederate side, assuming they'd win. Of course they didn't, and we took out every one of his followers who hadn't already been killed in battle. We've always managed to screw it up for him before he gets too far, but this time . . . " He shook his head. "He's never had people so high up before. He's learned new tricks. He's sneakier and more shrewd."

"I feel awful for my father. He's had such a hard time, and things have gotten so bad with the economy. People are so angry with him, and he keeps trying to make things better, but he has no idea those people are purposely screwing things up instead of helping him." She looked at Key. "I really, *really* want to be there when they get taken out."

"I understand, but you should know now, they won't care. They'll care that they're about to die, but they won't give a damn who's the executioner."

"I care. I want to be there. Promise me I can go."

"Only if you're ready, Jordan. Like I said, it's going to take a lot of training." He looked toward the dark TV. "It's also absolutely necessary for you to be completely changed to Mephisto. You have to be able to do what we do."

"I understand."

Key met her gaze. "Then will you come here and let me kiss you?"

Panic descended. "It's too soon. Matthew . . . I know I can never be with him again, but we were—"

"Time is a major factor, and you need to make the change as soon as possible."

"I thought I was already changing."

"You are, but only one kiss means the process will be very slow. If there was another way to give you what's needed to make it happen faster, I'd do it."

Was that a note of hurt in his voice? She looked at his expression, which gave nothing away, but somewhere in his eyes was a hint of anxiety. No, he wasn't nearly as unemotional as he wanted her to believe.

And she could still hear his voice on the wind, filled with grief and desperation.

She unfolded her legs and slid across the smooth leather until she was just next to him. For Matthew, she said, "This is just for Mephisto."

He nodded as he reached for her shoulders, pulled her toward him, and lowered his head to hers. There was no slow buildup. Just the meeting of their mouths. And tongues. And instant heat from deep within her body. Her mind registered a bizarre mix of pleasure and pain, an urgent impulse to get away from him and a contradictory need to get closer.

She wasn't exactly sure how long it was before it happened, but the reason for the kiss faded to irrelevant when they simultaneously embraced and fell against the back cushions. His skin was hot, even through the T-shirt, and the muscles in his back flexed beneath her palms. His kiss was deep and seductive, while his arms drew her so close she was practically in his lap.

Matthew's kisses were never like this—all-consuming and confident. There was no hesitation and no awkward fumbling. Key knew exactly what he was doing, and she didn't want to like it because it felt like yet another betrayal of Matthew, but she did. When he broke the kiss, they stayed almost nose to nose, staring at each other. "You've done this . . . before," she whispered, her breath coming in short little gasps.

"True."

"With who? The angel said the Mephisto can't be with anyone but an Anabo."

"Easy girls in dark places."

"More than kisses, I'm guessing."

"Does it matter?"

Yes. "No."

He kissed her again. And again. She lost track of time. "I hate you for this, Kyros."

"It's what you have to do, and there's no harm in enjoying it."

"How do you know I'm enjoying it?"

"You have no reason to fake it."

Guilt was an evil, unfamiliar foe. Closing her eyes, she dropped her forehead to his shoulder. "I love Matthew. You won't forget that, will you?"

His sigh was deep. "I won't forget."

She started to cry. Key didn't ask why, or tell her to stop. While tears leaked from behind her lids and dripped onto his shoulder until it was soaked, he held her tighter and closer and never said a word.

SEVEN

WHILE JORDAN CRIED ON HIS SHOULDER, KEY WONDERED what it was about Matthew that she loved so much? What had he done to elicit an attachment this strong?

After a while, she stopped crying, but he kept his arms around her and his cheek against her hair. She was so soft, and her scent of bluebells made him remember England. Maybe he'd take her there someday and show her where they'd lived in Yorkshire: the moors, the woods, and the bluebells.

When she dropped off to sleep, he popped them upstairs to her room and laid her on the bed, where she curled into a ball and sniffled against the pillow. He fought to get Mathilda's covers loose to spread them over her, then blew out the candles and left.

Headed back to his rooms, he admitted Matthew's existence

made no difference to his chances. Whether the guy lived or died, he was now off-limits to her. In truth, every male on the planet other than Key was out of the running, but he faced the real possibility that he would fail even without competition. If he couldn't figure out how to make her feel for him what she felt for Matthew, all he'd ever have of her was guilty lust.

And wasn't that the ultimate irony? He'd spent a lifetime appeasing his lust with girls who meant nothing to him. The one female who mattered, who had the power to redeem his debauched soul by loving him, felt as much for him as he did for all those long-forgotten girls.

In his bedroom, he found one of Ty's kittens asleep on his bed, along with a note: *For Jordan, because girls like baby cats.* He looked at the gray-striped kitten, who woke and mewed at him before pouncing on the Post-it note, which promptly stuck to his paws and freaked him out. It was war, and the sticky note was winning. Reaching down, Key scooped up the fur ball, pulled the note off of him, then popped back up to Jordan's room. He set the kitten on her bed and watched him explore until he found a spot against the curve of her belly and curled up to sleep.

Back in his room, he changed into sweats then popped out to the gym to get in a workout before breakfast. He felt more energized than he could remember, which was amazing, considering how close he had come to death.

He was only half surprised to find Phoenix in the weight room, on his back at the bench press. "Can't sleep?"

His brother grunted in reply, never slowing his up-and-down rhythm. Based on the sweat covering his body, Key guessed he'd been out here awhile.

Taking a seat on the rower, he wondered what sick twist of fate had brought him an Anabo before bringing one to Phoenix. Maybe he didn't talk about Jane, but Key knew he never stopped thinking about her. He emphatically said he didn't want another Anabo, but Key didn't believe him. If the right Anabo appeared, he'd leave Jane in his memory and move on with living his life.

Key waited until Phoenix finally rested his weights, then told him the new plan. His brother sat up, reached for a towel, and mopped the sweat from his face. "If you allow her to go on a takedown at her own funeral, you're even more coldhearted than I thought."

"She insisted. Said she'd do whatever is necessary to get ready for it." He kept rowing. "It's another pair of hands, and this is going to be extremely difficult."

"Don't do this, Key. I'll think of another plan."

"We'll discuss it at breakfast and see what the others have to say."

"I always knew you were different than the rest of us, and you take your job way more seriously, but I never figured you'd put what we do ahead of an Anabo." He stood and went toward the door that led from the weight room into the gym. "It makes me question just how much of our mother's light remains in your soul."

Key abruptly stopped rowing. "You didn't really just say that." It was maybe the meanest thing any of his brothers had ever said to him, and that was saying a lot.

"I'm sorry," Phoenix said, his hand on the doorknob. "You're doing it wrong,"

"I don't know how to do it right."

Looking at him over his shoulder, Phoenix said very quietly, "From now on, forever until the end of time, it's always about her. Always. It's just that simple." He sighed. "And just that difficult."

～～～

Jordan woke up with what felt like needles in her back. *What the . . . ?*

" 'Tis a wee kitty," Mathilda said from somewhere across the room. "Roll over gentlelike, so's not to crush the mite."

Jordan moved just slightly, and the kitten leaped onto her pillow, where he began a fight with her hair. Rolling to her back, she extracted him carefully, then held him suspended above her. She wasn't a big fan of cats, but this little thing was übercute. "Where did he come from?"

"I don't reckon I know, but I'm guessing he's a gift from Master Ty. He's a hopper, that one." Mathilda came closer and waggled a finger at the cat. "Use the box, little man, or ye'll be back in the stables."

The kitten mewed at her, and Mathilda harrumphed. "Ye'd best be getting up now, Miss Jordan. Breakfast is in half an hour, and Master Jax expects you in the gym just after for yer first training. You need to practice popping around, and God willing, ye'll be better at it than Miss Sasha. Puir lamb ends up in some strange places, she does, and it doesn't matter how hard she practices, she gets no better. Ye'll also be learning to use a blade. The brothers don't care for pistols and such, because they make noise and can't always be reliable not to kill. Blades will tame a lost soul long enough to take them out, but ye have to learn where best to attack."

The idea of cutting someone turned her stomach. Relaxing her arms, she put the squirmy kitten down and sat up in bed. "What do I wear for training?"

"Master Jax likes his pupils to wear what they wear in the field." She went to the closet and returned to the bed with a pair of black leather pants, a black silk long-sleeved T-shirt, and a black leather trench coat. She made another trip to the closet and this time returned with a pair of black boots. The Mephisto monochrome. "Why all the black? And why leather?"

"Takedowns are usually at night, and almost always a surprise to the lost souls and Skia. Black blends into the dark. Leather is warm, and more resistant to cuts than cloth."

Jordan pulled the kitten and his needle claws away from the coat, and he attacked a lump beneath the covers, which was her right foot. "Mathilda, how long have you been with the Mephisto?"

Smiling at the kitten, she said, "Since 1852."

She waited to hear why Mathilda was mad at God, but the

woman didn't say anything else, and Jordan didn't want to over-step or pry.

"What time is it?" She hadn't known what time it was since her kidnappers had taken her cell phone out of her pocket at Mat-thew's house, and it was making her crazy.

"Close to seven. Breakfast is always at seven thirty." Mathilda plucked the kitten from where he was batting at a loose string on the coverlet. "I'll look after yer kitty, Miss Jordan."

When she was gone, Jordan didn't waste any time getting ready. She was starving. While she braided her hair, she won-dered if Key's family would be friendlier now that he wasn't at death's door.

She had her answer ten minutes later when, on her way down-stairs, she met Zee at the landing of the second floor and he asked, "What kind of music do you like?"

"Mostly rock and some R and B."

"What's the last concert you went to?"

"I've never been to a concert."

He stopped her halfway down the steps with a hand on her arm. "Wait. Seriously?"

"It's not as if I haven't wanted to, but I've been the president's daughter since I was twelve, and my dad always said no, that it was too much trouble for the Secret Service."

He looked like he felt sorry for her. "That's it, then. First chance we get, I'm taking you to one. You think about who you want to see, and we'll go wherever they are."

Seeing the offer as an olive branch, an unvoiced apology for yesterday, Jordan accepted. "Thank you, Zee."

They continued down the stairs, then toward the back of the great hall and into the dining room, which smelled delicious and made her mouth water. Deacon stood in front of a buffet with an array of silver chafing dishes, staring straight through a large window with a view of the mountains. The only other person in the room was Denys, who spun a plate balanced on his forefinger. "Good morning, Jordan," he said with a grin while he gave her a once-over. "All set to start training, I see." He pushed the plate into the air, then caught it with his other hand and set it on the table. "Take my advice and eat a lot. Jax is a real gentleman until he gets into training. Then he becomes a maniacal hard-ass."

"I wouldn't say maniacal," Jax said as he walked around her toward the table.

"More like homicidal," Sasha said, following Jax.

Jordan noticed Sasha looked different today, but she couldn't decide why. Her blonde hair was in a ponytail, and she was dressed all in black just like yesterday, so what was unusual?

Zee said, "It's the Anabo glow. You can see it now, can't you?"

It wasn't what she expected, which was some kind of golden light. Instead, she thought Sasha looked . . . ethereal. Almost otherworldly, and so beautiful, it was hard to look away from her.

Sasha took a seat next to Denys and smiled at Jordan. "Now you can see how Jax and I knew you were Anabo the second we laid eyes on you at the National Cathedral on Christmas Day. It's kind of awesome, yeah?"

"Amazing. But I have to ask, how does a son of Hell go inside a church?"

Jax reached for Sasha's ponytail and smoothed the stray hairs. "I earned the right to stand on holy ground because of Sasha."

"How? What did she do?"

"It's the Mephisto Covenant," Key said as he came into the room and walked to the chair opposite Denys, "a deal made between our father and God when we became immortal. If any of us love a girl and she loves us back, we have the same chance of Heaven as anyone else, and we can go inside a church without burning to ash. We're limited to Anabo girls because they're not afraid of us, but finding one is rare, and even then, we're not really cut out for undying, noble love."

As if he hadn't just told her she was his only hope of Heaven in the same tone he'd tell her they needed a gallon of milk, he pulled out the chair and waved her toward it. "Have a seat and let's eat, Jordan. Lots to do today."

Behind her, someone cleared his throat. She glanced over her shoulder and saw Ty and Phoenix looking awkward. Darting a look at Zee, who was frowning, she walked toward Key and took the seat. He sat at the head of the table, just to her right, and Zee took the chair to her left. After Ty and Phoenix were seated, Deacon began to serve in the uncomfortable silence. Hoping to dispel the awkwardness of Key's casually delivered bombshell, Jordan said, "Ty, thank you for the kitten. I've never had a cat before."

"Give him a try, and if you decide he's not for you, he can go back to the stables."

Silence fell again, and as they all received their food, they became completely focused on their plates. She made herself concentrate on what she was eating, while she determinedly tried to avoid thinking about the Mephisto Covenant.

Eggs Benedict was one of her favorites. There were also bacon and scones. And kippers. She skipped those.

Holy crap. She could kiss him, and after what they'd done on the couch in the TV room last night, she could almost imagine sleeping with him somewhere down the road. She didn't doubt they could be friends. But love?

Hans was a genius. There were tiny pancakes. Or were they blintzes?

Key was a dictator, rough and curt, a son of Hell. Was he capable of sincere, unselfish love?

She wondered if she could have more bacon. How could she still be hungry? Why couldn't she make her brain stop thinking about the Mephisto Covenant?

Wasn't it enough that she had given up mortality for him, to stay here and be with him? How could she be his only chance of redemption? Mary Michael had failed to tell her about the Mephisto Covenant. Why would God lay something this heavy on her?

Into the exaggerated racket of cutlery clinking against china, Key said, "There's been a slight change to the plan."

Everyone stopped and looked at him.

"Jordan is certain her father wouldn't have a party to celebrate her return, which kills the original plan. Instead, the takedown will be during her memorial."

The table erupted in angry voices, until he held up his hand and said, "Unless one of you can come up with a better solution, this is the way it will be."

"Tell them the other part of the plan," Phoenix said in a deadpan voice.

"Jordan will be with us for the takedown."

They all turned their attention to her, and Jax said, "You don't have to do this. We can handle the takedown."

"I want to be there. I want those people who've screwed over my father to know I'm aware of what they are, and what their betrayal has cost them."

"We're not about revenge," Zee said. "They won't care anyway. All the lost souls give a damn about is Eryx, and saving their sorry asses from Hell on Earth."

"It's not right for her to be there," Phoenix said. "She needs time to come to terms with all that's already happened to her. Going to her own funeral, seeing her dad and family and friends— it's a recipe for disaster."

"She's a liability," Jax said. "If she wigs out, she can threaten the whole takedown."

"I'll take responsibility," Key said, now scowling.

"I won't wig out." Jordan could see from their faces that they all expected her to fly to pieces. "I'm not saying it'll be easy, but it's important to me to be there, and if I've done all I need to do to prepare, I don't see the big deal."

"You can physically prepare," Jax said, not unkindly, "but mentally, I don't think you can do it."

Key set his fork down. Loudly. "I'll make sure she has what she needs."

"She's going to be wiped out," Ty said, "and you want us to believe *you* can put her back together and make it okay?"

"I don't need anyone to put me back together." This was starting to tick her off, in spite of their concern. She wasn't some tender flower to be coddled.

"She'll be Mephisto by the time of the takedown, and that will make all the difference."

"No, it won't," Sasha said. "Her dad isn't a lost soul, and it's going to kill her to see him and not be able to speak to him. And even if she's Mephisto, it's still way freaky for her to be at her own funeral. I think it's a terrible idea, made worse because you're so sure you can help her. No offense, Key, but you're the last guy on Earth I'd look to for emotional support."

He had no expression on his face, gave no indication that their words fazed him, but how could he not be hurt? Jordan wanted to tell them to back off.

"I think you should sit this one out," Zee said to her. "It's a bad way to start, and Key's not going to—"

"*Okay.* I get it. I'm not Mr. Sympathy." He wasn't hurt. He was mad. Or maybe he was hurt and hiding it behind a ferocious scowl. He gave her a hard look. "Are you sure you want to do this, considering you'll have no *emotional* support?"

His anger toward her was unfair, and it pissed her off. "A lack of emotional support is one thing, but you're acting like a total tool."

The look went from hard to cold. "I asked a simple question."

"Loaded with an unjust accusation. I never said anything about needing help to get over being at my own funeral. And what's with that look? I get that you're the one in charge, but no way that gives you the right to glare at me like I'm a misbehaving child. Is this how you run things, Kyros? Maybe everybody here puts up with it, but I won't."

"No one ignores me." His voice was low, almost threatening.

"No one patronizes me. And since we're on the subject of your leadership skills, what's with tossing the Mephisto Covenant at me like it's an afterthought? That's seriously huge, and you didn't bother to mention it last night? I have to assume it's not important to you, so why should it be important to me?"

"What did you want me to do? Make a formal speech, with trumpeters and a scroll? It is what it is, and my opinion of its importance is irrelevant. Whether or not we grow to love each other has no bearing on what needs to happen right now, and what we have to do to prepare. I don't have any illusions or expectations about you and me, Jordan, and neither should you. All you need to worry about is completing your change to Mephisto."

"You're doing it again."

"What?"

"Telling me what to think, setting my priorities for me, and generally being a d-bag." She laid her napkin on the table and stood. "Jax, I'll wait for you in the hall." Turning, she grabbed her coat from the chairback and walked away. As she passed Deacon, she said, "Please tell Hans that breakfast was exceptional."

The Moor nodded, and she thought she saw a hint of a smile on his ordinarily so solemn face.

❧

Watching Jordan walk out, Key was struck by how quickly things had deteriorated and how thoroughly he'd been told. From the looks on the others' faces, they were equally stunned. Maybe if he was the joking kind like Denys, he'd say something flip, and they'd all laugh it off. If he was deliberate like Phoenix, he'd point out that Jordan had a lot to learn about being Mephisto. Or, if he was a gentle soul like Ajax, he'd say he clearly had a lot to learn about females. Especially one who had come of age in the White House.

But he wasn't like his brothers, and he would handle this in his own way. He'd keep his thoughts to himself and silently dare anyone to say a word. He swept his gaze around the table, glad when no one picked up the gauntlet.

"I'll be out most of the day, looking for something in Washington we can use for our base, but as soon as I'm back, we need to meet and talk about taking down those nut jobs in Texas."

"The ATF and the FBI are there now," Zee said, "demanding Red Out's surrender."

"I suspect Eryx told them to hold out and force the Feds to storm the place. If they die, he wins—not only because he gains that many more souls, but killing those people will make the president look like he was out for revenge."

He stood and walked toward the door, but slowed when Phoenix said, "Will you allow Jordan to be at the Red Out takedown?"

Without turning around, Key said, "No, it's too soon. We need to do it by tomorrow night, and she won't be ready."

"She could go along to observe. That'd be helpful."

Key continued walking. "We'll see."

In the front hall, he found Jordan staring up at Jane's portrait. When he reached her side, she asked, "Did he love her?"

"In his way, but it wasn't enough. She died too soon."

"Did Eryx find her because she was marked?"

"He can sense it as well as the rest of us, but we didn't know until it was too late. Jane was the first Anabo we found, and we didn't have a clue how things were supposed to happen."

"Phoenix must feel guilty."

"It makes him overprotective, which is why he'll continue to argue against your being at the takedown."

She turned toward him. "It's not as if you're completely sold on the idea."

"I'm not even partially sold."

"Then why are you letting me do it?"

Good question. "Because I don't want this to be something that defines the rest of our lives together. I lead, but this isn't an absolute monarchy. I have to let the rest of you do what you will, if it's within the rules. You don't know what it's like on a takedown, or how you'll feel about seeing your dad under those circumstances, but if I assume you're not up to it, what does that say about me?"

In boots, she was taller, but she still had to tilt her head back to look up at him. She'd pulled her dark hair into a fat braid that hung to just between her shoulder blades, and tiny wisps curled around her temples and forehead. Looking into her blue eyes, he wanted to kiss her, and he didn't know if it was a subconscious impulse to apologize, or simple biology. He supposed it didn't matter. The desire was there, and the convenient excuse of necessity. Reaching for her shoulders, he took a step closer.

"Really? You're going to kiss me? Do you think it will make me not be mad at you anymore?"

"On the contrary. Your anger and my d-baggery have no relation to kissing." He pulled her toward him and angled his head to meet her lips. Just like before, she was hesitant for a nanosecond, then fell into it with total abandon. Her arms slid around his middle, and he wrapped her up in his. She tasted like honey, smelled like bluebells, and made the world fall away until there was nothing but her, this kiss, and blessed, addictive peace.

It was over too soon when sounds from the dining room

signaled the end of breakfast and an approaching audience. She pulled away and stepped back, her lips wet and full, her cheeks pink, and her eyes slightly sleepy. His mind went somewhere it definitely didn't need to go, and he abruptly turned away. "Work hard and learn all you can today." He strode across the hall and was halfway up the stairs before his brothers and Sasha came out of the dining room.

❧

Well, great, there she went again, kissing Key like there was no tomorrow, like she was some impetuous adolescent hormone, like she didn't have a critically wounded boyfriend in a Washington hospital. The need for kissing was no excuse for how much she enjoyed it. Maybe it was the Mephisto now running through her veins. If she had the chance and it wasn't too horribly awkward, she'd ask Sasha if turning Mephisto was the reason she felt like this. She kind of hoped so. Otherwise, she had to face that she was willingly leaving Matthew behind, making her the worst girl-friend in the universe and a lousy human being.

Jax walked toward her while the rest of them headed up the stairs. "We'll go to the gym and get started, if you're ready."

She nodded, he reached for her hand, and everything went dark. Seconds later, they stood in the most unusual gym she'd ever seen, with soaring stone walls, windows set way up high, and an exposed wooden roof with log crossbeams. There were basketball nets at opposite ends of the gleaming wooden floor and a set of cabinets along one of the short sides of the rectangular building.

"This used to be the dairy, back in the day before grocery stores sold milk and butter. We turned it into a gym in the sixties." He pointed toward the southeast corner. "Through that door is the weight room. You need to work out at least five times a week, minimum two hours, and use every piece of equipment. Your goal is to bench-press three hundred pounds."

"You're funny."

"I'm not joking. With the changes you've already made, you can probably press close to one fifty now."

"No way."

"We'll check it out as soon as we have your first transporting lesson." He turned her so she was facing the corner. "Stare at a spot over there on the floor close to the door, then close your eyes, concentrate, and imagine you're standing on that spot."

She did exactly as he said, and when she opened her eyes, she was across the gym. Incredible. "How does it work?"

"We learned once, a long time ago, but I don't remember. Ask Zee. He's the brainiac in the family. Now come back."

She closed her eyes, and when she opened them again, Jax was right there.

"Let's try popping back to the house. Imagine the front hall, the big *M* on the floor, and go there."

A few seconds later, she was straddling the *M*, Jax nodding approval. "Now return."

Back in the gym, he looked pleased. "You're catching on so fast, later today, we'll try transporting off the mountain." He nodded toward the weight room. "Let's see what you can do in there."

It was a bigger room than she expected, but otherwise looked like any other workout gym, with all sorts of equipment, a plasma TV on one wall, and a freestanding shelf filled with white towels in the corner. Jax slid out of his trench coat and demonstrated how to use the bench press. She couldn't help but notice how he filled out his T-shirt. His muscles were like Key's—enormous. "Am I going to look like one of those bodybuilder ladies? I'm on board for being Mephisto, but I'm not going to be okay with that."

He grinned at her as he set the weights back in position. "Sasha can press three twenty and she's very fit, but trust me, she's not ripped." Back on his feet, he said, "Take off your coat and let's see how much Mephisto you've got."

Tossing the coat across an elliptical, she straddled the bench and lay back while he removed weights and explained dos and don'ts. Right up until she lifted her arms, curled her hands around the bar, and pushed, she expected not to be able to do it. She was wrong. It was heavy, true, but doable. She repeated the up and down five times, then set the weights back. "How much was that?"

Jax was staring at her. "Key's been kissing you, hasn't he?"

"A lot."

"You just pressed two hundred."

She sat up. "I feel like Popeye after he eats spinach."

Jax extended a hand. "Let's go get some knives."

Hesitating, she looked up at him but didn't take his hand. "I don't know if I'm up for knives, Jax."

"You have to be able to protect yourself in a takedown. The lost souls and Skia will go to any lengths to avoid capture, and even though we always recover quickly from wounds, the more severe ones will keep you down long enough to become a liability. Somebody will have to bring you back to the mountain, which means two of us out of commission. The other reason you'll want to protect yourself is because there's no bypass of pain. Getting stabbed, shot, strangled, kicked, and thrown from windows is as awful as it sounds."

He reached for her hand and tugged until she was standing. "You're also going to be less freaked about cutting someone when you confront a lost soul as a Mephisto. If you're anything like Sasha, it'll be a never-ending struggle to keep from killing them."

Unable to imagine actually wanting to kill someone, but accepting the necessity of learning knife skills, she followed him back into the gym and stood by while he opened one of the cabinets. Inside looked like a display case at Hunters-R-Us. Jax pulled one from its felt binding and handed it to her. "See if this fits your palm."

It felt heavy and cumbersome. "I don't think this is the one." He handed her another and another. She went through at least a dozen more until he found one with a white handle that fit her hand perfectly. "This one is good, I think."

"Nice. It's from a shop in Prague." He began replacing the discarded knives. "Now, let's see what you're made of, Jordan. Pretend I'm a lost soul and your job is to capture me and take me to the *M* in the front hall."

"I'm not really good at role-playing."

Still fiddling with the knives, he shrugged and said, "Not surprising. You're not very good at real life, either."

Stunned, she stepped back. "What?"

"You've had everything handed to you since you were four years old and your parents took you out of that hellhole in Bucharest. What do you know about life, really?"

Not sure where he was going with this, and not at all liking the hard edge to his voice, she said, "It's true I've never gone without material things, but I've lost people, and they're what matter."

"You mean your mom."

"And my friend Holly."

"Yeah, let's talk about Holly." He continued arranging the knives in the display case. "When she went off the rails, you felt bad for her, but you didn't really understand. How could you? You were popular and rich, and your parents adored you. Holly was a scholarship kid with a chip on her shoulder, an alcoholic mom, and a father who abandoned her. For you, she wasn't so much a friend as a project."

Jordan sucked in a quick breath, feeling like he'd punched her in the stomach. Where did he get off saying something like that? "I loved Holly! We grew up together."

"Only because she was the maid's daughter. While her mother was cleaning toilets in your family's Maryland mansion, your mother was picking out fabric for seat cushions in the family jet. Holly went home every day to a double-wide with a hole in the roof, a raving drunk for a mother, and a stepdad who knocked her teeth out because she refused to steal your jewelry. You ended up selling the jewelry to pay for her dental work, but what did it cost you to part with it, Jordan? Not nearly so dear as the price Holly paid for being loyal." He closed the door to the display case, then stared down at his hands. "The day she died, you told her a secret that changed everything. Remember?"

This could not be happening. Jordan took another step back and considered leaving. Why was he doing this? How did he know about the jewelry, or the day Holly died? The only person she ever told was Matthew.

"She came to say good-bye. She was running away, going to find her real father." He turned to face her. "You knew all about him because your dad did a background check on her mom before he hired her, and you snooped in his files."

That day was never far from her mind: Holly's desperation to get away from her stepfather, her certainty that finding her real dad was the answer to everything, the look of complete and total devastation on her face when Jordan told her the truth.

"He was a wife beater," Jax said, "in prison for murdering his second wife."

"How . . . do you know all this?"

"My father is the dark angel who carries souls to Hell. What's said about suicides is true."

She flinched and nearly dropped the knife.

He took a step toward her. "She was already desperate, and you pushed her over the edge."

"Don't say that."

He took another step closer. "How does it feel to be responsible for your friend's suicide?"

Images she'd worked hard to banish scattered across her mind, and she held up her hands, as if to ward them off. "Stop it. Just stop talking."

His next step brought him inside her personal space. "You didn't buy the rope, but you tied the noose."

Impulsively, she shoved him, but he didn't budge, and the knife in her hand sliced into his shirt. And his skin. Horrified, she was about to apologize when he spun her around and held her with one arm pressed against her throat and a switchblade aimed at her stomach. "I win this point, Jordan. If I was a lost soul, you'd now have a blade in your belly. Do you know why?"

"Because you're a mean son of a bitch?"

"I got inside your head. You allowed me to get this close, and you let me push you way too far. Now that I'm in a position to hurt you bad, what are you going to do?"

Swiftly lifting her foot, she slammed her heel down on his. Nothing happened.

"I'm wearing steel-toed boots. Try again."

She tried to bend at the waist to throw him over, but again nothing happened.

"Considering I have a knife pointed at your midsection, that'd be a disastrous move—if it had worked. What's next?"

"I don't want to hurt—"

"Do it!" His arm tightened, restricting her airflow, and the switchblade was suddenly slicing into her arm.

Grasping the knife, she lifted her hand and tried to cut him, but he moved too fast. He cut her again.

"Are you stupid? Should we assume you're too dense to be Mephisto and send you to work in the kitchen, chopping vegetables?" He cut her a third time, about the time the first two began to sting and burn.

"Time out," she gasped.

"F that, princess. Are you going to let me slice you into little pieces?" He cut her again.

Closing her eyes, she imagined she was standing on the Mephisto *M*, and just like that, she was free. In the front hall, she pumped a fist and hissed a triumphant *"Yes!"*

"Mathilda will be displeased, Anabo. You bleed on her floor."

Looking down, she saw a lot of crimson on white, but it didn't curb her enthusiasm. "Tell her I'm sorry."

"I will do no such thing. The apology is yours to make."

Deacon disappeared just as Jax appeared, looking aggravated. He clearly didn't approve. "You lose again, Jordan. No matter what the situation, never leave a takedown. I wanted you to transport, but not away from the fight. It defeats the purpose."

She deflated. "Oh."

"Let's head back before Mathilda wigs out about the blood."

Duly chastised, she closed her eyes, but hadn't even begun to imagine a spot inside the gym before she was knocked off of her feet by a force so strong, she flew through the air, landed on her back, and skidded all the way to the wall. While she was thinking this must be how victims of vehicular manslaughter feel, Jax was stalking across the marble with murder in his eyes.

Ignoring the pain in her back and the burning cuts in her arm, Jordan rolled to a sit and sprang to her feet. Incredibly, she still had the white knife in her hand, and she held it in front of her to keep him from attacking.

"Am I supposed to be worried?" He kept coming. "Because I'm not. You'll let me cut you again because you're a weak, soft, spoiled princess. It's why you never really understood Holly. She was a fighter."

"She killed herself! How is that fighting?"

They were circling each other now. "In every war, there's a loser, but not until there's a fight. She gave it all she had before she surrendered. You haven't given anything, so you don't win or lose. You just take up space."

She didn't move fast enough to get away before he lunged at her, and she gasped in pain and shock when his blade sank into her side. Jerking back, she spun around and ran to the stairs, up three steps, then shoved off on the fourth and did a backward flip, landing just behind him as he followed. Without hesitating, she stabbed him in the shoulder, and he let out a mighty roar before he turned and dove for her legs. Then they were rolling across the floor, through the blood, across the *M*, fighting for an opening to stab each other. She got him three times. He got her five.

She managed to get her legs beneath him, then bent her knees and shoved as hard as she could, gratified when he grunted in pain and rolled away. Scrambling to her feet, gasping for air because every breath was agony to her wounds, she stumbled for the door. She had to stop, at least for a while.

She was reaching for the egg-shaped knob when she felt his blade in her back, right between her shoulders. Then the door was meeting her face and she slid all the way to the floor. Dazed, she saw his boots next to her head, felt his hands against her back, watched while he wiped his blade clean on her sleeve. He squatted next to her and tipped her face to look up at him. "I win again, Jordan. Do you know why?"

"I hate you so much it's a sin."

"I was down. You kicked me in the nuts, which was a most excellent move, but then you walked away, leaving yourself wide open for my blade in your back."

"I needed a break."

"There are no breaks in takedowns. You should have incapacitated me while I was unable to defend my position. Best way to do that is to cut the hamstrings. Nobody can get to his feet with severed hamstrings. Got it?"

"I'd like to kick you in the nuts until you sing soprano."

"Your only objective is subduing your prey long enough to transport him to the gate. Once you're there, the pull of Hell will keep him pinned to the ground until you send him down."

She was in so much pain, her hair hurt. "The pull of gravity is keeping me pinned to this floor. I need a doctor."

He frowned and reached down to feel the pulse at her neck, which gave her the perfect opportunity to stab his arm. Seconds later, they were circling each other again. "Faked you out, didn't I?"

"Yeah, pretty much. I believed you because you're pale as a ghost and covered in blood. Mostly yours. Nice job."

"Give me a point."

"Done. So we're at five to one, which means you'd better get on it if you have a prayer of catching up."

"Five to two. That backflip totally counts."

"Agreed, but you're still three points behind, about to be four."

"Says you." Determined not to be stabbed even once more, she shoved everything out of her mind, focused only on Jax and the knife in his hand, and grimly soldiered on.

EIGHT

AFTER SEVERAL HOURS SPENT LOOKING AT PROPERTIES, KEY was hungry and frustrated. Adding to his annoyance, the leasing agent was overly anxious and jittery, even though Key wore Wayfarers to hide his eyes and kept his distance. He had to go through the usual Q&A about his age and his finances. He had an ID putting his age at twenty-two, and a wallet filled with cash and every major credit card. His credit score was sterling. He dropped a few well-placed comments about his trust fund, and eventually the guy lightened up and showed him the kind of places he was interested in. He settled on a Capitol Hill town house and signed a six-month lease, then ran an errand in New York and grabbed some lunch. It was almost three in the mountains when he popped back to Colorado.

The instant he landed in the front hall, he saw blood. Rivers of it. "Deacon, what's the meaning of this?"

"Ask me no rhetorical questions; I will give you no nonsensical answers."

Handing the Moor his portfolio to hold while he slid out of his blue wool overcoat, he asked a different question. "Why here? Training is in the gym."

"It would seem this Anabo sets her own rules."

He gave Deacon his coat, then turned toward the library. As usual for midafternoon, Phoenix was sprawled in one of the leather wingbacks in front of the fireplace, reading. He looked up when Key came in. "Did you find something?"

Unbuttoning his suit jacket, he nodded and took the opposite chair, then loosened his tie and leaned back. "Is she okay?"

Phoenix set his book aside and sat up. "Define okay."

"I'm going up to see her in a minute. What should I expect? Is she mad, sad, hurt?"

"All three. She was slow to attack, but Jax pissed her off enough that she finally went after him. She has a competitive streak a mile wide, and I think she really thought she could beat him. When she didn't, it bothered her, and she wanted to keep going, but as you can see from the front hall, neither of them was in very good shape by the end. Mathilda was so worried about her, she failed to get mad about the mess. She hustled her off to her room, and I suppose she's dressed her wounds and put her to bed."

Key stared across the library at dust motes in the beams of sunlight coming through the west window. "She isn't what I expected."

His brother didn't respond right away. They sat with only the crackle of the fire and the tick of the grandfather clock in the corner to break the silence. After a while, Phoenix said, "Jane wasn't what I expected."

Jerking his attention away from the dust motes, he saw Phoenix staring at the clock. "You never said so."

"I thought I'd find a girl who was strong and independent, who liked to ride as much as I did, who had a spirit of adventure and would go with me to places like the Himalayas, or the pyramids in Egypt. Instead, I got Jane, who couldn't walk and was afraid of horses. She was shy, reserved, and a homebody." Phoenix shifted in his chair and rubbed an invisible spot from the brown leather armrest. "Looking at it from her side, she thought she'd marry an aristocrat who would be as passionate about social change in England as she was, who could take her to church. Instead, she got me."

"Who healed her so she could walk. That had to rank higher than social change."

"Not to Jane."

Key was floored. "I thought you and Jane were crazy about each other."

"We were."

"But you just said—"

"All that was in the beginning, Key. Once I really knew her, I didn't care so much about the pyramids. She could be funny, which isn't something I ever considered important. She had quirks, like hiding dime novels inside her hat so she could sneak away from parties and read. You don't think about things like that while you're waiting. You build up this perfect girl in your head, but she doesn't exist. What you get instead is a real human being, and if you're lucky like me, she'll be a million times better than what you imagined and expected."

"In her hat? Really?"

Phoenix nodded and reached for his book. "She loved scary stories."

Key got to his feet and walked to the doorway into the front hall, then stopped and said over his shoulder, "Do you ever imagine another girl?"

"All the time, but now, instead of a girl who's into pyramids, she's always Jane."

He walked out and saw Mathilda and two other Purgatories scrubbing the marble floor. She looked up at him as he made his way toward the stairs. "Ye'll find her in yer greenhouse, Master Kyros. Said she wanted to practice traveling, so she popped there and here for a while, but the last time, she didn't come back."

He stopped walking, and a nanosecond later was inside the greenhouse. He saw her right away, sitting cross-legged on the glider, staring ahead at a bank of daylilies. She turned her head when he appeared and said, "Do you ever have regret?"

Taking a seat next to her, he moved the glider back and forth while he considered his answer. "I wouldn't call it regret. More like a lesson learned."

"What difference does it make to learn the lesson? It's not like you get a do-over."

She was dressed in a red hoodie and pair of black pants that were more like tights, with thick gray socks and no shoes. Her hair was loose, shiny, and clean. Below the scent of bluebells, he smelled shampoo. "Are you healed already?"

Tugging her hoodie up, she showed him her belly. He stopped the glider and stared. The wounds were almost gone, with only small red marks to indicate where they had been, but there were so many, he felt ill. "Holy hell, there must be a hundred." Jax had let things get way out of hand.

As if she could read his thoughts, she said quietly, "Jax looks just as bad."

"What happened? It was supposed to be an introductory training session, not a gladiator match."

"He called me a princess and said it was my fault my friend committed suicide."

"That explains why you jumped in, but why did he cut you so many times? Jax doesn't have accidents, which means every one of those was on purpose."

She didn't answer for a while, her concentration on his tie. Finally, she said, "I wanted to get inside his head, like he was in mine, but all I really know about him is that he has Sasha."

His eye twitched while he waited to hear what insults she had hurled at Jax about Sasha.

"I told him he was suffocating her, and the real reason she sucks at transporting is because that's her only chance to get out of here and do something on her own." She lifted his tie and brought it closer to her face to squint at it. "You had Italian for lunch."

Staring at her, he was overwhelmed with guilt. Not regret, but plain, simple guilt. It was the Mephisto in her that had made her say something like that to Jax. Yesterday, before she kissed him, she'd never have said it. Wouldn't even have thought it.

He sighed and set the glider moving again. "What you said to Jax . . . it's something he worries about."

"Did he tell you that?"

"He didn't have to. Last week, Sasha was watching some reality show about college girls spending a semester in London. She loves art, and had planned to become a restorer and work in a museum. Jax asked if she was sorry she couldn't go to college, if she feels like she missed out, and she said no, but in the next breath she asked me if she could take an art class. I had to tell her she couldn't, which she accepted, but I know it bugged the hell out of Jax. What you said hit him where he's vulnerable."

She sat silently staring at him for so long, he finally turned his head to meet her gaze. "Is something wrong?"

"You love your brothers, don't you?"

He looked away quickly. He hadn't seen that coming. "I'd kill for them. I feel responsible for them. If that means I love them, then yeah, I guess I do."

Jordan drew her legs up and hugged them, resting her chin on one knee. "Why did you say no to Sasha?"

Why had she asked him about his brothers? What difference did it make how he felt about them? "We're not safe in the real world for anything long term or routine because it'd give Eryx the opportunity to plan a capture. If he took any of us, it'd be difficult to escape."

While he continued to push the glider, listening to the bees and the fall of water in the koi pond, she said, "I told Jax I was sorry. You don't have to worry that we hate each other."

"I wasn't worried, but in the future, you don't have to make a sparring partner mad. Jax got under your skin only to coerce you to fight. In a real takedown, the less you engage with a lost soul, the better."

She turned her head so that her cheek was resting on her knee and gave him a look, almost a once-over. "I wouldn't have thought it, but you look mighty fine in a suit."

Her compliment was so unexpected, Key had no idea how to respond.

"Why are you wearing a suit? I thought you went to rent a house."

Recovering slightly, he cleared his throat and said, "It makes me look older. Since I take care of the money and all of our assets, I have to go a lot of places where people assume I'm too young to be taken seriously."

"In that suit, I'd guess you're in your early twenties, and if you didn't have a ponytail, I'd think you were even older. Why do you have a ponytail? It looks good on you, but they're kind of out of style for anyone but guys from eighties hair bands."

"I've had long hair my whole life, but it's not vanity. I was told to keep it long."

She lifted her head. "Why? Who told you?"

"I've never known why, but Lucifer said to keep my hair at least to my shoulders."

"You've talked to Lucifer?" Her eyes were wide with curiosity. "What does he really look like? Were you scared? Was he übercreepy?"

"I didn't actually see him. He was just a voice in the dark. And yes, I was scared. I was dead. My father told me I'd come back, but I thought maybe he got it wrong and Lucifer was there to give me the bad news."

"So instead of taking you to Hell, he just came to tell you how to wear your hair?"

Key smiled. "No, wise guy, that's not all he told me."

"Why would he tell you to wear your hair long? That's really random."

"I think it was sort of a test, to see if I'd rebel. He was very big on my doing what he told me to do." And even more emphatic about what would happen if Key failed. So maybe after so many centuries, keeping his hair long wasn't really necessary, but he wasn't willing to chance cutting it.

"What else did he tell you to do?"

"Lead my brothers. Work as hard as I could to take out Eryx."

He looked down into her bluebell eyes. "Since we'd lost Eryx, I was the oldest, and the first to die. He told me to let the younger ones do whatever they wanted until Denys turned eighteen, not to be hard on them. He knew, like I didn't, that everything would change once we all became immortal."

"Because you had to start looking for Eryx's Skia and lost souls?"

He stopped the glider and smoothed her hair. Nothing in the world was as soft as Jordan's hair. "Because we had to leave Kyanos. We'd never been in the real world before, or had any interaction with humans, other than our mother. It was an adjustment, and all of us were completely clueless."

"After your mom died, did no one stay with you?"

He dropped his hand and shook his head.

"So the six of you lived there, alone, and fended for yourselves?"

"Mostly. M came every few months and brought food stores like wheat, sugar, and salt. We had goats and chickens, and grew things like potatoes and cabbage."

"Since you were the oldest, did you take care of everyone?"

"We all had our chores, but yeah, I was the last word."

"Did you ever see Eryx?"

He tilted his head back and watched a bank of clouds roll across the sky above the greenhouse. More snow. "After he left Kyanos, he couldn't come back because of the mists. Not that he wanted to. The day he went away, the day we buried our mother after he murdered her, he said he wouldn't remember us." Key made it a point never to think about that day, and it bothered him that he'd done so now.

Standing, he moved away from her and went to the potting bench for his shears. "But we made sure he didn't forget us. After Denys made the jump and we left Kyanos, we lived in Greece because Eryx was there. We screwed things up for him as much as possible and captured a big percentage of his converts." The newest miniature orange tree was sprouting more rogue tendrils, and he took his time trimming them. "After a hundred years or so, he moved to Russia, and we followed. We were there for centuries, until he relocated to Romania. By then, we didn't see the need to be that close to him, so we moved to England."

"Is the painting in your room the house you lived in?"

"Yes. It was in Yorkshire."

"Will you show it to me?"

"I can't. It's no longer there."

"Why? How? It's a stone house, so it couldn't burn down."

"We can only have one protected home outside of Kyanos. When we moved here at the turn of the last century, the house in Yorkshire ceased to exist."

"How does a huge house just disappear?"

He looked across the twenty feet separating them. "It wasn't in the real world. Only in ours, on a different plane of existence. When we left, Lucifer made it disappear." He waved his arm to indicate the mountain. "Everything here can only be seen and felt by us, the Luminas, and the Purgatories. If people hike up here, they see only forest and meadows."

The intercom over the door crackled with static, then Phoenix said, "War room meeting in fifteen. Somebody remind Zee. He's got the Stones cranked to ten."

He was about to tell her he was going up to change clothes, but before he could, the intercom came on again, this time courtesy of Zee, backed by "Gimme Shelter." "I'll be there. Somebody needs to tell Kyros. He's making out with Jordan in the greenhouse."

Replacing his shears on the potting bench, Key waited for the inevitable next message.

Seconds later, Sasha said, "I can see in there, and he's trimming trees."

"Roger that," Denys said. "The guy's got a gorgeous girl in a hothouse, and he's holding gardening shears instead of her. I vote for an intervention."

Ty was next. "Maybe he's afraid she'll stab him."

Three heartbeats later, Jax said, "This is a valid fear."

Key walked to the glider and held his hand out to her. "Let's go inside."

She took his hand and was unfolding her legs to stand when a solemn voice came over the intercom. "A man disrespects a woman by expressing his affection in public."

He drew her closer and slipped his arms around her.

"I thought we were going inside."

"We have a long-standing policy of immediately doing whatever Deacon tells us not to do. It's our way of tweaking his nose to take him down a notch, which clearly hasn't worked because he's still here, but by now it's family tradition." He bent his head to hers and kissed her.

Applause came through the intercom.

⤜⤏

Thirty minutes later, sitting at a huge oval table in a basement room with stone walls, Jordan listened to them plan the Red Out takedown. The plasma screen was split, a map of central Texas on one side and a Google Earth image on the other.

From a laptop, Zee moved a cursor and dropped pins as he talked. "This is the main building of the compound, where they take their meals and hold meetings. The smaller building, here, looks like a barn, but it's a stockpile of weapons and munitions." He looked at Key. "They've got a rocket launcher in there."

"Why would Eryx have a rocket launcher?"

"He wouldn't. Red Out was formed six years ago by a Marine named Brandon Holder, after he got kicked out of the military for threatening a superior. He gathered like-minded wing nuts who helped him build this compound on his family's land. They started accumulating weapons and hiding them in a basement beneath the floor of the barn. Eryx probably did a lot of research to find a group to use as the scapegoat for Jordan's abduction. Once he chose Red Out, he turned Holder, made him Skia, and the others pledged because he told them to. They worship the guy."

"How many are there?"

"Eighteen men, fifteen women, and five kids under eighteen. With the exception of three toddlers, they're all lost souls." He moved the cursor and dropped more pins. "These long buildings are the living quarters, and this tiny structure is what Holder calls solitary. Somebody pisses him off, that guy gets stuck in solitary until Holder says he gets out."

Key looked at Phoenix. "Give us the plan."

"Mass suicide. The ATF and FBI are there now, surrounding the place, demanding Holder's surrender. He's the kind of guy who'd order his followers to off themselves before giving up, and they're the kind of people who'd do it. The takedown will be day after tomorrow at three in the morning. We'll throw a freeze, and half of us will take them to the gate while the other half transports doppelgangers. The freeze will fade before we're done, so plan on fighting."

Jax had been quiet, Jordan noticed, but he was clearly paying attention, frowning at the screen and Zee's pins. She wondered why he looked unhappy.

Sasha asked, "Is there a plan for how they acquired enough poison to kill thirty-five people?"

"Records Luminas are making it look like Holder bought small quantities over the past six years." Phoenix looked around the table. "Any other questions?"

"Just one," Jax said, still frowning. "If we're going into multiple buildings, are we recruiting Luminas to help? We're limited on freeze time, and unless every building is secure, we run the risk of a lost soul escaping."

This was evidently a touchy subject. Lots of looks were exchanged, and Jordan could feel the sudden tension. It wasn't long before they were all looking expectantly at Key. He shook his head. "No Luminas."

"Why?" she asked. "Do they suck at fighting?"

"No, some of them came to us as soldiers, but they're given immortality by God, not us, and violence affects them differently. If they're made to participate, it'll take weeks for them to recover." He looked at the screen again. "It'll be dicey, but we'll manage."

"I think we're making a huge mistake not using Luminas," Jax said. "This isn't like any other takedown because we have the added complication of Jordan. Some of us are likely to be distracted."

"Am I included in the takedown?" she asked, surprised. She had thought all along that she wouldn't be there.

"Phoenix thinks you need to observe," Key said.

Everyone around the table nodded in agreement.

"What do you think?" she asked Key.

"You haven't even transported off the mountain yet. No one can take you to where the gates are, because we'll already be carrying the lost souls. I'm not sure you're ready to pop halfway around the world, to a place you've never been."

"Jax can teach me tomorrow."

Sasha said, "I think it's important for her to be there, Key. She needs to know what she's up against." She looked at Jordan. "The lost souls will mess with your head. The brothers ignore everything they say, but it's impossible for me."

"Do they try to talk you out of taking them?"

"No, and that's what gets me, every time. It's their arrogance, like they don't believe I can do anything to them because they're some special snowflake. I never knew what rage was until I became Mephisto. I hate them, and what they say makes me so angry, it's seriously hard not to kill them."

Ty said, "Why don't we let Jax see how Jordan does tomorrow, then decide whether she should go?"

Everyone agreed, and Key gave her that hard look again. "No guarantees. Got it?"

He must have practiced that look for centuries. "Got it."

"All right," he said, "let's move on to plans for Washington. I rented a town house today, and Zee will begin reconnaissance after the Red Out takedown." He glanced at Jordan before looking at the screen, which was now a series of photos. "These are who we'll be taking out, and Zee will give everyone a printout to memorize their faces."

She was torn between crying and cursing. All those people her father had counted on, some of whom had been friends. Mr. McCall, the Senate majority leader, gave her a gift every year on her birthday, usually a book, but once he had given her a pearl necklace that he brought back from China. And Carla, who worked for the press secretary and had been so nice and helpful. It didn't seem real that all those people had turned their back on God to follow a spooky guy like Eryx.

While she was mourning the loss of their souls, another series of photographs appeared.

"These are potential lost souls who may or may not pledge between now and the memorial service," Key said. "We'll go over the final list before the takedown, but remember these as well."

Jordan felt short of breath, staring up at the faces. "Why is Matthew there? He's the least likely to pledge."

"Looking for a miracle, he might believe a Skia who tells him he can walk again."

"What are you talking about?" She was dizzy. *"Walk again?"*

He looked surprised. "I thought you knew. I thought you saw the news."

"No, you turned it off, and I haven't watched it since."

His gaze was direct. "The gunshot damaged his spine, Jordan. He's paralyzed from the waist down."

NINE

KEY KNEW HE'D NEVER FORGET THE LOOK ON JORDAN'S face in those few seconds after he told her about Matthew. It was more than shock, more than grief. She was devastated. She opened her mouth to speak, then closed it. She pushed back from the table, as if to stand up, then pulled close again.

He wanted to pick her up and carry her out of the war room and not stop until he'd walked a mile from the house, then set her down and let her scream. She needed that. As it was, all he could do was say, "You don't have to be here, Jordan. It's okay if you want to leave."

He ignored the looks from the others. Skipping out on a takedown meeting was grounds for a council. Nobody missed meetings for any reason. So maybe he was abusing his position.

At that moment, he didn't care. Watching the play of emotions across her face, seeing the horror in her eyes, he decided he'd beat the crap out of anybody who questioned his offer to let her leave.

She shook her head. "I'm okay."

She was so not okay, but over the next half hour, while they talked about possible plans for the Washington takedown, she was tuned in and added her own ideas to the mix. Through it all, she never lost the wounded look in her eyes, and as soon as he called an end to the meeting, before he could round the table to talk to her, she disappeared from the war room.

He was about to follow when Sasha laid a hand on his arm and said quietly, "Let her be. She'll come to you when she's ready to talk about it."

He stared at the whiteboard, covered in diagrams of the Red Out compound. "She shouldn't be alone. Maybe you should go talk to her."

"If it was me, I'd want to be alone." Sasha dropped her hand. "When she's ready to talk about it, *you* need to be there for her."

Jerking his gaze to hers, he didn't try to hide his astonishment. "I wouldn't have the first clue what to say to make this better."

"Nothing you or I or anybody can say will make it better, Key. She'll just need to talk about it. All you have to do is listen." Sasha turned away and vanished.

When Jordan didn't show up for dinner, he asked Mathilda where she was, expecting her to say Jordan was in her room, crying. Instead, she looked confused and said, "I thought she was here, at dinner."

He laid his napkin on the table, stood, and popped out to the greenhouse, but she wasn't there. He went to the TV room, thinking maybe she went to watch the news, but she wasn't there, either. He looked in the library and checked her bedroom again. Finally, he went to the intercom and said, "Jordan, where are you?"

No answer.

Back in the front hall, he asked Deacon if he'd seen her. The Moor said, "No, but I'm aware she learned of her friend's infirmity at the hands of Eryx's minions. Were I wearing her shoes, vengeance would be mine."

The men who'd kidnapped her were sitting in jail, without bail, awaiting trial. "Surely you don't think she's gone to do something to the lost souls who shot Matthew?"

"I believe she readies herself for what comes."

The gym. He hadn't considered that, but it made perfect sense. He went there and knew Deacon was right. The light was on in the weight room. Looking through the window in the door, he saw her on the bench press, covered in sweat, shoving the bar up and down while she cried. He watched until it hurt to look, then popped back to the house, to his bedroom.

He called Mathilda and asked her to tell him when Jordan returned from the gym, then sat down at his desk to write his journal entry for the day. Done with that, he went over the Red

Out takedown plan, looking for anything they might have missed. When he'd hammered it enough, he put it away and reached for a magazine, but after he read the same article three times and still had no clue what it was about, he tossed it aside and went out to the greenhouse.

Two hours later, Mathilda finally came to tell him Jordan was back in her room. She was in the shower, and Mathilda was on her way to the kitchen to get the "puir lamb" some supper.

He thought about going up to see her but had no idea what he would say, and he hadn't forgotten what Sasha had told him. Jordan would come to him when she was ready.

Setting aside his shears, he went to his room and got ready for bed. In the dark, he stared up at the ceiling and went over everything he needed to get done tomorrow, but her face kept intruding on his thoughts. When he fell asleep, her sad, wounded eyes were in his dreams. When he jerked awake, her face was there, just above his. "Are you okay?"

"I came to ask a question."

She wasn't crying. That had to be a good sign. "What time is it?"

"Almost four in the morning. Are you awake enough to answer?"

He stared up at her and had a good idea what her question would be. His answer was only going to make her sadder. "I'm awake, but couldn't this have waited until daylight, somewhere besides my bed? I'm naked under here."

She was so focused on the reason for her visit, she blew right past what he'd said. "When I was with Eryx, I felt sick, like I was about to throw up. He put his hand on me, and I instantly felt better. And when I died, you gave me part of your humanity to bring me back. I want to know, can you heal Matthew?"

Yeah, that's exactly what he had been afraid she'd ask. He sighed and reached up to stroke her hair. "I have the ability, Jordan, but we're forbidden to get in the way of free will and the progression of human life. If I were to heal him, I'd be sent straight to Hell."

"How do you know?"

He dropped his hand. "Lucifer told me. The powers we have were given to us only to fight Eryx, and using them for any other purpose means instant death and forever in Hell."

She pushed away and stood straight. "Do I have the power to heal?"

Key sat up. "You will when you're completely changed to Mephisto, but you have to live by the same law."

"I thought I was guaranteed Heaven, since I'm Anabo."

"True, but you're also going to be Mephisto, which gives you abilities you didn't have before. You'll have the same limitations as the rest of us, and if you break Lucifer's law, you'll have the same punishment we would."

"When will I be done changing, Key?"

"I can't say for sure, but I think you're close. Has your birthmark changed?"

Her eyes widened. "I *thought* it looked different. It's bigger, and kind of a weird shape, instead of an *A*."

"Sasha's is a perfectly formed *A* entwined with an *M*."

He could tell by her expression, she was considering making a sacrifice of herself for Matthew. "Do you think he'd be happy about walking again if he knew you had traded your soul to Lucifer?"

"He'd never know."

"Would he be glad that you threw your gifts away? He's paralyzed because of Eryx. People are suffering because of Eryx. You've been given the chance to work against him, but that's all history the instant you lay your hands on Matthew and fix him."

She turned away and walked to the painting of the house in Yorkshire. "It's dark in here, but I can see this as well as if it were light."

"We can see in the dark." Which meant he could see every inch of her slender legs, and the curve of her cheeks beneath a pair of pink knickers that her T-shirt didn't quite cover. He assumed her decision to pop into his room was impulsive. She was most likely unaware of how she was dressed, or that she was barefoot.

"What else can we do?"

"Think very hard about the lamp on my desk being on." A few seconds ticked by, and the lamp lit up. "You can move things with your mind, but usually only when you're in crisis. Telekinesis is tied to adrenaline."

The lamp went off and on a couple more times, then she moved back to the bed. "I want to see him, Key. Will you take me?"

"You can't talk to him. We'd have to go under a cloak so no one can see us."

"Please take me."

Beneath the covers, he drew his legs up and rested his arms across his knees. "If I do this, you have to swear to me you won't go back."

"Are you jealous?"

"My feelings have nothing to do with it. You're the one I'm concerned about. It's the same principle as not allowing the Luminas on a takedown. Seeing Matthew will only prolong your suffering, and to what purpose? He has his own journey, and you're no longer a part of it."

Turning around, she sat on the edge of the bed. "I feel responsible for what happened to him, Key. Wouldn't Lucifer maybe look at it like I've paid something I owe, instead of that I'm interfering?"

"He might, if that were the real deal, but it's not. I get that you think because you're the president's daughter this terrible thing happened, and if your dad was just an ordinary man, with an ordinary job, Matthew wouldn't have been shot, but that's like saying if it hadn't rained, our picnic wouldn't have been ruined. You have as much control over what others do as you have over the weather. If your dad was an accountant, or a butcher, and you and Matthew were going out, you might have been mugged and Matthew shot. This isn't your fault, Jordan."

Her spine relaxed slightly, and after several long moments, she said, "Can I tell you something that's eating me up? Something completely inappropriate?"

"You can tell me anything."

"I just don't want you to take this the wrong way."

"People usually say that just before they tell you something that can only be taken one way." He reached over, lifted a lock of her dark hair, and let it slip through his fingers. It was silky soft and had a gentle curl, like it had a life of its own. "Go ahead."

"He's paralyzed from the waist down. That probably means he can't . . . he hadn't ever, because he was waiting on me, and now, he won't ever . . . and . . . " She drew in a deep breath and let it out slowly. "If he'd gone out with Tori Kingman instead of me, he'd have had a chance. Lots of chances, actually, because Tori spreads it around."

Her guilt over something like this was unexpected, and as much as the cause of it made him feel ridiculously possessive—she wasn't his, after all—he appreciated the sentiment. Maybe because he was a guy. Maybe because he had a strong suspicion about what it'd been like for Matthew Whittaker.

He reached for her and hauled her backward, until her shoulders were against his chest, and wrapped his arms around her. "I don't know Matthew at all, but I think he stuck with you because you're what he wanted, and it was worth it to him to wait. If getting laid was his primary goal, trust me, he'd have ditched you and gone out with Tori."

"He'll spend the rest of his life never knowing."

"You had a reason for saying no, and it's still valid. There's no mandate that says you were responsible for Matthew's virginity."

"You're just not going to let me feel guilty, are you?"

"No, because it's unjust and unfair. You can spend days, weeks, even years feeling guilty, but it doesn't change anything. Look at Phoenix. Guilt over what happened to Jane defines who he is, so instead of living his life, he's given up everything he loved as some kind of sacrifice. But it changes nothing. Jane is still dead, and no amount of guilt is going to bring her back. Don't let that be you, Jordan."

She sighed, and he felt the tension ease out of her body. "When can we go?"

"Tomorrow at midnight, when we'll be sure of the fewest number of people in his room. Even if they can't see us, we still take up space, and I have no clue how big the room is."

"Can't we go now?"

"You need to get some sleep before tomorrow. Jax has all kinds of things planned, and none of them will be good without sleep."

Surprising him, she didn't argue. Shocking him completely, she turned in his arms and kissed him. "Good night," she said, just before she disappeared.

Lying back down, he thought, yet again, that she wasn't what he had expected.

❦

Jordan figured the following day would be a repeat of the day before, but she was way wrong, starting with how she dressed.

Mathilda told her to wear workout clothes instead of leather, which made sense when Jax told her to warm up in the weight room. When she went in, she saw Sasha on the elliptical. From the corners, Bose speakers were blasting a Pink song.

Jordan stepped on the treadmill and smiled back at Sasha while she started the machine.

"Are you okay?" Sasha asked, her ponytail swinging back and forth.

"It's better this morning, but not by much." Jordan increased her speed slowly. "I was so happy when I found out he didn't die. I had no clue he's paralyzed."

"It's a travesty." Sasha's voice was angry. "Another reason to hate Eryx, as if we didn't have enough."

Jordan had run a quarter of a mile when Sasha said, "It'll get better."

Jordan knew Sasha wasn't talking about Matthew. "I still feel like I'm dreaming, it's all so surreal."

"When you don't feel like you're dreaming, it'll be bad. Just fair warning. When reality sets in, you'll feel like a stranger here, like you don't fit, but that'll pass, and it gets better."

"Did you agree to become Mephisto because of Jax?"

"I didn't want it to be for him, because this is all so much bigger than any one of us, and what they do seemed so much more important." Sasha moved up and down on the elliptical for another minute before she looked at Jordan with a wry smile. "That's all true, but in the end, yeah, it was mostly about Jax."

She reached for a towel and swiped it across her face. Tossing it back, she looked again at Jordan. "It may sound funny, but I also did it for his brothers."

Jordan's surprise must have shown.

Sasha nodded and faced forward as she spoke. "It's true. The brothers are . . . well, they're sons of Hell. They mean well, mostly, and they can be extremely affectionate, but sometimes, for no apparent reason, they'll go off."

"Like how?"

"Like Denys will pick a fight with Zee, and it'll turn into a death match. It's horrible. And the things they say to one another turn my blood cold. I remember the first time it happened, I kept shouting for them to stop, even tried to get in the middle of them. Jax finally took me away from the mountain. Ty seems like the gentlest of them, but he has anger in him that runs so deep, it's scary. We were on a takedown in São Paulo a couple of months ago, standing outside the hotel we were about to go in, and Ty saw a guy kicking a dog." She looked at Jordan. "If Jax hadn't saved the man, he'd be dead. If he hadn't healed him, he'd be without a couple of fingers and an eye. Jax called a council, and Ty had to spend a month in exile on Kyanos."

"I thought it was forbidden to heal humans."

"Not if their injuries are caused by the Mephisto. Or if the human is Anabo. Not long after I met Jax, I broke my leg skiing." She smiled. "Totally wigged me out when he fixed it, and that's when I knew he wasn't just a guy."

Jordan looked down and realized she'd run another half mile but was barely breathing hard. "What about Phoenix?"

"Yeah. Phoenix." Sasha huffed out a breath. "He's his own kind of tormented and screwed up. He'll go off for a week at a time and won't say where he goes. Jax thinks he wanders around where they used to live in Yorkshire, where Jane is buried, but I went there once when he was away and didn't find him."

"Where do you think he goes?"

"Oh, I *know* where he goes." Sasha glanced over her shoulder toward the door, then said in a low voice, "It's kind of an unspoken agreement that, unless it's necessary, none of us mentally search for the others. Otherwise, nobody has any privacy at all."

"So you have to think about it to know where someone is?"

"Right, and it's not as easy as it sounds. You have to really concentrate and blank your mind of everything but who you're searching for." She glanced over her shoulder again. "I've never told Jax, because he'd give me a lecture about respecting Phoenix's privacy, and he'd be right. But, Jordan, I had to know."

She didn't judge or blame Sasha. She was just as curious. "So where does he go?"

"Right here, on the mountain. Way on the other side, away from all the Lumina cottages and the mansion and everything else, there's a tiny little one-room cabin, probably built by a rancher back in the olden days." Sasha slowed the elliptical until it stopped, then grabbed her towel, dabbed it across her face, and stepped down, moving closer to the treadmill. "It's got modern stuff inside, like a nice bed and a refrigerator and stove. And books. A crap ton of books. That's where he goes when he's away. He stays in that cabin, all by himself, for a whole week."

Jordan had to admit, she was a little disappointed. She'd expected something really off the wall. Instead, Phoenix just escaped the never-ending noisiness of the house, and his brothers. She could see why he'd do it, to be alone for a while.

"I can tell you're unimpressed," Sasha said, "but I haven't told you the sad part."

Jordan had run a mile, and she slowed the treadmill until it stopped, then stepped off and accepted the fresh towel Sasha handed to her. "Okay, hit me."

Sasha looked one more time toward the door, then said almost in a whisper, "He has Jane's things in that cabin. It's amazing all the stuff he has, like a fan, and a velvet cloak, and little paintings she did, and most of the books there are hers. She was an invalid until Phoenix healed her, and she read all the time. He has boxes of papers, and I didn't look that close, but I think they're manuscript pages. She must have been writing a book. He has her gloves, and opera glasses, and a hat."

Jordan felt her heart break a little. "What does he do with all of it, do you think? Just sit around and stare at it?"

"I don't know. I figured out where he was and popped over there to make sure I was right, but I didn't stay. I felt like a creeper." She smiled. "Let's be honest. I kind of am a creeper. Anyway, later, when I knew he wasn't there, I went back and went inside and looked around. It made me *so* sad."

"I wonder if he'll ever find another Anabo? And if he did, what would he do? If he has what amounts to a shrine for Jane, how's he ever going to let go of her and be with someone else?"

"Maybe he won't find one for a long time, and by then, he'll not be as obsessed with Jane's memory."

"I don't know, Sasha. She's been dead over a hundred years, and it sounds like he's still pretty extreme."

Sasha tossed her towel into a wicker basket against the wall then met Jordan's gaze. "I have to say, if another Anabo turns up, and she's meant for him, I feel supersorry for her. Can you imagine? It's hard enough to love a son of Hell, but having to replace a girl he still grieves for would be next to impossible."

"She'd have to be really strong, with the patience of a saint."

"True that." She cleared her throat and fiddled with the drawstring of her running shorts. "That's pretty much what Jax and I thought about Key, that whoever came along who was meant for him would have to be unique."

Jordan blinked. "Bummer she didn't show up, and he got me instead."

Shaking her head, Sasha said, "You're exactly what he needs. When you told him off yesterday at breakfast . . . " She grinned. "That was *epic*. He needs somebody who'll stand up to him. Somebody who can crack the wall he's built around himself. He's always so quiet, such a loner, and I'm not sure if it's because he's always been in charge, or if it's just his personality."

"You said the others twist off every so often. What about Key? Does he ever lose it?"

Sasha shook her head. "I've seen him get mad, and he can yell and give a lecture like nobody's business, but he never loses control."

"I wonder why. He's a son of Hell, same as the others."

"I think it's because everybody looks up to him and counts on his being steady. If he went off, it'd be freaky. So he keeps to himself, and if he ever has the urge to lose it, he manages to get past it. But I don't think he's anywhere near as cold as he seems, Jordan. I mean, look at his greenhouse. How many guys do you know who'd take care of a greenhouse like that, with so much time and attention to every little detail?"

"None. All the guys I know wouldn't have the patience, or the interest."

Sasha continued fiddling with the drawstring, wrapping it around her index finger, letting it go, then starting again. Like she was nervous. "I realize how awkward this must be, and you just got here, and you're still thinking about your boyfriend, but I hope when the time's right, you'll give Key a chance. He's so . . . he's always all about everybody else, and as strange as that sounds, because of what he is, it's the absolute truth. I'd bet money he's wondering why he was the one to find an Anabo, why it wasn't Phoenix, who's so miserable. Key is arrogant and proud, and if we'd let him, he'd be a total dictator, but there's so much more to him."

She should probably tell Sasha she knew that already. She had known it the instant she heard him calling her back from the dead. But that wasn't something she wanted to share, so she said only, "I wonder what he'd think about your pleading his case?"

Sasha laughed. "I can just imagine the look he'd give me and the lecture to go with it. Swear you won't tell him?"

Jordan found herself laughing, too. "Swear."

Without warning, Sasha was hugging her, whispering, "I'm always here for you, Jordan. I'm so happy you came to stay, and I'll do whatever it takes to make this easier for you."

Returning the hug, Jordan felt tears prick the corners of her eyes. "Thank you, Sasha."

Pink was starting a new song when Sasha pulled away and went toward the gym door. "I'm off to shower and get dressed. I'll see you in a while. Jax has some fun stuff planned for you today."

Then she was gone, and Jordan saw through the window when Jax dropped the basketball he'd been dribbling and rushed at her. Sasha laughed and ran. When he caught her and kissed her, Jordan turned away and went to the bench press.

An hour later, after she'd gone through the rest of the weight room equipment, she got a bottle of water from the mini-fridge next to the towels and went out to the gym. Leaning against the stone wall, she drank the water and cooled off while she watched Jax shoot hoops. She was impressed. He moved almost like a dancer, and he never missed a shot.

"Do you play basketball?" he asked.

"Too short, and my hands are too small.. I played volleyball."

"Any good?" He shot another one.

"Decent." She flexed an arm. "I bet now I'd be killer."

He laughed and came toward her, the basketball between his arm and his side. "Maybe we'll get a game together. I know a few Luminas who play volleyball."

"I'd like that."

"Are you ready for today's training session?"

She pushed away from the wall and stood straight. "More knives?"

He shook his head. "Not today." He walked to the cabinets and stored the basketball, then slid a T-shirt over his head and stepped into a pair of sweats he pulled up over his shorts. Turning, he came back to her and handed her a Telluride High cap and a pair of really nice Jackie-O shades, überdark and ginormous. "These are Sasha's, but we'll get you your own later."

"Why do I need sunglasses?"

"Put them on, and the hat, then take my hand."

She did, and moments later, they stood on the sidewalk of a busy street in London. She knew from the cabs and the double-decker bus that passed. It was almost dark, but the street was well lit from streetlamps and store windows.

"We're here to capture a lost soul—a little training and education before tomorrow morning's takedown. Look across the street and tell me what you see."

"A bank."

"And?"

"Pedestrians. A dog. A No Standing sign. A trash bin. A guy texting. Another guy wearing earbuds. A girl looking at a city map." She squinted. "She looks a whole lot like Sasha. And the guy with earbuds looks like Zee with shades and a hat."

"That's because that is Sasha, and it is Zee with shades and a hat. Rule number one in any takedown is that we all go, or no one goes. That's so we can cover any surprises, like more lost souls than we counted on, or one who's on top of his game, or one who might bring civilians into it. Ordinarily, we'd meet up on the *M* in the front hall and all take off together, but today's a little different. We're taking the lost soul during London rush hour, so we need to be less conspicuous."

"How did we appear out of thin air with no one seeming to have noticed?"

"It doesn't work as well when there are only a few people around, but on a busy street like this, especially at dusk, people tend not to see things that are right in front of them. We use that to our advantage. If anyone does notice, they convince themselves they imagined it. Okay, so here we are, waiting on our target to exit the bank. We know his schedule because Zee did reconnaissance. He leaves every day at five sharp, walks down there to the Rose and Crown for a pint, then hails a cab to take him to his flat in Kensington. Today, he's going to be robbed and stabbed by a guy who will jump in the cab after him."

"Who's the robber?"

"Phoenix. Key will be driving the cab, and the rest of us will cause a distraction so people won't be looking right at the cab when Phoenix disappears with the real guy and leaves behind a doppelganger." He looked at her. "Actually, the others are going to do that. You and I will only observe. Pay close attention. There'll be a test later."

"Seriously?"

"No. But pay attention. Look, here comes our guy."

She watched a middle-aged man step out of the bank and turn to the left. Right away, she noticed his face was weird, like he had a smudge across his eyes. "Oh, my God, I can see it! He really does have a shadow over his eyes."

"Wait until you see a Skia. It's hard to tell they have eyes until you get closer to them."

A lady with two big shopping bags slowed down and looked at her curiously. "Excuse me," the woman said in German, "but can you tell me where you bought those sunshades? They're just what I've been looking for."

"They were a gift," Jordan replied in German.

The woman smiled, nodded, and walked on.

"Jax, do you speak German?"

"I'm Mephisto. I speak all languages."

"That explains it then."

"Explains what?"

"I've never spoken a word of German before in my life, unless you count 'sauerkraut.'"

"I hate sauerkraut, and Hans cooks it a lot, because he's

German." He grabbed her hand. "Let's head toward the pub and wait for Mr. Mathers to have his pint."

They wandered down the street looking in windows until they came to a bookstore that was directly across from the pub. While they waited, they stood at the front window, pretending to discuss a display of travel guides, and watched the reflection of what went on behind them.

She was so focused on studying the door of the pub, it took her a moment too long to notice the girl inside the bookstore who walked right up to the window and waved. Jax moved so that he stood between her and the window and said under his breath, "That girl knows you. You've got to fake like you're someone else."

Turning quickly, Jordan took a deep breath. "It's Kristen Ahrens. She goes to my school. Her dad works for a congressman, and her mom's British. They must be here for the holidays. What do we do?"

"Pretend you're German," he said, just before Kristen came to stand right beside her. "We have only an hour before dinner," he said in German. "We should go back to the hotel now."

Kristen said, "Jordan? Oh, my God, Jordan, it *is* you, isn't it?" She looked at Jax, who was babbling on about their dinner reservations, and her eyes grew wide with fright. She grabbed Jordan's arm and began tugging her away from Jax. *"Hey!"* She turned her head and shouted, *"Somebody call the cops! This is Jordan Ellis!"*

Kristen continued pulling her arm, but Jordan stood fast and jerked away from her. "Leave me alone, or I'll alert the authorities," she said in German.

Jax shouldered between them and began yelling at Kristen, who backed off but kept screaming, "Help! Somebody help! This is Jordan Ellis! The American president's daughter! She's not dead! God, won't somebody *help*?"

Jax was reaching for Jordan when she was suddenly yanked backward. Within seconds, she was surrounded by people, and he was swallowed up by the crowd.

~~~

From the driver's seat of the cab, while Phoenix deposited Mr. Mathers's doppelganger in the back and subdued the real man, Key watched Jax lose Jordan. If he hadn't seen it happen, he wouldn't have believed it. One second that girl was shouting, and the next Jordan had disappeared inside a flash mob. His heart began to race, and he broke out in a cold sweat. "Phoenix, did you see that?"

"See what?"

"Jax just lost Jordan. Take Mathers, and I'm going under a cloak to find her and follow." He concentrated until he was cloaked, then got out of the cab and ran toward the crowd, shouldering his way through until he found her. A policeman had just swung her up to sit in front of him on his horse. The crowd cheered. Jordan looked panicked. Key pushed his way toward the horse and yelled up at her, "Go with it, and I'll stay with you, cloaked. Just be calm and we'll figure out a solution."

She looked down at him and nodded, just before the cop turned the horse around and started through the crowd, which followed all the way to the police station on Buckingham Palace Road. Once there, the policeman dismounted, then plucked Jordan from the saddle and carried her into the station, the crowd cheering.

Forcing himself to be calm, not to follow his instinct to grab her and pop out immediately, Key followed. As soon as she was on her feet, he went to stand next to her. "Don't look at or talk to me, or they'll think you're crazy. Tell them you've been locked in a room since landing in London, but you don't know where or why. This afternoon, you were taken by car to Hyde Park and left there. You never saw anyone's face, have no idea who took you, and you weren't mistreated in any way. Jax came along and offered to help, and you were on your way to the police when that girl saw you and started shouting. Can you do this, Jordan?"

She gave a tiny nod, even as she answered the policeman's questions, repeating what he'd just told her. There was a lot of commotion in the station as others became aware of who'd just arrived. A row of policemen lined up across the entrance, not allowing anyone to come inside.

Jordan smiled and nodded and answered questions without looking shell-shocked—just mildly frightened, and very relieved to be safe now. She played it well.

Jax popped in, cloaked, and completely freaked out. "Kyros,

I'm so sorry this happened. I tried to take her away from there, but some guy grabbed her, and before I knew it—"

"It's going to be okay, Jax. We'll deal."

"You're not mad?"

"No, I'm afraid."

Jax gave him an odd look. "You're never afraid."

"Untrue. I just hide it well."

A burly man in a suit came to the front of the station and patted Jordan's arm while he went on about his happiness that she was alive. "I've rung the U.S. ambassador and the prime minister, who's on his way here now. As soon as we can ensure you are Miss Ellis, the PM will call your father. Such a brave girl!" He patted her arm again, and she smiled, but Key could see the panic in her eyes.

He felt the same way. Completely panicked. He shoved his hands into his trench coat pockets and told himself there was a way to fix this. He just had to be calm, and the answer would come to him.

A tall woman stepped forward and waved Jordan toward a chair. "Let the poor girl have a sit, Mr. Lamb. Would you care for tea, miss?"

"No, thank you." She sat and cast a long look at Key.

"No matter where they take you, I'll be there, so no worries," he said to her.

"What are we going to do?" Jax asked. "How can we get her back?"

"We can't just take her. We're going to have to let her go back to her father."

"Then what?"

"I don't know. We'll have to think up a new plan, because the memorial obviously isn't going to happen."

Mr. Lamb had begun a series of questions for Jordan, and he wrote down her answers on a legal pad. "When's your birthday?"

"February second. Groundhog Day in the States." She looked toward Key. "It will be my eighteenth, and my father planned a large party. I hope he'll still do it. I have a lot to celebrate."

"Indeed you do," said Mr. Lamb. He asked more questions, designed to verify she was Jordan Ellis, although he didn't appear overly concerned that he had an imposter. Without the sunglasses, she was distinctive, her eyes an unusual shade of blue and her face exceptionally pretty. She held herself and spoke with the poise of a young woman who was comfortable in any situation. Like a First Daughter who'd taken on the duties of a First Lady.

"She's telling us about her birthday party," Jax said. "Do you think we could wait that long for the takedown?"

"It's a month away, Jax. Think of how many more souls might pledge during that time. Even worse, Jordan will be vulnerable to Eryx. It's not like she can live in obscurity. He's probably watching the news as we speak." He saw fear leap into her eyes and cursed himself for saying that out loud.

"True," Jax said, "but he has to operate within the same rules as we do, so he can't just grab her. He'll have to come up with another abduction scenario, and that's going to take some time."

A few minutes later, the police guard parted and Prime Minister Burton rushed through the front doors, trailed by a harried-looking female assistant and two solemn guys who were bound to be with Diplomatic Protection. "Jordan!" He reached out both hands and grasped hers, pulling her to her feet. "God be blessed, your father will be overjoyed! Are you well? Have those brutes hurt you?"

Jordan calmly repeated the lie, and the PM nodded as she spoke. "We'll have questions to ask, to try to determine who was holding you, but for now, I'd like to take you to Number Ten. I've asked the U.S. ambassador, Mr. Simmons, to meet us there. As you and I are old friends, I thought you might be more comfortable at Downing, instead of in the embassy."

Jordan looked genuinely glad to see the man. "Thank you, sir. I appreciate your help, and I know Dad will be glad to hear from us."

"Yes, of course. We'll call your father right away." He nodded at Mr. Lamb. "Good work, sir." He looked around at the others. "Most excellent, all of you."

Linking Jordan's arm in his, he led her out the doors to a waiting car, and just like that, she was gone.

"To Number Ten?" Jax asked.

"I'm going, but you go to the house and tell everyone what's happened. Phoenix needs to begin planning something immediately."

He was about to transport away from the station when Jax laid a hand on his arm. "They're likely to send her back to Washington within twenty-four hours. You can't stay on guard through all of this, Key. I'll come back in a few hours, and we'll make a rotation schedule."

Key nodded, even though he had zero intention of leaving Jordan. No matter how long it took, he'd be with her until he could return her to the safety of the Mephisto Mountain.

⁓

Sitting in a chair at a small conference table in the prime minister's office, Jordan waited for him to finish talking to Dad and hand her the phone. He was a nice man, if a little bit of an egomaniac. He made a lot out of her rescue, and assured her father the MI5 would find the people responsible for keeping her locked up.

She was thinking, *Good luck with that,* when he handed her the phone. "Dad?"

"Jordan! Are you okay?"

"I'm fine, Dad." Other than being shot, dying, and coming back immortal.

"Oh, God, I can't believe it! I'm so—" He began to cry, deep, hard sobs of relief and happiness. "We'll get you back home as soon as possible. You just hang in there a little bit longer."

His tears made her choke up, and she had a hard time saying, "I can't wait to see you."

"We'll take a few days up at Camp David. Would you like that?"

"Sure, Dad." Key appeared then, in a corner, and seeing him made her cry harder. Yes, she'd see her father, but it would be only for a short while. She'd be going back to the Mephisto Mountain as soon as Phoenix came up with a new plan.

"Let me talk to Burton again, and we'll make arrangements to get you home."

"I love you," she whispered around the enormous lump in her throat.

"I love you, too, Jordan. I've never been this happy."

He was happy, but it would last only until she had to go back to Colorado. She'd have to fake die again, and he'd have to go through all of this once more. Staring at Key while she handed the phone back to Prime Minister Burton, she couldn't stop crying.

"Now you can say good-bye," he said from the corner.

He was right, and she wouldn't dwell on how this would end. She'd see Dad, and Matthew, and when she left next time, things would be settled. There'd be some closure, and she'd go back to the Mephisto without any regrets.

She hoped.

One of the prime minister's assistants, Ms. Duplessis, bent low and said quietly, "If you like, Miss Ellis, I can show you to a room in the residence. You can freshen up and rest, and I'll see that your clothes are laundered. We've also a fine kitchen if you're hungry."

Standing, she nodded and followed the woman out of the office, into a hallway, and toward the stairs, well aware that Key was trailing just behind.

On the third floor, in the prime minister's personal residence, the room was beautiful, old-school London, with heavy brocade draperies and bedding. "There's a water closet just there," Ms. Duplessis said. "If you'd care to slip out of your clothes, I'll take them to the laundry. There's a robe hanging on the opposite side of the door, and a laundry bag just inside the cupboard beneath the basin."

She couldn't very well say no, so she did as the woman suggested and went in the bathroom to take off her clothes. When she came out, Key stood beside the window. She handed the bag to Ms. Duplessis, who offered food again.

"Yes, tea would be nice," she said, "and whatever is on hand to eat. I am a little hungry." She could eat a whole chicken, maybe two, she was so enormously hungry, but she was in the real world now, and eating enough to sustain Mephisto strength would cause questions she didn't want to answer. She kept reminding herself to act normal, to react as if she's been held hostage for two days. "Actually, I'm very hungry. The, uh, people who had me didn't feed me. I had some bottles of water and a package of crackers, but that's all."

"Oh, you poor girl! Yes, I'll pop down to the kitchen and bring you something marvelous. If you like, bathe while I'm gone, and I'll have the house steward come in and light the fire."

As soon as she left the room, Key said over his shoulder, "Go ahead and take a shower. I'll be right here."

"What are we going to do?"

"Phoenix will come up with something, so until then, we'll muddle through as best we can."

"Should you go back to Colorado and help with a plan?"

He turned to face her and shook his head. "I'm not leaving you."

She didn't admit to him that she was relieved. She also didn't suggest he come in the bathroom with her and face the other way while she took a shower, but she wanted to. She was scared, half expecting Eryx to show up at any minute. With one last look at Key, she went back into the bathroom and turned on the shower.

She was about to slip out of the robe and step into the tub when she heard her worst fear, just behind her. "Hello, Jordan."

Spinning around, she wanted to scream but knew she couldn't. Dizzy with panic, she clutched the robe against her body. "How did you find me?"

"All I had to do was find my brother." He crossed his arms over his chest and leaned against the opposite wall. "No worries, Jordan. I'm not going to steal you away, although it's tempting. I need you for one purpose, and until you agree to fulfill that purpose, there's no point in taking you with me."

The door opened abruptly, banged against the wall, and Key filled up the space. He looked straight at Eryx, and for one millisecond before his expression turned to rage, Jordan saw something in his eyes that blew her away. Instead of hate or anger, she saw something like joy. His instantaneous reaction on seeing Eryx was happiness, until he remembered in the next heartbeat that this was his sworn enemy.

Eryx never batted an eyelash. "Hello, brother. I was just telling your Anabo that I have no intention of taking her again. When she returns to Erinýes, and she definitely will, she'll do it of her own free will."

"You always were a smug son of a bitch. What makes you so sure of yourself?"

Eryx looked at her from his dead, flat eyes. "Her greatest quality will be her ultimate downfall, just like our mother. She could never accept that our father was irredeemable, and Jordan will never accept that you're a lost cause. She'll sacrifice herself for you, just as Mana did for Mephistopheles." He pushed away from the wall and gave Key a patient look. "You can leave off guard duty. When I come back, it won't be as a thief in the night but in the light of day, to take her away from you in plain sight."

Before Key could say a word, Eryx disappeared.

TEN

SIX HOURS LATER, AT MIDNIGHT, JORDAN TOOK OFF ON
a British government plane, accompanied by a small contingent
from the prime minister's office on board to ensure she made it
back to Washington without any problems.

There was a bedroom in the back of the plane, and as soon
as she was able to leave her seat, she excused herself and said she
wanted to get some sleep. No one questioned her, considering
she'd been unable to get any rest since arriving at Number Ten.
She'd answered a thousand questions, lied about where she'd
been, over and over, and tried not to feel bad that police and MI5
personnel would spend so many man-hours searching for a phan-
tom kidnapper and a place that didn't exist. She told them the last
time she saw Smelly and Stinky was in Washington, after they left

her on a plane. When it landed, she was blindfolded and gagged by a man in a ski mask who never spoke, but took her in a car on a very long drive that ended in a room where she was held until she was taken by the same man to Hyde Park. Key had said to keep it simple, and she did her best.

She didn't worry about Smelly and Stinky refuting her story. What could they say without mentioning Eryx, and how he transported Jordan off of a plane?

It was over now, and she was going home. Amazing how everything had changed in one second. All because Kristen Ahrens had recognized her.

As soon as she opened the door to the bedroom, she saw Key sitting on the end of the bed. Torn between relief and guilt that she was this glad to see him, she stepped inside the cabin and shut the door behind her. She hadn't seen him since he'd gone back to Colorado to meet with the Mephisto. After Eryx's visit, he'd been agitated and kept touching her, as if he was afraid she'd disappear. When Ms. Duplessis came to get her to return to the prime minister's office, he'd looked conflicted. He needed to go back to Colorado, but he didn't want to leave her. She had said to Ms. Duplessis, "I'm really nervous about all this. Will you stay with me?"

"Of course!" She was all smiles. "And there are two men from Diplomatic Protection right out there in the hall, and they'll stay with you until you board a plane for the United States. Don't be afraid, Miss Ellis. I promise you'll be safe."

She'd glanced at Key and silently told him to go, that she'd be fine.

He'd said, "I'll be back as soon as I can," before he disappeared.

And here he was, as promised, waiting for her. He stood and came toward her. "I'm putting you under a cloak so we can talk and no one will hear."

She felt an odd chill, then looked down and saw that her hand was not quite solid, like she was pixilated. Then he was sliding his arms around her, drawing her next to him where he held her for a long time. "Are you okay?"

With her head nestled in the nook between his shoulder and collarbone, she absorbed his warmth and inhaled the scent of him. "I'm fine. Just glad to be gone and on the way home." She tightened her arms. "Did you cancel the Red Out takedown?"

He shook his head. "They decided to go ahead with it."

"So you'll be leaving soon?"

"No, I'm going all the way to D.C. with you. We gain five hours, so we should arrive sometime around three a.m. As soon as you're with your father, I'll leave."

"Has Phoenix dreamed up a new plan for taking out the Washington people?"

He pulled her toward the bed, and when she was sitting down, he sat next to her and leaned forward to rest his elbows against his thighs. "It went to a vote, and they all decided to wait for your birthday party."

"You voted against that, didn't you?"

Staring at the carpet, royal blue with little golden jets woven into a pattern, he nodded. "I think it's too long for you to be in the real world; I don't trust Eryx; and so many more may pledge between now and then."

"Why did the others want it this way?"

He turned his head and met her gaze. "They think you'll be better adjusted when you come back if you have this time with your dad and your friends. Even the Luminas, before they cross over, have a month or so to prepare for leaving the real world behind. The way you came to us was so abrupt, they think it's only fair, since things happened the way they did, that you have the same concession as the Luminas."

"And you don't agree?"

He sat up and turned so he was facing her. "It's not the same for you, Jordan. People who become Luminas don't change until they cross over, so they're never in the world as a Lumina. You're well on your way to being Mephisto, and it's going to be difficult for you to live among humans. You'll have to continue lying about what happened to you, which is against your nature, and living alongside the lost souls and Skia without killing them will take an incredible amount of restraint. It's our instinct to take them out, and I'd like it if you didn't have to do this any longer than necessary."

She still couldn't wrap her head around the idea of wanting to kill someone. "I think I'll be okay."

"Maybe so, but you can't do this alone, which is why I'm going to stay as close as possible to you, especially when you're at school."

Here was something else she couldn't wrap her head around. She thought of Oates, and of the kids who went there, most of them preppy overachiever children of preppy overachiever parents. There was an emo contingent, but Key wouldn't fit there. There were the jocks, but Key grew flowers. And there were the potheads, who were into alternative literature and deep discussions about existentialism; Key would probably give them a lecture.

"You're thinking real hard about this, Jordan. Will it bother you if I'm at school with you?"

"No, I just think you're going to hate it. A lot."

"It's only for a month. I'll manage."

She eyed his black leather trench coat. "You're gonna have to get some new clothes, or everyone will think you're a *Matrix* wannabe."

"I want to be as inconspicuous as possible, so yeah, I'll find something that doesn't stand out."

"No matter what you wear, you're never going to be inconspicuous."

"Why not?"

"You're over six feet tall, you're built like . . . well, you're not average, that's for sure. And you have long hair. Nobody at Oates has long hair, except Ted the janitor."

He reached up and fiddled with his ponytail. "Nothing I can do about that, because cutting it isn't an option. I've done everything Lucifer told me to do, and so far, so good. I'm sure as hell not going to be a rebel so some kids with acne won't make fun of my hair."

"What would happen if you didn't do everything he told you to do?"

"Does it matter?"

"Of course it matters. Would you be sent to Hell?"

"No. Well, probably, but his trump card isn't what happens to me." He was so serious, staring at her. "I've never told anyone what he told me, and it's become a habit. Just know that I'm never going to step out of line."

Her curiosity went off the charts. "I won't tell anyone else. I think I should know."

"Why? It's not like it has anything to do with you."

"It has everything to do with me. Did you forget we're supposed to be together?"

"You're kidding, right?"

"If you expect us to build something beyond friendship, you're going to have to open up, Kyros. No secrets."

Frowning, he turned so he faced the bathroom again, then fell back on the bed and stared up at the sloped ceiling. "I keep my own counsel, Jordan, and have for over a thousand years, since I became immortal."

She stretched out next to him and rested her head in her hand.

"What about before, when you were a regular guy? Did you talk about stuff with your brothers?"

"Just one brother."

She understood then. No wonder he had looked glad to see Eryx for that nanosecond. "He was your best friend, wasn't he?"

"Yes."

Nothing else. Just, *yes*.

Sasha was so right. Key had built a wall around himself, and it was so tall, Jordan couldn't see the top. But she was compelled to try.

Reaching over, she traced one of the buttons on his coat with her finger. "When he died and came back as someone totally different, it must have been worse than if he'd actually died and gone away forever."

No answer. Just a slow blink.

"What was it like on Kyanos?"

❦

The seven-hour flight stretched before him, and he knew she'd never stop asking questions. His only hope was to talk long enough that she would become bored and go to sleep.

The Mephisto's gift of total recall was a blessing and a curse. Some things he'd just as well not remember. Like the day Eryx killed their *mitera*. She who was everything to them, murdered when Denys was just ten years old, killed by her firstborn and, arguably, favorite son. Eryx had come back from the cliffs, and they all knew what had happened. His eyes were like their father's, but darker, without a spark of life, of humanity. Their eyes changed when they became immortal, but not like Eryx's. The eyes were windows to the soul, and his were darker than the deepest pit of Hell.

It was the worst day of Key's life. At sixteen, he had lost his mother; and his beloved older brother, his best friend, had become his greatest enemy.

He was going to a place he'd sworn never to revisit, so he forced it from his mind, going further back to when Eryx was fourteen and Key was twelve, on the edge of adolescence, his body doing things that completely confused and embarrassed him. He never understood how Eryx knew things, but he did, and Key learned what he needed to know from the older brother he idolized. Fishing, hunting, scavenging for food on the island— Eryx knew how; he knew which were good things to eat and which would make them sick.

They often left the house and wandered miles away, leaving the younger brothers behind so they could do what they liked without fear of being ratted out. The two of them discovered all the secrets of the island: a labyrinth of caves accessed beneath one of the giant boulders clinging to the side of the tallest hill; a grove of crabapple trees on the western shore, almost unreachable because of the rocky hill and sheer cliffs that led down to the sea; and, maybe best of all, a spring-fed warm pool, sheltered by a rocky overhang, surrounded by the hardwood and evergreen forest that covered most of Kyanos. They learned to swim and spent hours diving to the bottom, competing to see who could stay down the longest. Strangely, they never questioned the warmth of the water. He realized now that it had been fed by a spring from far below, where the Earth was hot. The whole island was undoubtedly an inactive volcano, but they didn't know about things like volcanoes back then.

They were sons of Hell, but also sons of Heaven, and they grew up surprisingly innocent and carefree. M had been there a lot of the time, and maybe he'd never win Father of the Year, but he was generally benevolent, if not loving, and had seemed proud of them. They never knew, had no inkling they were a secret, that neither God nor Lucifer knew of their existence. He remembered feeling betrayed when he finally understood—why had Mana insisted they pray to God each night if he couldn't hear them?

He mentally shook himself. He wouldn't linger on details that made no difference now. Channeling his thoughts to those days on Kyanos when he and Eryx had rambled, he remembered things his brother said, what he taught Key, what he revealed about himself. One day in particular stood out in his memory.

They left early, just at sunrise, with dried apples and venison hardtack slung over their shoulders in fishing nets, headed for the crabapple grove and the ocean beyond. They planned to fish for a while, then go to the warm pool in the afternoon.

Sometime midmorning, they reached the hill that dominated the island, a small mountain, really, and began the hike to the summit, picking their way through crags and boulders, stopping every so often to drink from the freshwater brook that tumbled its way down and meandered to the eastern shore. Halfway up, a raven flew into a bush, and Eryx stopped, cocked his head, and stared. Key looked, too, but he didn't see anything except a raven in a bush. "What are you looking at?" he'd asked Eryx.

Instead of answering, Eryx pushed the branches of the laurel aside, scaring the blackbird away, and swept his hands across the face of the rock, knocking away the dirt collected in its cracks. Key stared in surprise as a picture was revealed. "Who do you think made a picture on a rock?" Peering at the figures, he was confused. "What are they doing?"

Eryx laughed. "Little brother, has M told you how babies are made?"

"What's to tell? A mother grows big, then they come out." He wasn't sure where they came out, or how, but he was okay with not knowing. When Denys was born, he remembered hearing his mother crying, but M wouldn't let them anywhere near her room, made them stay outside on the beach until Denys came. She seemed happy, and smaller, when he saw her again, and he forgot about her crying.

"Don't you wonder how babies get in there?"

Key shrugged. "I never thought about it."

Eryx pointed at different parts of the picture while he explained. Key was alternately freaked out and wildly interested. He was a little hazy on how long they stood there and looked at that picture, which he now knew was some prehistoric human's rendering of procreation, revealed to them when the rock shifted and slipped in the spring snowmelt. About the time the image was permanently etched into Key's brain, Eryx wrestled with the bush to cover it up.

"I can still see it," he told his brother. "Maybe we should find a bigger rock to put in front of it so the little ones don't see."

"They won't see it until they're ready."

"But, Eryx, it's right there, plain as day. That bush isn't covering it at all."

"You see the picture because you know it's there, because you're looking for it. The little ones, if they come up here, won't see it because they won't be looking for it. The best way to hide something is in plain sight, because no one sees the ordinary. A rock in front of this one would look out of place, out of the ordinary. They'd be curious and move it."

He was right. Eryx had generally always been right.

When Jordan shifted and laid her head on Key's shoulder, he wrapped his arm around her and drew her closer. "He still hides things in plain sight, and sometimes it takes me a while to realize what he's up to. That's how he managed to get so many powerful people in Washington to pledge without our knowing about it. About a year ago, we took down a Skia who had a whole lot of information about certain politicians on his computer. There were compromising pictures and personal e-mails and other things a politician really wouldn't want made public."

"Eryx blackmailed them?"

"We thought so, but when we checked them out, none were lost souls. Zee went back several times, but none of them ever pledged, so we decided the Skia must have been planning something for later, and since he was gone, we didn't need to worry about it. Now I realize it was a setup. Eryx had that Skia move to Telluride, right in our backyard, knowing we'd eventually take him out and find those files. While we were looking at the wrong people, he was busy converting the ones we weren't paying attention to."

"Hiding in plain sight."

Key sighed, frustrated all over again. "Even though I know how tricky he can be, he manages to fake me out. If we hadn't seen Ron Trent on TV, and suspected he was Skia, we might still not know about the D.C. lost souls. I'd bet money that Eryx told him to show some emotion if he had to be on television, and Trent either forgot or was just too arrogant to think it mattered."

"I'd vote for arrogant. He'd gotten really pushy with Dad the last few months." She moved even closer and slid her arm around his middle. "Tell me more about what it was like on Kyanos."

So much for his make-her-go-to-sleep plan. "I don't really want to. Remembering is painful."

"Just tell me if your younger brothers ever saw the picture on the rock."

"A few years later, Denys found it, because he was always a nosy, curious wild child. He came running home and told Mana all about it."

"How old was he?"

"Maybe eight. It wouldn't have been so bad, except he drew that picture on every rock around the house with a piece of charcoal. Eryx told him to wash them all off because if Mana saw them, she'd cry. If he'd threatened to take a switch to him, he'd have carved the picture in all the tree trunks. The only thing that worked on Denys was the idea of making our mother cry."

"Did she cry a lot?"

"Not a lot, but when she did . . . we didn't like it. And it bothered Denys so much, he'd run and hide in the caves." Key remembered all the times he'd gone to find his baby brother, and how he had to reassure him, over and over, that their mother wasn't crying because of something he had done.

"What were the others like back then?"

"Ty was always all about animals, and Zee always loved music. He was a strange kid, though. Sort of lived in his own world, talking to himself and the ocean sometimes. Phoenix was a daredevil, forever breaking something, falling out of trees or off the mountain. Once, he took off swimming in the Atlantic and said he wasn't going to stop until he reached England. When I took the canoe out to rescue him, he'd already gone almost a mile."

"Was Jane like that?"

"Not even close. She was shy and quiet and not much for adventure."

"That's . . . strange."

"I guess, but Phoenix didn't seem to mind."

"Tell me about Jax."

Key smiled. "After Eryx, he was Mana's favorite. He was affectionate and sentimental and just . . . solid. Loved any kind of sport and excelled at all of them."

"How did he and Sasha meet?"

"We found her during a takedown of a group of kids who went to school with her in San Francisco. Jax thought he'd have a better chance with her if she thought he was just a regular guy, so he erased her memory of us and approached her in the real world, but they'd only been with each other a few hours when she broke her leg. He panicked and healed it, and that pretty much killed his regular-guy idea."

"But she fell in love with him anyway, so it all worked out."

He really didn't want to talk about Sasha's falling in love with Jax. For some reason he couldn't explain, the topic made him uncomfortable. "You should get some sleep."

"I'm way too hepped up on English tea and adrenaline to go to sleep." She shifted so that she was even closer to him. "Tell me more about Kyanos."

"I'm tired of talking. I don't usually."

"I noticed."

"You talk. Tell me what it was like when you were little."

"Eh, what's to tell? Dad was a senator when he and Mom adopted me, so I've always lived in Maryland or D.C. Went to private schools, had a nanny, didn't see my parents all that much, and I thought I could be an Olympic gymnast. But you already knew that."

"Why didn't you see your parents very much?"

"Because Dad was a senator. He had something going most every night, and Mom went with him, of course. When the Senate wasn't in session, we'd go on trips, but they were usually something related to his being a senator, so I was mostly with my nanny."

"What was her name?"

"Betsy. She's still with us, sort of a pseudo housekeeper, stand-in Mom type, who cooks most of our meals and keeps an eye on the White House staff, even though it's not her job."

"What do you know about your biological parents?"

"Zero. The only thing left with me was that rabbit, and the nuns weren't big on investigating orphans' backgrounds. They took in foundlings and kept them until they were either adopted or old enough to be sent to work. I was there only a few months before I was adopted."

"Why did your parents go to Romania to adopt?"

"They didn't. They were there on vacation, and to visit the American ambassador in Bucharest. He arranged for the orphanage visit because he was urging Dad to run for president, and he thought photo ops at an orphanage would look good. He told the nuns to find the prettiest baby for Dad to hold, but that one peed on him so he was put back, and I happened to be handy. My mother wasn't able to have children, and she said when she saw me, she knew she wanted to take me home. So she did, and that was that."

"You sound okay with it."

"Why wouldn't I be? If they hadn't adopted me, I'd be working in a factory making tennis shoes or cheap watches. And no biological parents could have been kinder or loved me more than they have. It's like I won the adoption lottery."

He heard something in her words that didn't quite ring true. "But it bothers you that you don't know who your real parents are. You wonder what happened to them, and why they abandoned you. Did they die? Or were they just not up for being parents?"

She didn't answer.

"Am I right?"

"Maybe a little, but what difference does it make? Especially now."

"What if you found out your parents weren't human? What if you were born of angels and delivered to that orphanage by someone who had a master plan for your life?"

She sat up and looked down at him with wide eyes. "What are you saying, Key?"

"Nothing. It's just a guess. When I was dying, my father came to me and said something weird, about how there were no more Anabo, and how he had promised my mother that she would see us again, which means we'd have to find an Anabo. I asked what he'd done, but he never answered."

"Can he create babies that aren't his own?"

"No."

"How does he make doppelgangers?"

"He doesn't. Lucifer does, and they're not real people—just bodies. Only God can create a soul. M went behind Lucifer's back once before, when he fell in love with my mother, and I wonder if he did it again and asked God for help, to send more Anabo. Sasha was also adopted, and she has no clue about her biological parents."

"How is asking God for something going behind Lucifer's back?"

"M isn't supposed to have anything to do with God. Asking him for more Anabo might sound like a good thing, but Lucifer would see it as a betrayal. What he would never understand is that M did it for our mother, because as crazy as it is, he really did love her. He sees getting us to Heaven as a way to make up to her what happened to Eryx. She begged him to confess their relationship and our existence to Lucifer, but he refused, and you know the rest."

Turning away, she slumped over and stared at her hands.

Key sat up beside her and reached for one of her hands, gripping it tightly. "Even if it's true, it changes nothing, Jordan. You are your own person, with your own will. I know you died too soon, and for all the wrong reasons, but so do a lot of people. And it's not as if you were forced to do anything. You had the choice of Heaven or the Mephisto Mountain. You had the choice to become Mephisto, or not."

Falling against his arm, she sighed. "Those weren't really choices, Kyros."

"What do you mean?"

"How could I blow off humanity after I'd been with Eryx and *knew* what he is, what he does? And how could I let you die when Sasha and everyone else was telling me how important you are to them and what they do?"

"Are you saying you regret your decisions?"

She looked up at him. "No, but it's a hard truth to learn your whole life was planned before you were even born."

Nudging her off of his arm, he let go of her hand and stood. "You'll have to forgive me if I don't feel sorry for you, Jordan."

"I didn't ask you for sympathy."

"No, you've got enough self-pity to make do."

She scowled at him. "That's harsh, Key."

"It's not as if I or my brothers had great choices. We were born this way, same as you were born Anabo. We could choose not to hunt down the lost souls and let Eryx win the war, but what kind of choice is that? I could choose to go off on a ten-day rampage, destroy everything in my way, and kill people, which would land me in Hell and would mean the end of my father, but again, what kind of choice is that? I didn't draw the regular-guy, grow-up, get-a-job-and-have-a-family card. I got dealt the son-of-Hell card, which sucks, all day, every day, *for a thousand years*. But you won't hear me bitching about it, because it *is* what it *is*."

He expected her to jump to her feet and tell him off. Instead, she looked up at him with eyes full of sorrow. "That's what

Lucifer told you, isn't it? He threatened to take out your dad if you don't toe the line."

All his anger evaporated, and he turned away, not wanting to see her pity.

He nearly jumped out of his skin when her arms slid around his waist. He felt her cheek against his back and waited to hear her say she was sorry. He didn't want an apology. He wanted her to accept. Death. Mephisto. Him.

"I didn't come back for humanity," she whispered. "I came back for you."

He'd swear his heart skipped a beat. Letting out the breath he hadn't realized he was holding, he turned, drew her closer, and bent his head to kiss her. She pressed her body against his, and he deepened the kiss, vaguely aware that this was different than all the others they'd shared. Just like always, he was drowning in her, floating on the euphoria of peace that settled across his spirit, but for the first time, his mind didn't go where it usually went when he was kissing her. All he could think about was what she had said. He was blindsided. He was awed.

Ironically, while his thoughts about her were, for once, not headed toward taking her clothes off, she was kissing him as if she'd never get enough.

She moved her hands to the lapels of his coat and pushed. He dropped his arms so she could slide it from his shoulders and let it fall to their feet, but they never broke their kiss. Then she was pulling him with her until they were on the bed again; he was on his back and she was angled across his chest, still kissing him.

"I came back for you." Her words ran through his mind, over and over, while her soft, sweet mouth laid a kiss on him that made him dizzy.

She kissed him without the slightest bit of inhibition, so he wasn't surprised when she slid her hand beneath his shirt to stroke his belly and chest, and he was only a little bit thrown when she moved so that she was on top of him. It was when she made no protest at all after he unhooked her bra, actually shifted so he could palm her breast, that he was surprised. How far would she let him go? He wrapped his arms around her and rolled her to her back, broke the kiss, and opened his eyes. She stared up at him with a strange mix of desire and fear.

"You're not afraid, are you?" he whispered. "Tell me you're not afraid of me, Jordan."

He heard her swallow. "I'm afraid of how you make me feel. I don't . . . I'm never . . . it's always kind of gentle and easy." Her breathing was short and shallow. "I'm never the one who wants it to go further."

"Why do you think it's different with me?"

Now she was focused on his mouth. "Maybe Mephisto?"

He shook his head. "Mephisto makes you hate the lost souls and Skia enough to take them out, and because of that, you're a little more edgy, which is why you said what you did to Jax. But in everything else, you're still Anabo."

"Are you sure?"

"I'm sure." She wanted to believe her desire was caused by something other than her own will. He knew without asking that she was thinking about Matthew, feeling guilty, looking for an excuse for the way she kissed Key.

Jax had told him all about what Mephisto did to Sasha, and he made sure to tell Key he was on his own when it came to sex. "If it happens," he'd said, "it'll be up to you, so don't be thinking you'll get any help from the Mephisto in her."

"This just isn't like me, Key."

He kissed her nose, then her cheek, and said against her mouth, "It's exactly like you, Jordan, because here you are, of your own free will." He moved his lips across her beautiful face. "Would it be so bad if you liked kissing me just because you like it? Does there have to be a reason, or an excuse?"

"What does it say about me? Matthew is still fighting for his life."

Key looked deep into her eyes. "And you lost yours." They were so close, he could feel every breath she took. Their shirts were pushed up, leaving them skin to skin. He lowered his head until his lips were next to her ear, his nose buried in her silky hair, and asked the question he couldn't get out of his head. "Why did you come back for me, Jordan?"

Her hands were behind his head, tugging the ponytail loose, combing her fingers through his hair. "I heard you calling my name. Calling me to come back."

He kept his head next to hers, his face hidden. "I thought

you were gone. I thought . . . " Closing his eyes, he remembered every word he'd said, and *how* he said them. He'd been devastated, and the thought of being alone again, when she'd been right there within reach . . . he knew he had sounded desperate because he'd felt the agony of over a thousand years of loneliness.

His mood took a dive, and he sighed, feeling like a fool. "So you came back because you felt sorry for me."

"Pity had nothing to do with it, Key. The angel had already told me all about you and why you would want me to stay. I felt bad for you, and I liked the idea of fighting Eryx, but living forever seemed too huge and scary. I'd pretty much decided to go with her." Her hands stilled, and her voice dropped to a whisper. "Then I heard you calling my name."

He lifted his head and looked into her solemn eyes.

"I'd just met you, barely knew you, but in that one minute, I knew exactly who you are. I was blown away." She smiled softly. "So I came back, and no matter what happens between us, whether we're friends or . . . something more, I'll always be with you." She held his head within her soft, pretty hands, drew him down, and kissed him.

⁓⁓⁓

Three hours into the flight, Jordan had lost the caffeine buzz, and her adrenaline had slid back to normal. When Key insisted she get some sleep, she didn't argue, except to insist he join her. "You need sleep, too."

She took off her running shoes; he took off his boots. She removed her hoodie; he removed his shirt. She slid out of her sweatpants; he turned out the light.

Under the covers, he gathered her next to him and whispered in the dark, "I haven't ever slept with anyone. I don't know if I snore, or kick, or behave badly, so you'll have to let me know."

"Never? Like *ever*? I thought you'd been with . . . other people."

"We didn't sleep."

"Oh."

"Does that bother you?"

"No, but if you intend to be with me, like *with* me, it will bother me a lot."

He held her a little tighter. "Go to sleep."

She drifted off and was caught unawares by a nightmare. She was back in Washington, at Matthew's house. Every moment replayed in her dream exactly like it happened, except when she fell to her knees beside Matthew, screaming, he opened his eyes and looked up at her with accusation. "You betrayed me."

"Jordan, wake up! It's okay. *Jordan!*"

She woke up disoriented, crying and gasping for breath.

Someone was knocking on the door.

"You've got to answer," Key said somewhere close to her ear.

Sliding from beneath the covers, she went to the door and opened it just enough to see Ms. Duplessis standing there, looking worried. "I'm sorry," Jordan said, "I had a nightmare."

"Can I get you something?"

"No, thank you."

The woman took a step closer to the door. "If you'd rather not be alone, I understand, Miss Ellis, and I'd be only too happy to sit with you."

"You're very kind, but I'm okay. Will you make sure I'm awake for landing?"

"Of course! You'll need to take a seat and buckle up."

Closing the door, she made her way back to the bed and slipped beneath the covers, still trembling. "I thought I was under a cloak. How did she hear me?"

"I took you out of it before we went to sleep, in case anyone peeked in."

She couldn't shake the nightmare. "Key?"

"Right here."

"You were going to take me to see Matthew tonight."

"That was before everything went to hell."

"I still want to see him."

His reply took a long time. Finally, he said, "Then see him. You'll be in the real world again, so you can visit him all you want, and talk, and . . . whatever."

She rolled to her side, facing away from him, and didn't sleep again. She was pretty sure Key didn't either.

ELEVEN

WATCHING JORDAN REUNITE WITH HER FATHER WAS HARD. Under a cloak, Key stood on the tarmac a few yards away and heard her father cry. For all his faults as a president, and his weakness in not standing up to people who led him in the wrong direction, he was a good, decent man, and if Key had had any doubts about his love for Jordan, he didn't now. He felt sorry for Ellis, because in a month, he'd lose her forever.

Despite the falling snow, they hugged for an eternity, with a thousand cameras snapping pictures and an army of news cameras recording everything from a distance. Eventually, they parted and walked to the limousine that waited, door open. She glanced at Key, just before she ducked inside, and said good-bye with her eyes. He would see her again in a few hours, but watching the limo take her away made him anxious. Eryx had said he wouldn't take her until she would go of her own free will, but suppose he decided to take her anyway?

"If he does," she'd said while they got ready for landing, "he'll regret it because I'll make his life miserable."

"How?"

"I'll find his weakness and exploit it, over and over."

Key was doubtful. "You do understand he's a worse evil than Lucifer?"

"Don't worry so much. He really believes he can convince me to go with him willingly, so for now, at least, I'm not afraid. Besides, if he shows up, anywhere, at any time, I'll transport to the Mephisto house before he can touch me."

Watching the limo turn a corner and disappear around the hangar, Key wished he felt as confident as she did.

Back in Colorado, he went to his rooms, to his closet, and prepared for the Red Out takedown. He was slipping his switchblade into his trench coat pocket when he felt a piece of paper. She'd written a note on a teabag wrapper. *Thank you for telling me about Kyanos. Happy New Year, Kyros.*

Was it New Year's? He'd lost track of the days.

From his bedroom, he heard Jax on the intercom. "We have a situation. War room in one minute."

He immediately popped down, his heart in his throat, praying nothing had happened to Jordan. He was first to appear and looked straight at Jax. "Don't wait for everyone else. Tell me what's going on."

Jax nodded at the screen, at a news feed about Red Out. Less than an hour earlier, the ATF had stormed the gates and found every man, woman, and child dead.

"Something didn't feel right, so I went down to check things out," Jax said, "and they were all shot, mob style, with one single bullet to the back of the head. They were lined up in rows, as if they'd gotten to their knees and waited to be executed. When I got back, this was on the news."

The reporter voiceover said, "Brandon Holder was found inside the main compound, dead from an apparently self-inflicted gunshot. Federal agents won't comment, but the head of the task force will be giving a press conference in an hour or so. Speculation is that the recovery of Jordan Ellis prompted the Red Out leader to kill his followers and himself. There's still a lot of mystery surrounding her disappearance, reported murder, and reappearance in a London crowd."

All those lost souls were Eryx's now. "Holder was Skia, so if he's dead, there's no doubt Eryx did it. He's the only one who could kill Holder."

Jax nodded. "He knew we'd show up and take all of them, so he got them before we could."

Key thought of all the doppelgangers in the cooler that would have to be disposed of.

Suddenly, Jordan was there, wide-eyed and breathing hard. "Have you heard? They've all been shot!"

"Why are you here?"

"I'm supposedly in a bathroom at the hospital, peeing in a

cup, so I have to go right back. I wanted to see if you knew."

He pointed at the screen. "We just found out." He looked at her hospital gown. "Why are they making you pee in a cup?"

"To see if my kidnappers gave me any drugs, and to check for other . . . things that might have happened to me. They're taking blood next. Is it going to be weird that I'm immortal? Will something show up in my chemistry?"

"Your enzyme levels will be off the charts. Can you get them to skip the blood test?"

"I'll try." She glanced at the screen and grimaced, then said, "I gotta go," and disappeared.

⁓

She fake cried and got semi-hysterical when they said they wanted to take blood, claiming that she'd had enough and wanted to go home. "Please, Dad, I'm fine. They didn't do anything to me, didn't give me anything except water and crackers. Don't let them stick me!"

Poor Dad. Today, she could ask for anything under the sun, and he'd move mountains to get it for her. If she didn't want to get stuck, she didn't have to. He brushed off Dr. Kirk's insistence on the necessity of it, and Jordan went to get dressed.

In the hallway, before they began walking toward the entrance where the limo waited, she asked, "Can I see Matthew before we leave?"

"He's still in intensive care," Dad said. "Family only. You can visit him as soon as he's in a regular room."

She was disappointed, but then it occurred to her that she'd rather see Matthew without her dad waiting for her in the hall or, worse, standing right there in the room with them. A few minutes later, they were back in the limo, headed for home.

"Do you still want to go to Camp David? It's New Year's Day, so we can watch some football, maybe a movie. Whatever you want to do, Jordan."

Looking at his tired face, the mess he'd made of his graying hair, and the random coffee stains on his white dress shirt, she thought he needed a break even more than she did. "That sounds perfect, Dad. Maybe Betsy will make something delicious for dinner."

"Says she's making a ham and black-eyed peas for New Year's."

Looking out the window at Washington, at the newly fallen snow beneath circles of light from streetlamps, she wanted to be elated to be back, but it was bittersweet.

"Ron's funeral is scheduled for Thursday, so we'll have to be back tomorrow night, but one night away is okay, right?"

"Sure, Dad." She'd have to figure out a reasonable excuse to skip Mr. Trent's funeral. No way would she go and listen to a minister talk about how he was now in heaven and how God forgives, and yada yada. Mr. Trent wasn't in heaven, and God couldn't forgive him because he'd blown God off. She wondered what Dad would think if she told him his chief of staff and longtime best friend had known who was behind her abduction. Then she wondered who Eryx would choose to approach her father again. Key had said that

Dad didn't remember any of what Mr. Trent told him about Eryx, or even that he'd been there the night of her kidnapping. All he knew was that Ron Trent had a heart attack and died. "What about Maggie's and Paul's funerals?"

"Maggie was taken to Kansas, where she was from, to be buried with her family, and Paul was buried yesterday in Virginia."

"Oh." It bothered her not to go to Maggie's funeral. She'd been with Jordan so many years, she'd become like part of the family.

"Jordan, you don't have to talk about it, but I'd really like to know, did anyone hurt you?"

"No, Dad. I was alone most of the time." She squeezed his hand. "I'm mad and sad and all kinds of upset about Matthew, and about Paul and Maggie, and I hate that this has been so hard on you, and it was freaky wondering if they would kill me, but I'm okay."

He stared out the window with her. "Patricia suggested you see someone at Bethesda, a therapist who specializes in post-traumatic stress disorder. Will you do that?"

Someone else to lie to. Awesome. "Yeah, Dad, I'll see somebody."

Back at the White House, she went to her room, supposedly to rest before she got ready for their departure at eight, but she didn't feel like resting. Instead, she sat at her laptop and opened the First Daughter e-mail, watching in amazement as the program downloaded over fifty thousand, most of them sent since she had been discovered in London. She picked a few at random to read, and it made her sad that some of them were so hateful. Why did people think it was okay to write to tell her what an idiot her dad was? Or that she deserved to be kidnapped? How did somebody have such a cold heart that he could send a message that said her father was as guilty of what happened to Matthew as the guys who shot him?

Most of the ones she opened were sweet and kind, with wishes for her to be okay, but at least a third were just plain mean.

She went to her private Facebook page and saw a ton of posts on her wall from friends at school, which made her feel a little better.

Tessa had sent her a message. *I don't pray much, but God's sick of me after this weekend. I am SO grateful and happy, Jordan. I can't WAIT to see you and hug you and cry on you and make your sweater snotty. I LOVE you!* She followed the message with a stack of heart emoticons.

Somewhere around six thirty, her house phone rang. Thinking it must be Dad, checking to see if she was awake and packing, she grabbed it and said, "Hey."

"Why aren't you asleep?" Key asked in a low voice.

"How are you calling on a house phone?"

"I'm in the Oval Office, just because I can be, and thought I should call before I popped in. I thought you might be asleep. Or naked."

"No, I'm reading e-mails, fully clothed. Come on up."

The line went dead, and seconds later, he appeared in the middle of her room, his trench coat swirling around his biker boots. "What's the story?"

"We're leaving at eight a.m. for Camp David. I think I'll be okay there, Key, so you should maybe get ready for school. It starts Thursday." She eyed his boots. "You have to go shopping."

"I'll send Mercy to pick up some things."

She remembered Mathilda had mentioned that Mercy had purchased Jordan's new clothes. "Who's Mercy?"

"A Lumina who loves to shop. Trust me, she'll find the right stuff."

"So you're going with me to Camp David?"

"I'll just check in from time to time, so you and your dad can be together. He seemed pretty broken up."

She nodded, then got up and walked over to her closet to get a bag. She opened it on her bed and went to the bureau to get pajamas and underwear. "I didn't get to see Matthew because he's in intensive care and nobody but family is allowed."

He sighed. "And I suppose you want me to take you?"

"I'd take myself, but I haven't learned how to be invisible yet."

"I don't want to. You know that, right?"

"Please, Key. Just for a few minutes."

"Oh, hell." He sighed again before he set her bag on the floor, then went around the bed and tossed aside the covers. He arranged her pillows, then covered them up and tucked them in so it looked like she was under there, asleep. Turning, he looked at the light switch and it was instantly dark—except she could see him just as well—then reached for her hand. "George Washington University Hospital?"

"Right."

Seconds later, they stood in the entrance vestibule. Key scanned the directory, then they were gone again, to a dimly lit hallway. "He's in one of these rooms, and it looks like the names are posted by the room number." They started walking, looking at each name until they reached the end of the hall, and there it was: Matthew Whittaker.

"Are you sure you want to do this, Jordan? There's just no way this will end well."

"I'm sure." But she wasn't one hundred percent sure. Now that the moment was upon her, she had a million butterflies in her stomach.

"He can't see or hear you, but he can feel you if you touch him, so not too close."

She nodded, and they popped into the room.

Nothing could have prepared her for Matthew. He was hooked up to all kinds of wires and tubes, his hair was a tangled mess, his skin was white as snow, his eyes were sunken with deep, dark circles beneath, and he held a wrinkled picture of her in one hand. But that wasn't what made her burst into tears. He'd been shot. He was paralyzed. He still might die or he wouldn't be in ICU. He looked like he ought to look, considering all of that. But the look in his beautiful, soft brown eyes—always so full of life and warmth—was of a rage so violent, her heart broke all over again.

"You had to know he'd be extremely upset," Key said. He nodded toward the muted TV, tuned to CNN, which was replaying video of her arrival at Andrews. "He thought you were dead. Now he knows you're not. He's afraid you'll come here to see him." Key walked toward the door. "Don't do it, Jordan. If you love this guy, if you really care about him, don't come back in real life. Let him go home, or go to rehab, or wherever he'll be after this hospital. Let him get some help and regain at least some of his dignity before you see him. You can call him, send him text messages, e-mails, candy-grams. But don't come see him in person."

The door opened slowly, and there was Matthew's mom, a quiet, gentle lady who was old-school southern, complete with a soft drawl and a backbone of iron. "I checked, honey, and she's gone. As long as you're here in ICU, no one but family can visit."

"Then I'll stay here forever."

Wiping her nose on the back of her hand, Jordan cried harder. She looked at Key and felt her resolve harden into ice. "I hate Eryx. I want to stab him and poke his eyes out and cut off his arms and feed him to alligators. I want to make him suffer. I hate him so much, it's like I can *feel* the hate. I want to hit something!"

He held out his hand. "Let's go."

She looked once more at Matthew before she turned away and took Key's hand.

~~~

He'd known it wouldn't go well, but he hadn't anticipated a train wreck. He popped them back to her room at the White House, but left them under a cloak so she could get it all out. As soon as they arrived, she pulled her hand away and strode back and forth between the end of her bed and the window, dragging her hands through her hair and crying while she shouted her fury. She listed every possible way to hurt Eryx, and got downright personal by the end. He leaned against the wall with his hands in the pockets of his trench coat and let her go off until she tired herself out and slowed her pacing. When she came close again, he grabbed her arm and hauled her next to him, wrapping her up in his arms and stroking her hair. Clutching his shirt in two hard, angry fists, she cried and cried, until he wondered if she'd ever run out of tears.

Eventually, she quieted, her hands relaxed, and she slid her arms around him. She'd stopped talking. He couldn't imagine that anything he could say would make one iota of difference, so he didn't say a word.

She lifted her head from his chest to look up at him, and he blinked. Her eyes were incredible. He moved one arm, fished around in his coat pocket for a handkerchief, and dabbed the tears from her cheeks. "Maybe you don't believe it now, but everything will get better. It might be after you're gone, but he'll eventually accept it and make a life for himself."

"I hope so. He's such a good person, and he doesn't deserve—"

"Don't go there, Jordan. Nobody deserves bad things, even people who aren't good. But life dishes out the bad with the good, and some draw the short straw."

"But did he, really? It seems to me that Eryx isn't a short straw. He's a force in the world that screws up fate or destiny or whatever it is that directs people's lives."

"There really is no such thing as fate or destiny. There's free will, and choices, and a series of random events like fires and floods and car wrecks and plane crashes and criminal acts. People move through life; sometimes things work out, and sometimes they don't, but at the end of life, all that matters is how they treated others."

"What about people who pledge their souls to Eryx?"

"That proves my point. In what world would it be fate or destiny for a person to hand her spirit over to a liar? It's one of a million choices a human might make, but also the one that makes all the others meaningless."

She looked up at him again. "I still don't get why healing Matthew interferes with free will."

"It doesn't matter that those guys who shot him are lost souls. They came to abduct you, and whether they were working under Eryx's direction, or that nut job's in Texas, the goal was the same. The end result would have been the same. It happened, Jordan, and no amount of crying or shouting or wishing it was different is going to change it. Matthew has to work this out, and you have to back off and leave it alone."

"I want revenge. I want Eryx to pay."

"The best way to hurt Eryx is by taking out his lost souls and Skia. Every one he loses makes him that much further from having the power to get rid of Lucifer and take over Hell."

"Why does he want it so bad, Key?"

They were headed into choppy waters, and he'd had enough soul baring for the day. He didn't reply.

"Please answer. I want . . . *need* to understand."

He dropped his arms and sidestepped, forcing her to let go of him. He took up the pacing now and debated his capacity for this. He could tell her they'd talk about it later. He could go home to his greenhouse, to the only place where this didn't eat him alive.

"Please, Key."

Damn. He couldn't leave. Not now.

He kept pacing. "When Eryx died, all his light died with him, and when he came back, he was lost not only to God but to Lucifer. He's the only spirit ever in existence to belong nowhere. No one wants him. He wants Hell because he wants to belong. He believes ruling Hell, holding the spirit of all humankind in his power, will fill the empty place where his light used to live. He doesn't understand that if he wins, he's not going to be different. It'll just be more of the same hopeless, lonely rage."

"I can't believe it. You actually sound like you feel *sorry* for him."

Key stopped and wheeled around to face her accusing look.

"He's my *brother*, Jordan. I see what he does and hate it, but I can't hate him. You wanna talk about choices? He had to make the worst of all choices."

Her expression turned to dismay. "He chose to murder your mother, and you *admire* him for it?"

"Of course I don't admire him, but he did it for me! For *all* of us. Once she was gone, God knew we existed. He didn't have to jump when he did. If he'd waited even an hour, Lucifer would have interceded. Eryx would have had God's blessing. He'd have been like us. But he couldn't live with what he'd done, so he jumped. Now he's nothing to God, Lucifer's greatest enemy, and mankind's biggest threat, but is it his fault? What did he do except be born first? How close was I to the same fate?"

She held up her hands, as if in surrender. "This is so messed up, Key. You just said life is all about free will and choices, that fate doesn't exist."

"For *ordinary* people. We're not ordinary. Our father is the dark angel of death, and that makes us only two steps away from Lucifer. Think about that, will you? It's his temptation of the human spirit to darkness that causes all the horrible things in the world. My father is his first-ranking subordinate. He fell when Lucifer fell. He's capable of things you couldn't fathom in your wildest imagination, and *so am I*. Why do you think humans are afraid of us? They know what we are, can sense it better than a herd of gazelle senses when a lioness is stalking it."

"I'm not afraid."

"Because you're Anabo. Because you can't be tempted."

"People aren't afraid of Eryx. He said they're drawn to him, that he's charismatic."

"They are drawn to him, but it's because he's no longer of Hell. He's an anomaly, a freak of nature, something humanity can't fathom. He hides what he is behind his face and his charm, and people believe his lies. They believe he's the answer. Read the Bible. Revelation says the beast will come to the world as a false messiah, a charismatic leader who'll trick the people. Maybe the prophet who saw the end of times assumed the false messiah was Lucifer, but it isn't, Jordan." He walked away from her, all the frustration, grief, and anger of a thousand years tearing him to pieces once again. "It's my brother."

She was quiet, without any more questions, which should have been a clue to him, but it wasn't, so he was stunned when she said, "I don't think it's going to happen for you and me, Kyros. I hate him so much, if I could kill him, I would, and feel no remorse. Knowing how you feel, that while you fight against him and hate what he does, you still hold some twisted brotherly love for him, it's horrible to me. It's like there's a part of him in you."

He felt as though an eight-hundred-pound gorilla had just jumped on him. He tried to draw a deep breath and couldn't. "There is, Jordan. We share blood, a father, and brothers."

"Your brothers hate him."

He nodded.

"It's only you who feels this way. Do they know?"

"I've never spoken of any of this to anyone, until now."

"And you probably regret it, but you shouldn't. It was bound to come out, and it's just as well that it's now, before we went any further."

He hadn't expected her to be okay with how he felt about Eryx, but he never thought she'd be this upset. Enough to tell him it was over before it had even really started. "What about what you said on the plane?"

"I meant it, Key. I'll stay with you, but I don't know that I can ever . . . love you." She let out a soft sob. "You'll have to carry out the Mephisto Covenant with someone . . . another Anabo."

He turned away and took a blind step toward the window. "I'll have Phoenix or Zee check on you at Camp David." He didn't look back before he disappeared.

~~~

Jordan went through the day in a hazy fog of misery. She put on a good face for Dad, and if he noticed she was quieter than usual, he undoubtedly passed it off as a result of her abduction and didn't mention it. While they watched the Rose Parade and football, she replayed the visit to Matthew, over and over. When Dad popped a movie into the DVD, she looked but didn't watch, her mind turning over what Key had said.

She remembered when Eryx told her about himself, she'd felt something close to sympathy. He was what he was through no fault of his own. Now all she felt was hate. Just because he couldn't help what he was didn't make any difference. He was an evil force in the world. He was a threat to all humanity. All she had to do was remember the look in Matthew's eyes, and her fury returned as strong and all-consuming as before.

How could Key feel anything for him but hate? She couldn't understand it.

After dinner, she went for a walk while Dad was on the phone to his assistant, Patricia. Twenty or so feet behind her, a Secret Service detail followed.

Crunching through the snow, she drew frigid air into her lungs and wondered what would happen to her when she went back to Colorado. She'd never be marked as Mephisto, which would leave her vulnerable to Eryx forever. For the briefest moment, she considered telling Eryx she would go with him. There was an old saying about keeping friends close and enemies closer. If she was with Eryx, she could try to undermine everything he did. But could she succeed? Maybe not, but she'd still be stuck with him for the rest of eternity. Bad idea.

She rounded a bend in the path through the woods, and there was Phoenix. She could tell he was under a cloak because he looked less than solid. Walking past him, she whispered, "Meet me in my room in five minutes."

He nodded and disappeared.

Turning, she headed back to the house, and when she got to her room, Phoenix was already there.

She started to turn on the light, then changed her mind and crossed to the closet. While she shrugged out of her coat, she felt the chill of the Mephisto cloak and saw her hands lose solidity.

Phoenix leaned against the wall and crossed his arms over his chest. "Will you tell me what happened?"

"I don't want to talk about it." She *wouldn't* talk about it.

"Neither does Kyros, but we all know something bad went down, and I was elected to find out what."

She turned from hanging up her coat and met his dark eyes. "How do you know?"

"He destroyed the greenhouse."

Jordan slowly slid the knit cap from her head and sank to a chair.

"We heard glass breaking, and when we went to look, there he was, standing on top of it, smashing it with his bare hands. He threw all the plants out into the snow. He built a fire and tossed in the apiary box, the butterfly house, and the potting bench. He tore that old glider into a hundred pieces and threw them into the fire. I asked him why, and he said he didn't have the luxury of destroying the real world. Then he turned on me. Beat the crap out of me, and I let him, because I've never seen him like that. When the greenhouse was completely wiped out, he disappeared."

"Where did he go?"

"Kyanos. It's where he goes when things get to be too much for him. It's strange to us because we go there only when we have to, as punishment, or when one of us screws up enough that the others call a council."

She had a feeling that Key liked going back because he remembered how it had been before they became immortal. Before Eryx became a monster. "Will someone call a council on Key for what he did today?"

"No. It was his greenhouse, and he can do what he likes with it. But we're all very concerned, Jordan. We want to know what happened to upset him this much. He's been building that greenhouse since the early 1920s. Almost a hundred years. What would make him destroy it in three hours?"

She stood and went to the window to stare out at the woods behind the house, considering what she would say. She'd never tell anyone what Key had told her about his memories, or how he felt about Eryx. He'd said he kept his own counsel, and if he trusted her enough to share, she wasn't going to break the confidence. Even if she did think he was wrong-headed. "I won't go into the reasons," she finally said, "but I told him it's never going to happen for him and me."

Instead of asking why, which she expected, Phoenix said, "That explains everything."

She turned to look at him. "It does?"

"He's been waiting to find an Anabo for over a thousand years. He finds you, and you tell him it's over before it has even started. I'm amazed he didn't destroy more than the greenhouse. It's a miracle he didn't go out and murder someone, because that's a kind of rage that needs blood to satisfy it."

He didn't go out in the real world to ease his rage because

it would be stepping out of line, which would mean the end of Mephistopheles. But Phoenix didn't know that. No one did— probably not even Mephistopheles. "He'll find another Anabo, and she'll like him just the way he is."

"Wishful thinking, Jordan. If there've been only three in the past thousand years, what are the odds he'll find another one?"

Probably pretty good, if Key's suspicions about what M said were right. Who knew how many there might be out there? She imagined Key with another girl, kissing her, and her throat made a weird noise.

"Are you okay?"

"No. I saw Matthew this morning, and it was more horrible than I expected. I don't exactly understand blood rage, but I certainly get the impulse to break things. I wanted to hit something. I want to kill Eryx, slowly and painfully."

"We all do, but since that's not possible, we take it out on the lost souls and Skia."

He was wrong. Kyros didn't want to kill Eryx.

Phoenix cleared his throat. "Can you give me a hint?"

"It doesn't matter, Phoenix. It just is what it is."

"Christ, you even sound like him sometimes. You're dead-on perfect for each other, so what gives? Is it that he's a son of Hell and you can't get past it?"

"No. I told you, I don't want to talk about it. Leave it alone and go home."

"Is it the sex? Is that freaking you out? Because there's no pressure, Jordan. None at all. It's important, because of the mark, but you could go years without being marked."

She blushed and looked away. "It's not that." After what happened on the plane, the idea of sex with Key had become the least of her worries. She admitted to herself that, until the awful moment this morning when she learned how he really felt about Eryx, she wasn't worried at all. For the first time in her life, she was more than curious about what it would be like. She had begun to anticipate it.

But that was over. She couldn't let him get that close, not knowing how he felt about Eryx. Just thinking about what he'd said, how sad and frustrated he'd been, made her feel lightheaded.

Phoenix was staring at her, no doubt dreaming up alternate theories.

Her head began to pound. "I'm not going to talk about it, Phoenix. Please go home."

"Is there any chance you'll change your mind about Key?"

Was there? She rubbed the tension from her forehead while she stared down at the rug. "I don't think so."

"Well, then, that's that, I suppose. You can't avoid him. We live together, and the rest of us aren't going to put up with a feud, so make your peace with his presence. Understand?"

"I understand."

"He's still going to be in Washington to go to school with you, along with one of the Luminas, a guy named Brody, and you're going to need him, so don't be too proud to ask for help."

"I won't."

"Good night, Jordan."

He disappeared, and she was alone again.

TWELVE

BY LUNCHTIME THE FOLLOWING DAY, JORDAN WAS READY to go home. She asked Dad over ham sandwiches, "Would you mind leaving now, instead of tonight?"

"What's wrong, Jo? You love being here."

"I do, but school starts tomorrow, and I have to do some stuff to get ready. And I'd like to see Tessa."

Dad wiped his hands on a napkin and nodded. "Whatever makes you happy. I'll let Stu know we need a ride." He reached for a bowl of sweet pickles. "I worry about your going to school. You'll have a new Secret Service detail, but it's going to be hard for me to let you out there again. Maybe you should take some time, wait until next week to start back."

"I'd rather go see friends than sit around the White House,

Dad. I'll be okay." She picked up her second sandwich and took a bite. "And I don't think anyone will do anything stupid so soon after Red Out."

He flinched. "I should never have signed the Bingham bill. It seemed like such a good idea—who could have seen what an epic failure it would be?"

"Maybe you're listening to the wrong people." David Bingham was a lost soul, a powerful senator who'd helped her father get elected president. Jordan wondered what Eryx had promised Senator Bingham in exchange for his soul.

Dad smiled at her, but it had a note of falseness to it. "Nothing for you to worry about, Jordan. You just enjoy your last semester of high school. You'll be at Yale before you know it, and classes there will be a lot tougher than they are at Oates."

"Okay, Dad." She *hated* lying to him. She wasn't going to enjoy her last semester. She wasn't even going to finish it. She wouldn't graduate, and she'd never go to Yale.

"Baby, you're crying. I'm going to have Patricia make that appointment this afternoon."

She wanted to leave the table, but hunger won out. Taking another bite of the sandwich, she wished all over again that Kristen Ahrens hadn't seen her in London. It was all hard enough, dying, becoming Mephisto, learning that the guy she was supposed to fall in love with sympathized with a monster; but now, being forced to lie to the man she loved most in the whole world, knowing she'd have to lie to all her friends, including Matthew—she couldn't remember ever being this miserable. And there wasn't anything she could do about it.

So she ate her sandwich and cried, because she couldn't help it.

⤙⤚

After a snowy night on Kyanos, hunger forced Key to leave. But he didn't go home. Instead, he transported to England, to Yorkshire and the tiny hamlet close to where they used to live on the moors. The Pig Whistle pub was still there, and he walked into the dark interior to take a seat in the corner. A pretty girl came to take his order and never batted an eye when he asked for half the menu, along with two pints. While he ate, he stared at the only other patron, an elderly gentleman who wore a felt hat and smoked a pipe, just below the NO SMOKING sign.

The girl returned to collect Key's dishes and kept glancing at him from beneath her lashes. Even in the wilds of Yorkshire, here was a girl who wanted to flirt with danger. In his current mood, sex would be incredible, the very best release of his rage.

She was blonde, with blue eyes and a nicely shaped body. She was obviously willing. But she had one strike against her, and it overrode all the positives: she wasn't Jordan. He couldn't believe it, but he really, truly wasn't interested.

He gave her a credit card because all he had was American money, and she peered down at his name. "Kiros. That's a funny name."

"It's Kyros, with a long *e* sound, like Key."

"Is it Greek?"

"Yes." He looked away from her so she'd understand he wasn't interested, then glanced back again when she walked away. Was he going to spend the rest of eternity without sex?

He watched her talk to the guy behind the bar and almost wished he'd feel something, *anything*, remotely sexual, but none of his usual thoughts about pretty girls came to him.

Great. He was going to be a damned eunuch, just like Phoenix. How could this be happening to him?

Why did Jordan have to be so judgmental? She had no brothers, no sisters, no blood relations that she knew about, so it was natural that she didn't get how he felt about Eryx, but how could she turn her back on Key without even trying to understand? She was supposed to be an accepting, sympathetic soul. She was Anabo.

And Mephisto. He sighed and stared down into his glass. He'd seen her birthmark on the plane, and it was almost completely changed. She was close to fully Mephisto, and while her Anabo side was still there, wholly intact, the Mephisto in her wouldn't allow an inch of understanding when it came to Eryx. He was her enemy, someone she was supposed to destroy because of the instinct given to her through Mephisto, which she had because of Key. The irony was epic.

Blaming her inability to understand—hell, her refusal even to try—on the Mephisto in her kind of made him feel better. He was Mephisto, and he had the same instinct to annihilate Eryx, except his memories of his love for his brother always screwed with his head. He wanted to hate Eryx but couldn't, and it was a worse burden than being a son of Hell. It was torture.

After leaving the waitress a one hundred percent tip, he walked out, stepped around the building and into an alley with old cabbage crates, then disappeared and took himself back home.

It was midafternoon in Colorado, and Mercy was in his closet, hanging up new clothes she'd probably spent all morning buying. "Key, there you are!" She started showing him what she'd bought, but he didn't pay close attention. He had no intention of wearing any of it. Not now. He'd go to her school as himself, and if she didn't like it, he didn't give a damn.

"What's wrong?" Mercy asked, her face falling. "Do you hate all of it?"

"No, it's fine. I'm tired now, Mercy."

She backed out of his closet, looking wounded, but he didn't feel like making nice.

He stripped out of his clothes and took a shower, then dressed again and popped downstairs to his office. Reilly was there, working on the computer, a stack of bills next to her. She was their newest Purgatory, a seventeen-year-old girl who'd been murdered by a lost soul just over a year ago. She hated Eryx like everyone else hated Eryx. She glanced up when he appeared, then looked back at the computer. He didn't miss the look in her eyes. They must all think he was bat-shit crazy after what he'd done to the greenhouse. Maybe he was bat-shit crazy.

Taking a seat at his desk, he leafed through a stack of bank statements without really seeing them. He ordinarily didn't mind taking care of the Mephisto money, but he was way too restless to do this right now. "I'm going to be back and forth between here and Washington for the next month. Check the investments every day, and if anything takes a dive, call me."

"Okay." She continued clicking keys.

Looking at her long, auburn hair, he remembered she was supposedly a favorite at Telluride High, involved in everything, a natural leader. She'd had a very bright future ahead of her, until a kid who'd handed his soul to Eryx shoved her over a cliff, all because Reilly wouldn't go out with him. That was the thing about the lost souls—they always felt entitled. What Sasha called "special snowflakes." He wasn't sure if it was because they no longer had command of their spirits, or simply that they bought into Eryx's hyperbole. "Any suggestions for me, Reilly?"

Still clacking away, she said, "Just be yourself. Isn't Brody going with you?"

"Yes. We're doing the same thing he and Jax did at Telluride, posing as fraternal twins."

"Good. He's a total geek, but he's a Lumina and everyone will love him, which means they'll tolerate you." She stopped clicking and glanced over her shoulder at him. "You've changed enough; maybe no one will pee themselves when you walk down the hall."

Had he changed? He didn't feel different, but Jax had told him, the night Jordan came to the mountain, that as much as she would change because of Mephisto, Key would change because

254

of Anabo. "It's not like you'll be Mr. Sunshine," his brother had said, "but you'll see things a little differently than before, and people won't be as afraid of you."

Key stood and rounded the desk, headed for the door, thinking he'd find Jax and ask him what he should do about Jordan. He couldn't tell him the reason she had turned her back on him, but maybe Jax could give him some ideas of things to do that would make her change her mind. He didn't know details of what had happened between Jax and Sasha, but his brother clearly had done something right. Sasha was crazy in love with him. "Remember," he said to Reilly, "call me if you need me."

"Sure thing, Key. Good luck at school." She laughed. "I'd give anything to be there."

❧

Seeing Tessa was almost as wonderful as it had been to see Dad. She came over that afternoon, not long after Jordan arrived back in Washington, and after many hugs and lots of tears, they wound up in the living room on the couch, with *Love Actually* on the DVD. Not that they watched it. They'd seen it so many times, it wasn't necessary actually to watch.

"It's stupid news, considering what you've been through," Tessa said, "but Cory and I broke up."

Watching her friend braid her long, blonde hair, then undo it and start over, Jordan smiled. "It's stupid news only because you and Cory break up once a month. You'll be going out with him again by Friday."

"Not this time, Jordan." Tessa frowned. "He cheated on me with Tori."

"No way!"

"Oh, big way. Rick Durgin had a New Year's party, and I didn't go because I was too upset about you, but Cory went, and Megan said she walked in on him and Tori."

"Oh, man, Tess, I'm so sorry."

Her friend shrugged. "Honestly, I was kind of tired of his whining anyway. I'm not all that upset. And after what happened to you and Matthew, this just doesn't seem very important."

The mention of Matthew sent her mood due south.

Tessa dropped her braid. "Maybe we shouldn't talk about it."

"It's all right."

"I wanted to go see him, but my dad said since he's in ICU, only family is allowed."

"He may like it that way."

"Yeah, maybe so, but I bet he wishes he could see you, at least."

Jordan shook her head. "I texted him a few times, and he never replied. I called, and the hospital put the call through, but his mom said he was sleeping."

Tessa's green eyes were wide with surprise. "You think he's avoiding you?"

"It seems that way."

"That just makes this even more sad. You two were always so close, almost as much best friends as boyfriend and girlfriend."

Tessa shook her head and looked at the TV. "Maybe he's afraid you'll not like him anymore because he's paralyzed."

"He knows me too well to think I'd care. I think he just needs some time to accept what happened."

"Do you think he'll come back to school?"

"I hope so, because he has a lot of friends, and being there might make him feel better."

"Or worse. He's a guy, and being in a wheelchair is a huge blow to his manhood. He might resent that all his buddies are walking around while he's stuck in a chair."

"But he's alive. I'm hoping he'll realize life can go on, and he'll be able to do a lot, even in a wheelchair."

Tessa let go of her braid and fell back against the sofa cushions. "What about you, Jordan? You aren't injured, but what happened has got to have messed with your mind. I'm worried about you."

"I'm okay. Dad's insisting I see a shrink, someone who works with vets, for PTSD, so we'll see how messed up I am." She saw Tessa's look and smiled at her. "Hey, don't worry so much."

Tessa started to cry. "I feel so guilty."

"Why would what happened to me make you feel guilty?"

"You can't imagine what it was like, seeing the news after those guys were arrested in London and they told the cops they'd dropped you in the ocean. I barely slept for two nights, because every time I went to sleep, I'd have a nightmare about you . . . in the ocean."

Tessa pushed the tears from her cheeks and gave Jordan a

quivering smile. "When they found you in London, I was so happy, but I kept wondering what they'd done to you, and I was sure you'd be different, and we wouldn't be as close as we've always been. And I realized, I was totally looking at this like it was all about me, but you're the one who was kidnapped. You're the one who was there when Matthew was shot." She leaned over and slid her arms around Jordan. "I am *so* sorry this happened to you, Jo. I love you so much, and you're the best friend I've ever had."

Jordan hugged Tessa and couldn't speak around the lump in her throat. She hated knowing she would cause her friend so much pain a month from now, when the Mephisto faked her death so she could return to Colorado.

She swallowed hard and managed to whisper, "I love you, too, Tess."

❦

"Girls are completely different than guys," Jax said, just before he went for a layup.

From where he leaned against the side wall of the gym, Key said, "Yeah, I kinda figured that out, oh, I don't know, over a thousand years ago."

Dribbling the ball, Jax came closer. "I'm not talking about their lady parts, smart-ass." He pointed to his head. "Up here, they process certain things a little differently than we do. And they say one thing but mean something else. Like, if Sasha says, 'Hey, Jax, whatdya think about popping over to San Francisco for Chinese?' what she really means is, 'I'm feeling nostalgic and I want to see the house where I grew up with my father, who I loved.'" He dribbled away and went for another layup.

"If that's what she wants, why doesn't she just say that?"

"Because she knows I don't like to take her there. It's all real sweet until she starts thinking about his murder. That makes her think about her mom becoming a lost soul, and having to take her out, and instead of a happy trip down memory lane, she's depressed for three days. I know that's how it'll be, and I'm bound to argue against taking her, so she's figured out not to ask me directly."

Key started to ask why Sasha didn't just go by herself, if Jax was so opposed to her going, but realized almost at the same time that she wouldn't want to go alone. He also realized this was an insight he wouldn't have had a week ago. He must be changing, at least a little. "If it upsets her, why does she want to go?"

Jax dribbled to the free throw line and stopped. "She grieves, Key. It's no different than the Luminas, who sometimes take years to finally let go of their mortal lives. It's longer and longer between the times she wants to go to San Francisco, and there'll come a day when she doesn't want to go back at all, but until then, she's going to ask me to go for Chinese, and I'm going to know why." His shot *whooshed* through the net without touching the rim. He went for the ball and dribbled it back to Key. "Girls are also into drama. They get hyperemotional about something and tell you things they are entirely sure they mean, except they don't. What's an absolute today will sometimes become a maybe by tomorrow."

That was promising. "Like for example?"

"Remember when Sasha asked you if she could take an art class?"

Key nodded.

Jax stopped bouncing the ball and tucked it under his arm. "A couple of days later, I asked her if she was upset that you said no. She said she wasn't, but I couldn't leave it alone, and she said it was almost like I *wanted* her to be unhappy that she's stuck on this mountain forever. I was annoying the hell out of her, so she went off on me, said she'd just go ahead and move up to the third floor and I could sleep by myself and then we'd *both* be unhappy. The whole thing was ridiculous, and of course she didn't move upstairs, but I thought for a minute that she might. Which was the point. It freaked me out enough that I finally let it go."

"So she never intended to move upstairs? She faked you out?"

"No, that's what I'm trying to tell you. She was absolutely sure she would, until she wasn't. I think they're *all* like that, Kyros."

Maybe they were all like that, but Key couldn't see that his situation was the same. How he felt about Eryx was in a whole different category than Jax's insecurities about Sasha. Maybe she got aggravated at him, but she loved him.

Jordan wasn't just annoyed with Key. She saw this thing about Eryx as a game changer.

"Are you going to tell me why she said no way?"

He dropped his gaze from the windows at the top of the gym wall and shook his head. "It doesn't matter, Jax. She's made up her mind."

"Key, have you been listening? Nothing they say is written in stone. Everything is negotiable. Don't you remember what Sasha said about us, about me? It wasn't no, but hell no, and buddy bar the door."

"Yeah, but then you were kissing her every five minutes, and she let you, so I don't think she really meant it."

"Oh, she meant it."

"Then what changed her mind?"

Jax began dribbling the ball again. "That run-in she had with the lost souls from her school pissed her off so much, she knew she wanted to stay with us and do what we do." He dribbled to center court and made his shot, but didn't go after the ball. Instead, he walked to Key and leaned against the wall next to him. "But what sealed the deal was that she loved me."

He was so not good at this. Talking about it made him feel awkward. But he had no idea what to do or how to begin, and Jax was his best hope of figuring it out. "Why?"

"Why does she love me?"

Key nodded. "What did you do that made her love you?"

"It's not like it happened overnight. In the beginning, it was all about her being Anabo. Then I got to know her, found out what she dreamed about, what was important to her. I did things for her that she couldn't do for herself, and it took a while, but I finally realized I wasn't doing them to make her love me. I was doing them because it mattered to me that she was happy, that she had what she needed. I was doing them because I loved her."

"So she fell in love with you because you did things for her."

"No, I think she fell in love with me because she discovered my deepest, darkest secret."

Key jerked his head up and stared at his brother. "What secret?"

Jax smiled. "That I'm kind of a sentimental sap. It never occurred to me that a girl would find that appealing, but after she figured it out, everything changed."

"How did she figure it out?"

"None of your business." He caught Key's look and shook his head. "It doesn't matter. The point is, what I considered to be a negative turned out to be the turning point."

"What if she had discovered your secret and didn't like it, couldn't get past it? What if you were convinced that nothing you could do would make any difference?"

Jax stared down at his shoes for a long time. Finally, he said, "Jordan is an Anabo who's becoming Mephisto, so the only thing in this world she wouldn't be able to get past is something to do with Eryx. With *you* and Eryx." He looked up at Key, his eyes full of sympathy. "You think we don't know, but you're wrong. We've always known how you feel about him. We don't like it, but we get it, because we were there. We all know what it cost you, Key, and what it did to you. And maybe I know more than anyone because I was there when he jumped. I was there with you."

Key stared at his brother and wanted to say a million things, but he was afraid if he opened his mouth, nothing would come out. Nothing could get past the knot in his throat.

"You're not easy to reach, Key. You're my brother and I'd do anything for you, but no way I could have told you I know how it is with Eryx. You'd have denied it and kicked my ass."

"True," Key managed to say.

"But it's different now, because so much is at stake. So maybe this is uncomfortable for you to talk about, and maybe it bothers you that we've known all along, but you gotta set all that aside if you have a prayer of making it work with Jordan."

Key looked up at the windows. It was snowing again. "She wasn't there."

"No, but you can tell her how it was. You can explain how close you and Eryx were."

"I did."

Jax was quiet again, until he said, "It wasn't in our nature to forgive and accept, but we did, because we love you. If Jordan were to fall in love with you, there's no way she wouldn't accept this part of you. She's Anabo before she's Mephisto. It's totally her nature to be forgiving."

"But there's a fundamental difference. We were brothers before Eryx jumped. We shared a home, and parents, and our childhood. All we had was one another. Jordan and I have known each other only a few days. There's no investment, nothing to fall back on."

"You brought her back to life, and she saved yours. I'd call that a ginormous investment. I'd call that a bond that'll take a lot more than this thing with Eryx to break."

For the first time, Key felt hopeful. "It was already hard enough because of what I am, and like you said, I'm not easy. I know that. But this takes the level of difficulty into the stratosphere."

"Difficult, but not impossible."

"I don't know, Jax. She sounded pretty certain."

"Yeah, and Sasha was actually packing her stuff to take up to the third floor."

"You never did say what changed her mind."

"My supreme power of persuasion."

"No, really. What changed her mind?"

Jax shoved away from the wall. "I groveled."

"No, you didn't."

"Yeah, I did. I'd die for Sasha . . . in fact, I *did* die for Sasha, so laying my pride at her feet and telling her I'm sorry for being a jackass isn't such a big deal."

"*Were* you a jackass?"

Jax turned to face him. "I'm a son of Hell. Of course I was a jackass."

❧

Late in the night, unable to go to sleep, Jordan was lying in bed staring at the ceiling when her phone dinged. Thinking it would be a text from Tessa, she grabbed the phone off of her nightstand and sucked in a breath.

It was from Matthew. I'm glad you're alive, Jordan. I wish I wasn't. I'm calling it good between you and me—it's over. Please don't call or text or come see me. Just forget me. This is the way I want it, and it's never going to change.

She texted him back. I never got the chance to say I love you, Matthew, but I do. Please don't shut me out.

Two seconds later, he replied. I don't want to hurt you, but I guess I have to. I don't love you, Jordan. I just said it because I was hoping to get lucky.

He was lying. He had to be. She could remember his face and his eyes so clearly, and the way he said it. Just before Eryx's minions busted in and shot him. You're lying.

Not lying. I cheated on you with Tori, because you held out on me so long.

You're still lying.

Ask her.

Why would she admit it? She's easy—not stupid.

He didn't answer for a long time; she was just about to text a line of question marks when her phone dinged.

It was a picture of Tori. Naked. On Matthew's bed. I'm sorry.

She didn't text him back.

Rolling into a little ball, she cried herself to sleep.

THIRTEEN

BETSY WOKE HER BEFORE HER ALARM EVEN WENT OFF. "Upsy-daisy, young lady. Your papa wants you in the kitchen for breakfast ASAP so you can meet your new Secret Service detail." The older woman stood with her arms crossed over her chest and looked down at Jordan with her usual drill-sergeant expression, which made total sense because Betsy used to be a drill sergeant. "They're both built like tanks, and one of them is named Gunther."

Jordan sat up and rubbed the sleep from her eyes. "You are so not funny, Betsy."

"Who's kidding? The other one's named Hank. The night-shift guys will be here at seven tonight, so don't make plans until after that. In fact, maybe you shouldn't make any plans.

You need to stay home with your father until he feels better."

Alarmed, Jordan asked, "Is he sick?"

Betsy dropped her arms and turned to walk toward the door. "If you'd seen what he went through after you were taken, you'd stay right here in this room until he dies, just to make sure he never has to worry again." She stopped at the door and said over her shoulder. "Be careful out there, Jo."

"Aw, Betsy, you really *do* love me, don't you?"

"Humph! Hard enough, what with you being such a problem child. Now up and at 'em. Don't keep the president waiting."

Jordan slid out of bed and headed for the bathroom, taking off her T-shirt as she went. Flipping the light switch, she blinked and moved closer to the mirror to look at her birthmark. The tiny *A* had morphed into a bigger *A*, twined within an *M*. It was weird and way more conspicuous than the tiny *A* had been, but beautiful. So this was it. She was now fully Mephisto.

Her first impulse was to call Key to tell him, but then she remembered how it was between them and knew she shouldn't. That made her feel very alone. And sad.

She got in the shower, and the whole time she was getting ready for school, she thought about him, imagined his destroying the greenhouse; she wondered if he was calmer now. She refused to feel guilty. And she wouldn't think about the Mephisto Covenant. He would find another Anabo someday, and *she* could love him and ensure he earned a chance of Heaven.

Her throat made that weird noise again. She tossed the tube of lip gloss back in the drawer and faced the fact that she didn't want Key to find another Anabo. How could she be this unfair to him? She told him she could never love him, but she didn't want him to be with anyone else.

Dammit, why did he have to feel this way about Eryx, and worse, why couldn't she forgive him for it? Lots of people were together who didn't see eye to eye on certain things. Her own parents had been miles apart on several issues. So why couldn't she see past this thing with Key and Eryx?

Anticipating seeing him today, even if it was awkward, she grabbed her backpack and headed for the kitchen. Turned out Betsy hadn't been kidding.

"Jordan," Dad said from his usual seat at the table, "I'd like you to meet Gunther and Hank."

Gunther had a shaved head, and Hank had short, curly, dark hair. They stood and offered their hands to shake, and she noticed they were twice the size of hers. They both wore dark suits, and she wondered if they had to get them specially made to fit their huge bodies.

When she was seated, they also sat, and Betsy served Jordan her breakfast. As usual, she gave her a small bowl of granola with half a banana and a teeny glass of orange juice. Yeah, this wasn't going to work. She'd have to hit the vending machine at school.

"If you need to come home," Dad said, "do it. I don't want you feeling miserable."

"I'll be fine."

"I know how you like to dodge your detail, but you won't do that anymore, will you?"

Glancing at the two giants assigned to protect her, she shook her head. "I may be more afraid of them than the bad guys."

Hank smiled. Gunther didn't look up from his eggs. Which looked delicious. "Betsy, can I have some eggs?"

"Why? You never eat eggs. You said the egg people are mean to the chickens."

It pained her to put her stomach ahead of her principles, but she was starving. The granola and the banana hadn't made a dent. "I think I need protein."

"I have some protein powder I can make into a shake."

That sounded just awful. "How about some eggs, instead?"

"Whatever you want, precious."

"Can you leave off the side of sarcasm?"

"Killjoy."

Dad finished his coffee, got to his feet, and came around the table to kiss her cheek. "Have a good day, Jo. Call me later, will you?"

He never asked her to call him. He was seriously worried about her going to school, being out there, exposed. "I will, Dad. Bye."

When he was gone, Hank asked, "What time does the bell ring?"

"Ten after eight."

He stood, and Gunther followed suit. "We'll be down at the side portico."

As soon as they were gone, she asked Betsy, "Are they going to have breakfast with us every day?"

"No, just today. It was supposed to be a chance for all of you to get to know one another, but between Gunther, who evidently never speaks, and you with your fixation on eggs, you're all still strangers. Here're your eggs."

She tried to eat slowly, then didn't, while Betsy did dishes and hummed the theme from *Hawaii Five-0*.

From behind her, a woman said, "Good morning, Jordan."

She turned quickly and saw Carla standing there in the doorway, her eyes smudged by the shadow of Eryx. She was young, probably in her late twenties, and so pretty, with dark eyes and hair and the most beautiful skin. Jordan had always admired Carla because she was so kind and thoughtful.

But not anymore.

Feeling slightly sick, Jordan turned back to her eggs. "Since when do you not call ahead, or knock? This is our private residence, Carla."

Betsy turned, eyes wide, probably shocked by her tone. Carla had been a favorite staffer for a long time, so it must have been odd to hear Jordan talk to her that way.

Finished with the eggs, Jordan pushed away from the table and stood. "Thanks, Betsy. I'll see you around five. It's Thursday. Student Council day." She picked up her backpack and turned toward the doorway into the dining room. "Let's go in the living room, Carla."

She walked out, and when she was standing next to the mantel, she turned to Carla and waited for her to speak. Dad always said, in a confrontational meeting, let the other guy talk first. See where he was coming from.

Carla didn't disappoint. "No point beating around the bush, is there?"

"No."

"I know what you are now, but don't think you can intimidate me. You probably expect me to quit, but I'm not leaving this job."

Was she serious with that attitude? "Eventually, you'll be leaving life."

"Eryx promised me immortality." She sounded completely confident.

"Big deal. All that means is that you'll live forever in Hell on Earth. It must be the worst kind of horror down there, all those rotting bodies, and the immortals who wish they could die but can't."

She was gratified when Carla took a step back.

"Eryx will protect me," she said. "He'll make sure I don't end up there."

"What else did Eryx promise you, Carla? What was worth your soul?"

Carla sort of preened and actually looked down her nose at Jordan. "I'm going to be the chief of staff."

Her soul for a stupid job. Jordan clenched her fists. "When? Dad just appointed Mike Willis."

"Mr. Trent told me—"

"What difference does it make what he told you? He's gone, so he can't keep any of his promises." Jordan took a step closer. "If you mention Eryx and your twisted agenda in a reply to even one kid who sends an e-mail to the First Daughter account, I'll make sure you're fired. I'd do it now except I have no cause other than that I despise you. That's not intimidation. That's a fact."

"You think you scare me?"

"I don't give a damn if you're scared. I won't tolerate you or Eryx jacking around with any kid who writes to me. I'm pretty sure Mike Willis, your new boss, will feel the same way."

Carla smiled like she'd just won the lottery. "Why don't you ask him, Jordan?"

Oh, no. "Is he . . . did he—"

"Yes, he did. And Robert Threadgill."

Mr. Threadgill was the press secretary and Carla's direct boss, reporting to the chief of staff. If all three of them were lost souls, where did that leave her? She had no leverage.

Carla knew it, too. She looked ready to laugh with glee. "I'll be replying to lots of e-mails today, and every single kid with a problem will get a thoughtful, compassionate response, along with a suggestion to join their local Ravens group. If there isn't one, I'll invite them to start one. Do you know about the Ravens, Jordan?"

Jordan remembered Jax telling her that some of the kids at Sasha's school in San Francisco had pledged to Eryx; they had called themselves the Ravens. Then she moved to Telluride, where there was another group of Ravens.

Feeling all the weight of all those kids who wrote to her looking for help, for answers to their problems, Jordan clenched her fists and took a step closer to Carla. "You will *not* mention—"

"Yes, I will, and there's *nothing* you can do about it."

Rage slammed into her, turning her vision blood red. All she could see was Carla and her damned shaded eyes. She dropped the backpack and went for her throat, knocked her down, and straddled her, pinning her to the floor while she choked the life out of her.

"Jesus, Joseph, and Mary!" Betsy cried, her hands on Jordan's arms, trying to pull her away.

If it had been anyone but Betsy, she'd have shoved him back so she could finish off Carla. But somewhere in her wrath-induced mania, she remembered Betsy was older now, with arthritis. And she loved Betsy. She couldn't hurt her. So she allowed the woman to drag her off of Carla, who was rubbing her throat, coughing, and glaring at Jordan.

"I'm bringing charges," she said hoarsely, sitting up with a cell phone in her hand.

Betsy said, "You punch one number on that phone, and I'll be telling President Ellis what you and Mr. Threadgill really do in his office." Carla lowered her hand and looked surprised. "Yeah, I know what goes on. Now put your phone away, get up, and leave. If you speak a word of this, especially to the president, count on getting fired."

Carla gathered up her leather portfolio and got to her feet. Jordan could see bruises forming on her neck, which meant Carla didn't have to tell anyone. They'd know she'd been attacked, and she'd tell them Jordan had done it. There'd be more trouble for Dad, more bad PR, and another giant problem for him to take care of. His daughter getting charged with assault just might be his breaking point.

Now she understood what Key had meant about how hard it would be for her in the real world. He'd said she'd want to kill the lost souls. She wondered if maybe Eryx had told Carla to egg her on, hoping Jordan would lose it and do something that would get her into trouble. Then Eryx would show up and offer to fix it for her if she'd agree to give him what he wanted.

From now on, she was going to have to be way more careful.

"Wait," she said to Carla before she left the residence. "Sit down on the couch."

"Why? So you can try again?"

"Just do it. I need to tell you something."

Undoubtedly full of questions and fear, but always Jordan's champion, Betsy went to stand between Carla and the door. "Do as she says, Carla." Betsy looked across at Jordan. "I'm still bigger than you, so don't get funny."

Carla went to the sofa and sat down, glaring at Jordan as she came close and wrapped her hands around her neck again. Except this time, Jordan didn't squeeze. This time, she concentrated on Carla's creamy skin, on the pulse she could feel beneath her fingers, on smoothing away the bruises. She felt warmth travel through her arms, into her hands. It was amazing.

When she let go of Carla, she heard Betsy gasp. "Saints alive, child, how did you do that?"

"She's sold her soul to Satan," Carla said.

Betsy opened the door. "Time for you to go."

Springing to her feet, Carla walked away, shooting a murderous look at Jordan as she went.

When she was gone, Betsy looked at Jordan with tears in her eyes. "I should tell your father, but I can't stand to break his heart. Swear to me you won't attack anyone again, and promise me you'll go to that appointment and work through this."

"I swear and promise."

Betsy looked behind her at the door. "I can't hardly believe she said you sold your soul to the devil. I always thought she was so nice." She looked again at Jordan and crossed herself. "I'll be taking you to mass with me Friday afternoon, and no arguing."

"I'm not Catholic, Betsy."

"Been taking you to mass since you were a grasshopper, and it hasn't hurt you any. I want to pray for you, and it's easier when you're there. I can show you to God."

Jordan retrieved her backpack from the floor, then walked over to Betsy and hugged her, accepting her old nanny's bearlike embrace, which nearly crushed her spine. "I'll go, Bet. I'll even be nice to Father Simon."

"Aw, Jo, I worry so about you. And now this healing thing. How did you do that?"

Still hugging her, Jordan wished with all her heart that Betsy hadn't seen her do that. For that matter, she wished Betsy hadn't seen any of it. She hated for her old nanny to think badly of her, and how could she help it? Jordan had almost killed someone, right here in the White House. She sighed. "It's just something I realized I can do."

Betsy pulled away, looking confused. "What did you realize you can do?" She looked around and became more confused. "Where's Carla? Why are we hugging?" Betsy put her hand to her head and shook it. "Glory be, I must be going senile. I came in here because . . . I was doing dishes, and . . . "

Reeling with the sudden understanding that she could make someone forget something, Jordan led Betsy to the sofa and sat down with her. "I was having an argument with Carla, and you came in to see what was going on. You were upset, so I hugged you and Carla left. It's not a big deal, Betsy. You talked about how much stress Dad's been under, but I know you have, too." She patted her arm. "Why don't you take the rest of the day off and go see a movie or something? I'll fix dinner tonight."

Still looking addled, Betsy nodded. "Maybe you're right. I think I'll go bake some cookies." She smiled at her. "You have a good day at school, and don't be worrying any about me. I'm old, but I'm tough. Even if I do lose my wits, I'm still going to look after you."

Jordan kissed her cheek, then stood to leave. She said as she walked to the door, "You really *do* love me."

"Nonsense! Love is for saps."

⤬

As soon as Jordan and Gunther hit the front doors of the school and walked into the entry hall, she was surrounded by people, all asking at once how she was doing. She said, "I'm okay," over and over, and accepted a lot of hugs and well wishes; after a while, people began to drift off toward the main hall and their lockers.

She was feeling glad to have the initial bit over with when Courtney Byrd and her four besties, publicly known as the Bible Bees and privately called the Buzzkills, descended on her. She cursed not having seen them coming so she could escape, but she was in it now with nowhere to run. She glanced at Gunther and wished the Secret Service also provided protection from obnoxious people.

"Jordan, I just wanted you to know how hard the Bees prayed for you."

"Thank you, Courtney." She glanced around at the others and smiled. "Thank you all. It's good to be back."

"We also wanted to let you know about a problem," Courtney said solemnly. "Since you're the president of the student body, we think you should put a stop to the prom committee's plans. The theme they've chosen is completely inappropriate."

Oh, boy. Some things she wouldn't miss after she went back to Colorado. Like Courtney and her over-the-top, fanatical religion.

"How is the Garden of Eden inappropriate? It was a beautiful place, made by God."

"Invaded by Satan! He spoiled it, and that's exactly what will happen if this prom theme is the Garden of Eden."

"You think Satan will invade our prom?"

She totally saw Gunther's lips twitch while he stared ahead from behind his aviators.

"There are people at this school who'll use the prom to tempt others to sin, maybe even to give their souls to Lucifer."

She shouldn't encourage Courtney, but she felt compelled. "If we don't use the Garden of Eden theme, what sort of prom do you have in mind?"

Eyes bright with excitement, Courtney stepped closer and said in a conspiratorial voice, "Rapture."

"You mean, like, end of times?"

Courtney nodded eagerly. "It'd be amazing, Jordan! We'd have decorations like the four horsemen of the apocalypse, and we could serve punch that looks like blood. Instead of music, we'd have someone reading from Revelation, with the sound of earthquakes in the background. Dancing encourages impure thoughts, so instead, we'd have games."

"Games? At a prom?"

"We'll play the rapture game and see who will be taken by Jesus and who'll be left behind."

Courtney, of course, would sit in judgment. She was a master at it by now.

Gunther wasn't smiling any longer. And Jordan was all out of patience. "The purpose of a prom is fun. People expect to dance, and drink pink lemonade punch, and look at the pretty decorations. The Garden of Eden is a universal concept everyone can accept."

She expected Courtney to argue with her, but instead the girl began to back away, her brown eyes huge in her long, narrow face as she looked over Jordan's shoulder.

Then Jordan caught the scent of evergreens and knew Key had walked in. She felt his heat when he came to stand just behind her, making her suddenly breathless. Courtney nearly tripped over her Bees, she was in such a hurry to go.

Turning, Jordan took one look at him and knew why Courtney had run away. He was dressed in the Mephisto monochrome, and the hard look on his face did nothing to dispel his menacing appearance. He wasn't trying to fit in at all, and she kind of admired him for it. She was also way too glad to see him. She'd planned to dial everything back to how it was before their time on the plane, but how could she do that if the first thing she wanted to do when she saw him was throw her arms around him and kiss him? It didn't matter that she could now kiss him without guilt, since Matthew was no longer her boyfriend.

But she wasn't going to think about that. Not yet. She couldn't get that picture of Tori out of her mind, or the anger she felt toward Matthew, which felt wrong even if it was justified. She was all mixed up and didn't want to think about it now.

Aware of Gunther's presence, and the kids passing by on their way to class, she knew she had to pretend she'd never met Key. Ruthlessly shoving away thoughts of kissing him, she pasted on a smile and said, "You must be one of the new students. I'm Jordan Ellis. Welcome to Oates."

From behind a pair of Wayfarers, in a deep, warm voice that didn't match his cold expression *at all*, Key said, "Hello, Jordan. It's really nice of you to be so . . . nice."

A nerdy guy in a blue oxford and a pair of khakis stepped around him and smiled at her. "Hi, I'm Brody DeKyanos, and this is my brother, Key."

"Hi, Brody," she said, instantly liking him. He had the sweetest eyes behind geeky glasses. "The office is just over there," she pointed to her right, "where you can check in with Mrs. Black and get your schedule, unless you already have it."

A piece of paper appeared from his back pocket. "Yeah, got that. Key and I are in all the same classes."

He handed it to her, and in one glance she saw they were in every one of her classes. Even AP government. No doubt the records Luminas had taken care of their schedules.

Before she could make any comment, she heard Tessa calling her name. She sounded way excited.

When Jordan turned around, she went stiff, and a giant rock of anxiety lodged in the pit of her belly.

Headed her way down the main hall was her best friend, holding hands with Eryx.

FOURTEEN

SHE FELT KEY'S HAND ON THE SMALL OF HER BACK, THEN heard him say in the softest whisper, "Take it easy, Jordan."

Tessa practically skipped up to them, beaming with happiness. "Jordan, this is Eryx DeKyanos, one of the new students I was telling you about."

She was speechless. All she could manage was a nod.

"He's living with Senator Markham and his wife while he finishes school here because his parents were called to Uganda on a missionary trip."

Jordan nearly choked.

"We went to dinner at the Markhams' last night because the senator wanted to talk to Dad about contributing to a new wing at the school, and Eryx and I hung out."

Senator Markham was on the list of lost souls Key had told her about, one of the ten they would take out at her birthday party. No doubt Eryx had put him up to inviting Mr. Barnes and his family for dinner, just so he could start something with Tessa.

She looked into Eryx's dead, flat eyes and couldn't fathom how her friend could be attracted to him. More than attracted. She was practically drooling on him. Sure, he had an incredible face, with a five o'clock shadow, he was tall and built, and he was dressed in übercool clothes—a frayed white oxford with its tail out, a loosely knotted skinny black tie, and black trousers—but his horrible eyes overrode everything else. How could Tessa see past those eyes?

His arrogance was infuriating, and she imagined how it would feel to stab him. It wouldn't be like it was with Jax during training. She'd hold nothing back. She'd go for Eryx's heart, and when he was out, she'd drag him over to the school chapel, to holy ground, and watch him burn.

The way he was looking at her, she suspected he knew exactly where her thoughts had gone. He looked smug, like he was completely confident that she had no chance of taking him down. Key's hand was still on her back, silently telling her to relax. She took a breath and asked Eryx, "Besides spreading the word about Jesus, what are your parents doing in Uganda?"

"Our family aren't Christians, but another faith, so it's not about Jesus. Dad's helping build a water-purification facility, and Mom's administering inoculations to children."

He sounded so sincere, so *real*, if she didn't know it was a giant load of BS, she'd be swallowing it the same as Tessa. "I took a religious studies class at church, so I'm all kinds of fascinated. What faith is your family, Eryx?"

"True Messiah. Like the Jews, we don't believe Christ is mankind's savior; but unlike the Jews, we believe the messiah has arrived and walks among us."

"Is this messiah a son of God?"

"He's a son of the world."

Tessa was never big on religion, but she was gazing at Eryx as if he was the second coming. How long would it be before he told her he was the true messiah? How long before Tessa pledged to follow him? What could Jordan do to keep it from happening? Panic nearly choked her, and she caught Eryx's meaningful look. He knew she was freaking out. He'd designed this little scene for just that purpose. *Go with me,* his eyes said, *and I'll leave her alone.*

Tessa was staring over Jordan's shoulder, frowning. Jordan knew just what she was thinking—who was this hard, rough biker-looking guy, and what was he doing dirtying up the front hall of Oates? "Tessa, this is Key, and his brother, Brody. Key, Brody, this is Tessa Barnes."

Tessa looked at all three of the new arrivals, then focused on Key and Eryx. "Y'all look so much alike. You're related, aren't you?"

Before Jordan could make up something, Brody said, "Eryx is our cousin. We lost our parents, so we live with our aunt, our mother's sister. She decided we should move to Washington from London. Eryx could have stayed with us to go to school, but our aunt doesn't like his father."

"Your aunt is a witch," Eryx said. He saw Tessa's shocked look and smiled. "Not in the bad sense. I mean, she really does think she's a witch."

"That's a lie," Key said, not bothering to put a fake face on it like Brody did.

"So you're not a True Messiah?" Tessa asked Brody.

"No, we're . . . something else."

"Wiccan?"

"Does it matter?" Jordan interjected, wishing Tessa would get off the religion train.

"No, of course not." Tessa smiled at Brody. "It's very nice to meet you. If you need anything, let me know. I kind of have an in. My dad's the headmaster."

"I'll keep that in mind," he said, "and so will my brother."

Tessa missed Brody's point—that she'd completely ignored Key. Smiling at Eryx, she tugged on his hand. "Come on, I'll show you around some more before first period starts."

Eryx shot Jordan another look before they turned and walked away.

Gunther said, "I'm switching out with Hank. Stay here until he gets inside." Turning, he walked to the doors and exited.

"Gunther's probably going to run a background check on you," Jordan said to Key. "I thought you were going to dress to fit in."

"I changed my mind. How are you?"

"Not so good. I attacked Carla, the press secretary's assistant, this morning."

His expression was instantly concerned. "What happened?"

She told him, and he asked, "Are you sure the nanny doesn't remember?"

"Positive. I didn't know I could do that."

"Just don't abuse it, and next time you feel that kind of rage, try to remember that killing a lost soul is a win for Eryx."

"I'm not sure I can, Key. I've never felt like that. It was as if my brain had checked out and I had no control. If Betsy hadn't made me stop, I'd have killed Carla." She looked at the buttons on his coat and sighed. "And I can't believe it, but I don't feel bad about that at all."

"For Mephisto, this is totally normal, and it's why I'm here, why we need to stay together as much as possible. It's going to be hard for you because Eryx has already collected followers at this school. His being here will make it way worse because he sets you off, and because he'll have told the lost souls who and what you are. They'll taunt you on purpose, hoping to get you into trouble. His goal is to make you desperate enough to give him what he wants, and he's got a good start already. You're so pumped on adrenaline right now, you could probably burn the place down."

"Is that so surprising? Tessa is my best friend, and she was practically climbing into his pocket."

Key looked like he almost felt sorry for her. "Right now, she's more at risk than anybody else at this school."

"I know." She stared after Tessa, who'd walked Eryx all the way to the end of the main hall and was showing him the photo gallery of all the famous politicians who'd given commencement speeches at Oates.

"Tessa may resist," Brody said.

"Don't give Jordan false hope," Key said. "He'll suck more and more of them in before her birthday."

"Maybe we should plan something else," Brody said. "Something sooner."

"It wouldn't make any difference. We take out ten, he's got ten more a week later. As long as he stays here, it's a losing battle. Skia have a harder time convincing people to pledge, but Eryx is the original, and it's like people can't help themselves."

And yet, he didn't hate him. "Let me tell Tessa," Jordan said.

"You can't tell her about us, about you. It's grounds for taking you out, and your sacrifice would be for nothing, because no matter what you tell her, in the end it all comes down to her faith. If she's strong enough, she won't pledge."

"You don't think she is, do you?"

He stared down at her for a long time before he said, "Most people aren't, Jordan. Some will pledge for something incredibly trivial, but even people with deep faith and a firm belief in God will pledge if they're desperate enough. Eryx has a talent for figuring out people's weaknesses."

Hank came inside and smiled at her. "Gunther is rechecking the perimeter, then he'll be back." He gave Key a look, maybe because he was standing so close to Jordan.

Key nodded at him and held out his hand. "I'm Key DeKyanos. This is my brother, Brody."

Hank smiled and shook Brody's hand just as the first bell rang.

With a frown, Key asked, "Why is that annoying bell ringing?"

"It's to let everyone know we have five minutes to get to class." She looked at Brody. "Ready?"

He sighed. "I can't believe I'm doing this again, but yeah, I'm ready."

She turned and headed down the main hall toward the science rooms, to chemistry, followed by a Mephisto who looked like a Hell's Angel, a Lumina who looked like a chess champion, and a Secret Service agent who could be on tour for the WWF.

As soon as she rounded the doorway and stepped inside the room, she knew Key hadn't been exaggerating. Three of her classmates, guys she knew and liked, stared at her from behind the shadow across their eyes. She was feeling grief at the loss until they looked at Key and Brody and laughed. One of them, a guy named Mark, who she'd had a crush on in seventh grade, said to the others, "Hey, look, it's the League of Nerds." He focused on Key. "Are we supposed to think you look like Neo from *The Matrix*?"

Key walked toward Mark, who was stupid enough not to back off. Jordan was beginning to understand that lost souls gave away more than their spirit—they also tossed their common sense.

"Ooh, I'm so scared," Mark said. "What are you gonna do? Force me to eat a blue pill?" His buddies all laughed, and others in the class joined in.

At Mark's desk, Key stopped, reached out his hand, and placed his index finger on Mark's forehead. Mark tried to jerk away, but was clearly stuck in his seat. When Key lifted his finger, there was a ginormous zit on Mark's face, oozy and disgusting. Key turned and walked back to stand next to Jordan, while everyone who was watching gasped. Six more zits appeared, and Mark looked around at the faces, his eyes wide. "What? Why is everyone staring at me? *Hey*," he called after Key, "what did you do to me?" He bolted from his chair and ran out of the room.

Key said to Mr. Shelley, who was staring with his mouth open, "Pretty weird when boils come up like that. That guy's got some infectious disease. Maybe you should send him home."

"Why did you touch him?" Mr. Shelley asked.

"I thought he looked like he had a fever. He does. Really, he should get out of here before he infects everyone else." Key took off his shades and looked pointedly at Mark's lost soul buddies, who shifted in their chairs and became interested in their chem books.

Mark ran back in the room, his face covered with more boils. While everyone gasped and made ick sounds, he rushed at Key, fists raised. "You sick bastard, you're going down!"

But Mark was the one who went down. He'd barely moved a foot before Hank took him to the floor, facedown, and placed his wrists in handcuffs.

Jordan blinked. Secret Service never hesitated when dealing with a threat, real or perceived, but she couldn't remember anyone moving as fast as Hank.

He looked up at Mr. Shelley. "I believe school policy is zero tolerance for physical assaults. I assume this young man will be taken to the headmaster?"

Nobody ever got in fights at Oates. Kids argued, and there were asshats who liked being mean to the geeks, but Jordan couldn't remember anybody actually getting violent. Maybe that's why Mr. Shelley looked like a deer in headlights. This wasn't something he usually had to deal with.

He looked toward the desk closest to the door. "Benjamin, go ask Mr. Barnes to come here."

Mark was struggling to get up, but Hank had a death grip on the back of his neck, and his other huge hand pressed against his back.

"Do you *know* who my dad is?" Mark yelled. "He'll get you fired for this!"

Hank evidently didn't care who Mark's dad was. He ignored him.

Moments later, Gunther came in, took one look, and immediately said, "Everyone take a seat."

Maybe because he was Secret Service, or maybe because he

was huge and his voice practically boomed, everybody who'd gotten up to take a closer look hurried back to their chairs.

Mr. Barnes came in, looking worried. "What's going on here?"

Hank said, "This boy threatened another student. He was about to punch him."

"Mark, why would you do this? Fighting means automatic suspension."

"The freak made me get boils!" Mark shouted. "If anybody gets kicked out of school, it oughta be *him*."

"Mark needs to go home, Mr. Barnes." Jeremy Speight said from the back of the room. "He's got something foul."

Tessa's dad moved closer and peered down at Mark's face, only half of it showing because the other half was against the floor, then he looked at Hank. "I'll take care of the situation now, unless you need to do something with him?"

Hank shook his head. "He didn't directly threaten Jordan, so he's all yours." He released his hold on Mark and took off the handcuffs. Mark got to his feet and glared at Key, but he didn't make another move to hit him.

Mr. Barnes took Mark's arm and walked him out the door.

Jordan cleared her throat. "Mr. Shelley, this is Key and Brody DeKyanos. They're new today."

Their teacher still looked weirded out. "Pick up a book from that back shelf and take a seat anywhere."

While Gunther went out into the hall and Hank went to stand at the back of the classroom, Jordan headed for her usual seat, between Cory and Megan, then felt Key's hand on her arm, propelling her toward the empty desks at the back of the room. "Why?" she whispered under her breath.

"I want to sit with you," he said out loud.

Everyone turned to look, and she blushed with embarrassment, then hurried to sit down so the kids would stop staring. Brody took a seat on one side of her and Key took a seat on the other.

Mr. Shelley asked Key and Brody about some principles and formulas he'd covered last semester and seemed impressed when they both knew everything he threw at them.

Mrs. Montoya was equally impressed with their command of Spanish in second period, and Mrs. Silver nearly danced for joy when she realized what they could do in advanced calculus. As for Jordan, she was elated not to see Eryx in any of her classes, and only one more lost soul.

Fourth period was when her luck ran out. Tessa, Eryx, Mark's buddies, and another lost soul were in AP government. Adding to the fun were Courtney and two of her Buzzkills.

Key insisted on sitting next to her again, and as soon as they took their seats, he leaned close and said, "Who's the horse-faced girl?"

"That's mean, Key."

"It's the truth. And she's looking at me like I have horns and frowning at you like you have a scarlet A on your blouse. What gives?"

Leaning toward him, she explained about Courtney.

He stared back at the queen of the Bible Bees and said, not in a whisper, "Boo!"

Courtney jerked around to face the front, and Jordan smiled behind her hand.

Class began, and their teacher, Mr. Hopper, a retired senator from New Hampshire who now worked as a pundit and taught this class because he said he loved shaping young minds, said in his deep, dramatic voice, "First off this morning, we will all pay homage to the First Daughter for her courage and resilience. Let's show her how glad we are that she's back with us, safe and sound." He began to clap, and everyone except Courtney and her Buzz-kills joined in, turning in their seats to look at her. Even Eryx clapped, probably because he was trying to make everyone think he was a nice guy. A regular guy.

"Ms. Byrd, Ms. Kendrick, Ms. Fair," Mr. Hopper said to Courtney and her friends after the applause died down, "is there some reason you didn't join us?"

Jordan couldn't see Courtney's face, but she didn't need to. She undoubtedly had her lips pursed and a disapproving wrinkle across her forehead. "I'm sorry she was kidnapped, but it's not like she made a daring escape. She was rescued. Seems to me we should applaud the guys who saved her."

Jordan couldn't help it. She looked at Key, and they each smiled.

"I'm also really disappointed that Jordan won't make the prom committee change this year's theme," Courtney added with a little bit of a whine in her voice.

"Is there something wrong with the current prom theme?" Mr. Hopper asked.

"It's the Garden of Eden, and everyone associates Eden with Satan."

"Everyone, Ms. Byrd? I'd say that's a stretch. Take me, for instance. I associate Adam and Eve and the tree of life with the Garden of Eden. Those who associate the garden with Satan may have a different perspective, but you can't assume the entire population of this school shares it with you."

Courtney's shoulders became more rigid, if that was possible. "I also didn't clap because she's cheating on her boyfriend, who's in critical condition and *paralyzed*. I refuse to applaud her for that, Mr. Hopper."

Everyone turned to look at Jordan again, but she didn't say anything. Mr. Hopper didn't tolerate people speaking out in class. Besides, what could she say?

"Are you aware, personally, of the state of Ms. Ellis's relationship with Mr. Whittaker?"

"They've been going out for two years."

"Yes, but are they going out now? Are you privy to this information? If so, Ms. Ellis might like to know how, because unless she or Mr. Whittaker discussed it with you personally, we have to assume you were with them at all times during all discussions about the status of their relationship. Were you?"

"No, sir."

"Then your accusation is not based on fact, but on your own opinion. Opinions can be dangerous when confused as fact."

"It's a fact that she's hanging out with that spawn of Satan sitting next to her."

Mr. Hopper frowned. "Those are strong words, Ms. Byrd."

It was obvious Mr. Hopper didn't like Courtney, and maybe she was a pain in the neck, but Jordan wished the man would back off. So what if she didn't clap? Did he have to call her out like this?

"He caused Mark Summers to get *boils*," Courtney said. "All he did was touch Mark's face, and all of a sudden, he was covered in boils. He's evil!"

"How do you know Mr. Summers wasn't already ill?"

"I don't, but I do know that Jordan is cheating on poor Matthew. I saw the new guy come into the school and the way he looked at her, and no way did they just meet. Now they're inseparable, and it doesn't take a genius to figure out that they've got something going on. She's blowing Matthew off because he's paralyzed, and he got that way *because of her*. I think it's disgusting. *She's* disgusting."

Jordan flinched as if she'd been hit. Courtney gave voice to all the things that had been in her head since the first time Key had kissed her, except she hadn't blown Matthew off because he was paralyzed. She didn't think she'd blown him off at all.

Or had she? Turning her head to look at Key, who was

scowling at Courtney, she remembered all over again why she came back. Pleading with her to stay, his raw despair had exposed what was deep within his soul, and it had nothing to do with Hell. It made no sense, considering she was dead at the time, but she'd never felt so alive, as if something inside of her that had been asleep her whole life had woken up.

Being with him hadn't changed that feeling. He could be hard, cold, and autocratic, but all of that was only one side of him, something he'd grown into after over a thousand years of leading his brothers. She'd witnessed another side of Key, and that was what she was drawn to, what she couldn't stay away from. Even now, knowing how he felt about Eryx, her blood practically hummed when he was around. And while she loved Matthew, and always would, she was beginning to realize that it was more about friendship than romance. That's why she'd never gone all the way with Matthew. And why it was difficult to stop with Key.

Still, she felt guilty, and Courtney had managed to say it out loud, and everyone was darting glances at her and Key, obviously beginning to think along the same lines as Courtney. Jordan could almost feel the tide turning against her.

Mr. Hopper stared at Courtney for a long time, clearly angry, but when he finally spoke, his voice was even and calm. "Ms. Byrd, please leave my classroom and don't return. I'm certain Mr. Barnes can reassign you to another section of government."

"You're kicking me out? You can't do that!"

"I can, and I am."

"I have to have this class to be admitted at Princeton!"

"Then you'll have to meet the requirement elsewhere. You are unteachable." He went to the door and opened it. "Good-bye."

Courtney gathered up her backpack while everyone stared in shock.

Jordan disliked Courtney as much as anyone, and pretty much everyone did, except her silly Bees. She thought the girl did more harm to Christianity than good, turning people off before they ever heard a word of the real message.

But there was some truth to what she had said, and it wasn't as if she had spread gossip, whispering behind Jordan's back, accusing her of being a cheat. No, she'd been forced to say what she thought, and now she was being punished for it.

Courtney was almost to the door when Jordan called out, "Mr. Hopper, may I say something?"

The queen of the Bible Bees turned around, tears streaming down her face, and looked across the room at Jordan.

Mr. Hopper said, "If you have something to add, yes. If you merely want to chastise Ms. Byrd, then no."

She glanced at Key, who was staring at her with the strangest look in his eyes, then looked at Brody, who was smiling his sweet smile. He gave a tiny, almost imperceptible nod of his head.

Swallowing hard, she said, "Courtney is right that Key and I are more than friends, but she's wrong about Matthew. We aren't going out anymore."

Key said, "Jordan, you don't owe any of these people an explanation."

"I'm not saying this for anyone but Mr. Hopper and Courtney. She was forced to say what she believes to be true, and I don't think it's fair for her to be punished so harshly."

"We'll put it to a vote," Mr. Hopper said. "All those in favor of Ms. Byrd remaining in this class, raise your hand."

Jordan, Brody, and the two Buzzkills were the only hands. Courtney was turning away when Eryx said, "Jordan has a point. Courtney may be judgmental, but she's not a liar. I say she stays." He raised his hand.

Jordan wondered what he was up to. Why stand up for Courtney? If he thought he could collect her soul, he was way wrong. Courtney's faith in God was solid.

Since Eryx's hand was in the air, all the girls in the room raised their hands, too, along with the lost souls—of course. With so many voting yes, the rest of the class followed suit. Except Key.

"Mr. DeKyanos, do you abstain," Mr. Hopper asked, "or is your vote no?"

"My vote is no."

"Because she called you a spawn of Satan?"

"She can call me whatever she likes. I vote no because she insulted Jordan, who went to Hell and back, then accused her of cheating on the guy who was shot trying to save her. The fact that Courtney got a little bit of it right, which is that I did stare at Jordan when I came into the school, and sat next to her in every class because I'm extremely attracted to her, doesn't qualify her for a pass, even if Jordan thinks it does. She's too nice for her own good."

Most of the hands went down again.

Mr. Hopper said, "The nays have it, Ms. Byrd. Good-bye." After she walked out, he closed the door and returned to his lectern. "Now then, let's discuss judicial process and the necessity of evidence."

❧

Lunch was just after government, and Jordan said to Key, "I usually stay on campus for lunch, because it's easier for the Secret Service, but I really want to get out of here for a while. Let's get Hank and Gunther to take us for a cheeseburger."

So he, Brody, and Jordan wound up in the backseat of a Suburban with dark windows, on their way to Five Guys for a burger. Gunther drove, and Hank rode shotgun. When they arrived, Hank looked back at Jordan. "Stay here with Gunther while I run a sweep. If anything looks weird, I'll get takeout and we'll eat it in the car."

Jordan nodded, and as soon as the man was out of the SUV, Key said, "Tell me what you meant in Hopper's class about Matthew."

Without a word, she pulled her cell phone out of her purse, tapped a few buttons, and held it up to show him. It was a blonde with an amazing body, lying naked on a bed.

"This is Tori," she whispered, "and this is Matthew's bed."

Key took it from her and peered at it closely. He was almost certain it had been altered. There was a rim of dark around Tori's blonde hair, as if her image had been placed on top of someone else's. Someone with dark hair. Like Jordan. He glanced at her and saw the hurt in her eyes. He didn't have to tell her. It'd be better for him if he didn't tell her, because it would be easier for her to leave Matthew behind. But the look in her eyes bothered him. She was so hurt, so stung by betrayal, that he couldn't let it be. "Did Matthew ever take your picture, lying on his bed?"

"Yeah, but I wasn't naked."

He held the phone between them and pointed to the dark rim. "Somebody Photoshopped her into a picture of you."

"Why?"

"Maybe they sent it to Matthew as a prank, and he never deleted it off his phone."

"Could be," Brody said. "Guys do stuff like that."

"But why?"

Brody smiled. "Because naked girls never stop being interesting."

"Why Photoshop her into a picture of me so it looks like she's on Matthew's bed?"

"It's twisted," Brody said, "but it's kind of a turn-on to see a naked girl on your bed, even if it's not real."

"Look, don't try to analyze it," Key said. "Just know that Matthew didn't take a picture of that girl on his bed, so whatever he told you is a lie."

She was peering at the picture, wanting to believe what they said. "When I said I didn't believe him, he told me to ask her. Why would he say that if it wasn't true?"

"He knew you wouldn't ask her," Brody said. "Some girls would, but you wouldn't, and he knows it."

"I'm something of an expert on photo alteration," Gunther said. "Mind if I have a look?"

"Only if you swear not to ogle Tori when you see her at school," Jordan said.

"Never been much of an ogler, especially of children." He reached his hand back, and Key set the phone on his palm. Gunther took one look and said, "Yep, Photoshop. A really bad job, too." He handed the phone back. "Your boyfriend wants you to think he slept with her so you'll stay away from him. I'd run with it, at least until he comes around."

Hank returned and said, "Everything looks okay. Let's eat."

As they got out of the car and walked toward the restaurant, Key watched Jordan's face, expecting her to look happy. Instead, she looked more gloomy than she had before. While they stood in line to order, he bent low and whispered in her ear, "Aren't you glad it's not true?"

She nodded, then turned her head and replied, "He had to know how bad that would hurt, and he did it anyway, because he's that desperate to keep me away from him."

"So you're still hurt, even though he didn't actually sleep with her. I don't get it."

"I'm not hurt that he lied. Just terribly sad that he'd go to such an extreme."

Afraid she was about to get wound up on the Eryx subject again, he stood straight and nodded toward the gap in the line. "It's our turn to order."

She moved up and ordered a double cheeseburger, large fries, and a large Coke. Key noticed Hank raised a brow, but Gunther made no indication that he noticed this small young woman just ordered the same thing he had.

～⚬～

Key remembered Jax complaining about school, and now he understood why. Over the years, they'd recruited extremely bright people to be Luminas, some of them specifically as tutors. He and his brothers were well educated, so sitting through classes, hearing lectures on material he already knew, was mind-numbingly boring. The afternoon classes were no better than those of the morning, and he chafed under the realization that he had an entire month of this ahead of him. Why couldn't President Ellis have planned a party for Jordan's return? They'd probably be done with the takedown by now and back at home, working on another takedown somewhere else in the world. Something that wouldn't require Jordan to be this exposed.

Eryx was sly, as always, and Key was constantly on guard and nervous, wondering what he might have up his sleeve.

As was his usual MO in the real world, Eryx was charming, attractive, and always knew exactly the right thing to say. Just

301

like when they had been boys and Eryx had instinctively known things, he knew how to play people because it came naturally to him. By the end of the school day, Eryx had been asked to be on three committees, to play on the soccer team, and to join the yearbook staff. Everyone loved him.

Even Brody found his spot, asked to join the computer club after demonstrating his impressive brainiac tendencies in computer lab.

Key, however, wasn't asked to do anything. Everyone but the lost souls were afraid of him, which he found funny, considering he planned to kill the lost souls by sending them to Hell on Earth and had no interest at all in the others.

When they walked out of the day's last class, English lit, Jordan said, "I have a Student Council meeting, then I'm going home to cook dinner for Dad so Betsy can have the night off. She was pretty upset about her memory lapse this morning."

Aware that Hank was ever present, Key said, "You have my number, so call if you want to talk." He had no intention of leaving her until she was on her way home with Hank and Gunther, but he'd stick around under a cloak so no one would accuse him of stalking.

Thirty minutes later, he was glad he had made that decision.

It started when she walked into the room where Student Council met, and two of the twelve members were lost souls. She hesitated slightly, then continued on to take a seat at the head of the table. After she called the meeting to order, one of the lost souls, a blond guy with a neck like a tree trunk, said, "I'm making a motion for a recall vote for student body president."

Jordan sighed, like she'd known it was coming. "On what grounds, Randy?"

Randy said in a superior tone that was typical of a lost soul, "You're seeing a doctor for post-traumatic stress disorder, and I think we need someone as president who isn't a basket case."

Her cheeks went pink, and Key could see she was furious. She looked toward the corner where he stood, and he said, "Ask him how he knows."

"How do you know anything about my private medical information, Randy?"

"From Tessa."

Her eyes widened in surprise, but whatever she thought about her best friend telling others about her doctor appointment, she kept to herself.

A girl who looked at Jordan with sad eyes, said, "Maybe this *is* too much stress for you right now. I mean, you just got back a few days ago. No one would blame you if you wanted to step down."

Jordan focused on the nice girl. "I haven't even seen a doctor yet. I'm going only because my dad insisted. There's nothing wrong with me, and no, I'm not going to step down. Let's put Randy's motion to a vote. All in favor of a recall vote, raise your hands."

Seven hands went up.

"All opposed?"

Five hands.

"The ayes have it," she said. "I'll have Mrs. Black post the notice in tomorrow's newsletter, and schedule the recall vote for next week. Now, let's have committee reports."

"Aren't you mad?" Randy asked.

She looked to Key again.

"He wants you to be mad," Key said. "Eryx put him up to this to make you mad, hoping you'll lose it in front of all these people."

Focusing on Randy, she said in a dead voice, "I'm not mad. I just wish you weren't a douche."

❧

By the time she got home, Jordan was over Randy's stupid stunt and just wanted to put on a pair of sweats, have a cup of cocoa, and do her homework. First, however, she was going to call Tessa and ask her what she was thinking, telling Randy something so personal.

Tessa answered on the first ring. "Finally! I thought you'd never get out of that meeting. I've been dying to talk to you. Are you at home?"

"Yeah." What was she so excited about? "And I want to talk to you, too. Randy brought a motion for a recall of my office because he says you told him I was seeing a doctor for PTSD. Why would you—"

"I didn't, Jordan! I mentioned it to Eryx, because he seemed so worried about you, and he must have said something to Randy.

I'm so sorry, but no one will vote you out, so no worries. Listen, I've got the most excellent news!"

Wow, way to blow her off. Like sharing something that personal with a guy she barely knew was just a-okay.

"Eryx asked me to Winter Ball! I figured I wouldn't go, since Cory is a jerk face, so I haven't looked for a dress. Will you go shopping with me?"

Jordan paced back and forth between her bed and the window, wanting to go off about Eryx. She wanted to shout, she was so frustrated. But all she could do was say, "I don't like him, Tessa. He's not right, and he scares me."

"You're kidding with me, aren't you?"

"No. I really don't like him. And his eyes are freaky. How can you get past those eyes?"

"Jo, you're crazy! Eryx has the most beautiful eyes I've ever seen. He's smokin' hot and swoon worthy. You need glasses."

Why couldn't Tessa see what Jordan saw? She'd think it was immortality, or Mephisto, but she'd noticed his dead, flat eyes the instant she met him, when Smelly took her blindfold off on the plane. She decided it must be the Anabo in her that allowed her to see who Eryx really was. "I think your hanging out with him is a very bad thing."

"You're blowing my mind, especially considering you were glued to Biker Boy all day. Everyone's talking about it, Jordan. Eryx said he got arrested for too many DUIs, and that's why his aunt moved them here."

305

Jordan's instant reaction was fury, but she swallwed it, telling herself it didn't make any difference what lies Eryx spread, or what people thought. She and Key would be gone in a month. "It's a lie, and you shouldn't believe anything he says about Key. Eryx hates him, and he'll do anything to screw him over."

"How do you know it's a lie? You just met him. And what about Matthew? Since you're stuck on the new guy, everyone thinks you broke up with him because he's paralyzed. I know it's not true, but that's what people are saying, Jordan."

"I didn't break up with him. He texted me last night and broke up with me."

Tessa instantly lost her defensive tone. "Aw, Jordan, I'm so sorry. Are you okay?"

"It just feels strange not to think of him as my boyfriend anymore." In more ways than she could tell Tessa.

"Maybe it's like you said before. He needs some time."

"Maybe, but he sounded pretty certain." He even sent a fake picture and lied to make sure she got the point. But she didn't say anything about that to Tessa. She just didn't have it in her to talk about it.

"Eryx said there's a chance Matthew will get well." Tessa was no doubt trying to make her feel better. "He said there've been cases of people regaining the ability to walk, even after they've been paralyzed."

Jordan went cold all over, horrified at the thought of Eryx offering to heal Matthew, because she knew the payment he'd demand in return. Imagining Matthew as a lost soul made her a little hysterical. And the thought of Tessa pledging the oath made her crazy. She continued pacing. "Please stay away from Eryx. He's going to hurt you, I know it."

"You're such a mother hen. Can't you just be happy for me?"

She'd be happy if Tessa would get over this infatuation with Eryx. "Has he asked you to join his church?"

"No, he's not like Courtney and her Buzzkills, shoving Jesus down people's throats."

He would, eventually, except it wouldn't be Jesus he was selling.

"Please go shopping with me. Don't you want a new dress for Winter Ball?"

"I'm not going with a date, so I'll wear something I already have."

"You're not going with Biker Boy?"

"His name is Key, and he's not the type to go to something like Winter Ball."

"I rest my case. Why are you hanging out with him anyway? Are you rebelling? Is this something to do with your kidnapping? When *are* you seeing that doctor?"

"If I tell you, will you blab it to Eryx? Because I can't lie, Tess. It really bums me out that you told him I'm planning to see a doctor. He spread it around, and now everyone in StuCo thinks I'm too stressed to be president."

"I really am sorry, Jordan, and I swear I won't tell Eryx

anything else. I'm just really worried about you. So do you have an appointment?"

"Next week, on Wednesday."

"Good. Maybe he can tell you why you're interested in a criminal in leather."

"He's not a criminal." He was a son of Hell. She wondered what Tessa would say if she told her. No doubt she wouldn't believe her, and would think it was further proof that Jordan was one step shy of going off the deep end.

Unless Tessa pledged. Then Jordan wouldn't have to tell her. Eryx would. And her best friend would become her enemy.

She thought of Sasha, whose mother had become a lost soul, and her sympathy was so huge, tears pricked her eyes. Now she understood in a way she hadn't before. "I'm really not up for shopping, Tess. Why don't you call Megan?"

"Can I bring what I buy over to show you later?"

It'd be difficult to fake enthusiasm for a dress Tessa would wear on a date with Eryx, but she said yes anyway.

When she was off the phone, she went to her closet to see what she might wear to the ball. She didn't want to go, but it was part of her duty as president to be at school functions.

Except she might not be president by the time of Winter Ball.

FIFTEEN

FRIDAY CAME AND WENT PRETTY MUCH LIKE THURSDAY, except Gunther and Hank took them to a Thai restaurant in Georgetown. Megan Thompson was having a party that night, but Jordan didn't feel like going. Key wasn't invited, and after what happened with Carla, she was a little afraid to be around the lost souls when he wasn't with her. Not to mention, Eryx would be at the party with Tessa, and Jordan couldn't take watching them together.

So she spent Friday night with her dad, which turned out to be a very good thing. They watched a movie, then played Scrabble, and for the first time in months, he didn't look totally stressed out. She avoided asking him anything about politics and instead asked him to tell her about his and her mother's first date. She'd heard it before, but it never got boring.

"I was a geek in high school. You knew that, right?"

Jordan smiled. "Yeah, Dad. I've seen pictures."

"Connie was a year behind me, and we didn't have any classes together, but her locker was next to mine. I used to mess up my stuff during lunch so it'd look legit when I hung around to clean it up after school. I liked waiting for her, just to see her and hear her laugh. It's not like I ever spoke to her. Then, right before graduation, I decided that, since it was close to the end, I might as well go for it." He sat back on the couch and looked up at the portrait of Jordan's mom above the mantel. "I said I'd miss having my locker next to hers, and she said they didn't have lockers at Yale. I was shocked that she knew where I was going." He looked back at Jordan with a wry smile. "I didn't realize she was on the committee that worked on the graduation program, so she knew where everyone was going. I thought she'd actually noticed me, so before I chickened out, I asked her to go to dinner. She said no."

"Poor Dad. Were you crushed?"

"Humiliated." He leaned his head back and stared up at the ceiling. "I was hurrying to grab my books and get out of there when she said she couldn't go that night, but she could go the next. I dropped one of my books on her foot." He chuckled. "Damn, I was smooth."

Jordan laughed. "She should have known then what the date would be like."

"Funny thing about your mother. In spite of all evidence to the contrary, she never stopped believing I was really something. The next day, when my boss at the museum wouldn't let me leave early, I didn't want to be late to pick her up, so I showed up at her house still dressed like George Washington. We were on the way to my house so I could change when I ran into a parked car. I had to call my dad, who came and gave me a lecture about watching where I was going. I didn't confess I'd been staring at Connie. So there I was, in the middle of Constitution Avenue, looking like old George, with my dad fuming, the car wrecked, and the prettiest girl at Oates smiling at me. Even counting election days, that was one of my best days, ever."

Nope, the story never got boring. It was kind of weird to think about them in high school, and not all that easy to think of Dad as Captain Awkward, because he certainly wasn't now, but she had no trouble at all imagining how they fell in love. For as long as she could remember, until the day her mother died, they'd been devoted to each other.

He got to his feet and stretched. "I'm off to bed. Thanks for tonight. We should do this more often." Moving to where she sat cross-legged in a club chair, he bent and kissed her cheek. "Good night, sweetheart."

"Good night, Dad." After he left the living room, she stared up at her mother's portrait for a long time, wishing all over again that she was still here. Jordan sometimes missed her so much, she could almost imagine she heard her voice in the other room.

Feeling sentimental and sad, she went to her bedroom and dragged out the boxes where she kept old photos, cards, and other mementos, taking one last look because she'd have to leave it all behind when she went back to Colorado. Key was adamant about that. The Luminas weren't allowed to bring anything with them, because hanging on to remnants of mortal life made it more difficult to adjust, and Key had said the same rules applied to her.

She slept well that night, for once not waking up in the middle of a nightmare. On Saturday, she cleaned out her closet, bagging up things to be auctioned for charity, then spent the rest of the day going through some of the First Daughter e-mails. She checked a few of the responses Carla had sent and was relieved when she saw nothing in any of them about the Ravens, or Eryx. Key had said he didn't think she'd really do it, because it'd be grounds to get her fired. "Eryx wants her in the White House as long as possible so she can spy for him and keep provoking you."

On Sunday she did homework, but it was hard to stay focused. All she could think about was Key, the Mephisto, Eryx, and the lost souls.

Just before dinner, she was putting her books away when Jax called her cell. "How's it going?" he asked.

Her answer was automatic. "Okay. It's okay."

He took a moment before he said, "How's it really going?"

She sighed and sank down onto the floor, leaning back against her bed. "Awful, Jax. Just terrible. I can't wait to get this done because every day we wait means more lost souls for Eryx, but knowing I'm about to leave for good is so depressing. And it feels as if I'm mad all the time, which isn't like me, and it's exhausting."

"Part of the problem is that you have ten times the strength and energy you had before, and you're not doing anything with it. You need to work out. And you need more training before your birthday party."

"I can work out, but how can I train while I'm living here?"

"It'll have to be at night, after you've supposedly gone to bed. Brody will sit in your room under a cloak, and if someone comes in when you're not there, he'll let us know. Leave the bathroom light on and the door closed to buy some time until you can pop back."

She already felt better. Training was something she could do now, something more than just waiting and worrying. "Okay, I'll be in the gym at around ten, my time."

"That'll work."

She intended not to ask about Key, but before she could stop herself, she did. "Jax, what's he doing now that he doesn't have his greenhouse?"

"I'm not exactly sure. He's been gone since Friday after school and didn't tell anyone where he would be. It's his business, and he deserves his privacy, but Sasha kept wigging out about it, so I did a mental search."

"Did he go to Kyanos?"

"That's what I figured, but no. He's in Bucharest. Sasha thinks he went there to find out who your real parents were."

That seemed like a strange thing for Key to do, because if he believed her parents were angels, he'd know he wasn't going to find them in Bucharest.

"But Sasha tends to be a romantic," Jax said, "and I'm more practical. Since you were most likely born in Romania, I believe he went to see if there are any other Anabo."

That made a lot more sense than looking for her parents. "For your brothers?"

"Yeah, maybe, or he could be looking for another one for himself. If I were him, that's what I'd do."

Her heart began to race. "Wow, Jax, you always know just the wrong thing to say to me."

"What? The truth? If Sasha had stuck to her absolute certainty that she wouldn't become Mephisto and would never be with me, I'd have been out looking for another Anabo every chance I got."

"Your brothers don't search."

"If they had the slightest inkling what it's really like to be with an Anabo, trust me, they'd be searching day and night."

"What about Phoenix? He knows, but he isn't looking."

"Jane accepted him. She was leaving that night to be with him. It's not the same." He was quiet for a while, then said, "You can't have it both ways, Jordan."

"Do you really think he's looking for someone else?"

Silence again, until he sighed. "No. He would never do that, and neither would I. I was just hoping to shake you up a little. Besides, we aren't supposed to search for an Anabo. If it happens, great, but we can't spend time searching for Anabo when we should be looking for lost souls and Skia."

Jordan stared down at the pattern in the rug, thinking about Key in Bucharest, wondering why he was there. As much as she was curious, she wished she was with him. "I'm so confused, and it makes no sense because I meant what I said to him. I still feel exactly the same way about . . . I mean, nothing's changed. So how can I be this ambivalent?"

"Do you want me to give you a nice, politically correct answer, or tell you what I really think?"

If it was anyone else, she'd see the question as condescending. But this was Jax, a Mephisto, a son of Hell, the guy who told her she pushed Holly that last final step. What he really thought could possibly be brutal. But it wouldn't be a lie. "I want you to be honest."

"We've known since before we left Kyanos how he feels about Eryx, so when he told me there was one thing you couldn't get past, I guessed this was it, and he confirmed it."

"Was he upset when you told him you've always known?"

"Well, yeah, because it messes with how he thinks we see him, makes him wonder if maybe we don't respect him as much as he thought."

Her heart swelled with sympathy for Key. His whole identity, everything he did, was wrapped up in leading his brothers. "This is huge, Jax. Even bigger than my telling him I don't think it'll ever happen for us."

"*Nothing* is bigger than that, Jordan. But it goes to the heart of the problem, and why you think you're confused. I don't believe you're confused at all. You know exactly what you want, and you're frustrated and angry because you can't have it."

She'd known this wouldn't be easy. "What do I want?"

"You want Key, but only if he'll change to be *how* you want him. We all want an Anabo who'll like us enough to stay, and we want there to be love because it means we have a chance of Heaven. But as much as anything, we want to be accepted, in spite of what we are. Key has the added burden of what Eryx's death did to him. He's always been a loner because he never wanted us to get close enough to know he doesn't hate Eryx. He let you get that close, and you burned him."

"Should I have lied? It's not some no-big-deal thing, like he asked if I think he's funny, and I said yes so it wouldn't hurt his feelings. This is *who he is*."

"I'm not suggesting you should have lied. But you came back from death, then saved his life because there's something there you can't resist. You want that part of who he is, but you can't accept the other, which is, ironically, the flip side of the same coin. That's why you're constantly conflicted."

"I hear you saying that I just need to get over it, but don't you think I've tried?"

"You've been through a helluva lot, ever since those lost souls broke into Matthew's house, and you've been bombarded with an enormous amount of information and change in a very short time. Why don't you slow down, not fret so much about Key, and enjoy these last weeks with your dad and your friends? Nothing's going to be any different because you freaked out about it. Key's not going anywhere, and neither are we. Eryx will do what he will do, people will pledge or they won't, and nothing you do or say will change that."

"I'll try, Jax." She really would, she promised herself. "And you're right about Key, but you're wrong about my being confused. When he's with me, I'm constantly on edge. When he's not, everything feels wrong."

"Oh, that. You're not confused. You're falling in love. And it sucks almost as much as it's amazing."

"You're as unfunny as Key."

"Who's trying to be funny? I'm dead serious."

❧

From a dark corner of a dirty, smoky bar in the sketchiest part of Bucharest, Key drank cheap whiskey and watched a waitress in a low-cut blouse and skintight pants serve drinks to very drunk patrons. She danced away from their hands, ignored their lewd come-ons, and somehow managed to keep smiling. He supposed it was difficult, but she pocketed a lot of tips, so maybe to her it was worth it.

She came back to his table and gave him that bright, happy smile. "Can I bring you another whiskey?"

He couldn't stop staring at her, unnerved by her resemblance to Jordan. "Where do you go after you're done here? Where do you live?"

She never lost her smile. "In an apartment, with a cat and the mice she's too lazy to kill. How about another drink?"

Nice side step. "Yeah, I'll have another one."

Turning, she walked away, back toward the bar and the husky guy who tended it.

When she returned, he accepted the drink and handed her a hundred-dollar bill. She grinned. "I had a feeling you're American." The bill disappeared into her pocket.

He pointed to the chair across the table. "Give me two minutes."

"I can't sit down or Gustav will be angry. I'm sorry."

Her voice was low and sexy, but he didn't think it was on purpose. She'd been born this way. "I know who you are."

She laughed and pointed to the name badge she wore above her left breast: MARIAH. "It's not a secret."

"I know a lot more about you than your name. You were born in a tiny village fifty miles from here to an older couple who thought they couldn't have children. Not quite two years later, they had another daughter. When she was four, they were killed in a car wreck, and you and your sister came to live with your mother's cousin here in Bucharest."

Her smile had faded as he spoke, and now she was eyeing him apprehensively. "Who are you?"

"My name is Kyros."

She darted a glance toward Gustav, then said softly, "What do you want?"

"I want to know how your sister wound up at an orphanage. Did your mother's cousin take her there?"

"My sister died. You've got the wrong story, or the wrong person." Turning, she walked away from him.

He stayed where he was and drank his whiskey while he continued watching her. As it grew closer to two in the morning, the drunks began to shuffle out, headed for home and hangovers. When he was the only patron left, and she couldn't avoid him any longer, she came to the table and picked up his empty glass. "We're closing now. You should go, because if you don't, Gustav will make you."

"I know she didn't die, Mariah. She was adopted by a man who became the U.S. president."

Her face became more pale. "Please tell me who you are."

"I'm a friend of your sister's." He pulled Jordan's stuffed rabbit out of his trench coat pocket and handed it to her.

Tears instantly filled her blue eyes. "Oh, my God." She inspected it carefully, running her slender fingers across its stitches and its button eyes.

"I came to Bucharest to find who made it, to have it repaired. It took all day yesterday and most of today, but I finally found a little shop in a village fifty miles from here, and the woman who made this was still there. She remembered your family. All I want to know is why your sister wound up at an orphanage."

"If you're her friend, you'll leave right now and never, ever tell her what you've learned."

"She and I are a lot more than friends, and I can't keep something like this from her. I'd like to keep it from everyone else in the world, but not from her. She's going to want answers, and there's no doubt she'll want to see you, but for now, I just want to know why she was in an orphanage."

She took a step closer. "How did you get the rabbit? Did you steal it when you stole her? Did you have something to do with her kidnapping?"

That surprised him, and he blinked, answering automatically. "I rescued her."

"You're a liar. She was left in Hyde Park by her captors."

"That's what the world believes, but that's not what happened. You tell me about the orphanage, and I'll tell you the real story of her abduction." He intended to erase her memory of him before he left, so he'd tell her anything if it would make her open up.

She glanced at Gustav again, then turned and whispered, "I took her there."

"Why? How? You were six."

Gustav's voice boomed across the bar. "That floor's not going to mop itself, Mariah."

She handed the rabbit back to Key and said in a hurry, "I'll be done here in an hour. Meet me outside, down at the corner."

Key got to his feet and walked out of the place, glad to breathe some clean air. Leaning against the building, he looked up at the night sky. His theory that Sasha and Jordan were born of angels was shot to hell, but he still wondered if M had asked God to provide more Anabo. The woman in the shop had told him Jordan's parents were in their forties when they had Mariah, whom the doctors had called a miracle because her mother had been told she couldn't have children. When she got pregnant again about a year later, she had actually been written up in a medical journal because it was so incredible. They were warm, generous, kind people, delighted beyond all reason over their beloved daughters.

If God in his infinite wisdom were to handpick parents for an Anabo, wouldn't he choose people like that? Not only kind, but older, so when and if their daughter was discovered by the Mephisto, if she left real life, it wouldn't be so long for them to grieve the loss.

Except a car wreck had ended their lives too soon, long before Mariah and Jordan were grown. The shopkeeper hadn't known what had happened after the couple died and their daughters went to live with other family members.

In the grand scheme of things, what happened after that didn't make any difference, but he was compelled to find out. Jordan would want to know. *He* wanted to know. How had she wound up in an orphanage? Why had she been separated from her sister?

He'd called Brody, sworn him to silence, and asked him to find out what he could about Mariah. When he called back and said there was an eighteen-year-old Mariah Ardelean in Bucharest and her work records showed she was employed at a place called Gustav's, Key got the address and went there first, hoping she was working tonight, hoping it was the right Mariah. He'd taken one look at her and had no doubt. Her resemblance to Jordan was still blowing his mind. She was taller and curvier, and her blue eyes were a shade darker than bluebell, but she had the same dark hair, and her features were uncannily similar.

As promised, Mariah was done in an hour, and when she stepped outside, bundled in a ratty-looking coat and an old scarf, she looked up at him and said, "Let's walk."

He fell in step with her as she went down the street, impatient for her to tell him what he wanted to know.

At the corner, while they waited for cars to pass, she looked up at him again. "Is there any way I can convince you not to tell my sister about me?"

He shook his head. "Not a chance. Why don't you want her to know? Wouldn't you like to see her?"

She focused on the top button of his coat. "It's just that I want her to be happy, and nothing about any of this is good. I thought that someday, when we're older, when she's settled and not living in the White House under a microscope, I'd see her and explain. She'd want to know. But she's still so young, barely seventeen."

"Barely? She'll be eighteen in three weeks."

Mariah raised her gaze to his. "She was born on Christmas Day. She just turned seventeen. I turned eighteen last February."

"Did the orphanage not know how old she was?"

Mariah shook her head. "They didn't know anything about her.

Either they made up a birthday for her, or her adopted parents did."

"Please tell me what happened."

She studied him for a bit. "You're in love with her, aren't you?"

"Does it matter?"

"How are you here? And why? No guy I know would come so far to get a girl's stuffed animal repaired. There must be a million places you could have gone to in the States."

She was extremely suspicious, which said a lot about her. Mariah wasn't the least bit naive. Or trusting. What had happened to make her this way? Why was a girl so young working in a dive like Gustav's?

He could see that he had to do something to win her trust. So he lied. "I'm here for a family funeral. Jordan's rabbit was torn up because of me, an accident, and she's so attached to it, I thought it'd make her happy if I found where it had been made and took a picture. I didn't expect to find out so much, but now that I know, I'd like to have the whole story."

Mariah dropped her eyes to his button again and sighed. "My mother's cousin, Nadia, was married to a horrible man named Emilian. We'd been living there only a week when he broke my arm. He'd get angry and lock me in a closet and wouldn't give me any food for days at a time."

Clenching his fists, Key felt an overwhelming need to choke the life out of Emilian.

"It's said that very young children who are abused don't know it's not normal, because that's all they know. So maybe if our parents hadn't been so loving, I wouldn't have understood how wrong it was. But I knew he was evil, and as much as I hated what he did to me, I couldn't bear watching him torment Viorica. She was so happy, so sweet, and I didn't want what happened to me to happen to her. So I took her and ran away."

Viorica. Jordan's birth name was Viorica. Romanian for bluebell. "Where did you go? Where did you *plan* to go?"

"As you said, I was six. I had no plan. I just knew I had to get her out of there. Emilian was already pinching her hard enough to leave bruises. I sometimes wonder if God led me, because I took refuge inside a church that happened to have an orphanage. I hid there for two days, trying to decide if I should ask the priest for help, but I was afraid he'd call Emilian and we'd be sent back. I'd been watching what went on at the building across the street, the children in the play yard, and the nuns who looked after them. I realized those children lived there, that they had no parents, no family. So I took Viorica late in the night and left her on the doorstep, rang the bell, then hid to watch, to make sure the nuns took her in."

The cars had long since passed, and she stepped off the curb.

"Why did you leave her? Why didn't you stay, as well?"

"I knew if I didn't go back and make up a story about Viorica, Nadia would search for us, and she might look where orphans live." She walked with her head down, her hands in the pockets of her coat. "So I went back and told her I had gotten lost when

Viorica and I followed a dog down the street. We couldn't find our way home, and when we were in a crowd of people, a lady picked up my sister and took her away. Maybe because Viorica was such a beautiful child, Nadia believed my story. She made a halfhearted attempt to find her, but I know they were glad to be rid of her."

"Didn't they call the police?"

She glanced up at him. "Emilian wouldn't let Nadia call."

"What about neighbors? Didn't anyone ask what had happened to your sister?"

"If anyone noticed one of us was missing, they must have assumed she'd been visiting or something. We'd only been there two months when I ran away. And even if they were curious, no way they would have knocked on the door and asked. Emilian and Nadia never spoke to their neighbors and had no friends. You really can't imagine what horrible people they were."

"You'd be surprised. I'm kind of an expert on evil people."

Her eyes were assessing. "You seem . . . different. How do you know my sister?"

"It's a long story." As they turned a corner, he asked, "Didn't Emilian and Nadia recognize Jordan when her adoptive father became president and she became a public figure?"

Mariah's speed increased just a little, enough to clue him in that she was nervous. "Nadia died from cancer before he was elected president, but yes, Emilian knew it was Viorica, and he had big plans to demand money in exchange for not taking her back. He also wanted to extort money for his silence. How would it look if the American president had adopted a child with legitimate guardians? That President Ellis didn't know wouldn't have made any difference, because there would be people who'd insist he *did* know. Emilian would have threatened to go public and play up how Viorica was stolen from him. I was so afraid for her. She didn't know any of this, and having that slime crawl out of the gutter and come after her family . . . I couldn't let it happen. By then, I was almost fourteen, and after all that time, after what I did to save her from Emilian, I wasn't going to let him screw up her life."

"How did you stop him?"

Her steps became more brisk. "It turned out I didn't have to do anything. He died when his house burned down. He was a drunk, and a smoker. He passed out with a cigarette, and that was that."

She was extremely anxious and scared, which made him wonder if Mariah had had something to do with the fire. "When did Nadia die?"

"When I was twelve. After she was gone, Emilian started . . . everything got worse."

Key wished he didn't know it could get worse than what she'd already described, but he knew all too well the unimaginable things humans were capable of.

Watching her, seeing how afraid she was, knowing all the grief and horror she'd endured in her life, he felt like a stone had settled in his heart. And yet, in spite of what she'd lived through, there was goodness in her, so powerful he could feel it. "After he died, what did you do?"

"I lived with the woman across the road, who wasn't unkind, but she expected me to work for my keep. I cooked and cleaned, and when I was old enough, I went to work for her son."

"Gustav?"

She nodded. "He's gruff and hard, but generous, and he makes sure none of the customers get out of hand. About six months ago, his mother passed on, and he sold her house. That's when I got my own apartment."

"Are you . . . with someone?"

"No. I'm never going to be with someone. I don't even date." She shot him another glance. "I don't like men."

"You mean, you're—"

"No, I just don't like guys. You saw, in the bar. You know. And after Emilian . . . " She sighed. "So are you going to tell me how you met my sister, and about her kidnapping, and who you really are? Because I'm pretty sure you're not a regular guy."

"What makes you think so?"

"There's something about you, a little bit spooky. No offense."

"None taken. As soon as we get to your apartment and you get your cat, I'll tell you everything."

"What do you mean, get my cat? Do you think I'm going somewhere with you?"

"I'll explain when we get there, and you can decide if you

want to go, or not." He'd already decided to take her to Colorado. He and his brothers had always discussed whether or not to recruit someone as a Lumina, but this time he wasn't going to wait. He wasn't going to ask. Jordan's sister was as close to Anabo as any human could be. He could feel the warmth of her soul, knew as well as he knew his name that she needed to be with them. She needed Jordan. Maybe she wouldn't agree to stay and become a Lumina, but he had to ask.

"Just so you know, if you didn't have her bunny, I wouldn't be taking you to where I live, and I wouldn't have told you anything. I don't ever talk about her with anyone."

"How do you know it's the same bunny?"

"Viorica's initials are embroidered inside its ear."

She slowed down, then stopped at a door in a building that looked ready to be condemned. He followed her inside and up seven flights of rickety stairs. Despite the fact that it was past three in the morning, loud music came from behind a few of the doors they passed in her hallway, and he heard a guy shouting at someone, then glass breaking. The disgusting stench of meth permeated the place. He definitely needed to get her out of here. Immediately.

Her apartment was like her coat—old, shabby, and too small, but clean.

The cat was there, winding between her legs, meowing. As soon as Mariah picked her up, Key reached for her arm and popped them to Colorado, to the front hall of the house.

She blinked and stepped away, clutching the cat. "Holy God, *what* just happened?"

Key was about to reassure her that she was safe, but before he could say anything, he heard Phoenix say from the upstairs hall, "It smells like Yorkshire in here. Like heather."

Sasha said, "All I smell is short ribs. I'm starving."

Key looked up as his brother and Sasha came to the top of the stairs. They both stopped dead and stared at Mariah. Phoenix went pale, clearly stunned.

"Key, who is this?" Sasha asked with a note of wonder. "Oh, wow, she's got to be Jordan's sister. Is she? Where was she? Does Jordan know?" She said all of this as she hurried down the stairs.

Phoenix remained on the top step, completely still.

"Hello, I'm Sasha. Poor thing, you look scared to death. Please don't be. You're safe here." She turned to Key, and her smile nearly blinded him. "This is absolutely incredible! Another Anabo!"

Key jerked his gaze to Mariah. "I don't think so, Sasha. She's exceptional, but not Anabo."

Mariah's cat meowed, probably because she was being squeezed too tightly.

"Of course she is! Can't you see her glow? It's very dim, but maybe she's not feeling well." She smiled at Mariah. "Are you okay?"

Eyes wide with bewilderment, Mariah said in Romanian, "I don't speak English."

Sasha repeated what she'd said in Romanian, and Mariah took a step back, looking desperately at Key. "Please take me home."

"I know this is confusing," he said, "but no one's going to hurt you, I swear it."

Mariah didn't relax at all, clutching her cat to her chest as if she were a lifeline.

Key couldn't see the glow, but he felt the brightness of her spirit. Maybe Sasha was right and Mariah was Anabo. Maybe her glow had dimmed because of what Emilian had done to her. Maybe Sasha could see it because she was Anabo.

Looking up, he asked Phoenix, "Can you see it?"

Phoenix was staring hard at Mariah, as if he was powerless to look away. "No, but I can feel . . . I can . . . " His voice was low and rough.

Key thought about what Phoenix had said before he saw Mariah. His brother smelled heather, but Sasha didn't. Key didn't. There was no heather anywhere in the house.

There was only Mariah.

Oh, hell, no. It couldn't be.

But it was. Mariah must be Anabo, and, incredibly, Phoenix was the lucky one who caught her scent. Except he didn't look like he'd just been blessed with the best thing to happen to any Mephisto. He looked like his whole world had been sucked into a black hole. Here was another Anabo meant for him, another chance, but in his brother's twisted mind of guilt and grief, the instinctive need to pursue her meant he had to leave Jane behind.

Phoenix's greatest wish and his worst nightmare stood on the Mephisto *M*.

Key looked at Mariah, who was staring back at Phoenix much like a small animal would look at a lion, and wondered what he had done.

SIXTEEN

IT WAS PAST MIDNIGHT IN D.C. WHEN JORDAN POPPED BACK
to the White House from the Mephisto gym, and she was surprised to find Key instead of Brody waiting for her. Dressed in
jeans and a long-sleeved black T-shirt, he sat in the chair by the
window, cloaked, staring down at her rabbit, which she could see
had been repaired.

So that's why he went to Bucharest. That he'd do something
like that made her heart turn over. Moving to stand in front of
him, she saw uncertainty in his dark eyes when he lifted his head
and looked up at her. He held the rabbit out, and she blindly
accepted it, unable to tear her gaze away from his. "Thank you,"
she whispered.

He stood slowly, and she stepped into his arms, dropping the bunny to the chair behind him at the same time he bent to kiss her, his lips deliberate and gentle. When he lifted his head, she stared up into his eyes and knew something was different. The hard edge was gone, and in its place was . . . sympathy? "Why are you looking at me like that?"

"I have something to tell you, Jordan. It's easier if I show you, so Brody will be back in a minute and stay while we're gone."

"What's going on? Is there something wrong?"

"No, it's . . . why don't you put on some jeans and a sweater and a jacket?"

"Just tell me if everything's all right."

"It's fine. Go on and change."

She went in her closet, pulled off her workout clothes, then grabbed a pair of jeans and a sweater. She was ready in less than three minutes, just about the time Brody popped back into her room.

"We'll be back in a couple of hours," Key said as he turned on the bathroom light and closed the door.

"I'll be here," Brody said.

Then Key took her hand, put her under a cloak, and everything went dark. When she could see again, they were standing in a copse of trees, facing a narrow road. A small cottage of stone and wood was on the other side, a compact red sedan parked in front. It had foreign plates. The sun was up, but it was still early. "We're in Europe, aren't we?"

His hand tightened around hers. "Romania, about fifty miles

from Bucharest. That's the house where you lived until you were almost four."

Getting the rabbit repaired wasn't all he'd done over the weekend. He'd searched for her past and found it. Staring at the little house, she waited for anything resembling a memory, but there was nothing. "How do you know?"

While they stood there in the trees, he told her how he had looked for the shop where the rabbit came from, and was about to give up when a guy in an antique store told him about a woman in this village who made stuffed animals from scraps of cotton. The world went dark again, and when she could see, they were in a narrow alley between two buildings, looking across a cobblestone street at a small tailor's shop. Lined up in the window was a collection of stuffed animals. "She remembered your family, Jordan. Your parents were older, and very kind."

"So they weren't angels."

He told her his new theory, and it sounded a lot more reasonable.

"But why are you so sure your father asked God for more Anabo? I know he said something to you, but maybe you misinterpreted it. Maybe it's just coincidence that Sasha and I were born a year apart. For all you know, there could be lots of Anabo out there, and you just haven't found them. There could have been Anabo born all through the centuries, and the Mephisto just weren't aware."

"Maybe a few, but not many. We spend a lot of time searching for the lost souls and Skia. For some of the Luminas, it's a full-time job. If an Anabo was out there, chances are good one of us would have seen her." He shook his head. "Knowing my father and his obsession with making sure we get to Heaven, I'm convinced this isn't a coincidence. I'll never know for sure, because he'll never admit it, but I think he asked for more Anabo, and God came through. He gave you to an older couple who thought they couldn't have children."

That she didn't know them, would never know them, pulled at her soul. "What happened to them?"

Once more, everything went dark, and the next place they landed wasn't nearly so quaint and pretty as before. The street was lined with very old, run-down houses. "They were killed in a car accident when you were three, and you came here, to Bucharest, to live with your mother's cousin and her husband. Their house was right over there, where there's now a newer house. The one you lived in burned down several years ago."

"If I lived with family, how did I end up at the orphanage? Did they die, too?"

Again, he transported them, and they were standing on the steps of a church. Across the street was a youth center in an old building made of red bricks. "That was the orphanage."

"But how did I come to be there, Key?"

Still gripping her hand, he turned toward her and reached up with his free hand to smooth her hair away from her face. "Your sister took you."

"My *sister*? Wait. What? I had a *sister*?"

"You *have* a sister."

Stunned, she sank down to sit on the step, and Key sat beside her. For the next half hour, he told her about the sister she never knew she had, and what she'd done for Jordan. Staring across the street, she imagined a child of six taking her sister there, late at night, and leaving her, to save her. The building blurred as tears gathered in her eyes. "How can I not remember her?"

"You were barely four. Most people don't remember anything of their childhood earlier than five or six."

"How did she do that when she was only six?"

"Desperation and fear. Emilian was the worst kind of human being."

And Mariah had gone back to him, instead of staying at the orphanage. She'd sacrificed herself for Jordan.

All her long-avoided, deeply buried memories of Holly came to her, one after the other—the bruises, the burns, the haunted look in her eyes, and when she was older, the most evil violation. She hinted, she said strange things, she insinuated, but she wouldn't admit it, no matter how many times Jordan had asked, because she knew her stepfather would be arrested, and he was all that kept them from being homeless. By then, her mother was too deep into alcoholism to hold a job. Jordan had pleaded with Holly to let her tell her father, or take her to the police, or call the child-abuse hotline, but Holly always said no, and she had threatened to kill herself if Jordan didn't leave it alone.

Jordan had never doubted it wasn't an empty threat.

Then, on a bright, sunny autumn day, she came to see Jordan, to say good-bye, and finally said out loud what she'd denied for so long. Her stepfather had raped her. She'd taken her mother's old beater car, planning to leave Washington to find her real father. Jordan had to tell her why she couldn't do that, and she'd never, ever forget watching hope die in Holly's eyes.

After much cajoling, Holly finally agreed to let Jordan talk to her dad, and let him get help for her, but before he'd even left the Oval Office to come up to the residence, Holly ran. Jordan went after her, with Maggie driving, but by the time they got to Holly's house in Virginia, she was dead. She'd hanged herself from a two-by-four, exposed by a hole in the roof.

Had it been like that for Mariah? Had she lived through the same horror that Holly had? She couldn't stand this, couldn't bear the weight of crushing, terrible guilt. Bending forward, she hugged her thighs and rocked back and forth, silently sobbing. She felt Key's hand gently stroking her back, heard his soothing words, but she couldn't be consoled. "Why would she do that? *Why* did she go back . . . to him . . . why did she *stay there*?"

"Because if only one of you could be safe from him, it had to be you, because you were younger. Because she loved you."

All because she was born second, instead of first. And because her sister loved her. A sister she didn't know at all. Her sister, who may have killed a man to keep him away from Jordan. She cried harder, her stomach twisting into a knot, her whole body shaking. "Do you . . . think she . . . started the fire?"

His hand stopped, and he didn't answer.

Jordan looked up and saw her misery reflected in his eyes. "Key?"

He withdrew his hand and turned to face the street. "I haven't told you everything about Mariah. I took her to Colorado because, in spite of all she's been through, there's this incredible goodness in her, so strong, I could feel it. When we got there, she was freaking out because I hadn't explained anything yet, but before I could even start, Sasha saw her." He looked up at the now cloudy sky. "She saw that Mariah is Anabo."

Jordan sucked in a quick breath, astonishment quickly followed by dread. How had Sasha seen it, but Key hadn't?

"I called my father, because I had to know if Emilian was a lost soul. It would be hard for an Anabo with no Mephisto in her to kill a lost soul, but it'd be impossible for her to kill a human who still belonged to God."

Wiping tears from her cheeks, she whispered, "Was he a lost soul?"

He shook his head slowly. "Just evil in person. M said he shouted all the way to Hell. Most damned souls cry and beg to be forgiven, or allowed a second chance, but not Emilian."

Jordan stuffed her freezing hands into the pockets of her jacket. "So she didn't kill him?" *Say no. Please say no.*

"I don't think she set the fire, but I think she knew when it started and did nothing to stop it. She was so afraid, she did the impossible." His expression was tormented. "That's why I couldn't see that she's Anabo. What he did to her, and what she didn't do for him, is destroying her."

Unable to speak because she was crying so hard, Jordan could only stare back at him.

"And as if everything wasn't bad enough for her, she's meant for Phoenix."

Jordan wiped the tears from her face and rubbed her nose on the back of her hand. "How . . . how do you . . . know?"

"He caught her scent like ten seconds after we arrived at the house." He rested his forearms against his thighs and bent his head to stare at the ground between his boots. "Even after all my time in the world, I don't understand how life can be so cruel. She needs help. She needs somebody who has a way with the wounded. Why couldn't it have been Ty? Phoenix looked at her as if she were Lucifer, come to take him to Hell."

She remembered the day she came to the Mephisto Mountain, how frightened and unsure of everything she was, but at least she'd known who they were and what they were about. Mariah must have been scared out of her mind, and to have Phoenix look at her like *she* was the scary one? Jordan wanted to go punch him in the face. "If she's meant for him . . . why, Key? Why would he do that?"

"He had no warning, nothing at all to prepare him. He hit the top of the stairs, and there she was in the front hall." Key took a deep breath and huffed it out, like he was trying to control the urge to cry. "He'll want *so much* to be with her, but he'll make her suffer for it. He'll resent her for interfering with his obsessive need to keep Jane's memory alive. I've hoped for another Anabo for him, but I imagined she'd be strong and independent, someone who'd give him whatever it is he needs to finally forgive himself and move on. Instead, it's Mariah, and after all she's been through . . . *why* did it have to be Phoenix?"

Watching him agonize over his decision to take Mariah to Colorado, Jordan forced herself to pull it together and moved closer to him, until she was pressed against his side. "She's hurt, true, and it'll take her a long time to heal, but she must be insanely strong and independent to do what she did. And it's not like she'll be alone on the mountain with just Phoenix. I'll be there, and Sasha, and Jax." She rested her head against his shoulder. "And you."

He let out a short bark of a humorless laugh. "Yeah, like I'll be so much help to her."

"You've already helped her. She wouldn't be better off staying in Bucharest."

"I'm not so sure. I feel like a traitor to my brother for saying it, but I did her no favor by bringing her to Phoenix. He's incredibly screwed up, and she's in so much pain, her light's all but gone out. With everyone on the mountain being there for her, especially you, she could get better and even be happy, but not if Phoenix won't leave her alone. And he won't. He'll most likely ignore her for a while, which will be a blessing, but eventually, he'll be absolutely compelled to be with her. He won't be able to help himself."

As it began to snow, she slipped her arms around his neck. "Is it that strong, Kyros?"

He lifted his head and met her eyes. "I'd risk everything just to stand next to you. Yeah, it's that strong."

Pulling him toward her, she kissed him, and he turned and wrapped his arms around her, burying his face in her hair. They sat like that for a long time, on the steps of the old church, hugging each other in the falling snow.

❦

Half an hour later, Jordan stood with Key in the third-floor hallway at the door to the bedroom next to hers. She was shaky and anxious as he knocked, and she felt relieved when Sasha opened the door. She hated to think of her sister being alone right now. Sasha smiled at her. "Mariah and I were just talking about cats."

As Jordan stepped into the room, a big orange tabby wound around her ankles, meowing loudly, but Jordan didn't pay it much attention; all of her focus was on the dark-haired girl getting up from where she'd been sitting at the end of the bed. It was there, the unmistakable glow of Anabo, but not nearly so obvious as Sasha's. She was pretty, with big blue eyes and a soft, hesitant smile.

"Mariah," she whispered.

"Viorica," her sister replied.

Then they were hugging and crying, and Jordan didn't notice when Key and Sasha left.

❧

It had been snowing in Bucharest earlier, and it was snowing in Yorkshire now. Carrying two rapiers, Key materialized in the countryside close to the moors where they used to live, next to Jane's grave, and looked through the falling snow at his brother.

Phoenix glared at him. "No. Just . . . *no*."

He hadn't expected Phoenix to welcome him, especially here, where his love was buried, but he wasn't leaving until they'd had it out. His brother needed to see blood, particularly Key's.

Sliding out of his coat, he tossed it aside and moved toward Phoenix, gripping the hilt of one sword in position to begin a match. He tossed the other into the air, and for a nanosecond, he thought Phoenix might let it split his head in two, but he caught it in the nick of time and immediately pointed it directly at Key. "You arrogant, overbearing piece of *shit*, you had no right. *None*. There was no discussion, no request."

His brother didn't know anything about Mariah, because he'd popped out almost as soon as she'd arrived. He had to know she was Jordan's sister, because the resemblance was so strong, and he definitely knew she was Anabo, because he'd caught her scent. But that was it for him. He didn't want to know anything more. He had come to Jane immediately. It was just as Key feared, and he didn't have any idea what to do about it.

Except fight. And so, here he was, sword in hand, about to

spill a lot of blood because Phoenix couldn't handle Mariah's existence. "She's all that's good. And she's Jordan's sister."

"I don't give a damn if she's *our* sister. Nobody brings a Lumina recruit to the mountain without asking."

"Let's skip the bullshit, Phoenix. Do you want to fight, or do you want to stand there and yell at me?"

"I'd like to cut your heart out and feed it to the buzzards."

Key whipped his rapier through the air. "Bring it."

Phoenix lunged, and Key parried, the loud ping of steel against steel ringing through the cold morning air. Next to Jax, Key'd always been the best of them when it came to swords, but not today. Phoenix had cold, steady rage running through him. It wouldn't last, but for now, Key knew his brother hated him as much as he hated Eryx. And no one hated Eryx as much as Phoenix. Not even Jordan.

His brother fought with single-minded purpose, fierce and powerful, his black eyes hard with hate. Key wasn't going to hold back and let him win, but when Phoenix thrust his blade into his only weak spot and skewered his side, he realized he just might lose. He redoubled his effort, but Phoenix forced him into retreat, and they moved around the perimeter of Jane's grave. He hadn't eaten, so he was weakening, and Phoenix knew it.

"Take her back."

"You can't be serious. Her life is crap, Phoenix." He made another thrust, but his brother easily deflected and countered with his own, slicing into Key's upper arm. "She's not just some girl, not just Jordan's sister. She's Anabo, and we need her."

"*I* don't need her." He was savage in his attack, his rapier moving with lightning speed.

Grimacing in pain when Phoenix sliced across his chest, Key came back and slipped beneath his guard, landing a hard jab into his brother's shoulder. "She's another soldier in our dirty war."

Phoenix came after Key and made another slice across his chest, shredding what was left of his shirt so that it hung in tatters from his shoulders. The snow on the ground was stained with blood, mostly Key's. Phoenix was practically snarling. "*Always* about the job, isn't it, brother? God forbid you do *anything* that isn't about Mephisto."

Key waited to feel righteous, to be pissed off enough really to go after Phoenix. He *hated* it when one of them accused him of caring more about their war with Eryx than about his brothers. Didn't they realize what he did for them? Did they have no clue how much he cared about them?

Seeing the pure hatred in Phoenix's eyes, he knew the answer was no. They saw him as an asshole dictator, a machine without feelings.

His righteousness never materialized, and he wasn't angry. Instead, he was overwhelmed with sorrow. His brothers didn't know him at all, and it was his own fault for distancing himself from them. And as much as they didn't know him, did he really know them? They had formed alliances with one another centuries ago, while Key had held himself apart, always the watcher, the referee, never in the game. He had grieved for Eryx, living in the past, and had missed what had been in front of him all along.

He was tired. So tired. But Phoenix needed a real fight, so he carried on until he couldn't anymore, and when his brother went for his heart, he didn't raise his sword to protect himself.

Phoenix stopped with the tip of his rapier an inch from Key's chest. "You're going to let me take you out?"

"I'm not *letting* you do anything. I'm fucking exhausted. Just do it." He saw his brother hesitate. *"Do it!"*

The sword slowly moved away from him, and Phoenix said in a dead voice, "No." He held the rapier hilt toward Key, and after he'd taken it, he turned and walked back to the foot of Jane's grave. "You need to think real hard about talking her into staying, Kyros, because she won't be Mephisto, and if that's all she means to you, it's cruel to keep her on the mountain."

He was telling Key that he'd never kiss her. Key wanted to believe his brother would cave, eventually, but Phoenix had kept Jane in the forefront of his mind for over a century, her memory so strong, he wouldn't even touch an ordinary human girl. A guy with that kind of iron will wasn't going to cave easily, if ever. Key had the urge to weep again, and he wondered at himself because he never cried; but knowing how horribly conflicted Phoenix was made him painfully sad. "That's not all she means to me." He was aware that blood was dripping into his boots. "She's Jordan's sister. She's been through a lot, and she needs us to help her find her way back to her own humanity."

"If you think I'll feel sorry for her, you've—"

"She wouldn't want anyone to feel sorry for her. She's all about Jordan, and if all she can ever be is a Lumina, I think that's just fine. There's no rule that says a Mephisto has to accept an Anabo, just like they don't have to accept us."

Phoenix was staring at Jane's headstone. "So there's no way you'll take her back?"

"If you knew . . . if you could see where she lives, and what she's got in this world, and if you could understand how she feels about Jordan, you wouldn't want her to go back. Besides, it's not as if her being away from the mountain will make any difference. She'll still be Anabo, and you're still Mephisto, and you know she exists. It's not going to make her any less tempting."

Jerking his gaze to Key's, he scowled. "I'm *not* tempted. I'm not interested at all. And that's not going to change, *ever.*"

Key's gaze moved to the headstone. "Of course Jane would want you to stay true to her, and you're nothing if not loyal, Phoenix." He was lying, because no way did he think Jane would be happy with Phoenix burying himself for over a century, or ignoring Mariah, whom Jane would see as a gift directly from God. He remembered Jane well. She was sweet and gentle and kind, and as much as she would want Phoenix to let go and move on, she'd want Mariah to find happiness.

He hoped his words would go a little way toward waking Phoenix up, but no, he took them at face value and nodded as he said, "She's got nothing to worry about."

Jordan had pointed out that Mariah must be very strong to have done what she did, and that gave him a measure of comfort. So maybe his brother was determined to make himself miserable, but that didn't mean Mariah had to join him.

"I'm sorry, Phoenix."

His brother looked up and turned his head. "Did the mighty leader of the Mephisto just *apologize*? Is this the apocalypse?"

Key bent to get his coat so Phoenix wouldn't see that he had tears in his eyes. When he straightened up again, he had himself back under control. "I wish I'd known she's Anabo so I could have warned you. I'd never have done that to you, but I just didn't know."

Phoenix stared at him for a while before he said, "Why can't we see it?"

"Because of her life. She's been . . . things have happened that caused her to . . . " He sighed and watched snowflakes land on his brother's dark hair. "She's broken."

He'd swear Phoenix flinched before he quickly refocused on Jane's grave. "Go home and eat, Key. You're still bleeding, and you're pale as a ghost."

Knowing that the conversation was over, Key left his brother to his memories and disappeared from England.

❧

Jordan's reunion with her sister was bittersweet: extremely joyous and heartbreakingly sad, all at once.

Before she'd say a word about herself or any of their history,

Mariah insisted that Jordan tell her about her life, about her parents and being the First Daughter. Then she wanted to know about Key, and Sasha, and where this room was where they were visiting. She had no idea they were in Colorado. Jordan knew Key intended for Mariah to stay, if she wanted, and Jordan was over the moon at the prospect of having her here, so she carefully sidestepped certain details, like Phoenix and the Mephisto-Anabo scent thing, and, most especially, the Mephisto Covenant. But she told her about Eryx, and the lost souls, and what the Mephisto did, and what had happened to her after she was abducted.

She found it extremely strange how Mariah accepted all of it, asking a few questions but never appearing anything more than curious. After a while, she realized her sister was completely insulated. She'd wrapped herself within a blanket of safety that didn't allow anything—good or bad—to filter through to her heart. Or her soul. That was why her light was so dim.

Jordan had talked for almost an hour when she finally said, "Okay, you know everything about me. It's your turn."

With that soft, hesitant smile, Mariah said, "I'm happy to talk about our parents, what I can remember of them, or my life now, but everything in between is best left unsaid, Viorica. I hope you understand."

Just like Holly. Don't talk about it, shove it under the rug, pretend it didn't happen. Jordan knew that pushing would only make Mariah close up more, so she let it go for now and said, "What did our parents look like?"

"I have some photographs I can show you, if Kyros will take me home to get them."

"If I take us to the orphanage, can you direct me from there?" Jordan asked, way too eager and excited to wait for Key.

Mariah nodded, and two minutes later, they stood on the steps of the old church. They were holding hands, and they stood and looked across the street for a while before Mariah turned to Jordan and said, "I live close enough to walk, if you like."

Jordan nodded and wished she knew how to put them under a cloak, but since she didn't, she pulled up the hood of her jacket, effectively hiding her hair and shielding her face. As they walked, she couldn't stop imagining the two of them walking this way fourteen years ago, except in the opposite direction. Her hand tightened around Mariah's, and her sister looked at her, silently telling her that she had the same thought.

Several blocks later, she stopped in front of a building that made Jordan want to cry. She'd lived in the beauty, comfort, and security of the White House for the past five years, while her sister had lived on poverty row. Upstairs was worse. She would tell Key the minute she saw him that he'd absolutely done the right thing getting Mariah out of here. There were cockroaches everywhere, making her skin crawl, but Mariah didn't appear to notice.

She tried to hide her revulsion over the place. Her sister was obviously humbly proud of her apartment. Jordan wasn't sure if it was because she'd provided it for herself by working and earning her own money, or if it was because this was the first thing in her life that was truly hers.

Mariah offered her tea, but Jordan didn't want to stay. She could hear someone shouting, the smell in the building was awful, and she was freaking over the roaches. There was also something making her very antsy, some sixth sense of danger nearby. "If I'm caught here, there'll be no way to explain it, like there was in London. Is it all right if we go back to Colorado?"

Mariah nodded, her expression never changing from easy acceptance. "The pictures are here, in this album," she said, pulling a book from a shelf that held a few chipped dishes and an ancient toaster.

Jordan noticed she had a copy of the book her mom had done for charity before she died—homey stories about life in the White House, with pictures of the three of them. Just next to that was a Bible, and next to that was Kafka's *The Metamorphosis*. It was a strange collection.

Mariah turned with the photo album in her hand. "I promised I'd stay for a few days, and I've already called Gustav to tell him I'm taking off of work, but I don't have any clothes in Colorado. Maybe I should get some while I'm here."

If Mariah decided to stay on the mountain, she'd have to give up her things, including the photos, and allow all of it to be returned to this apartment. For now, however, she was simply a guest, so Jordan nodded her agreement.

Jordan nodded. "Good idea."

Her sister went to a flimsy curtain in the corner of the small room, just next to the narrow bed, and pushed it aside, revealing a tiny space with a pathetically small amount of clothes hanging there. She took out a pair of jeans—the only pair—a couple of simple cotton blouses, and a threadbare sweater. Jordan thought of her closet at home, stuffed with designer jeans and couture ball gowns. As soon as she was back in Colorado for good, she was taking Mariah shopping. She'd buy her anything she wanted, in every color.

She supposed Mariah didn't have a bag, because after she added two pairs of panties and an old T-shirt that Jordan decided must be a sleep shirt, she rolled the clothes up into a tidy ball, then strapped a belt around it. Turning, she smiled again at Jordan. "I'm ready."

Jordan was moving closer to reach for her hand and pop them back to Colorado when the door to the tiny apartment flew open and a guy in blue coveralls and a shadow across his eyes came in. A superfast glance at Mariah told her this wasn't a neighborly visit. Her eyes were wide with surprise. Jordan simultaneously remembered the night she was abducted and Jax's lesson from just a few hours ago. *"Assess the situation and stay cool. You're ten times stronger than any lost soul, and equal in strength to a Skia, but that's not much help if you panic. Stand your ground."*

This lost soul wasn't going to take her. Not this time. She faced off against him and wished like everything she had a knife. She couldn't pop out without Mariah, who was just out of reach.

He stared at her for three beats, then stunned her completely when he turned toward Mariah. Before she could register that he was after her sister, not her, he'd pushed Mariah to the bed and was shoving her blouse up and over her bra.

Filled with rage, Jordan grabbed the old toaster, launched herself onto the guy's back, and smashed his head as hard as she could, gratified when she saw blood. He grunted and collapsed on top of Mariah.

"Creepy son of a bitch," Jordan mumbled in English as she shoved him off of her sister. "Do you know this guy?"

"No, I've never seen him before." Mariah smiled up at her. "You're really strong, aren't you?" She'd just been attacked by a stranger, but there was no fear in her eyes. Only that calm acceptance. And she hadn't fought. For those few seconds that guy had been holding her down, Mariah had passively lain there and made no move to fight him off.

With her heart shattering into a million pieces, Jordan returned her sister's smile. Her whole life, it was the hardest thing she'd ever done. "Yes. Very . . . strong," she managed to whisper around the ginormous lump in her throat. "Let's go home now."

As if nothing had happened, Mariah sat up, tugged her shirt down, reached for her bundle of clothes, and accepted Jordan's hand. "Maybe we should drag him out into the hall."

"I'll get Key and come back for him, Mariah. He's a lost soul."

Her sister never looked at the guy. She nodded and said, "Okay."

Key had stripped out of his bloody clothes and taken a shower as soon as he got home. He was looking forward to getting something to eat after he dressed, but before he was even finished drying off, he heard Jordan calling his name. Wrapping the towel around his hips, he went into the bedroom and saw her standing next to the bed, eyes wide, looking at him like he was all that stood between her and Hell. Hurrying to her, he grabbed her next to him just as she began to cry. "What's happened, Jordan? Shhh, it's okay. I'm here. Tell me what's wrong. Is it Mariah?"

She nodded against his chest and explained that they'd gone to her apartment for some pictures, and a lost soul had busted in. "I thought he was there for me, but he went after Mariah, and I smashed his head with a toaster. She never fought, Key." She clung tighter to him, her fingers digging into his back. "She just . . . lay there."

All kinds of alarms were going off in his head. "You say he pushed her shirt up?"

She leaned her head back and looked up at him. "I think he intended to rape her."

"If that was his intention, he would have done something to restrain you first so you couldn't run for help. I think he was looking for her birthmark."

Her face went white. "How would he . . . " She looked totally confused.

"Were you on the street at all?"

She nodded. "We started at the old church."

His first inclination was to give her a lecture about going into the world as Mephisto when she was still faking real life at the White House, but he decided that was something for later. "Did you see the guy anywhere on your way?"

"No, and Mariah said she'd never seen him before."

"Where is she now?"

"In her room. I called Mathilda to look after her while I came to see you."

He dropped one arm and kept the other around her while he walked her toward the bathroom and guided her toward the chair next to the sauna. "Wait right here while I get some clothes on."

She was staring at his chest. "My God, Key, what happened to you?"

"Phoenix was visiting Jane's grave, and I figured he'd talk himself into doing something extremely stupid, so I took a couple of swords and let him work a little of it out."

She was still staring at his chest. "I think he worked a lot of it out. Is he this wounded?"

"No, but I managed not to lose my dignity completely. It's all okay, Jordan. Just wait a minute, and I'll be ready."

She nodded, and he went in his closet, quickly got dressed, and pocketed his switchblade. Back in the bathroom, he took her hand. "I'm running on empty. Can you transport us to Mariah's apartment?"

Seconds later, they stood in the cramped room. There was no

one there, but he saw the toaster and a stain of blood on the old blanket covering the bed. He looked down at Jordan. "You're awesome."

She gripped his hand. "I wonder where he went?"

He stepped to the door, which was standing wide open, and looked down the hall. "Let's follow the trail." She closed the door behind her and went along with him as he walked toward the stairwell. Drops of blood were here and there, all the way down to the fifth floor, where they meandered off into the hall. Key saw the guy slumped against the wall, a cell phone in his hand. "Is that him?"

"For sure. He had on blue coveralls."

"I was kind of joking, Jordan." He looked down into her surprised eyes. "I mean, the guy's bleeding all over the place. You seriously nailed him, didn't you?"

She looked at the lost soul, and her eyes hardened. "I wanted to kill him."

"But you didn't. Like I said—you're amazing." Still holding her hand, he walked toward the guy, who saw them coming and tried to get up but couldn't. "I need you to transport us to the gate, Jordan."

"But I don't know where it is."

"Just keep holding my hand." He reached down and grabbed the lost soul's arm, ignoring his feeble protests. Closing his eyes, he concentrated on the gate, and the well of energy inside his Anabo. He heard her gasp, then they were moving, and when he opened his eyes, they were in the desert. He let go of the lost soul but not Jordan's hand.

"Where are we?" she asked, looking all around them.

"Saudi Arabia, close to the Yemen border."

"Can you send him down, Key? Jax said everyone goes on a takedown, or no one goes. He said there has to be a doppelganger. We don't even know this guy's name."

He bent and took the cell phone from the lost soul. "Now we will." He dropped it into his pocket. "I'll call M, and he'll provide a doppelganger; Phoenix will come up with a plan for where to leave it. For now, however, this one's got to go, because he saw Mariah's birthmark." He looked down at the lost soul, noticing how very young he was. Probably eighteen or nineteen. "What were you looking for?" he asked him.

He stared up at Key, a glazed look in his eyes. He was close to death. He didn't seem to realize where he was, or what was about to happen to him.

"Tell me what you were after," Key said to him.

Dazed, the man blinked and looked at Jordan. "Beautiful, just like he said."

"Who said?" Key asked.

"Eryx," the guy whispered. "Said she was in Bucharest, and to follow and see why she was there. I . . . saw look-alikes. Sent a photo and he said see if taller one had . . . Anabo mark."

Key felt cold all over. "How did Eryx know she was in Bucharest?"

He looked surprised at the question. "Her cell phone. Has someone track . . . and tells him . . . " He stopped and looked up at the sky. "I'm . . . my head . . . hurts so much." Tears began to roll down the sides of his face. "Let me die. Please don't send me down."

Key looked at Jordan. Her eyes were wide with apprehension but no sympathy. She'd changed completely to Mephisto, without an ounce of compassion for the lost souls.

The guy began to shake and mumbled, "Mercy . . . have mercy."

Before he could die and become another win for Eryx, Key raised his arms, still holding Jordan's hand, and began the chant, drawing from her energy again.

When it was done, he saw her staring at the place where the lost soul had been. "I bet he was texting Eryx when we found him, and he'd already told him about Mariah."

Key looked at the guy's cell and wished they'd found him sooner. "You'd win the bet, because that's exactly what he was doing." The last text was from Eryx, telling his lost soul to stay in Mariah's apartment until she returned, then keep her there and let Eryx know immediately. He'd already been planning her capture, and if he'd been successful, Key didn't know if he would have used Mariah as leverage to get at Jordan or kept her instead. Probably leverage, because Mariah would be no challenge to him, and Key was beginning to believe his brother was enjoying this cat and mouse game with Jordan.

Eryx had lost all capacity for empathy, was detached from most every human emotion, but he still had likes and dislikes, and he was still an eighteen-year-old guy. Key had always wondered if cruelty to Phoenix wasn't Eryx's only reason for killing Jane. Since she carried his mark, he could have tried to bring her back, and if she'd chosen immortality, he might have convinced her to have his sons. But she wasn't his type of girl, at all. Jane was quiet and proper and, in some ways, very passive.

Jordan was none of those things. She was outspoken and strong, a natural-born leader. She would never be easy, would always be a challenge. She was also petite, dark-haired, and beautiful. Every girl Key had ever seen with Eryx was small, dark-haired, and beautiful. He wanted Jordan badly enough to come out of his reclusion and go about in the real world, so Key had his doubts that Eryx planned to capture Mariah as a substitute. She was all about leverage.

He made a mental note to talk to the Mephisto about this, to ensure Mariah didn't leave the mountain again for any reason.

Jordan was still staring at the sand. "What you said," she murmured, "it's a language I've never heard before."

"It's ancient and tied to the underworld. Lucifer gave us the words, and he hears when we say them and allows us to open the gate. It means—"

"Commit this soul that defiles humanity to eternity within. Grant no mercy. Hear no plea." She looked up at him with a small smile. "I understood. But how do you make the gate open?"

He brushed her windblown hair away from her face. "It's like when you turned the lamp on and off in my room that night. I willed it to open, and Lucifer allowed it. But it takes energy, and I haven't eaten since lunchtime yesterday, so I drew on yours."

"Then you need me to get you back home."

"Well, yeah."

"So you're kind of at my mercy, aren't you?"

"Jordan, I'm at your mercy wherever we are, whatever the circumstances."

"It's just that I want to tell you something, and since we're all alone here, it seems like the right time." She turned her head to stare down at the spot in the sand that hid the gate. "When this guy went after Mariah and she didn't make the tiniest effort to escape him, I realized she's closed herself off so completely—just to cope—that she's even buried her instinct to survive." Raising her gaze to the soaring dune in front of them, she held his hand a little tighter. "I feel insanely protective of her, and I'm humbled and heartbroken, but what's eating me alive is guilt. I can't stand that she's this way because of what she did for me."

She turned her head and gave him a solemn look. "I get why you can't bring yourself to hate him, Key." Fat tears welled in her eyes and clung to her lashes. "I can't imagine how you've lived over a thousand years with this unbearable guilt, and it's a billion times worse for you, because he became a monster, with no chance he'll ever be different. Mariah's lost right now, but she's still Anabo, and I'll never give up hope that she'll find her way back. If I didn't have that, I think maybe I'd self-destruct." Her tears spilled over. "I'm sorry for what I said, and for causing you more pain. I can't help hating him, Key, but I can't hold it against you that you don't." She squeezed his hand. "I'm in awe of you."

The tears he'd managed to keep at bay all day popped into his eyes, and no amount of swallowing or deep breaths would make them go away. Finally, he gave up trying, hauled her into his arms, and silently wept.

SEVENTEEN

BY THE TIME JORDAN GOT BACK TO HER ROOM AT THE White House and apologized to Brody for being gone six hours instead of two, it was quarter-past six and sleep was out of the question. She seriously considered taking a sick day, but she hated to waste any of the time she had left in the real world. She could sleep when she was back in Colorado, three weeks from now.

Her dad wasn't at breakfast, and Betsy said as she set a plate of eggs in front of Jordan, "A riot broke out in Atlanta late last night, and he decided to go down there to show support for law enforcement and talk to the people who instigated all the trouble."

"Who is it? Should Dad be doing that? Is it safe?"

"It's just people. No group, or anything. They're out of work, and another plant closed on Friday. And I'm sure he'll be safe.

With things so crazy right now, I think the Secret Service is more diligent than ever. You know there've been protests and riots popping up all over, don't you?"

Jordan was ashamed to admit that she didn't know. "I've been kind of preoccupied, Betsy, and haven't watched any news. And Dad doesn't tell me stuff like he did before—I guess because he worries it'll upset me."

Betsy had always urged Jordan to be active and up to speed on what was going on in the world, so it surprised her when she said, "Probably just as well, Jo. Someday, it'll be you and your generation running things, and it'll be more of the same problems, because it's always the same problems. You need to enjoy what's left of your childhood, because one day you'll wake up with heavy responsibilities."

Jordan ate her eggs and thought it was kind of funny that Betsy had hit the nail on the head, except her old nanny didn't know that her childhood was going to last only three more weeks, and her responsibilities would be heavier than she could imagine.

When she arrived at school, Key was waiting for her in the front hall. She saw him and grinned because she was glad to see him, but also because of how he was dressed. In a long-sleeved blue polo, dark blue Levi's, and contacts that turned his eyes to smoky blue, instead of pitch black, he would look like most every other guy at Oates, except that he was over six feet tall and wore his hair in a ponytail. She noticed the other kids were checking him out as they passed, especially the girls, as if they'd only just noticed he was hot. "You're a sheep," she whispered to him.

"I'm totally whipped," he whispered back.

"Are you saying you did this for me?"

He met her eyes. "I gave serious thought to being less obviously stuck on you so you could spend this time doing what you'd normally do, and it'd maybe change people's mind about kicking you out of office. But I decided to try to fit in instead; that way I can stay close to you, and maybe people won't be so judgy about your being with me."

"Because you're worried about me taking out a lost soul?"

"Because I'm stuck on you."

"It's only the Anabo thing."

Reaching for her hand, he took off walking, all the way to the end of the hall, to his locker. Hank and Gunther took up positions several feet away, huge and out of place in the middle of the mass of moving kids.

Key opened his locker and crowded her against it, holding the door to give them the maximum privacy possible under the circumstances, which wasn't much at all. He stared down into her eyes while he said in a low, even voice, "If I didn't like you, do you think I'd still want to be with you just because you're Anabo?"

"Yeah, I kinda do. It's pretty huge, especially the covenant."

He sighed. "Am I that much of an ass? My brothers think I'm a robot, and you think I want you only because of what you can do for me."

"You're not an ass, but you can be pretty harsh. As for me, I think you want me to listen when you're worried and help you when you're trying to make a decision. And you want me for . . . to . . . well. . . . " She blushed, but didn't look away from his eyes. She dropped her voice to a whisper. "You want a girl who'll stay all night and be there when you wake up in the morning."

"And you think just any girl would fit the bill, so long as she's Anabo?"

"It's okay, Key. You've waited over a thousand years, and now I'm here, and we get along, so you don't have to pretend you like me. I mean, *like* me. I know you like me enough to be friends."

"Don't you know I like you a helluva lot more than *friends*?"

"How would I?"

Confusion came into his eyes, and he said, "I don't know." Then he brightened and said, "But now you know, because I just told you."

He wanted so badly to do what he needed to do to make it work between them, but he went at it like everything else in his life. Make a plan, make a list, check off each task; when he reached the end, it was done. Move on to the next problem or project. "Yes, Key, now I know."

He was looking at her expectantly, waiting to hear how she felt about him. She remembered telling Mary Michael that this sounded as romantic as cold oatmeal, but the reality was worse. He didn't have a romantic bone in his body. He had created a miniature Eden in a greenhouse, but he'd never send her flowers. He sometimes looked at her as if she was the most beautiful girl on the planet, but he'd rarely say it out loud. He'd be pushy and arrogant and spend a lot of time looking at her just like he was looking at her right now, impatiently waiting for an answer.

But he went to Bucharest to get her bunny fixed and look for her past. He brought her sister to her. And when she told him she was sorry for what she'd said, the Mephisto leader who never cried lost it.

He got up every day and toed the line for his brothers, his father, and everyone on the mountain. For all of humanity. He might never find it in himself to love her enough to earn Heaven, but he'd be true to her forever. He was way more than romantic. He was deep, strong, and completely devoted to those he cared about.

Yesterday Jax had said she was falling in love, but she kind of wondered if she'd already landed.

One of Matthew's best buddies passed and gave her an accusing look, but she didn't let it get to her. She loved Matthew, and she'd make sure he knew it before she had to go away again, but she'd never felt this way about him, like she was skating across the universe. Matthew had been her escape from all the crazy that came with being the First Daughter, and she'd been his refuge from his hypercritical father.

Key would never be an escape. If anything, there might be times when she'd need an escape from him, because he was a son of Hell. Because he was Key. But he'd also always be that voice on the wind. He'd never take her for granted.

Reaching out, she hooked a finger through one of his belt

loops and tugged until he moved a few inches closer. "You're a lot more to me than just a friend, Key."

He looked relieved. "Good. So will you just believe that if I had a whole roomful of Anabo to choose from, I'd pick you?"

"Would you?"

"No question. I admit, you're not what I expected, but you're exactly what I want."

"What did you expect?"

"A sweet, reserved girl who wouldn't provoke my brother into stabbing her a hundred times."

"A wilting violet? Oh, come on, Key. You'd run all over her and forget about her in a week."

"I see that now." He grinned at her. "I keep trying to run all over you, but you're just so . . . stabby."

The final bell rang, and they were late to class, so Mr. Shelley gave them each a tardy slip. On their way to the back of the room, where Brody was already sitting, they passed Mark, whose boils were all gone. She expected him to say something to Key, but he never looked up from his desk.

After they sat down, Key took her tardy slip and his and folded them together into the shape of a heart, then leaned over and set it on top of her chemistry book. She was feeling all warm and wonderful that he'd surprised her and done something romantic, when she noticed he'd written a note on the heart. *You're tired, but I know you're going to want to see Mariah. After your visit tonight, skip training and get some sleep.*

Okay, so it wasn't romantic in the usual way, but it was for Key.

Before she could slip the heart into her backpack, he took it back to write something else.

And don't forget to let me kiss you.

She looked across the aisle at him, but he was looking straight ahead, seemingly engrossed in Mr. Shelley's lecture about emulsifying agents.

⟳

The rest of the day passed entirely differently than the week before. People didn't seem as freaked out by Key, and she didn't think it was just the change in what he was wearing. He was different. Granted, he would never be Mr. Popular, because it wasn't as if he suddenly became extroverted, but he sat with her at lunch in the dining hall and joined in the conversation. He smiled and remembered people's names.

Eryx sat next to Tessa at the other end of their table, and every time Jordan glanced their way, she caught him looking at her. She knew Key also noticed, but he continued acting like a regular guy, and when lunch was over, he held her hand as they walked to their next class and never mentioned Eryx. It was odd, but he seemed to want to pretend they really were just ordinary kids.

She went to see Mariah that night, and they looked through the pictures in the album. It was surreal to see her biological parents, and supersad to see her and Mariah, so young and small, smiling at the camera. There were pictures of them playing with dolls, swinging on swings, standing in front of a Christmas tree, and sleeping curled up together, Mariah with a protective arm across Jordan, who was clutching the bunny. All this time, lost to each other. But she had all the years ahead to be with Mariah, and she would focus on that, on getting her sister back to the happy girl she was in those pictures.

She didn't forget to let Key kiss her. When she left Mariah, who said Sasha was going to teach her to paint the next day, Jordan popped to Key's door and went in after he answered her knock. He was at his desk, writing in a journal. "Do you do that every day?" she asked.

He leaned back in his chair and nodded. "Since the middle of the eighteenth century. There are boxes and boxes of my journals in a room in the basement."

"Why? You have a photographic memory."

He stood and came toward her. "Only for events and people. Not how I felt about them."

She was surprised. And fascinated. "Can I read them?"

"I guess, but I'm not sure why you'd want to."

No, he wouldn't understand her interest in knowing more about him, or how much he probably revealed in his words. "Do you write about me?"

He was standing right in front of her now. "Of course. I was just writing about our conversation this morning."

"And what did you say?"

Resting his hands on her shoulders, focused on her mouth, he was clearly losing interest in discussing his journal. "I wrote that it bothers me that you think my only interest in you is that you're Anabo, and I wish I was more creative and could think up ways to prove it to you. Then I made a note that I should ask Jax, because he's good at things like that." He moved closer.

"I told you I believe you. Do you think I was lying?"

His hands slid into her hair to hold her head, and his cheek was warm against hers. "You'd never lie to me, but you still doubt. I know you do. And that makes me nuts. I wish I knew exactly the right thing to say, so you'd know you're all I'd ever want. You'd know how much I love that your scent is bluebells, and that you're maybe the softest thing on God's earth, and just putting my arms around you is like a gift. You'd know I dream about you every night." He kissed her almost reverently. "And you'd know that I was a goner from the moment you kissed me and saved my life. Maybe another Anabo would have had the guts to do that, Jordan, but I don't think so. You're brave and strong. My biggest regret is that God can't hear me thanking him for sending you to me."

And she'd thought she had him all figured out. Tightening her arms around him, she whispered just before he kissed her again, "Don't bother talking to Jax."

⚬⚬⚬

Tuesday passed pretty much like Monday. Eryx was always around, it seemed, looking at her with that freakish intensity. Tessa didn't appear to notice, thank God, but Key did, and after lunch, he went to Eryx and said something Jordan couldn't hear. Eryx shrugged and walked away. "What did you say to him?" she asked when Key came back to her locker.

"I told him he needs to give up, because you're way too strong-willed ever to give in."

"Have you noticed, there've been no new lost souls since last week? And none of the ones here now has even spoken to me, much less tried to get me to lose my temper. This morning, Carla came to the residence, and it was almost like business as usual. She told me about a talk I'm supposed to give at a school next week, and an ambassador dinner at the White House a month from now." She watched Eryx and saw Tessa hurry to catch up. "What's he up to?"

Key was also staring after him. "Something, that's for sure. Dammit, I wish we could do the takedown right now and get you out of here."

Just as Eryx and Tessa reached the end of the hall, he looked back at her and *smiled*. Cold dread slid down her back.

The next day was Wednesday, and she had to leave school early to go to her doctor appointment. Key wanted to go with her, under a cloak, but she told him she'd rather do this alone. So after sixth period, Hank and Gunther drove her to the military medical center in Bethesda. Hank ran a sweep of the doctor's office, then she went in for her visit, and they both stayed just outside the door.

Since the doctor's name was Terry Meyers, she had expected

a man, but it was a middle-aged woman with short brown hair and glasses she wore at the end of her nose while she sat in a chair and paged through Jordan's file. "Are you having any difficulties? Nightmares? Changes in appetite? Things like that?"

Boy, if she only knew. "I've had a few bad dreams about Matthew, but not really what I'd call nightmares."

"Have you seen Matthew since you returned home?"

"No," she lied, "I can't. He's in ICU, and it's family only, but as soon as he's in a regular room, I plan to visit him."

Dr. Meyers asked her more questions, and Jordan did her best to answer honestly, except when she couldn't. Toward the end of their hour, the woman came back to Matthew. "You've said that you feel guilty about what happened to him, and from our conversation, I believe this is what's troubling you most, even more than being held captive."

She told the doctor about Matthew's texts, and the Photoshopped picture. "All that said to me is that he's in a terrible place, emotionally, and I can't help but feel guilty about it."

"You said you plan to visit him, but do you think you should, when he's so adamant about not wanting to see you? Should you wait until he changes his mind?"

She couldn't tell the doctor that she was running out of time. It was only two and a half weeks until the takedown. "If he tells me to leave, I will, but he's one of my best friends, and I think maybe I could help him."

"I've worked with a lot of paraplegics, Jordan, so you need to be prepared. It's a grieving process, and until he reaches the stage where he's ready to accept his new life, he's going to be angry and bitter. I don't want you to push things and then feel more guilty because of his reaction."

She hadn't thought about it that way, but it didn't matter. She had to see him before she left Washington for good.

On the way back to the White House, she stared out the window and thought a lot about what Dr. Meyers had said. At dinner, Dad asked how her appointment had gone, and she wasn't lying when she said, "It was a big help, but I don't think I need to go back."

"Are you sure, Jo?"

"Yeah, Dad, I'm sure. I'm doing all right."

He looked supertired and stressed again, and she almost asked about the Atlanta riot, then didn't. Instead, she told him stories about people at school, hoping to take his mind off of things, even if it was just during dinner.

When she visited Mariah later that night, she saw her first attempt at painting. Jordan didn't say so, but she didn't think her sister had a future as a painter.

Mariah said, "It sucks, I know, but it was fun to do. Tomorrow Zee's going to give me a piano lesson."

Everyone had taken Mariah under his wing, and she seemed content to stay awhile. Jordan hadn't broached the subject of staying forever, because she didn't want to scare her sister with the specter of Eryx. Not yet. She also hadn't told her she was Anabo.

But it was a conversation that had to happen, because now that Eryx knew what she was, she'd never be safe in the real world. Key had agreed that they should wait to tell her and let her get more comfortable with life on the mountain.

In a way, Mariah was being courted by Sasha and the brothers, and even Mathilda, who loved and adored anyone who needed her. Everyone liked Mariah. Everyone except Phoenix. Her sister had asked why he was so rude, when the others seemed so gracious, but all Jordan said was that he'd lost his fiancée and was still grieving. Mariah asked, "When?" and Jordan gave a vague, "Oh, a while ago."

Watching her sister drink the tea Mathilda had brought, she said, "So, piano lessons. Do you like music?"

"I love music." Mariah smiled at her. "We used to sing all the time. Mama taught us some of the old folk songs, and we'd sing them for Papa when he got home from work."

"Would you sing one to me now?"

Mariah looked toward the fire and began. By the third note, Jordan was mesmerized. Mariah's low, smoky voice was beautiful, and she lit up when she sang, giving Jordan a glimpse of the person her sister was meant to be.

After their visit, she went to Key's room, but she didn't stay as long as she had the past two nights. She had tons of homework, and even though it didn't matter in the long run, she couldn't bring herself to blow it off.

Thursday was the recall election, and by lunchtime, she was

no longer president. As she and Key walked toward the dining hall, he said quietly, "I'm sorry, Jordan. As much as I'd like to blame it all on Eryx for spreading it around about your doctor visit, I know it's partly my fault."

"It doesn't really matter, Key. I'll be gone soon, anyway." But it still stung, and later, after school was over, she wanted to get out of the building as fast as possible, to avoid hearing anyone apologize and having to say it was okay when it wasn't.

She was digging around in her locker, searching for her history book, when she heard Key mutter under his breath, "Holy shit."

Then she heard Courtney say, "I'm really sorry about the recall vote, Jordan."

Of all the people she wanted to escape, Courtney was top on the list, so of course she was standing just behind her, pretending to be sorry Jordan had just been kicked out of office. "Yeah, me, too." With the history book finally found, she unbent, turned to face Courtney, and had one of the biggest shocks of her life. There was a shadow across Courtney's eyes. Jordan stared in disbelief. "No way. Of all people, not you."

Courtney shrugged, as if it was no big deal to blow off God and pledge her soul to a con artist. "Eryx promised he could get me back into Hopper's class so I could still go to Princeton."

"But you wanted to go so you could major in theology and become a minister. You can't do that now, so what difference does it make?"

"I didn't realize what it really meant until after I did it, so there is a lot of irony. He got me back into Hopper's class, but now I don't want to go to Princeton."

"You won't be going to college anywhere," Key said.

She gave him a look. "You don't scare me, so don't even try." She turned away. "I'll say hello to Matthew for you, Jordan."

"What?" Jordan jogged after her and reached for her arm, making her stop. "You're going to see Matthew?"

"He was released from ICU this morning, so I'm going to see if he'd like to be healed. Eryx could do it, you know." She smiled, but it wasn't real, didn't reach her eyes. "Matthew loves you so much, I guess he'd do just about anything to walk again, so he wouldn't lose you to . . ."—she nodded toward Key—"that."

Watching Courtney walk away through the sea of kids in the hall, panic clawed at Jordan's throat. She wanted to stop her, but she couldn't, and even if she did, Eryx would send someone else. Turning, she slowly walked back to her locker, feeling as if her whole world had just tilted.

"Maybe he won't do it," Key said.

She turned and stared after Courtney, who was almost to the front doors of the school. "I saw Randy outside of Mr. Barnes's office today, and I asked him what Eryx had promised him." She looked up at Key. "He wants to play football for Notre Dame. He gave up his soul to play football. Matthew could walk again. That's so much bigger than football, how could he resist?"

"It's not really about what a person wants, Jordan. It's how he thinks it will change his life. Zee's already doing reconnaissance, and he says Randy's here on scholarship. He's a low-income guy in a school full of über-rich kids. It could be that he believes he'll be drafted to play pro ball and become rich and famous if he plays for Notre Dame. All those government friends of your dad's probably thought they'd become more powerful, or more respected, or whatever they think is missing that would make them feel more worthy. For Matthew, if he pledges so he can walk, it won't be just because he can get out of a wheelchair. It'll be because his ability to walk is tied to something else, something he thinks he has to have to feel whole. That's why Eryx is so good at this. He can figure out what a person wants, way deep inside, what they would never say out loud, or maybe even admit to themselves."

Now she was even more depressed. "Matthew's dad is a hard-ass who always expects him to be perfect. When he falls short, his dad treats him like dirt, and he always falls short because no one is perfect." She watched as the front door closed behind Courtney. "I'm not sure when, but I have to see him, Key."

He didn't argue or ask to go with her. Just looked at her with sad understanding. "I know."

⁓❦⁓

After he watched Jordan head back to the White House with Hank and Gunther, Key went to his Capitol Hill town house, where he was pretending to live with Brody and a Lumina named Mirabelle, who was posing as his aunt. He collected two weeks'

376

worth of junk mail out of the box and decided to thumb through it before he tossed it. He spied one interesting piece and pulled it out to read.

He and Brody were cordially invited to the Winter Ball, to be held in the dining hall at Oates this Saturday night. He'd heard people talking about it but hadn't paid much attention. Looking at the invitation, he could see that this was a big deal at her school.

And this would be her last school dance.

Holding the invitation, he popped into her room, cloaked, with his eyes closed.

"I'm decent."

He opened his eyes and walked toward where she sat cross-legged on the bed, reading her history textbook. "Are you going to this?" he asked, showing her the invitation.

She shook her head. "Tessa will be there with Eryx, and they're sure to win king and queen of the Winter Court, which will make me happy for Tessa, but furious with everyone who voted for Eryx."

"I think you should go. With me."

She gave him an odd look. "You would hate it."

"Probably, but I want to take you because this will be your last school dance."

The look became more odd. Sort of dreamy. "I don't have anything to wear."

"I've seen your closet."

She lay back on her pillows. "All right, but you can't make

fun of anyone, and no griping about the music, and don't eat all the cupcakes."

"Can we dance?"

She smiled. "*I* can dance. Can you?"

"I've waltzed across some of the finest ballrooms in Europe."

"This won't be ballroom dancing."

He groaned. "I was afraid of that."

"Do you still want to go?"

"Can I take you off into a dark corner and kiss you?"

"I certainly hope so."

"Then yes, I still want to go." He started to pop out, then noticed she was wearing one of his dress shirts. He knew because a very small KdK was embroidered on the breast pocket. It was ginormous on her small body. "Hey, Sticky Fingers, have you been raiding my closet?"

"Maybe." She blushed. "I like the way this smells."

"What? Like starch?"

Her smile was kind of funny and shy. "Like you."

<hr/>

Jordan ditched school the next day, in spite of Hank's and Gunther's protests, and told Hank she wanted to go to George Washington University Hospital. Key texted her at 8:15, five minutes after first period began. Is today the day?

Yes.

I'm right here. No matter what.

I'm nervous.

You've been friends a long time. It'll be okay once you get there.

Unless he's pledged.

Leave. If he's done it, promise me you'll leave.

I promise.

Inside the hospital, she asked at the information desk for Matthew's room, then, after taking an elevator upstairs, she walked down long hallways and through multiple doors before she finally found it.

Gunther went in before her, because he had to, killing whatever element of surprise she'd had; when he came out, he said, "Matthew asked me not to let you come in."

"Is there anyone in there with a gun?"

"Of course not. We wouldn't be standing here if there was."

She pushed open the door and stepped inside the room, leaving Hank and Gunther out in the hallway. Matthew had no shadow across his eyes, and she was so relieved, she felt weak in the knees. He was alone, for which she was grateful. She'd have a lot harder time saying what she came to say with his mom staring at her.

"God, Jordan, don't do this. Please don't do this."

"I had to see you, Matthew."

He wouldn't look at her, but kept his focus on the muted TV, tuned to ESPN.

She stood next to the bed and wasn't sure where to begin. He looked so much better than when she'd seen him after she returned from London. He wasn't hooked up to nearly as many tubes and wires. His hair was back to its usual shaggy softness, with a lock that drifted across his forehead. His eyes didn't have that wild, violent look, but instead held a sad resignation.

"I know you made it up about Tori, and the picture you sent was Photoshopped."

"I did it so you'd get that I meant what I said. But here you are anyway. I don't know why I'm surprised, because it's what you do. You have to fix everything and everybody, always the avenging angel. I don't need an angel, Jordan. I need my damn legs to work, and not even you can fix that."

Yes, she could, and it made her crazy with frustration that she couldn't use her ability to heal him. "I'd give anything if this hadn't happened to you. I'll always feel like it was my fault."

"How? Two guys with guns decided to bust into my house and kidnap you. They shot me. How is any of that your fault?"

"They wanted me because I'm the president's daughter."

"I made a choice to go out with you, and I knew you weren't going to be like an insurance salesman's daughter. They assign Secret Service agents to protect you because there's always a risk of something happening. I knew that going in. So maybe I should feel like an idiot for dating the First Daughter."

"Maybe you should. Or at least be mad that I said no that night."

He turned his head and looked right at her. "I know what you're thinking. If we'd been upstairs, we'd have had a chance to get away. But you're wrong. Outside my window it's a twenty-foot drop to the street. The bathroom window is too small to get out of. My parents' window also drops to the street. And the guest room window is a twenty-foot drop to the alley. We would have been at just as much risk upstairs. Maybe worse." He looked at the TV again. "So save your guilt. Jordan. Shit happens, and we don't get a do-over."

As many times as she'd thought of how they might have gotten away, he must have done so endlessly. "That night, I never had the chance to tell you that I love you."

He closed his eyes and laid his head back against the pillow. "You sure have a funny way of showing it. Courtney told me about the new guy."

She'd given a lot of thought to how she'd confront this if he said anything, but she still wished he hadn't. "When I was . . . away, some things happened to me. I feel weird and different. He's new, so he has no expectations, and he made a point of meeting me because he's had some bad things in his own life. I can be with him, and I don't have to pretend."

"Or feel guilty?"

She hated hurting him when he was already in so much pain. But they'd been friends for way too long, and she loved him too much to lie about it. "Guilt has nothing to do with why we're not together, Matthew."

"Of course it doesn't. I broke up with you, and that's why we're not together."

"When you get out of here and put your life back together, I don't want you to feel any regret or guilt for pushing me away."

He opened his eyes and gave her an angry look. "What are you saying? That if I hadn't broken up, you would have?"

"I'm not the same person, Matthew."

All the anger went away, and he looked like he might cry. "Me, neither." He swallowed hard and looked up at the TV hanging in the corner. "I miss you, Jo. Since the day we met, not one single day has gone by that we didn't talk to each other. I can't . . . it's never going to be how it was."

She wasn't going to cry. Matthew hated it when she cried, and no matter what, she was going to hold it together. But God it was hard. "If you want me to go away, if it's better for you not to see me or talk to me, I'll do that. But we've been like best friends for a long time, and it seems to me that now, more than any other time, is when that friendship means the most."

He swallowed again. "I'm just so . . . humiliated."

"With me, Matthew? I'm the one who knows you, who loves you. You're paralyzed because you tried to save me. Do you seriously believe I'd ever, in a billion years, think less of you because you can't walk?"

"That's not all I can't do, Jordan."

"And you feel like less of a human being because of it? The world doesn't start and stop because of sex. You are an *amazing* person, with so much to give."

"It's going to be a while before I can get there."

"I know."

He bent his head and stared at his hands, resting on the blanket. "So this new guy. Courtney says he's a creeper. She hates him."

"Is that the reason she came to see you? To tell you I've become friends with the new guy?" She hoped he'd say yes. She hoped Courtney hadn't asked him to pledge his soul to Eryx.

He looked up and shook his head. "I thought about having the nurse throw her out, because I figured she was here to preach at me. She drives me crazy anyway, but no way could I take that right now." His soft brown eyes reflected confusion. "But she never mentioned Jesus. First, she went off about you and the new guy, then she asked me what I was willing to do to be healed. I was imagining she was about to lay hands on me and speak in tongues or something. I had my finger on the nurse call button. But she said she'd found a new way of thinking, that she was no longer a Christian. My mind was blown."

Jordan didn't say so, but she had to agree. Of all the people who might have pledged, she thought Courtney would have been way at the bottom of the list.

"You know me and God. We're tight, so I told her whatever she was selling, I wasn't interested."

"Did she really say she could heal you?"

"She said she knows someone who could. And get this—he's started some kind of alternative religion and goes around looking for people to pledge to follow him. I told Courtney, I think I saw that episode of *Twilight Zone*, and it didn't end well for anybody. She got all mad and said this was serious, that this guy has powers I can't imagine." He shook his head. "It's like she traded one kind of crazy for another."

"What if it was real? What if someone really could heal you? Would you give up God, if that's what it took?"

He stared up at her for a long time before he answered. "No, never. I'd like to be normal again, but that's too high—" Matthew stopped talking in the middle of his sentence and went inhumanly still.

Jordan blinked. For a nanosecond, she thought he'd died, and her heart skipped several beats.

Then the bathroom door opened, and Eryx stepped into the room. No wonder Matthew was still as a statue. Eryx had frozen him. "I suppose you're very happy that he refused Courtney's offer."

So angry, she forgot to be afraid, she glared at him. "Tracking my cell phone again? How long have you been in there?"

"Long enough." He looked down at Matthew. "It'd mean a lot to you if he could get up out of this bed, wouldn't it?"

"A lot, but not enough to go with you."

"No, I didn't think so." He leaned across the bed rails and slid his hands behind Matthew's back. "But I'm going to fix him anyway. For you."

"Why? Do you think I'll feel like I owe you? Because I won't. He's in that bed because of you."

"Yes, I know. So think of this as my way of apologizing."

"You haven't apologized for anything in over a thousand years."

He was quiet for a while, focused on Matthew's still form,

then he withdrew his hands and stood straight. "Remorse is pretty essential in an apology, and since I never regret anything I do, I never ask anyone to forgive me."

"If you want me to believe you feel bad for what happened to Matthew—"

"I'd never insult your intelligence like that. Of course I don't feel bad, but I don't want you to live with guilt and regret for the rest of eternity."

"Why would you care?"

He stared at her with those dead, flat eyes. "When you come to be with me, and you will, I want your conscience clear."

"So all of my misery can be because of you?"

"I don't want you to be miserable. I want you to have my sons."

She could almost laugh, he was so clueless. "Yeah, because giving birth to your children would never make me miserable."

"They'll be your children, too. I think you'll love them, no matter who their father is." His gaze was intense, and she could swear she saw something in his eyes, something behind the deadness. "I want a son, Jordan, and I want you to be the one to give him to me."

Intensely uncomfortable with both the subject and his nearness, she dropped her gaze to Matthew. "For your own purposes. You're incapable of love. It's all about you, and no kid should have a parent like that."

"Lots of kids have parents like that."

She jerked her gaze back to him.

"They write to famous strangers, like you, looking for what their parents can't or won't give them. Maybe I'm incapable of love, and what I'd feel for my own offspring would be narcissistic obsession instead of self-sacrificing adoration, but I want a child. I want something that belongs to me."

Jordan slowly shook her head. "People don't belong to people, even if they're your children. And a child of yours would also be mine. Even if you locked me away and never let me see him, he'd still have a part of me in him, and that would make all the difference."

"I'm aware. It's the Anabo in you that will make him great."

"I'm also Mephisto, or had you forgotten? Suppose my son is born with Mephisto, and his DNA ensures he hates you? What if he grows up and turns on you?"

"How did you become Mephisto?"

"Key kissed me."

He looked surprised. "That's all?" He saw her nod, then shrugged. "It may be that the Mephisto in you won't always pass down. I'll take my chances that one of my sons will be like me. He'll see the possibilities in ruling Hell the way I envision."

She looked away from him again. "I'm seventeen, Eryx. I don't want to have babies. Not for a long time."

"I can wait."

She was astonished. "Did I just hear you being considerate?"

"I'm a son of Hell, and some would call me a monster, but I'm not an animal. Our mother was very big on manners."

"What is it that you think you can do to me that'll convince me to give you what you want?"

"Not what I can do *to* you, Jordan, but what I can do *for* you."

"Like healing Matthew?"

Eryx shook his head. "He's not the most important thing in your life, is he?"

"He's one of them."

"But he's not Kyros."

She took a step back from the bed. "Lame threat, Eryx. You can't do anything to Key."

"No one knows my brother like I do." He moved around the bed and stopped when he was still several feet away. "All of my brothers are way closer to the barren wasteland that's my soul than they'll ever be to the Eden that's yours, but Key's different than the others. For whatever reason, he never had as much of our mother's light as the rest of us. There's a certain kind of darkness in him that was there even before he jumped. He hides it well, and it might be that you'll never see it, even in an eternity with him, but never doubt that it's there. Has he told you about Kyanos? What it was like when we were boys?"

She was afraid to hear what he would say. She told herself over and over that he was a liar, that he'd do anything to get what he wanted. So why was it that she was listening to him? Why did she have the terrifying feeling that he wasn't lying? Slowly, she nodded.

"Our mother loved each of us, but it was a little different

with me. I was her firstborn, and since Mephistopheles couldn't be there all the time, she leaned on me. Key was always insanely jealous of how it was between our mother and me. I was never sure if his jealousy was toward me, or our mother, because as much as he loved her, he loved me. He'd act out sometimes and say cruel things to her. He'd turn on me when I least expected it—so vicious, he almost killed me, twice."

"I don't believe you."

"I don't care. Maybe you want to think he's different now that you're with him, but that dark side of him will never go away."

"I could never be afraid of Key."

"No, you're strong enough to withstand whatever he does, and the Anabo in you will always forgive him."

"Then I don't understand why you're telling me all of this."

"Because he's closer to what I am than any of them, Jordan. He doesn't hate me like they do." He took a step closer. "If you refuse me, I'll convince him to give up what small glimmer of light is still in his soul and pledge to join me. We'll be like Lucifer and Mephistopheles, working together for one common purpose. Key will be just like me."

The horror of that was too huge to imagine. He'd have no chance of Heaven. His brothers would hate him. *She* would hate him, because she was Mephisto, now hardwired to despise Eryx and his followers. "He would never join you."

"Are you absolutely sure? He still loves me, and he feels just as guilty now for what happened to me as he did a thousand years ago. I know. I see it in his eyes, every time we meet. You've seen it, too. You know."

"If Key hasn't felt guilty enough to join you in over a thousand years, why would he now?"

His smile was diabolical. "I've never asked. If I do, I'll remind him what I did for the rest of them, and what I lost. I'll tell him I can't stand the loneliness, and he'll know exactly what I mean, because it's the same for him."

"Not anymore. Now he has me, and he'll never leave me." She said it, but inside she was screaming, *What if he did?* She'd never known just how strong guilt could be until she found out about Mariah. How far would she go to help her sister? She honestly didn't know.

"See if you can convince yourself that he'll tell me no. And if you have the smallest doubt, agree to be with me at Erinýes and give me the sons I want, and I'll leave Key alone."

He looked toward Matthew. "When he unfreezes, he'll know immediately that he's well because he'll feel his legs. He'll think it's a miracle, and everyone will give thanks to God, but you and I will always know the truth." He looked at her again. "Won't we?"

He disappeared, and Matthew blinked.

EIGHTEEN

SATURDAY NIGHT, WHEN KEY POPPED FROM HIS CLOSET IN Colorado to the D.C. town house, Mirabelle and Brody were watching *Dr. Who*. Brody paused it when Key came in, and whistled. "Nice tux."

"Thanks. Why aren't you going to this hoedown?"

"Not much for dancing."

That was bullshit. Key knew he was still hung up on Jenny Brown, the girl he'd met at Telluride High last year, when he was going to school with Jax. He had fallen hard and couldn't get past it. Key had gone into town to check her out, hoping she'd have some qualities that would qualify her as a Lumina. She was a nice, sweet, quiet kind of nerdy girl—a perfect fit for Brody—but she would never be a Lumina. Her dark side was too strong.

So Brody was stuck pining for a girl he could never have. He'd shown zero interest in any of the girls at Oates, despite their obvious interest in him, further indication of just how gone he was on Jenny.

"Kyros," Mirabelle said in her heavy British accent, "you look positively dashing!"

"Thank you." The doorbell rang, and he was unaccountably nervous when he opened the door, relieved when it was Gunther in his dark suit.

"Who is this, Key?" Mirabelle asked from behind him. "Oh, hello! Are you Jordan's Secret Man?"

Gunther stared and didn't bother correcting her. "Uhm, yeah. Uh . . . yes. Yes, ma'am."

"Mirabelle is my aunt, Gunther," Key said.

"Yes, I see." Gunther seemed to appreciate Mirabelle, and she was all kinds of fascinated by Gunther. Key expected a lightning bolt to land right between them. Then Gunther smiled, which was highly unusual, and Key blinked. The big man had Lumina written all over him. At the first possible opportunity, he'd ask his brothers to come to see him.

For now, Gunther needed to drive. "Ready?" Key asked, hoping to break the spell.

Gunther stepped back. "Yeah . . . yes, ready. Jordan's in the Suburban, waiting." He smiled again at Mirabelle. "Very pleasant to see you."

"Yes, lovely! Do come in when you return Kyros home, and

we'll have a bit of tea. I'd offer you my finest Irish whiskey, but you're on duty and all that." She beamed up at him, and he almost tripped over the potted plant on the top step outside the town house.

Key went around him and down to the back door of the SUV. When he opened it, he had a hard time taking his next breath. Jordan was dressed all in white, in a long velvet dress that had crystals sprinkled all over. Her arms were bare, but partially covered by a flimsy-looking scarf. Her hair was up, and she wore dangly diamond earrings. With all that, and the glow of Anabo, she was the most beautiful thing he'd ever seen. *Ever.*

He climbed in to sit beside her and immediately reached for her hand because he had to touch her. Her bluebell scent mingled with her perfume and he felt light-headed, it was so provocative.

"You look amazing in a tux," she murmured.

He squeezed her hand and said, "Not as amazing as you look in that dress. I didn't think you could get more beautiful."

She looked up at him and smiled, but it was kind of sad.

"Is everything all right?"

"It's fine."

He hadn't seen her since Thursday night because she hadn't come to school yesterday. While she was at the hospital, Matthew had made a miraculous recovery, and she wound up staying with him the rest of the day, to help get him settled back home. She swore she'd had nothing to do with his healing, and he had to believe her, because if she'd fixed him, she wouldn't be here. Lucifer would have taken her out immediately. Still, it seemed extremely strange.

Last night, she'd said she wasn't coming to visit because she was emotionally exhausted, and she'd promised to tell him tonight how it had gone with Matthew. But that would be later, after the dance.

Hank turned around from the shotgun position and eyed Key. "You clean up nice."

"Thanks. Hey, why are you guys on duty? Don't you always have the day shift?"

"We switched out with the night guys because Miss Princess wanted it that way."

Jordan explained, "Hank and Gunther know you better. The night guys would hover too much. And Hank and Gunther . . . wait, where is Gunther?" She leaned forward to look past Key to the front door of the town house. "Key, he's totes flirting with your aunt."

"Who could blame him?" Hank asked. "The woman is beautiful." He rolled down the window. "Hey, Casanova, there's this thing called your job."

A minute later, they were on their way to the school, and when they arrived, Hank and Gunther were all business. Hank said to Jordan, "We'll try not to be too intrusive, but we need to stay closer to you than we do at school. It's bound to be crowded, so don't stray too far. Keep one if us in sight at all times." He looked at Key. "You're taller than most, so help out Shorty here, will you?"

"If you'll look the other way when I kiss her."

"Done." He got out of the Suburban and ten minutes later

gave the go-ahead to Gunther for them to come inside.

Key was actually vaguely interested, and as they went through the front doors of the school, then the security gates just inside, he noticed the lighting had been dimmed in the hallways. Everyone was dressed to kill, and some kids he hadn't thought particularly attractive looked damn good tonight.

At the end of the main hall was the dining hall, a cavernous room with walnut-paneled walls, an arched ceiling, and Gothic stained-glass windows. It was usually filled with rows of tables, but tonight, it had been transformed into a winter palace, with fake snow along the edges of the floor, on the refreshment tables, and across the stage that had been erected at the front of the room. Thousands of snowflakes in all shapes and sizes, made from some kind of glittery white paper, hung from the ceiling and swayed gently above the heads of the kids on the dance floor. From a side wall, a hipster DJ was doing a show that would rival any in the high-dollar clubs the Mephisto frequented. At the moment, he was playing Jay-Z.

He heard Jordan say, "Where did all this come from?"

Behind them, Megan Thompson said, "Eryx contributed a whole lot of money."

Jordan immediately frowned, her obvious pleasure in the decorations and the DJ tainted because they had come from Eryx. Key wished he'd thought of it. He'd have given a boatload of money to spiff things up, but he didn't know jack about how high school dances were done.

"Come on," he said to Jordan, taking her hand and leading her into the room. "Do you want cupcakes or dancing first?"

"Cupcakes."

He smiled. "Of course you do."

And of course the cupcakes were elaborate confections, each with its own unique sugar snowflake, arranged in an enormous tower that looked like a snow-covered peak in Colorado.

Jordan looked more annoyed. "The cupcakes were supposed to come from the Women's Center, a fund-raiser for them, and something the women could do to help boost their confidence."

Megan was still behind them. "Eryx had this made by the cake guy in Baltimore. I heard it cost three thousand dollars."

Key removed a cupcake from the display and held it out to Jordan. She shook her head.

"It's not the cupcake's fault Eryx paid for it."

She relented and bit into it, then moved closer and said around the bite, "Best freakin' cupcake I've ever had in my life." She swallowed. "Dammit."

Key joined her, then carried one over to Hank. He shook his head. "We never eat food served at private functions."

"Why? Because it might be drugged?"

"Something like that." He was looking around constantly, methodically sweeping his gaze around the room, always ending up at Jordan, who'd polished off her first cupcake and was well into her second. "That kid eats an amazing amount of food for such a small body. Wonder where she puts it?" Hank said.

"She must have an extra fast metabolism."

"Yeah." He glanced at Key. "You gonna eat that cupcake or stand here and taunt me with it all night?"

"Oh. Sorry." He ate it in three bites, then went to get Jordan. She handed her tiny little silver purse to Hank, who hung it over his arm while he continued his vigil, and they went out to the dance floor. But not too far away from Hank. Gunther was on the other side of the room, also scoping out possible threats.

Key was careful to steer clear of Eryx and Tessa, not wanting to spoil Jordan's fun. Except she didn't look like she was enjoying herself. When a slow song began, he pulled her close, and as they moved around in the sparkles from the mirror ball above, he asked, "What's wrong? And don't tell me nothing. You're sad, or worried, or something. Is it Matthew? Did it go that badly?"

She looked up at him. "It didn't go badly at all. We're still friends, and he's accepted that it won't ever be what it was before."

"You don't seem very happy about it. Are you having regrets?"

Her surprise was genuine. "None at all, Key. I'm happy to be with you."

"You say you're happy that it's all good with Matthew, and you're happy he can walk again, and you're happy to be with me, but your eyes are making you a liar. What's going on, Jordan?"

"Nothing, Key. Maybe it's just sinking in that I'll be leaving soon." She was staring at his bow tie. "I'm kind of hot. Let's get something to drink."

He led her off the dance floor to the table with lemonade

punch. After she'd drained three glasses, he took her hand, pulled her into the darkened kitchen, and hauled her into his arms. Well aware that Hank was on the other side of the door, and that the receiving door to the outside was locked and bolted, he had no worries about someone walking in on them.

He settled his lips over hers and tasted sugar. He dipped his tongue and touched hers and tasted more sugar. When she turned her head slightly, he kissed her more deeply, holding her small body against his, inhaling her scent of bluebells and reveling in indescribable peace.

It occurred to him that the music had stopped, but he didn't think much about it until he heard Mr. Barnes, the headmaster, say Jordan's name. He lifted his head just as Hank opened the door.

"You were just crowned Winter Queen. Better stop sucking face and get out here to rule your kingdom."

Blinking up at Key from sleepy, sexy eyes, she said, "This must be my consolation prize for getting booted out of office."

"It's because they love you, Jordan."

"Well, it *is* nice, and it does make me feel better, but if Eryx is Winter King, I'm throwing the damn crown at him and leaving."

"Deal." He let go of her, then offered his arm. Hank opened the door wide, and they walked back into the dining hall, turning right to head through the crowd to the stage. People were applauding as she climbed the five steps, and she smiled and waved when she was next to Mr. Barnes.

He spoke into the cordless mic in his hand, "Now, we crown the Winter King, whose word is law, just for tonight."

Key stood in front of the stage, Hank right beside him, and Gunther on the other side. He saw Eryx standing maybe a yard behind Gunther, his entire focus on Jordan. Lately, it seemed as if every time Key turned around, there was Eryx, staring at her like she might disappear if he looked away. His brother was completely obsessed, which was scary as hell.

Standing next to Eryx, Tessa moved her gaze between him and Jordan, her big green eyes filled with hurt and anger. Was she just realizing that her new boyfriend couldn't care less about her? Key might have felt bad for her, except this meant she'd be far more likely to ditch Eryx and keep her soul. While he watched, she turned and walked away, disappearing into the crowd. Eryx never noticed.

He suddenly turned his gaze to Key's, and that moment passed between them, just as it always did—a microsecond of remembrance of how it was before Eryx became a monster. And just like always, it was gone so quickly, Key wasn't quite sure it had been real. Then Eryx's dead eyes refocused on the stage, on Jordan.

Mr. Barnes was clearly excited about announcing whom the students had elected as Winter King. "Are you ready?"

The entire crowd shouted, *"Yes!"*

"All right, then, I give you this year's Winter King—Matthew Whittaker!"

The doors at the back of the hall opened, and a collective

gasp circled the room when Matthew walked in. As he made his way toward the stage, everyone was clapping, yelling his name, or whistling. The swell of affection for him was palpable. Key glanced at Eryx and knew from his look of smug satisfaction that he was behind this. But why?

He looked up at Jordan and knew in an instant that she was upset. Her smile was more fake than the plastic snow scattered around the room. He decided she must be bothered that she was to be in the spotlight with Matthew, like it was business as usual.

As Matthew climbed the steps, the crowd went even more nuts and began to chant, "Kiss! Kiss!" Key could see now how it had been before the kidnapping, before Matthew was shot. He and Jordan were much beloved by the other students. As a couple, they must have been sweet, and everyone loved a sweet romance.

He didn't, but he was a son of Hell. Watching Jordan stand there in that incredible dress, he didn't think she did, either. Not anymore. He thought of her stabbing Jax a hundred times. He remembered the morning she went off the page, screaming about Eryx and how much she hated him, swearing in graphic detail which of his body parts she wanted to cut off and feed to alligators. He recalled the flight from London, and how every night of the past week had been a repeat, and they had taken things a little further each time. His pint-sized Anabo was almost as aggressive as he was. Nobody would call what was between them sweet.

She shot him a resigned look, then turned to Matthew, who awkwardly gave her a quick peck.

Mr. Barnes handed him the mic, and as the room quieted, Matthew sobered and looked out across the sea of faces. "These days, especially for those of us who live in D.C. and have family members in the government, it's easy to become jaded, and maybe lose faith and hope, but I'm living proof that miracles exist."

Key saw Jordan shoot a quick glance at Eryx, who had a knowing look on his face. He knew then how Matthew was able to walk into this dance and stand up there and give an inspirational speech. There was no miracle. Eryx had healed him.

His nerves went from mildly agitated to full attention. What was going on? Why would his brother heal Matthew, then make sure he was here tonight? Had he decided to go the opposite direction and ingratiate himself to Jordan, instead of threatening her? He remembered her comment about there being no new lost souls since last week, other than Courtney, and that none of them were trying to jack with her. Even Carla had backed off. It dawned on him, suddenly, that none of the lost souls were here tonight. Had Eryx told them to stay home?

He looked again toward Jordan, who was standing stiffly, staring off into the distance. Like she was trying hard not to listen to Matthew's words. Of course she wouldn't want to hear him waxing on about miracles if she knew Eryx was behind his recovery. As soon as possible, he would ask her what exactly had gone down in Matthew's hospital room.

"I don't know how it happened," Matthew continued, "or why, but it changed everything for me, and not just because I'm able to walk again. I had planned to go to Yale with Jordan next fall, then I thought I wouldn't be going anywhere, at least for a while." He ducked his head for a moment, then looked up and smiled. "But that's all changed now. This afternoon I accepted an offer from Princeton, because I intend to become a minister. It's radical, I guess, since I'd originally planned to be an attorney and work here in Washington, but I figured out that this is what I'm meant to do. So I'd just like to say, I hope you all can find what you're meant to do without having to be shot, paralyzed, and miraculously healed." He waited for the laughter to die down, then said, "Thanks to everyone who sent cards and left messages, and thank you for electing me Winter King. Now, go forth and have fun, or heads will roll."

The applause and shouts and whistles were deafening, and they didn't stop until Matthew had escorted Jordan to the dance floor and music began for their inaugural dance.

At the edge of the crowd, Key watched, and he was thinking hard about what Eryx was up to when his brother came to stand next to him.

"Why'd you do it, Eryx?"

"For her," he replied. "She shouldn't spend any more time feeling guilty."

"Surely you don't believe this will change her mind. Do you *seriously* think she'll stay with you of her own free will and give you what you want?"

"No, I don't. I concede defeat, brother, and leave her to you."

He peered at Key curiously. "Why you? Did you have to fight the others for her?"

"She smells like bluebells."

"What?"

"Never mind. She's with me, and that's never going to change."

"Yes, I see that now. So I'll go back to Romania, and be alone. Like always."

"Oh, come on. Don't play the lonely-hearts card. I counted five girls at Erinýes, and I doubt you granted them immortality and had them move in so they could scrub the floors. You're like the Hugh Hefner of the dark side." He shook his head. "You're a lotta things, Eryx, but alone isn't one of them."

"There's a difference between alone and lonely."

"If you somehow coerced Jordan into coming to Erinýes, you'd still be lonely. She hates you, and that'll never change. She's not going to fix you. Nobody can fix you."

Eryx met his gaze. "But you wish someone could, don't you?"

Key's bow tie was suddenly way too tight. "Yes."

"Maybe you think I don't remember how it was, Kyros, but I do. And as hard as you try to hide it, I know you don't hate me. You're the only soul in existence who doesn't."

Was he really having this conversation? "It changes nothing, Eryx. You'll always be the enemy, and my only purpose is to defeat you, so how I feel about the past, or you, makes no difference."

Eryx looked toward Jordan and Matthew. "Who says what

your purpose is? By what right does anyone tell you what to do with your life?"

Key remembered the day he jumped, hanging in the balance between death and resurrection, hearing that deep, frightening voice in the dark. *"There may come a time when your brother will tempt you to join him, to take up his fight. Don't let your love for him blind you to what he is, or lead you into believing he can change. If you do, you're lost."*

He watched Jordan, who kept looking toward them as she and Matthew moved around the dance floor, and said to his brother, "Lucifer told me the day I jumped that it's my obligation to lead the others and kick your ass."

"Who are you obligated to, Key? What's Lucifer ever done for you, or for our brothers?"

Turning his head, Key looked into Eryx's dead eyes and said simply, "He didn't take out Mephistopheles for falling in love with our mother."

"So you'll spend all of eternity fighting me, just to save our father from execution?"

He nodded toward Jordan. "I'm beginning to understand why he did what he did, so yeah, now more than ever, I'll do what Lucifer asks."

"Think about it, Key. It'd be like when we were boys, you and me. We could—"

"Get away from him!" Jordan had booked it across the dance floor, rushed Eryx, and shoved him hard, sending him staggering

backward into the crowd of kids who'd been watching the dance. She was righteous, following Eryx and shoving him again. "Take your bullshit lies and *get out!*" She had the element of surprise on her side, because Eryx was clearly stunned, so when she doubled up her fist and clocked him with all the power of the Mephisto in her, he went down hard.

Hank and Gunther were there instantly, but in the nanosecond it took them to process the reality that their charge wasn't the one in danger, Key had his arms around Jordan, restraining her from jumping on Eryx and continuing to punch his face. She struggled to get loose while she shouted at Eryx. "No more threats, no more tricks, and I'm all done with games. This is war! It is *on*, you sick fu—"

Key put his hand over her mouth, and she bit him, but he kept his hand there and said in a low voice against her ear, "You're awesome, and we're leaving." Swinging her up into his arms, he turned and walked toward the doors of the dining hall, past the wide-eyed stares of her classmates, past Mr. Barnes, who stepped up like he intended to stop Key, then stepped back again when Hank moved in front of him.

Jordan clung to his neck and burst into tears about the time they passed Matthew. Key noticed the kid had tears in his eyes, staring at Jordan with grief and shock on his face. Tessa stood just next to him with the same expression.

As he walked down the main hall toward the front doors, he heard Jordan whispering through her sobs, "Don't go, don't . . .

change. Don't leave me. Oh, God, please don't . . . leave me, Key. I love you so much. I'd die if you were . . . if I had to . . . if you became what he is. Please, *please* don't . . . leave."

"Shhh, it's okay now, Jordan. Everything's going to be good, and I'm not leaving. I'd never leave you. Did you think I'd go with Eryx?"

"Not . . . no, but you looked so sad, because you . . . love him . . . and I could tell he was trying to talk you into—"

"I'd never do it, Jordan. If there was anything at all I could do to help him become what he once was, I'd do it. But there's not." They'd reached the doors, and while Hank moved to open them, Key looked down at Jordan's face, wet with tears. "I'll never forget that you punched him out, thinking you were protecting me. My whole life, I don't remember anyone ever doing something like that for me."

"Your whole life, nobody ever loved you like I do."

He wanted to kiss her, *so much*, but Hank was waiting at the open door, and Gunther was right behind them, so he carried her outside to the Suburban and said, as he set her into the backseat, "Will you come to my room tonight?"

She accepted the handkerchief he handed her and nodded. "Key?"

He hesitated before closing her door. "Yeah?"

"I'm sorry I lost it," she whispered. "I'm not exactly sure what I said back there."

"We're okay," he said softly. "If you'd gone too crazy, I'd have thrown a freeze, but we're okay. They probably think this is you acting out because of the kidnapping, and no one will hold that against you." He closed the door, went around to the other side, and when he was in his seat, Gunther drove away from the school.

~~~

An hour later, Jordan was dressed in her favorite sweatpants and a Library of Congress T-shirt, waiting for her dad to come in to talk to her about what had happened. He'd returned home early from a fund-raiser dinner for Senator Markham, just in time to get a phone call from Mr. Barnes. After he hung up, he told her to wait in her room and he'd be along as soon as he changed out of his tux.

She sat in the middle of her bed, looking at the bunny, and called Key. When he answered, she said, "It's going to be a while. Mr. Barnes called Dad, and now he wants to talk."

"How are you feeling?"

"Still a little shaky."

"Whatever gave you the idea that I'd sell out and join Eryx?"

"He told me if I'd give him what he wants, he'd leave you alone, and when I saw him talking to you, and saw the look on your face, I knew he was trying to talk you into it."

He was quiet for a long time before he asked in a low, funny voice, "Did you think about going along with him, even for a second?"

"No, because I didn't believe you'd ever go to his side."

"Then why'd you go after him?"

"Because he was hurting you." She smiled at Mr. Bunny. "And because I love you."

"Are you sure about that, Jordan? We haven't known each other all that long, and I'm a son of Hell; my brothers tell me all the time that I'm hard and difficult."

"Are you trying to talk me out of it? Of course I'm sure. I don't need to know you another year or two or fifty to know how I feel." She heard a knock. "Here's Dad. I gotta go, but I'll call Brody as soon as I can, and then I'll be there."

"Good, because I have something to tell you."

She smiled at the rabbit again. They said good-bye, and she called out for her dad to come in. But it wasn't her father who opened the door.

Still dressed in his tux, Eryx walked in. He came to the edge of the bed and glanced at the rabbit before he said, "I've frozen your father and the housekeeper, to make sure we're not interrupted. That gives me about ten minutes to say good-bye."

"Ten minutes is a long good-bye." She slid to the other side of the bed and got to her feet. "Also, I don't believe you."

"It's true. I realize there's nothing I can do to convince you. I thought about taking out Tessa, Matthew, and your father, but you'll be gone from here soon, and their loss would fade in your mind as years went by. You'd know that, of course, so even though it would cause you terrible pain, it still wouldn't convince you. Persuading them to pledge to me would also hurt you, but you'd still stay with Key. I'm all out of ideas, so as much as I hate it, I'm giving up."

She could think of no reply, so she kept her eyes on him, ready to pop out, and said nothing.

"I'm incapable of love, as you said, but I wanted you to know that I admire you. What I like best about you is your strength, and ironically, that's why you won't go with me. At no time in all the years since I jumped have I ever resented my brothers, until now. I don't understand what it is about Key that inspires such blind devotion, but I envy him that."

"You do realize that I don't believe a word you're saying?"

He looked surprised and damn close to hurt. "That's your prerogative, but I'm not lying. I've never known a girl like you. I've never wanted a girl the way I want you."

"Even after I decked you?"

"Especially after that." He rubbed his jaw. "Where'd you learn to do that?"

"Jax taught me."

He gazed at her from those dead, flat eyes, and she'd swear again that she saw a flicker of life somewhere in the shadows. "As much as anything," he said, "I like being around you because you know what I am but you're not afraid of me."

"I'm incredibly uncomfortable. It's taking all my self-discipline not to pop out of here."

"Why do I make you uncomfortable? Because I'm always talking about babies?"

"Because you have the power to alter the entire course of my life."

"True, but if I were the one to mark you, I'd want it to be because you chose me over Key."

Why was he beating this to death? Again, she made no reply because she didn't have anything to say that hadn't already been said.

"Will you let me kiss you before I go?"

He just didn't get it. She slowly shook her head. "No."

"One kiss. Then I'll leave."

"I don't trust you, Eryx. You're going to try to take me to Erinýes."

"I won't, Jordan. I know you're never going to give me a son, even if you were marked as mine forever. It's just a kiss."

"I owe you nothing. I don't feel sorry for you. I'm sworn to fight you for the rest of time. And I'm still seriously pissed off that you tried to talk Key into joining you. Where in all of that does kissing you fit? It doesn't. You need to leave. I'll see you at the next knife fight."

He moved around the bed, but stopped when she stepped back. "I just want to touch you, to be near you, even if it's only for a minute. I want to know . . . " He suddenly looked very sad. "I want to remember what it feels like to stand in the light. It's been a long, long time."

He took another step closer, and she took another one back. "I see right through you, Eryx. You think if I let you kiss me, I'll change somehow, the way I did after Key kissed me. But it won't work. I became Mephisto because I chose to, of my own free will.

The only way I'd ever go with you is by choice, and that's never going to happen, whether I let you kiss me, or not."

He moved closer and inhaled. "You always smell like bluebells."

Stunned, she scrambled for an explanation. How could he catch her scent, the one only Key knew?

"There were bluebells on Kyanos. They grew in the meadow, and Key always got mad at me for picking them to take to Mana. He said what made them beautiful was the company they kept, so he'd take her there to see them. Like I said, he was always jealous, always trying to one-up me."

Knowing Key's love of flowers, she didn't think he'd done that to one-up Eryx. He wanted his mother to see their beauty the way he saw it. "If he knew you were here now, asking me to kiss you, he'd be a lot more than jealous. Aren't you worried he can sense you're here? He might show up at any second."

Eryx shook his head and took another step toward her. "I eavesdropped, so I know he thinks you're having a heart-to-heart with your father, and he knows I'm giving up, so he isn't mentally searching for me." One more step. "If you're sure it won't change you, because you choose not to let it, why not kiss me?"

Why was he so determined? "Because I don't want to."

He took another step. He was close enough to grab her now, but she didn't back up again. She stood her ground and began to imagine Key's room, the chair before the fire. Was he sitting there, right now, waiting for her? If Eryx so much as twitched, she would pop out instantly.

"What if your kiss could change *me*? Would you do it?"

"If I knew for sure it would work, I'd do it in a heartbeat. But you'd have to choose to change."

He stared hard at her and she was absolutely certain she saw a flicker in his eyes of something besides infinite evil. "I'd change for you," he whispered.

"You're lying." He had to be lying.

But if he was lying, how could he fake what she saw in his eyes? How was he able to smell bluebells? That had to mean something. What if she really did have the ability to change him? He'd be like he was before he jumped; the brother Key missed so much. He'd cease to be a threat to humanity, and the Mephisto would no longer have to spend their days hunting the lost souls. They could search instead for their own Anabo, for love and redemption.

Key's words about Eryx replayed in her head. *"He's the only spirit ever in existence to belong nowhere. No one wants him. He wants Hell because he wants to belong. He believes ruling Hell, holding the spirit of all humankind in his power, will fill the empty place where his light used to live."*

"If I knew you'd stay with me," Eryx said into the silence surrounding them, "I'd accept your light and end the war for Hell."

"You said yourself, you're incapable of love. This is only an obsession for you. What is it that you want from me? Because you've gone way beyond the baby thing."

"I can't explain it, because I don't understand it myself. I realized while I was at your school that being close to you makes me feel different. Almost calm. It's completely addictive. I can only imagine what it would be like to hold you next to me and kiss you."

She shook her head. "If you ever felt any love for Kyros, you wouldn't ask me to do this."

"*If* I ever felt love for my brother?" He took one last step, so close now, she could feel his inhuman heat. "I loved him so much, I sacrificed my soul." He reached out and touched her cheek. "I don't know if it's possible, but maybe you can get it back."

"If you changed, you wouldn't want me to be with you. You'd see how badly it would hurt Key, and you couldn't do it to him."

His fingers were hot, gently stroking down, to her throat. "Then you'd be free to go back to him, so you have nothing to lose. Say you'll stay with me. Kiss me and give me what you will of your light." He was bending slightly, coming closer and closer. "Change everything," he whispered. "Say yes."

She'd begun to shake, but not because she was afraid. Every nerve in her body was at attention, every muscle stretched taut, and her heart beat erratically. All she could think about was Key, and the centuries he'd grieved for his brother while leading the Mephisto, day in and day out. If she did this, he'd understand why, but would he forgive her?

Eryx's hand at her neck was gently pulling her toward him, until his face was inches from hers. "Being this close to you is amazing," he said with a soft smile. "Please say yes."

"I don't . . . I can't . . . yes," she whispered, just before his lips met hers. When he drew her next to him and deepened the kiss, she kissed him back, praying it would work, that he'd become something besides a monster.

But kissing monsters was dangerous, and it took less than a minute for her to realize she'd made a fatal mistake. Intense heat was already racing through her body, and when she broke the kiss and looked into his eyes, that spark of life was gone. In its place was triumph.

"Oh, God, you *tricked* me." She shoved away from him and backed toward the window, staring at him in horror.

He shrugged. "Yes, I suppose I did, but not exactly intentional, Jordan. I really did think you could give me some of your light, that it would make a difference. Now I know, I'm truly lost for all time."

"This will kill Key. Take it back, Eryx. Let me go."

He looked sad. "I can't do that. You said yes. You committed to stay with me. You turned away from God and you can never go back."

She couldn't cry. This was beyond crying.

"There's a certain symmetry to this, Jordan. All those centuries ago, Eve believed Lucifer when he told her she would be like God if she ate the fruit of the tree of life. She changed the fate of all mankind." He watched her bump against her desk. "For a moment, you believed you had greater power than Lucifer, that you could do something he can't, which is to change me so I'm no longer a threat to the world. You'll be with me forever, and just like Eve, you'll alter the course of humanity." He came toward her, but stopped when she held up her hands. "I'll go now, and let you say your good-byes. Your father is on his way to your room. I hear his footsteps." He gave her a strange smile. "It only hurts for a little while. Then you won't know the difference."

He disappeared just as Dad knocked at her door.

She moved toward her bed as if she were in a trance, sat at the edge, and determinedly pulled herself together. "Come in," she called.

Dad opened the door and came to sit next to her on the bed. "How're we doing, Jo?"

She wanted to scream that she was about to become a monster. But she didn't. "I had a reason, Dad. That guy has been going out with Tessa, and he was awful to her."

Dad sighed and reached for her hand. "It's admirable of you to take up for Tessa, but I think you know punching someone in the face isn't the best way to handle a situation."

"I know, and I'm sorry."

"You've never been violent a day in your life. I have to think this is because of what happened. I want you to see Dr. Meyers again, and keep going until you've resolved it. Will you do that?"

She gripped his hand and nodded. "I love you, Dad."

He slipped an arm around her shoulders and hugged her next to him. "I love you, too, Jordan. I want you to be happy, and I don't think that's possible as long as you avoid dealing with the abduction. You can't ignore things like that, or they eat at your soul."

She leaned her head against him, suddenly feeling very young. "I'm sorry everything's so bad right now. I see how stressed out you are all the time, and I wish I could do something to make you feel better."

"How are you at writing tax legislation?"

She kissed his cheek. "I predict things will turn around, very soon. Keep the faith, Dad."

"I'm doing my best." He squeezed her, then dropped his arm and got to his feet. He walked to her bulletin board and stood staring at the dried flowers, campaign buttons, and Post-it notes Matthew had stuck in her textbooks over the past two years. "Speaking of faith, this is never to be repeated, but I discovered something unusual about Tom Markham tonight. He's keeping it very private, because he's certain if it becomes public it'll cost him the election, but he's dropped Christianity for some alternative religion."

She felt a little panicky. "Did he tell you that?"

"It was the strangest thing, and damned awkward, but yeah. I went into the men's room, along with half the Secret Service guys, and Markham came in right behind us. He started whispering to me about this new religion, and how I should look into it because it had changed his life."

"What kind of religion?"

"I'm not sure, but he's completely convinced it's the answer to all my problems. If I join with him and the others who've converted, we'll see a way to get the country out of the mess it's in."

"Does it seem like something that might interest you?"

He crossed the room and looked at her photos. "Nah, I'm too traditional to go for something like that." He smiled at her. "It's a pretty big deal to me to make sure I get to Heaven. I want to see your mother again."

"So no matter how bad things get, you're sticking with the Episcopalians?"

"These are hard times, but there've been hard times before, and this country has weathered them. We will again. I'll keep right on doing what I've always done." He walked toward her and bent to kiss the top of her head. "Good night, sweetheart."

"Good night, Dad."

He stopped with his hand on the door and looked back at her. "I almost forgot to tell you: you're suspended for three days, so no school until next Thursday." He gave her a sad smile. "We'll work through it, Jo."

When he was gone, she lifted her hand and touched her lips. "I don't think so."

⁓

An hour later, the heat in her body was more extreme. It wasn't like Mephisto, which had made her feel hot from the inside out. This actually burned, and she was in pain. It wasn't a gradual change, like Mephisto. This was like being electrocuted, realigning all the neurons in her brain, confusing her. She sat on her bed and stared at the bunny and prayed for God to have mercy on her, because she was certainly losing Anabo. Her birthmark was fading.

At first, she'd thought about going to Key, telling him what Eryx had done, but then she'd have to tell him she had let Eryx kiss her, and no matter how much she wanted to believe he'd understand why she did it, she knew he'd never understand. And she couldn't see any way at all that he could fix what was happening to her.

The only good thing in any of this was the irony that Eryx would still lose. As the Anabo seeped away from her spirit, she lost the ability to bear his children. His deviousness had cost him what he wanted most.

She thought of Jane and what she must have suffered at Eryx's hands. Did he kiss her when he marked her? Had she lost Anabo? Maybe that's why Phoenix couldn't bring her back, not because she carried Eryx's mark. If she'd lost Anabo, she couldn't carry anyone's mark. She'd simply be another human, who couldn't be resurrected.

Jordan was already immortal, and her loss of Anabo would mean something entirely different than what it would have meant for Jane. She couldn't be human again, and if she wasn't Anabo, or Mephisto, she would become like Eryx.

Before she lost it all, she sat down at her desk and wrote Key an e-mail, but by the time she finished explaining what was happening to her, she'd lost the inclination to send it and so didn't bother.

Another hour passed. She was sad, then angry, then confused because it didn't seem so bad. She felt as if she were seeing things for the first time, and nothing in the world of her bedroom made any sense at all. She went to her bulletin board and ripped every single thing off of it, throwing it all to the floor. She took the pictures of Matthew and Tessa, Mom and Dad, friends and family, off the wall, removed them from the frames, and ripped them to shreds. She went into her closet and pulled out the boxes of cards and letters and other mementos and carried them to the elevator. Downstairs, in the basement, she took them down the hall to the incinerator room and tossed all of it.

Back upstairs, she returned to her bedroom and stared at herself in the mirror. Her birthmark was gone. Her eyes were no longer blue, but gray so dark, they were almost black. When her cell rang and she saw it was Key, she put it on silent and dropped it in the trashcan. She was all done with Key, and the Mephisto. She thought of Mariah and felt a twinge of regret, but it was gone as quickly as it had come and she decided not to think about her again.

Back on her bed, she stared at the rabbit and wondered why on Earth she'd ever liked the pitiful old thing. His black button eyes seemed to be mocking her, and she turned him facedown.

"I've come back for you," she heard Eryx say, and when she looked across the room toward the window, he was there, gazing at her with beautiful black eyes, full of lust and longing.

"Maybe you won't want me anymore. I've lost Anabo."

"I'll always want you, Jordan, and who knows? It could be that because you became immortal as an Anabo, you'll still have the ability to conceive." He smiled. "That's something to worry about later. For now, I want to take you home with me. I want to talk to you, know you, plan our life together."

She was like him now, but she was still a seventeen-year-old virgin, and nervous about what he had in mind. "The mark . . . I don't know that it will work."

"We'll see." He gave her a patient look. "When you're ready, we'll see. Come with me, Jordan, and don't be afraid."

Standing, she went to him and stepped into his arms, accepting his kiss with no hesitation. This was where she was supposed to be. She knew that now. He had her scent. He'd known, all along, as she didn't, that they were meant to be together.

"Are you ready to go?"

"Yes, but I can't just disappear."

"I have a plan."

"You always have a plan, don't you?"

"Yes. Always. Do you want to take anything with you?"

She looked over her shoulder at the rabbit, then turned back to Eryx. "No. Nothing."

NINETEEN

SITTING IN FRONT OF THE DYING EMBERS OF THE FIRE HE'D built and rebuilt three times, next to a tray of food and drink Mathilda had brought hours ago, Key stared up at the portrait of himself and his brothers that hung above the mantel in his room. The clock on his bookcase chimed the hour. Midnight here; two a.m. in Washington. Why hadn't she come? Why had she never answered his calls and texts? He was worried about how it had gone with her father. Andy Ellis was a decent, honest man, but he was under a tremendous amount of stress, and learning his daughter had punched a guy at a dance might have set him off.

Maybe she'd been too upset to talk about it right away.

He thought of what now lay in the cooler and hoped that whatever had passed between her and her father had been resolved.

That she'd told him she loved him. Because she didn't know it yet, but she was going to die in her sleep tonight, the victim of an aneurysm, a congenital defect she'd been born with.

After what happened at the dance, his brothers and Sasha had insisted, and he'd agreed. She was suffering in the real world. She needed to be here, where everyone knew what she was, where she was safe from Eryx, where she could be with her sister. And with Key.

So he'd waited for her to be done with her dad, to come here, to him, and he would tell her it was over. He'd tell her they were back to planning a takedown during her memorial, for all the government people, as well as the kids from school. Anyone who was a no-show would be taken out later, individually. He had a feeling she'd be relieved, even while it made her sad.

But as the hours passed and he had no word from her, he became more anxious. He was about to pop into her room to check to see what was going on when his phone dinged, signaling the arrival of an e-mail. He picked it up from the side table, hoping the message was from her.

It was.

He read and reread it, over and over, but it always said the same thing. And the last line never changed. *She wrote this, but didn't hit send. I did. I'm sorry, son. ~M*

Shaking violently, he dropped the phone. His chest hurt. He couldn't swallow. Swiping his arm across the side table, he sent the dishes and cold food flying. He surged out of the chair and flew around the room, hurling furniture through the windows, smashing priceless Chinese vases against the wall, chunking books into the fireplace.

Sweet Christ, he couldn't bear this. He *couldn't.*

Staggering to the destroyed windows, he leaned into the freezing snow and screamed until he was hoarse. He didn't know anything could hurt this bad.

"Kyros."

He wheeled around and saw Phoenix standing in the midst of the wreckage, Key's phone in his hand and horror on his face. "Now you know."

Until that bleak moment, he had never understood his brother. Now he did. Now he knew.

"Your whole life, nobody ever loved you like I do."

Falling to his knees, he buried his face in his hands and sobbed.

TWENTY

FOR MAXIMUM ENERGY, IN A LONG-STANDING PRETAKEDOWN ritual, they ate as much as possible, and today, as fast as possible, then convened around the onyx *M* in the front hall. Each of them held a box of plastic explosives, and Jax held the detonators. He grimly looked around the circle. "Is everyone completely clear on what you're to do?"

They all nodded, except Zee, who said, "I still think it's dicey to blow up Erinýes. There's no reason to do it other than revenge, and it's going to take time, which means more opportunities to be discovered by Eryx's Skia. If he realizes we're there before we're ready for him to know, he'll take Jordan somewhere else and we'll have to start all over." He looked at Key. "Time is all important, and what you plan to do won't make any difference if she's already crossed the line. No way she's getting into Heaven if she's helped him take a soul."

"She's been with him ten hours, at the most," Sasha said, "and they haven't left Erinýes, I know, because I've been holding on to my mental search ever since I found out what happened. It's not like he's going to go hunt down a convert when he just got her there."

Zee shot a fast look at Phoenix, then said, "There's also the possibility he'll try to mark her, which may or may not be possible, but once she's taken that step, getting her back to God might be a lost cause."

Hands gripping the box, Key forced himself not to think about Jordan with Eryx in that way. It was horrible enough thinking of her kissing him. If his mind went anywhere else, he'd lose it again. "This will work, Zee, and it's not just about revenge. You saw the text he sent me." His blood was still boiling. "He's so pleased with himself for having the ability to trick an Anabo, comparing it to Lucifer's temptation of Eve, he's certain he's close to being powerful enough to confront Lucifer. He has to know that he's not. We have to show him he's nowhere close, because if he openly declares war, it'll be chaos and anarchy of biblical magnitude. Humanity will suffer because he's still tied to the world, and the only way he can draw Lucifer out is by trying to destroy it."

"And you think blowing up his castle is the way to show him he's not ready to take on Lucifer?"

"It's that we *can*, Zee. You went there and saw for yourself that he's allowing everyone in the castle to slack off. He's so cocky right now, he thinks we can't touch him. He thinks we're *afraid* of him. We have to make it real clear that he's not as powerful as he believes, and he won't win if he calls Lucifer out. Stealing Jordan and blowing up Erinýes will do that."

Zee shifted the box he held and said, "I wish to God what she tried to do had worked."

"We all do," Ty said, his voice hard. "But it didn't, and we owe it to her to get her out of there, to save her from what she's become."

Jax began a count.

On three, Key transported back to Romania, back to Erinýes, his mind filled with thoughts of the last time he'd been there. He'd found her in that disgusting bathroom, wigging out about the roaches, and knew she wasn't going to be anything close to what he'd expected. She wasn't as afraid of Eryx as she'd been of the bugs. She was strength and courage, wrapped up in all girl.

He materialized in the library and quickly set the plastic, affixed the charge, then moved across the hall to the billiards room and set another. Most of the Skia were in the great hall, dancing to hip-hop tunes and getting crazy drunk, but one occasionally came his way and he ducked and hid as they passed. He stealthily worked his way down the hall, and set the last charge in the dining room, then stepped away to slip his mask across his face. He could already hear gunfire coming from the other side of the castle. Reaching into his pocket, he pulled out his switch-blade, then swung the assault rifle around from where it'd been riding his back.

In the hall, he moved through quickly; any Skia who wasn't already passed out from inhaling the canister gas Zee and Sasha were dropping across the castle he shot. If one came at him before he could get off a shot, he plunged his blade into their heart. Some of them rallied enough to get pistols and rifles, but other than a hit in his arm, Key managed to make it to Eryx's bedroom without wounds.

He kicked the door open, threw a canister inside, then followed it, repeatedly firing the rifle, taking no chances that Eryx would get away from him.

They were sitting at a table in front of the fire while a Tchaikovsky waltz swelled the air. Jordan's skimpy black dress just matched her dead, black eyes. Eryx looked genuinely surprised by Key's appearance. He was so obsessed with her, so sure of her, he'd assumed Key wouldn't come after her.

He was dead-ass wrong.

She lunged from her chair, but before she could run, he shot her. Eryx raised a handgun and fired, but the shot went wild because he was losing consciousness. Key shot him, then shot him again.

Sliding the rifle to his back, he bent and picked Jordan up from where she'd fallen to the floor. Turning, he left as quickly as he'd come, and half ran toward the front of the castle, leaping over unconscious Skia, then through the open doors, and down the steps to the grocery truck Ty had commandeered from the village ten miles away. He handed Jordan up to Zee, then jumped in and removed his mask. Jax was right behind him, and Phoenix was last, leaping toward the truck as they sped away.

Fifty yards from the castle, Ty stopped and they all jumped to the ground. Key took Jordan from Zee and laid her across a stack of boxes, then joined the others.

Jax handed each of them a detonator. "On three."

They punched the remotes and felt the ground shake while they watched Eryx's castle explode, blasting everyone inside to bits. They were immortal, so they'd be back, but it would be a while. It took several weeks to come back from being blown to pieces. And it would take months, even years, for Eryx to rebuild and replace what he'd lost. When he came back, he'd know the Mephisto had won this round. He'd know he wasn't ready to take on Lucifer.

Key climbed into the back of the truck, sat on a cabbage crate, and settled Jordan in his lap, holding her against his chest. He tried not to think about bluebells, or how she no longer carried their scent. He tried not to remember her beautiful twinkling eyes. Or the sound of her breathless voice in his ear while her soft hands wandered across his body. He tried not to think of any of that. He had to stay focused.

Another five minutes and the truck passed through the gates that marked the edge of Eryx's land, freeing them to transport again. As they slowed, he looked across at Phoenix, who solemnly looked back at him. He didn't need to say anything. Key knew if he'd had the choice Key now had, he'd have done it. He looked at Sasha, who was sobbing. He looked at Denys, who said, "I'm glad you're my brother." His gaze moved to Zee, who lunged across the space between them to hold Key's face in his hands and kiss his forehead. "I love you," he whispered before he disappeared.

He looked to where Ty was standing behind the truck. His tallest brother swallowed hard and said, simply, "Good-bye, Kyros."

Finally, he looked at Jax. "You'll make sure Mariah is safe?"

He nodded.

"You'll be oldest now. You'll be the one who leads. Keep these filthy animals in line, understand?"

Jax gave up trying not to cry. "I'll miss you all the rest of my life."

Key looked down at Jordan's beautiful face, clutched her a little tighter to his chest, and disappeared from Romania.

He materialized on the frozen, narrow road that ran through the village in Yorkshire, near the moors, only a few miles from where they'd lived all those years. He wished it was springtime. He wished he could have shown Jordan the bluebells.

Turning, he looked at the small, Gothic church he'd passed so many times, but had never stepped inside of. He glanced at the adjoining churchyard, where stones in a weighted casket were buried beneath Jane's marker. She was buried in the countryside, where Phoenix could visit her, away from holy ground.

As he started to walk toward the doors of the church, Jordan began to regain consciousness. He slowed to a stop and watched her eyes open. She looked up at him accusingly. "You shot me."

"I had to get you away from Eryx."

"But I don't want to be away from him, Key. He caught my scent, did you know?"

Eryx had even lied about that. "You thought you could save him, didn't you, Jordan?"

She closed her eyes, as if she couldn't stand to look at him. "I don't know why, because I realize now that he doesn't need saving. He's been right all along, Key."

Stay focused. Don't let it get to you. She's out of her mind, and it's not her fault. He resolutely continued toward the doors of the church.

She opened her eyes, saw where they were headed, and immediately began struggling to get away. "No, Key! We can't go in there! We'll die!" She tried to get her arms free so she could hit him, but he held fast to her small body and climbed the three steps that led to the doors. Without a free hand, he concentrated on the oak, on the hinges, on the old iron locks.

Slowly, the doors opened. He could see dark wood pews marching toward the front of the church, to an altar with a cross hanging above it. It was dusk on a Sunday in Yorkshire, and no one was inside.

She began to cry, begging him not to do it. "Please, *please*, don't do this! I'll come back to you. I'll do whatever you want!"

He stepped across the threshold and immediately felt heat travel through his body.

He kept walking and mentally closed the doors behind him, even as his clothes caught fire.

Jordan was hysterical, fighting with all her strength to get away from him. "It hurts, Kyros! Have mercy!"

He reached the steps that led up to the altar and fell to his knees.

"Why?" She sobbed against his shoulder, her body stiff with the pain of the flames consuming them. "Why do you want to kill me?"

"Because even though you've lost Anabo, you're not yet lost. Not until you do what he does. I won't let you cross that line. I love you too much to let you become what he is."

Her sobs were heartbreaking. "You can't love me! Can't you see what I've become? The Mephisto in you has to despise me."

She was suddenly too heavy, and he laid her down and rested his weight on top of her, as much because he wanted to feel her against him one last time as to keep her from escaping.

Although she was past that now. She was dying.

As darkness began to shadow his vision, he felt her arms circle his neck and heard her say against his ear, "Please, forgive me."

"I will always love you," he thought he whispered, but maybe he didn't. He wasn't sure his lips worked any longer. He waited for darkness to come, to relieve him of this agony, but it never did. He knew when Jordan's spirit left him and he was alone, but he didn't feel the ache of it in quite the same way. She must surely be with God now, where she belonged.

The horror of burning to death lingered, and just when he was sure he couldn't take another second, he felt arms slide beneath them and lift them up, and heard a soft voice murmuring comfort and love. Still holding Jordan, he was laid on something soft and cool. Something that smelled of bluebells. Gentle hands smoothed his brow and cradled his cheeks, and his vision slowly returned. He blinked up at the face above him. "Mana?"

She smiled and ran her hand through his hair to hold his head. "It's been harder for you than the others, Kyros, and here you are, at the end, and it's still more difficult. You have to make a choice. Will you come with me, or stay behind and continue to lead your brothers?"

He turned his head and looked at Jordan, whose face was no longer burned, but as smooth and perfect as the first time he saw her. Her eyes were closed. "I want to go where she goes."

"Even if it's to—"

"Even there." He looked up at his mother. "Please tell me that's not where she's going."

"No, Kyros. She lost her way for love of you, imagining she could change Eryx to be how you remember him. And now you're both on the other side because you loved her enough to sacrifice yourself and bring her back to God." Her smile was joyful. "You've fulfilled the Mephisto Covenant, and you can choose Heaven now or return to your brothers and live a life that will bring you back here at the end."

"Does Jordan have the same choice?"

"She's been asked, and says she will go where you go."

"When will she wake up?"

"When you decide." She cradled his face in her hands and kissed his forehead. "If you keep this knowledge of me only in your soul, you'll never forget. If you speak of it, the memory will dissolve. Either way, I pray you'll always remember how much I love you, Kyros."

"I love you, too, Mana." She'd always been beautiful, but the light of divinity in her awed him. "I never noticed how much Zee takes after you. From now on, I'll see you in him." He realized she was fading. "Why are you leaving? I haven't told you my decision."

"Yes, love, you have. Your brothers . . . you're an unlikely shepherd, Kyros, but there is none more devoted."

"Good-bye," he whispered, but she was already gone. His vision fully returned, and he saw that he was in Jordan's room in the Mephisto house, with Jordan still wrapped up in his arms, lying on her bed, which was covered in bluebells.

She stirred, and when her eyes opened, they were blue once again. "You chose to come back," she whispered. "I'm glad."

"I love you, Jordan."

"Most guys send flowers to show how they feel. You died to save me."

"Yeah, I'm a master at subtle gestures."

She nuzzled his neck. "Did you meet Mary Michael?"

"She never said her name."

"Was she wearing a Woodstock T-shirt?"

"Come to think of it, she was." He smiled. So the Anabo angel was their *mitera*. He wondered if she was who M asked to make the plea to God for more Anabo. Had they broken all the rules of Heaven and Hell to bring more Anabo into the world? He'd probably never know, and maybe that was best.

He looked into this Anabo's eyes and whispered, "Here's to eternity, Viorica."

With her arms still around his neck, she shifted closer. "I love you, Kyros." She kissed him, and in the middle of it, he heard loud voices that became louder, until they were at the door. Just as Jordan lifted her head and turned to look, it flew open. There were the Mephisto, the Purgatories, and the Lumina, crowding into the room, surrounding the bed, spilling into the hall.

Key looked up at Jordan. "Honey, the neighbors are here. Better hide the good cookies."

They were bounced off of the bed in the midst of laughter, and lots of tears, and many embraces.

Jax said over his shoulder while he hugged him so hard he nearly broke his back, "We wouldn't have known you were here, except Sasha wouldn't let go of her search. She started shouting, and everyone came running." He eased up and stepped back, but his hands continued to grip Key's shoulders. "God, I'm glad."

"Kinda freaked about leading, bro?"

Jax laughed and ducked his head before he nodded. "Yeah, okay, that, too."

Watching Jordan and Mariah hug each other, he sobered and met Jax's eyes. "Did Zee take care of her doppelganger?"

Jax shot a glance at Jordan before he nodded. "It was pretty rough, Key. Zee said her dad's in bad shape. I really don't think she should be on the takedown at her memorial."

"It'll be hard for her, Jax, but she'll do it anyway. It's who she is."

He caught her smiling at him from across the room and knew exactly what she was thinking. Forever, until the end of time, they'd exchange looks across rooms and tables and takedowns and would always know, because the message would always be the same: *I love you.*

ACKNOWLEDGMENTS

MY SINCERE THANKS TO EVERYONE AT EGMONT USA FOR ALL their hard work and effort bringing this book to life, especially Senior Editor Greg Ferguson for your patience and vision. Thank you, Katie Halata, for all your marketing effort with *The Mephisto Covenant*, and talking me off the ledge a time or three.

Thank you, Meredith Bernstein, for your guidance, and your kindness when life took an unexpected turn.

Heartfelt, loving thanks to Alison Kent, HelenKay Dimon, Kassia Krozser, Wendy Duren, and Jill Monroe, who I'm so very fortunate to call friends. Thank you for being there during a difficult time.

My sincere gratitude to the Class of 2K11 for your wonderful wisdom and support. I'm in awe of all of you.

A thousand thanks to the blogger community, who so graciously spread the word about *The Mephisto Covenant*. Your love of reading is a beautiful thing. Thanks especially to Maria Cari Soto, Jen Bigheart, and Kari Olson.

As always, thank you to my family. I love you.